STAR WARS®

CROSSCURRENT

STAR WARS®
CROSSCURRENT

PAUL S. KEMP

BALLANTINE BOOKS • NEW YORK

Star Wars: Crosscurrent is a work of fiction. Names, places, and incidents either are products of the author's imagination or are used fictitiously.

2010 Del Rey Mass Market Edition

Copyright © 2010 by Lucasfilm Ltd. & ® or ™ where indicated. All Rights Reserved. Used Under Authorization.

Excerpt from *Star Wars: Fate of the Jedi: Outcast* copyright © 2009 by Lucasfilm Ltd. & ® or ™ where indicated. All Rights Reserved. Used Under Authorization.

Published in the United States by Del Rey, an imprint of The Random House Publishing Group, a division of Random House, Inc., New York.

DEL REY is a registered trademark and the Del Rey colophon is a trademark of Random House, Inc.

ISBN 978-0-345-50905-5

This book contains an excerpt from *Star Wars: Fate of the Jedi: Outcast* by Aaron Allston. Published by Del Rey Books.

Printed in the United States of America

www.starwars.com
www.delreybooks.com

987654

For my two little Padawans,
Roarke and Riordan

THE STAR WARS NOVELS TIMELINE

BEFORE THE REPUBLIC
37,000–25,000 YEARS BEFORE
STAR WARS: A New Hope

c. 25,793 *YEARS BEFORE STAR WARS: A New Hope*

Dawn of the Jedi: Into the Void**

OLD REPUBLIC
5000–67 YEARS BEFORE
STAR WARS: A New Hope

Lost Tribe of the Sith†
Precipice
Skyborn
Paragon
Savior
Purgatory
Sentinel

3954 *YEARS BEFORE STAR WARS: A New Hope*

The Old Republic: Revan

3650 *YEARS BEFORE STAR WARS: A New Hope*

The Old Republic: Deceived

Lost Tribe of the Sith†
Pantheon
Secrets
Red Harvest

The Old Republic: Fatal Alliance

The Old Republic: Annihilation

2975 *YEARS BEFORE STAR WARS: A New Hope*

Lost Tribe of the Sith†
Pandemonium

1032 *YEARS BEFORE STAR WARS: A New Hope*

Knight Errant

Darth Bane: Path of Destruction
Darth Bane: Rule of Two
Darth Bane: Dynasty of Evil

RISE OF THE EMPIRE
67–0 YEARS BEFORE
STAR WARS: A New Hope

67 *YEARS BEFORE STAR WARS: A New Hope*

Darth Plagueis

33 *YEARS BEFORE STAR WARS: A New Hope*

Darth Maul: Saboteur*
Cloak of Deception
Darth Maul: Shadow Hunter

32 *YEARS BEFORE STAR WARS: A New Hope*

STAR WARS: EPISODE I
THE PHANTOM MENACE

Rogue Planet
Outbound Flight
The Approaching Storm

22 *YEARS BEFORE STAR WARS: A New Hope*

STAR WARS: EPISODE II
ATTACK OF THE CLONES

22-19 *YEARS BEFORE STAR WARS: A New Hope*

The Clone Wars
The Clone Wars: Wild Space
The Clone Wars: No Prisoners

Clone Wars Gambit
Stealth
Siege

Republic Commando
Hard Contact
Triple Zero
True Colors
Order 66

Shatterpoint
The Cestus Deception
The Hive*
MedStar I: Battle Surgeons
MedStar II: Jedi Healer
Jedi Trial
Yoda: Dark Rendezvous
Labyrinth of Evil

19 *YEARS BEFORE STAR WARS: A New Hope*

STAR WARS: EPISODE III
REVENGE OF THE SITH

Dark Lord: The Rise of Darth Vader

Imperial Commando
501st

Coruscant Nights
Jedi Twilight
Street of Shadows
Patterns of Force

The Last Jedi**

*An eBook novella
**Forthcoming
† Lost Tribe of the Sith: The
  Collected Stories

THE STAR WARS NOVELS TIMELINE

*An eBook novella
**Forthcoming

dramatis personae

Drev Hassin; Jedi Padawan (Askajian male)
Jaden Korr; Jedi Knight (human male)
Kell Douro; assassin/spy (Anzat male)
Khedryn Faal; captain, *Junker* (human male)
Marr Idi-Shael; first mate, *Junker* (Cerean male)
Relin Druur; Jedi Master (human male)
Saes Rrogon; Sith Lord; captain, *Harbinger* (Kaleesh male)

CROSSCURRENT

A long time ago, in a galaxy far, far away . . .

chapter one

THE PAST:
5,000 YEARS BEFORE THE BATTLE OF YAVIN

THE CRUST OF PHAEGON III's LARGEST MOON BURNED, buckled, and crumbled under the onslaught. Sixty-four specially equipped cruisers—little more than planetary-bombardment weapons systems with a bit of starship wrapped around them—flew in a suborbital, longitudinal formation. The sleek silver cruisers, their underbellies aglow in reflected destruction, struck Saes as unexpectedly beautiful. How strange that they could unleash annihilation in such warm, glorious colors.

Plasma beams shrieked from the bow of each cruiser and slammed into the arboreal surface of the moon, shimmering green umbilicals that wrote words of ruin across the surface and saturated the world in fire and pain. Dust and a swirl of thick black smoke churned in the atmosphere as the cruisers methodically vaporized large swaths of the moon's surface.

The bright light and black smoke of destruction filled *Harbinger*'s viewscreen, drowning out the orange light of the system's star. Except for the occasional beep of a droid or a murmured word, the bridge crew sat in silence, their eyes fixed alternately on their instruments and the viewscreen. Background chatter on the many comm channels droned over the various speakers, a serene counterpoint to the chaos of the moon's death. Saes's keen olfactory sense caught a whiff of his human crew's sweat, spiced with the tang of adrenaline.

Watching the cruisers work, watching the moon die, Saes was reminded of the daelfruits he'd enjoyed in his youth. He had spent many afternoons under the sun of his homeworld, peeling away the daelfruit's coarse, brown rind to get at the core of sweet, pale flesh.

Now he was peeling not a fruit but an entire moon.

The flesh under the rind of the moon's crust—the Lignan they were mining—would ensure a Sith victory in the battle for Kirrek and improve Saes's place in the Sith hierarchy. He would not challenge Shar Dakhon immediately, of course. He was still too new to the Sith Order for that. But he would not wait overlong.

Evil roots in unbridled ambition, Relin had told him once.

Saes smiled. What a fool his onetime Master had been. Naga Sadow rewarded ambition.

"Status?" he queried his science droid, 8K6.

The fires in the viewscreen danced on the anthropomorphic droid's reflective silver surface as it turned from its instrument console to address him.

"Thirty-seven percent of the moon's crust is destroyed."

Wirelessly connected to the console's readout, the droid did not need to glance back for an update on the information as the cruisers continued their work.

"Thirty-eight percent. Thirty-nine."

Saes nodded, turned his attention back to the viewscreen. The droid fell silent.

Despite *Harbinger*'s distance from the surface, the Force carried back to Saes the terror of the pre-sentient primates that populated the moon's surface. Saes imagined the small creatures fleeing through the trees, screeching, relentlessly pursued by, and inevitably consumed in, fire. They numbered in the hundreds of thousands. Their fear caressed his mind, as faint, fleeting, and pleasing as morning fog.

His fellow Sith on *Harbinger* and *Omen* would be feeling the same thing as the genocide progressed to its inexorable conclusion. Perhaps even the Massassi aboard each ship would, in their dim way, perceive the ripples in the Force.

Long ago, when Saes had been a Jedi, before he had come to understand the dark side, such wholesale destruction of life might have struck him as wrong. He knew better now. There was no absolute right and wrong. There was only power. And those who wielded it defined right and wrong for themselves. That realization was the freedom offered by the dark side and the reason the Jedi would fall, first at Kirrek, then at Coruscant, then all over the galaxy.

"Temperature in the wake?" he asked.

The science droid consulted the sensor data on its compscreen. "Within the tolerance of the harvester droids."

Saes watched the cruisers slide through the atmosphere and light the moon on fire. He turned in his command chair to face his second in command, Los Dor. Dor's mottled, deep red skin looked nearly black in the dim light of the bridge. His yellow eyes mirrored the moon's fires. He never seemed to look up into Saes's eyes, instead focusing his gaze on the twin horns that jutted from the sides of Saes's jaw.

Saes knew Dor was as much a spy for Naga Sadow as he was an ostensible aide to himself. Among other things, Dor was there to ensure that Saes returned the Lignan—*all* of the Lignan—to Sadow's forces at Primus Goluud.

The tentacles on Dor's face quivered, and the cartilaginous ridges over his eyes rose in a question.

"Give the order to launch the harvester droids, Colonel," Saes said to him. "*Harbinger*'s and *Omen*'s."

"Yes, Captain," Dor responded. He turned to his console and transmitted the order to both ships.

The honorific *Captain* still struck Saes's hearing oddly. He was accustomed to leading hunting parties as a First, not ships as a Captain.

In moments hundreds of cylindrical pods streaked out of *Harbinger*'s launching bay, and hundreds more flew from her sister ship, *Omen*, all of them streaking across the viewscreen. They hit the atmosphere and spat lines of fire as they descended. The sight reminded Saes of a pyrotechnic display.

"Harvester droids away," 8K6 intoned.

"Stay with the droids and magnify," Saes said.

"Copy," answered Dor, and nodded at the young human helmsman who controlled the viewscreen.

The harvester droids' trajectories placed them tens of kilometers behind the destruction wrought by the mining cruisers. Most of them were lost to sight in the smoke, but the helmsman kept the viewscreen's perspective on a dozen or so that descended through a clear spot in the sky.

"Attrition among the droids upon entry is negligible," said 8K6. "Point zero three percent."

The helmsman further magnified the viewscreen again, then again.

Five kilos above the surface, the droids arrested their descent with thrusters, unfolded into their insectoid forms, and gently dropped to the charred, superheated surface. Anti-grav servos and platform pads on their six legs allowed them to walk on the smoking ruin without harm.

"Give me a view from one of the droids."

"Copy, sir," said Dor.

The helm worked his console, and half the viewscreen changed to a perspective of a droid's-eye view of the moon. A murmur ran through the bridge crew, an exhalation of awe. Even 8K6 looked up from the instrumentation.

The voice of Captain Korsin, commander of *Harbinger*'s sister ship, *Omen*, broke through the comm chatter and boomed over the bridge speakers.

"That is a sight."

"It is," Saes answered.

Smoke rose in wisps from the exposed subcrust. The heat of the plasma beams had turned the charred surface as hard and brittle as glass. Thick cracks and chasms lined the subcrust, veins through which only smoke and ash flowed. Waves of heat rose from the surface, distorting visibility and giving the moon an otherworldly, dream-like feel.

Hundreds of harvester droids dotted the surface, metal flies clinging to the moon's seared corpse. Walking in their awkward, insectoid manner, they arranged themselves into orderly rows, their high-pitched droidspeak mere chatter in the background.

"Sensors activating," intoned 8K6.

As one, long metal proboscises extended from each of the droids' faces. They ambled along in the wake of the destruction, waving their proboscises over the surface like dowsing rods, fishing the subsurface for the telltale molecular signature of Lignan.

Thinking of the Lignan, Saes licked his lips, tasted a faint flavor of phosphorous. He had handled a small Lignan crystal years before and still remembered the charge he had felt while holding it. His connection with that crystal had been the first sign of his affinity for the dark side.

The unusual molecular structure of Lignan attuned it

to the dark side and enhanced a Sith's power when using the Force. The Sith had not been able to locate any significant deposits of the crystals in recent decades—until now, until just before the battle for Kirrek. And it was Saes who had done it.

A few standard months ago, Naga Sadow had charged Saes with locating some deposits of the rare crystal for use in the war. It was a test, Saes knew. And Los Dor, his ostensible aide, was grading him. The Force had given Saes his answer, had brought him eventually, and at the last possible moment before the conflict began, to Phaegon III. The Force had used him as a tool to ensure Sith victory.

The realization warmed him. His scaled skin creaked as he adjusted his weight in his chair.

He would harvest enough Lignan from Phaegon III's moon to equip almost every Sith Lord and Massassi warrior preparing for the assault on Kirrek. If he'd had more time, he could have mined the moon in a more methodical, less destructive fashion. But he did not have time, and Sadow would not tolerate delay.

So Saes had created his own right and wrong, and the primates and other life-forms on Phaegon III's moon had died for it.

He tapped his forefinger on his lightsaber hilt—its curved form reminiscent of a claw—impatient to see the results of the droids' sensor scans. He leaned forward in his chair when an excited beep announced the first discovery of a Lignan signature. Another joined it. Another. He shared a look with Dor and could not tell from the fix of Dor's mouth, partially masked as it was by a beard of tentacles, if his colonel was pleased or displeased.

"There it is, Saes," said Korsin from *Omen*. "We've done it."

In truth, Saes had done it. Korsin had been simply following his lead. "Yes."

"It appears to be a large deposit," said 8K6.

More and more of the harvester droids chirped news of their discovery over the comm channel.

"Perhaps more than we have time to acquire," said Dor. "Shall I recall the mining cruisers, Captain? Further destruction seems . . . unwarranted."

Saes heard the question behind the question and shook his head. Dor would find no pity in Saes. "No. Incinerate the entire surface. What we cannot take before the battle at Kirrek, we will return for after our victory there."

Dor nodded, and a faint smile disturbed the tentacles. "Yes, Sir."

Saes fixed his colonel with his eyes, and Dor's gaze fell to Saes's jaw horns. "And when you report back to Lord Sadow, you tell him all that you saw here."

Dor looked up, held Saes's eyes only for a moment before his tentacles twitched and he turned away.

Saes allowed himself a moment's satisfaction as drill-probes extended from the droids' abdomens and began pulling the rare crystal from the burning corpse of the moon. The Force continued to carry the terror of the primates to Saes's consciousness, but with less impact. There were fewer left. He could not help but smile.

"Use the shuttles to collect the ore," he said to Dor. "*Omen*'s, too. We take as much as we can as quickly as we can."

"Copy."

Several standard hours later, Phaegon III's smoking moon and all its inhabitants were dead. The mining cruisers, having finished their work, had jumped out of the system. A steady stream of transport shuttles traveled between the moon and *Omen* and *Harbinger*'s cargo holds, filling both ships with unrefined Lignan ore. The presence of so many crystals so near caused Saes to feel giddy, almost inebriated. Dor and the other Force-sensitives aboard *Harbinger* and *Omen* would be feeling much the same way.

"Extra discipline with the Massassi," Saes said to Dor. The Lignan would agitate them. He wanted to head off outbreaks of violence. Or at least he wanted the violence appropriately directed.

"I will inform the security teams," Dor said. "Do you . . . feel that, Captain?"

Saes nodded, drunk on the dark side. The air in the ship was alive with its potential. His skin felt warm, his head light.

With an effort of will, he regained his focus. He had little time before he would rendezvous with Naga Sadow and the rest of the Sith force moving against Kirrek. He opened a comm channel with *Omen*.

"An hour more, Korsin," he said.

"Agreed," Korsin answered, and Saes felt the human's glee through the connection. "Do you feel the power around us, Saes? Kirrek will *burn*."

Saes stared at the incinerated moon in his viewscreen, spinning dark and dead through the void of space.

"It will," he said, and cut off the connection.

Relin stared out of the large, transparisteel bubble window that fronted the cockpit of his starfighter. Beside him, his Padawan, Drev, tapped hyperspace formulae into the navigation computer. Drev's body challenged the seat with its girth. His flight suit pinched adipose tissue at neck and wrist, giving his head and hands the look of tied-off sausages. Still, Drev was almost thin by the standards of Askajians. And Relin had never before met an Askajian in whom the Force was so strong.

Their Infiltrator hung in the orange-and-red cloud of the Remmon Nebula. The small ship—with its minimal, deliberately erratic emission signature, sleek profile, and sensor baffles—would be invisible to scans outside the swirl.

Lines of yellow and orange light veined the super-heated gas around them, like terrestrial lightning frozen in time. Relin watched the cloud slowly churn in the magnetic winds. He had been across half the galaxy since joining the Jedi, and the beauty it hid in its darkest corners amazed him still. He saw in that beauty the Force made manifest, a physical representation of the otherwise invisible power that served as the scaffolding of the universe.

But the scaffolding was under threat. Sadow and the Sith would corrupt it. Relin had seen the consequence of that corruption firsthand, when he had lost Saes to the dark side.

He pushed the memory from his mind, the pain still too acute.

The conflict between Jedi and Sith had reached a turning point. Kirrek would be a fulcrum, tilting the war toward one side or the other. Relin knew the Jedi under Memit Nadill and Odan-Urr had fortified the planet well, but he knew, too, that Sadow's fleets would come in overwhelming force. He suspected they would also strike Coruscant, and had so notified Nadill.

Still typing in coordinates, Drev asked, "We will be able to pick up the beacon's pulse once we enter hyperspace?"

"Yes," Relin said.

At least that was the theory. If they were right about the hyperspace lane *Harbinger* and *Omen* had taken; if Saes had not diverted his ship to another hyperspace lane; and if *Harbinger* and *Omen* remained near enough the hyperspace lane for the beacon's signal to reach them.

"And if the agents did not place the hyperspace beacon? Or if Saes located it and disabled it?"

Relin stared out at the nebula. "Peace, Drev. There are many *ifs*. Things are what they are."

Matters had moved so rapidly of late that Relin had not had time to report back to his superiors as regularly as he should, just the occasional missive sent in a subspace burst as time and conditions allowed.

He had picked up Saes's trail near Primus Goluud. There, he'd seen the armada of Sith forces marshaling for an assault; he'd seen Saes's ship leave the armada with a sister ship, *Omen,* falling in behind.

After sending a short, subspace report back to the Order on Coruscant and Kirrek, Relin had received orders to follow Saes and try to determine the Sith's purpose. He had learned little as *Harbinger* and *Omen* moved rapidly from one backrocket system to another, dispatching recon droids, scanning, then moving on.

"He is searching for something," Relin said, more to himself than Drev.

Drev chuckled, and his double chin shook. "Saes? His conscience, no doubt. He seems to have misplaced it somewhere."

Relin did not smile. The loss of Saes cut too sharply for jest.

"I worry over your casual attitude toward matters of import. Many will die in this war."

Drev bowed his head, his shoulders drooping, trying to look contrite under his mass of thick brown hair. "Forgive me, Master. But I . . ." He paused, though his round face showed him struggling with a thought.

"What is it?" Relin asked.

Drev did not look at him as he said, "I sometimes think you laugh too little. Among my people, the shamans of the Moon Lady teach that tragedy is the best time for mirth. Laugh even when you die, they say. There is joy to be found in almost everything."

"And there is also pain," Relin said, thinking of Saes. "Are the coordinates ready?"

Drev stiffened in his chair and in his tone. "Ready, Master."

"Then let us find out what it is that Saes is looking for."

Relin maneuvered the Infiltrator out of the nebula and checked it against Drev's coordinates. Stars dotted the viewscreen.

"We go," Relin said.

Drev touched a button on his console, and the transparisteel cockpit window dimmed to spare them the hypnotic blue swirl of a hyperspace tunnel. Relin engaged the hyperdrive. Points of light turned to infinite lines.

THE PRESENT:
41.5 YEARS AFTER THE BATTLE OF YAVIN

Darkness plagued Jaden, the lightless ink of a singularity. He was falling, falling forever. His stomach crawled up his throat, crowding out whatever scream he might have uttered.

He still felt the Force around him, within him, but only thickly, only attenuated, as if his sensitivity were numbed.

He hit unseen ground with a grunt and fell to all fours. Snow crunched under his palms and boots. Gusts of freezing wind rifled his robes to stab at his skin. Ice borne by the wind peppered his face and rimed his beard. He still could see nothing in the pitch. He stood, shaky, shaking, freezing.

"Where is this place?" he called. The darkness was so

deep he could not see his frozen breath. His voice sounded small in the void. "Arsix?"

No response.

"Arsix?"

Odd, he thought, that the first thing he called for in an uncertain situation was his droid rather than a fellow Jedi.

He reached for the familiar heft of his primary lightsaber, found its belt clip empty. He reached around to the small of his back for his secondary lightsaber—the crude but effective weapon he had built as a boy on Coruscant without any training in the Force—and found it gone, too. His blaster was not in his thigh holster. No glow rod in his utility pocket.

He was cold, alone, unequipped, blind in the darkness.

What had happened? He remembered nothing.

Drawing his robes tightly about him to ward off the cold, he focused his hearing, but heard nothing over the wind except the gong of his heartbeat in his ears. With difficulty, he reached out with his Force sense through the fog of his benighted sensitivity, trying to feel the world around him indirectly. Through the dull operation of his expanded consciousness he sensed something . . .

There were others there with him, out in the darkness.

Several others.

He sharpened his concentration and the tang of the dark side teased his perception—Sith.

But not quite Sith, not entirely: the dark side adulterated.

He tried to ignore the familiar caress of the dark side's touch. He knew the line between light and dark was as narrow as a vibroblade-edge. His Master, Kyle Katarn, had taught him as much. Every Jedi walked that edge. Some understood the precipice under their feet, and some did not. And it was the latter who so often fell. But it was the former who so often suffered. Jaden frequently wished he had remained in ignorance, had stayed the boy on Coruscant for whom the Force had been magic.

Summoned from the past, his Master's words bounced around his brain: *The Force is a tool, Jaden. Sometimes a weapon, sometimes a salve. Dark side, light side, these are distinctions of insignificant difference. Do not fall into the trap of classification. Sentience curses us with a desire to categorize and draw lines, to fear that after this be dragons. But that is illusion. After this is not dragons but more knowledge, deeper understanding. Be at peace with that.*

But Jaden never had been at peace with that. He feared he never would. Worse, he feared he never *should.* After completing his training, Jaden had done some research into unorthodox theories about the Force. He had come to think—and fear—that his Master had been right.

"Show yourselves," he called into the darkness, and the howling wind devoured his words. He knew the Sith would have sensed his presence, the same as he had sensed theirs.

They were all around him, closing fast. He felt vulnerable, with nothing at his back, unable to see. He sank into the Force and denied his fear.

Finding his calm, he stood in a half crouch, eyes closed, mind focused, his entire body a coiled spring. Even without his lightsaber, a dark side user would find him a formidable foe.

"Jaden," whispered a voice in his ear, a voice he'd heard before only on vidscreen surveillance.

He spun, whirled, the power of the Force gathered in his hands for a telekinetic blast, and saw . . . only darkness.

Lumiya.

It had been Lumiya's voice. Hadn't it? But Lumiya was long dead.

A hand clutched at his robe.

"Jaden," said another voice. Lassin's voice.

He used the Force to augment a backward leap, flipping in midair, and landed on his feet three meters behind Lassin, a fellow Jedi Knight who should have been dead, who had died soon after the Ragnos crisis. Lassin's voice unmoored him from his calm, and Force lightning, blue and baleful, came unbidden and crackled on his fingertips . . .

He saw nothing.

The hairs on Jaden's neck rose. He stared at his hand, the blue discharge of his fingertips. With an effort of will, he quelled it.

"Jaden Korr," said a voice to his left, Master Kam Solusar's voice, but Jaden felt not the comforting presence of another light-side user, only the ominous energy of the dark side.

He spun, but saw only darkness.

"What you seek can be found in the black hole on Fhost, Jaden," said Mara Jade Skywalker, and still Jaden saw nothing, no one.

Mara Jade Skywalker was dead.

"Who are you?" he called, and the wind answered with ice and screams. "Where am I?"

He reached out again with his Force sense, trying to locate Lumiya, Lassin, Solusar, and Skywalker, but found them gone.

Again, he was alone in the darkness. He was always alone in darkness.

It registered with him then. He was dreaming. The Force was speaking to him. He should have realized it sooner.

The revelation stilled the world. The wind fell silent and the air cleared of ice.

Jaden stood ready, tense.

A distant, sourceless cry sounded, repeated itself, the rhythm regular, the tone mechanical. It could have been coming from the other side of the planet.

"Help us. Help us. Help us. Help us . . ."

He turned a circle, fists clenched. "Where are you?"

The darkness around him diminished. Pinpoints of light formed in the black vault over him. Stars. He scanned the sky, searching for something familiar. There. He recognized only enough to place the sky somewhere in a Rimward sector of the Unknown Regions. The dim blue glow of a distant gas giant burned in the black of the sky, its light peeking diffidently through the swirl. Thick rings composed of particles of ice and rock belted the gas giant.

He was on one of the gas giant's moons.

His eyes adjusted more fully to the dimness and he saw that he stood on a desolate, wind-racked plain of ice that extended as far as he could see. Snowdrifts as tall as buildings gave the terrain the appearance of a storm-racked ocean frozen in time. Cracks veined the exposed ice, the circulatory system of a stalled world. Chasms dotted the surface here and there like hungry mouths. Glaciers groaned in the distance, the rumbles of an angry world. He saw no sign of Lumiya or Lassin or any of the other Sith imposters he had sensed. He saw no sign of life anywhere.

His breath formed clouds before his face. His left fist clenched and unclenched reflexively over the void in his palm where his lightsaber should have been.

Without warning, the sky exploded above him with a thunderous boom. A cloud of fire tore through the atmosphere, smearing the sky in smoke and flame. A shriek like stressed metal rolled over Jaden. Ice cracked and groaned on the surface.

Jaden squinted up at the sky, still lit with the afterglow of the destruction, and watched a rain of glowing particulates fall, showering the moon in a hypnotic pattern of falling sparks.

His Force sense perceived them for what they were—the dark side reified. He disengaged his perception too slowly, and the impact of so much evil hit him like a punch in the face. He vomited down the front of his robes, fell to the frozen ground, and balled up on the frozen surface of the moon as the full weight of the dark side coated him in its essence.

There was nowhere to hide, no shelter; it fell all around him, on him, saturated him . . .

He woke, sweating and light-headed, to the sound of speeder and swoop traffic outside his Coruscant apartment. The thump of his heartbeat rattled the bars of his rib cage. In his mind's eye, he still saw the shower of falling sparks, the rain of evil. He cleared his throat, and the sensors in the room, detecting his wakefulness, turned on dim room lights.

"Arsix?" he said.

No response. He sat up, alarmed.

"Arsix?"

The sound of shouts and screams outside his window caused him to leap from his bed. With a minor exercise of will, he pulled his primary lightsaber to his hand from the side table near his bed and activated it. The green blade pierced the dimness of his room.

The black ball of Korriban filled Kell's viewscreen. Clouds seethed in its atmosphere, an angry churn.

He settled *Predator,* a CloakShape fighter modified with a hyperspace sled and sensor-evading technology copied from a stolen StealthX, into low orbit. The roiling cloak of dark energy that shrouded the planet buffeted *Predator,* and the ship's metal creaked in the strain.

Kell attuned his vision to Fate and saw the hundreds of *daen nosi*—fate lines, a Coruscanti academic had once translated the Anzati term—that intersected at Korriban, the planet like a bulbous black spider in a web of glowing potentialities. The past, present, and future lines of the galaxy's fate passed through the Sith tombworld's inhabitants, threads of glowing green, orange, red, and blue that cut it into pieces.

Space–time was pregnant with the possible, and the richness of the soup swelled Kell's hunger. He had first seen the *daen nosi* in childhood, after his first kill, and had followed them since. He thought himself unique among the Anzati, special, called, but he could not be certain.

Thinking of his first kill turned his mind to the food he kept in the cargo hold of *Predator,* but he quelled his body's impulse with a thought.

His own *daen nosi* stretched out before him, the veins of his own fate a network of silver lines reaching down through the transparisteel of the cockpit and into the dark swirl, down to the tombs of the Sith, to the secret places where the One Sith lurked. He had business with them, and they with him. The lines of their fates were intertwined.

He punched the coded coordinates of his destination into the navicomp and engaged the autopilot. As *Predator* began its descent through the black atmosphere, he left the cockpit and went below decks to the cargo hold. He had half a standard hour before he would reach his destination, so he freed his body to feel hunger. Growing anticipation sharpened his appetite.

Five stasis freezers stood against one wall of the hold like coffins. Kell had given them their own clear space in the hold, separated from the equipment and vehicles that otherwise cluttered the compartment. A humanoid slept in stasis in each freezer, three humans and two Rodians. He examined the freezers' readouts, checking vital signs. All remained in good health.

Staring at their still features, Kell wondered what happened behind their closed eyes, in the quiet of their dreams. He imagined the zest of their soup and hunger squirmed in his gut. None were so-called Force-sensitives, who had the richest soup, but they would suffice.

He glided from one freezer to the next, brushing his fingertips on the cool glass that separated him from his prey. His captives' *daen nosi* extended from their freezers to him, his to them. He stopped before the middle-aged human male he had taken on Corellia.

"You," he said, and watched his silver lines intertwine with the green lines of the Corellian.

He activated the freezer's thaw cycle. The hiss of escaping gas screamed the human's end. Kell watched as the freezer's readout indicated a rising temperature, watched as color returned to the human's flesh. His hunger grew, and the feeders nesting in the sacs of his cheeks twitched. He needed his prey conscious, otherwise he could not transcend.

He reached through the *daen nosi* that connected him to his meal.

Awaken, he softly projected.

The human's eyes snapped open, pupils dilated, lids wide. Fear traveled through the mental connection and Kell savored it. The freezer's readout showed a spiking heart rate, increasing respiration. The human opened his mouth to speak but his motor functions, still sluggish from stasis, could produce only a muffled, groggy croak.

Kell pressed the release button, and the freezer's cover slid open. *Be calm,* he projected, and his command wormed its way into the human's mind, a prophylactic for the fear.

But growing terror overpowered Kell's casual psychic hold. The human struggled against his mental bonds, finally found his voice.

"Please. I have done nothing."

Kell leaned forward, took the human's doughy face in his hands. The human shook his head but was no match for Kell's strength.

"Please," the Corellian said. "Why are you doing this? Who are you? *What* are you?"

Kell watched all of the human's *daen nosi,* all of his potential futures, coalesce into a single green line that intersected Kell's silver one, where it . . . stopped.

"I am a ghost," Kell answered, and opened the slits in his face. His feeders squirmed free of their sacs, wire-thin appendages that fed on the soup of the sentient.

The human screamed, struggled, but Kell held him fast.

Be calm, Kell projected again, this time with force, and the human fell silent.

The feeders wormed their way into the warm, moist tunnels of the Corellian's nostrils, and rooted upward. Anticipation caused Kell to drool. He stared into the human's wide, bloodshot eyes as the feeders penetrated tissue, pierced membranes, entered the skull cavity, and sank into the rich gray stew in the human's skull. A spasm racked the human's body. Tears pooled in his wide eyes and fell, glistening, down his cheeks. Blood dripped in thin lines from his nose.

Kell grunted with satisfaction as he devoured potential futures, as the human's lines ended and Kell's continued. Kell's eyes rolled back in his head as his *daen nosi* lengthened and he temporarily became one with the soup of Fate. His consciousness deepened, expanded to the size of the galaxy, and he mentally sampled its potential. Time compressed. The arrangement of *daen nosi* across the universe looked less chaotic. He saw a hint of order. Revelation seemed just at the edge of his understanding, and he experienced a tingling shudder with each beat of his hearts.

Show me, he thought. *Let me see.*

The moment passed as the human expired and Kell let him drop to the floor of the bay.

Revelation retreated and he backed away from the corpse, gasping. He came back to himself, mere flesh, mere limited comprehension.

He looked down at the cooling body at his feet, understanding that only in murder did he transcend.

He retracted his feeders, slick with blood, mucus, and brains, and they sat quiescent in their sacs.

Sighing, he collected the human's corpse, bore it to the air lock, and set the controls to eject it. Through the centuries, he had left such litter on hundreds of planets.

As he watched the automated ejection sequence vacate the air lock, he consoled himself with the knowledge that one day he would feed on stronger soup that would reveal to him the whole truth of Fate.

Reasonably sated, he returned to the cockpit of *Predator* and linked his comm receiver to the navicomp, as he had been instructed. In moments the autopilot indicator winked out—reminding Kell of the way the Corellian's eyes had winked out, how the human had transformed from sentience to meat in the span of a moment—and another force took control of *Predator*. Kell settled into his chair as the ship sped through the malaise of Korriban's atmosphere toward the dark side of the planet.

A short time later *Predator* set down in the midst of ancient structures. Lightning illuminated weathered pyramids, towers of pitted stone, crystalline domes, all of them the temples and tombs of the Sith, all of them the geometry of the dark side. Black clouds roiled and jagged runs of lightning formed a glowing net in the sky.

Kell rose, slid into his mimetic suit, checked the twin cortosis-coated vibroblades sheathed at his belt, and headed for *Predator*'s landing ramp. Before lowering it, he took a blaster and holster from a small-arms locker and strapped them to his thigh. He considered blasters inelegant weapons, but preferred to be overarmed rather than under.

He pressed the release button on the ramp. Hydraulics hummed and the door lowered. Wind and rain hissed into *Predator*. Korriban's air, pungent with the reek of past ages, filled his nostrils. Thunder boomed.

Kell stared out into the darkness, noted the clustered pinpoints of red light that floated in the pitch. He shifted on his feet as the lights drew closer—a silver protocol droid. He attuned his vision to Fate, saw no *daen nosi*. Droids were programming, nothing more. They made no real choices and so had no lines. The false sentience of the droid unnerved Kell and he cut off the perception.

The anthropomorphic droid strode through the wind and rain to the base of the landing ramp and bowed its head in a hum of servos.

"Master Anzat," the droid said in Basic. "I am Deefourfive. Please follow me. The Master awaits you."

The droid's words rooted Kell to the deck. Despite himself, Kell's twin hearts doubled their beating rate. Adrenaline flowed into his blood. The feeders in his cheeks spasmed. He inhaled, focused for a moment, and returned his body to calmness, his hormone level to normal.

"*The* Master? Krayt himself?"

"Please follow," the droid said, turned, and began walking.

Kell pulled up the hood of his suit but did not lower the mask; he strode down the ramp and stepped into the storm. Korriban drenched him. With a minor effort of will, he adjusted his core body temperature to compensate for the chill.

The droid led him along long-dead avenues lined with the ancient stone and steel monuments of the Sith Order. Kell saw no duracrete, no transparisteel, nothing modern. On much of Korriban, he knew, new layers had been built on the old over the millennia, creating a kind of archaeological stratification of the Sith ages.

Not here. Here, the most ancient of Sith tombs and temples sat undisturbed. Here, Krayt wandered in his dreams of conquest.

A flash of lightning veined the sky, painting shadows across the necropolis. Kell's mimetic suit adjusted to account for the temporary change in lighting. As he walked, he felt a growing regard fix on him, a consciousness.

Ahead, he saw a squat tower of aged stone—Krayt's sanctuary. Spirals of dark energy swirled in languid arcs around the spire. Only a few windows marred its otherwise featureless exterior, black holes that opened into a dark interior. To Kell, they looked like screaming mouths protesting the events transpiring within.

The droid ascended a wide, tiered stairway that led to a pair of iron doors at the base of the spire. Age-corroded writing and scrollwork spiraled over the door's surface. Kell could not read it.

"Remain here, please," the droid said, and vanished behind the doors.

Kell waited under Korriban's angry sky, surrounded by the tombs of Korriban's dead Sith Lords. Checking his wrist chrono from time to time, he attuned his senses to his surroundings and waited on Krayt's pleasure.

Footsteps sounded behind him, barely audible above the rain. He changed his perception as he turned, and saw a thick network of *daen nosi* that extended through the present to the future, wrapping the galaxy like a great serpent that would strangle it.

chapter two

THE PAST:
5,000 YEARS BEFORE THE BATTLE OF YAVIN

RELIN AND DREV SAT IN PENSIVE SILENCE AS THEIR Infiltrator streaked through the churning blue tunnel of hyperspace. They watched their instrumentation intently, hoping for the telltale beep denoting detection of the hyperspace beacon secreted aboard *Harbinger*. Lingering silence would mean they'd lost Saes.

"Scanners functioning normally," Drev said. After a sidelong glance at Relin, he began to hum, a free-form, lively tune from his homeworld.

"Must you?" Relin asked, smiling despite himself as he adjusted the instrumentation.

"Yes," said Drev, also smiling, but without looking up from his instruments. "I must."

Relin admired his Padawan's ability to find joy in everything he did, though Relin thought—and taught— that it was more important to maintain emotional evenness. Extremes of emotion could lead to the dark side.

Still, he wondered sometimes if Drev was the only one doing the learning in their relationship. It seemed Relin smiled only when in Drev's presence. Saes's betrayal had cut the mirth out of him as skillfully as a surgeon.

Drev tapped the scanner screen with a thick finger. "Come out, come out, whither you hide."

Presently, the scanner picked up a faint signal. Relin and Drev exhaled as one and leaned forward in their seats.

Drev chuckled and put a finger on the scanner screen. "There. They did it."

Relin let the navicomp digest the scanner's input and cross-referenced the coordinates. "The Phaegon system."

Without waiting for instruction, Drev pulled up the onboard computer's information on the system.

"There's nothing there," Drev said, eyeing the readout. "What is he doing?"

"Still looking, maybe," Relin said, and took the controls. "We will know soon enough."

The signal grew in strength as the Infiltrator hurtled through hyperspace.

"He's deep in-system," Relin said. "We emerge ten light-seconds out."

Drev nodded and input the commands into the navicomp. "The system has four planets, each with multiple moons. An asteroid belt divides the third from the fourth."

"Use it as cover until we understand what Saes is doing."

"Deactivating the hyperdrive in five, four . . ."

"Activating signature scrambler and baffles," Relin said. At the same moment, he used the Force to mask his and Drev's Force signatures, lest Saes perceive their arrival.

". . . two, one," Drev said, and deactivated the hyperdrive.

The blue tunnel of hyperspace gave way to the black void of stars, planets, and asteroids.

Instantly a wave of dark side energy, raw and jagged,

saturated the ship. Unready for the assault, Relin lost his breath, turned dizzy. Drev groaned, lurched back in his seat as if struck, then vomited down the front of his robes.

"Where is that coming from?" Relin said between gritted teeth.

Drev shook his head, still heaving. He reached for the scanner console.

"Leave it," Relin said, and adjusted the scanners himself.

They showed nothing nearby but the spinning chaos of the asteroid belt, and Phaegon III and its many moons.

Relin took a moment to clear his head, then drew on the Force to shield them from the ambient dark side energy. With his defenses in place, he felt the energy as only a soft, unpleasant pressure in his mind, incessant raindrops thumping against his skull, but it no longer affected his senses.

"All right?" he asked Drev.

Drev cleared his throat, eyed his flight suit and robes in embarrassment. "I am all right. Apologies, Master."

Relin waved away the apology. He had been unprepared, too.

"My meal tasted better the first time," Drev said, smiling, his cheeks bright red.

"Smelled better, too," Relin said, chuckling as he pored over the scanner's output.

"So, it's vomit that looses your sense of humor," Drev said. He stripped off his robe, balled it up, and retook his seat. He took a gulp of a flavored protein drink in a plastic pouch, swished it around his mouth. "I will keep that in mind. Maybe scatological humor will amuse you also?"

Relin only half smiled. His mind was on their situation. What had they stumbled onto? He had never before experienced such a wash of pure dark side energy. Whatever Saes had been searching for, he must have found it in the Phaegon system. Drev must have sensed his seriousness.

"What do you make of it?" Drev asked. "A dark side weapon? A Sith artifact maybe?"

Relin shook his head. The energy was not intense, simply widespread. "We will soon know."

He engaged the ion drive and started to take them into the asteroid belt, but thought better of it. He took his hands from the controls.

"Take us in, Drev," he said.

He felt his Padawan's eyes on him. "Into the belt?"

Relin nodded. The Infiltrator's sensor scrambler and the churn of the asteroid belt would foil any Sith scanners.

"Are you certain, Master?"

"Still your mind," he said to his Padawan. "Feel the Force, trust it."

Drev was one of the best raw pilots in the Order. With time and training in the use of the Force, he would become one of the Jedi's finest.

"Take us in," Relin repeated.

Drev stared out of the cockpit, at the ocean of whirling rocks. He paused for a long, calming breath, then took the controls and piloted the Infiltrator into the asteroid belt.

He accelerated without hesitation and the ship darted through the field of slowly spinning rock, diving, ascending, rolling. Pitted stones flashed on the viewscreen for a moment, vanished as Drev cruised under them, over them, around them. One of the Infiltrator's wings caught an oblong asteroid and the ship lurched, started to spin.

"Master—"

"Calm, Drev," Relin said, and his Padawan zagged

out of the way of another asteroid as he righted the starfighter.

"Well done, Padawan," Relin said. "Well done."

A smile split Drev's face as he continued through the belt.

Relin monitored the sensors. "There is an asteroid on the edge of the belt, more than ten kilometers in diameter, in a very slow spin."

"I see it."

"Set us down there but stay powered up. Let us see what we see."

Drev maneuvered them over the asteroid and set down the Infiltrator. Phaegon III loomed large in their viewscreen against a backdrop of stars.

Drev was still smiling. Relin chose to ignore his Padawan's emotional high.

"Give me a heads-up display and magnify."

A HUD appeared off center in the cockpit window. Drev input a few commands and magnified the image.

Plumes of smoke spiraled from the charred surface of one of Phaegon III's small moons. Saes's dreadnought and its sister ship hung like carrion birds in low orbit over the moon's corpse. A steady stream of transports moved between the moon's surface and the belly-slung landing bays of the two Sith ships.

Drev lost his smile as he worked the scanners. "That is not—how can—? Master, that moon should be covered in vegetation." He looked up from his scan. "And life."

Relin felt his Padawan's anger over the destruction. He knew where anger led. The young man moved from joy to rage as if his emotions were on a pendulum.

"Stay focused on our task, Drev. The scope of the matter cannot affect your thinking. Do not let anger cloud your mind."

Drev stared at him as if he were something appalling

he'd found on the bottom of his boot. "The *matter*? It is not a mere matter. They incinerated an entire moon! It is an atrocity."

Relin nodded. "The word fits. But you are a Jedi. Master your emotions. Especially now. *Especially* now, Padawan."

Drev stared at him a moment longer before turning back to the scanners. When he spoke, his voice was stiff. "There are hundreds of mining droids on the moon."

More to himself than Drev, Relin said, "Saes incinerated the crust, then loosed the mining droids." He focused his Force sense on the transports and their cargo. Though he had been ready, the dark side backlash elicited a gasp and set him backward in his chair.

"It is the cargo."

"The cargo? What did he pull out of that moon?"

Relin shook his head as he took the controls. "I do not know. An ore of some kind, something attuned to the dark side." Relin knew of such things. "Whatever it is, it is powerful. Maybe powerful enough to determine the outcome of the assault on Kirrek. That's what Saes has been searching for, and that is why Sadow delayed his assault. We cannot allow it to get out of the system."

"You have a plan, I trust," Drev said, not so much a question as an assertion.

"We take those dreadnoughts out of the sky. Or at least keep them here."

Drev licked his lips, no doubt pondering the relative sizes of the Infiltrator and the dreadnoughts, not unlike the relative difference between a bloodfly and a rancor. "How?"

Relin lifted the Infiltrator off the asteroid and flew it into open space. "I'm going aboard. Saes and I should get reacquainted."

He expected at least a chuckle from his Padawan, but

Drev did not so much as smile. He stared out the viewscreen at the dead moon, at the Sith ships, his lips fixed in a hard line.

Relin put a hand on his Padawan's shoulder and unharnessed himself from his seat.

"You have the controls. The scrambler and baffles will not keep us invisible for long. I just need a little time."

Drev nodded as the Infiltrator sped toward the dreadnoughts. "You will have it. You'll try to board a transport?"

"That is what I am thinking," Relin answered as he moved to the cramped rear compartment of the Infiltrator. Rapidly he peeled off his robes and donned a vac-ready flexsuit, formulating the details of a plan as he went.

The ryon shell of the suit, lined with a flexible, titanium mesh as fine as hair, felt like a second skin. He checked the oxygen supply and the batteries and found them both full. He slipped the power pack harness over his shoulders, around his abdomen, and clipped it in place. The power umbilical fed into the suit's abdominal jack with a satisfying click, and the suit hummed to life. The energy running through the mesh hardened the suit slightly and caused Relin's skin to tingle. He put the hinged helmet in place over his head and an electromagnetic seal fixed it to the neck ring, rendering the zipper and power jack airtight.

The suit ran a diagnostic, and Relin watched the results in the helmet's HUD. His breathing sounded loud in the drum of the transparisteel and plastic helmet. He activated the comlink.

"Testing."

"Clear," said Drev, his voice like a concert inside the helmet.

The diagnostic came back clean.

"Suit is live and sealed," Relin said.

"We remain unnoticed," Drev said, his tone sharp, serious. "For now."

While Relin had been trying to encourage seriousness in his Padawan for months, at the moment he regretted the turn of Drev's mood. He missed his Padawan's mirth in the face of danger. To craft Drev into a Jedi, it seemed that Relin would have to turn him into something other than Drev.

"How close?" Relin said. He slipped a dozen maggrenades and a variety of other equipment into one of the suit's ample thigh pockets, then strapped a blaster pistol to his belt, beside his lightsaber and its power pack.

"Twenty thousand kilometers and closing fast," Drev said. A hitch in his voice told Relin something was wrong. "That moon. Master, it's a ruin."

"I know," Relin said. "That is what Sith do. They destroy. They take. That is all the dark side can offer. Now focus, Padawan. Match vectors with the nearest transport returning to *Harbinger,* but only for a moment. I will board it, and that will get me into one of the dreadnought's landing bays." He considered the grenades in his pockets. "From there, I'll see what I can do."

For a time, Drev said nothing, then, "Are you sure this is the way, Master? If you succeed, that takes care of only one of the dreadnoughts."

"That we may not accomplish everything is no reason to do nothing. We cannot let that cargo get to Kirrek. Or at least not all of it. We stop what we can here, doing whatever we must. If I destroy or disable the first ship, we'll figure out a way to do the same to the other."

"Understood."

"Entering the air lock," Relin said. He opened the interior air lock door, stepped inside, and closed it behind him. He disengaged the safety and pressed the button to open the exterior door. A red light flashed for three seconds to indicate the pending evacuation. Relin held the safety bar as the hatch slid open and the air rushed out into space.

"Coming up on the transport now, Master."

Relin moved to the open hatch as Drev eased the Infiltrator over the transport and matched its course and speed as best he could. The awkward transport was a flying storage crate, a gray wedge of a hold with a transparisteel bubble cockpit tacked on to its underside. Like all Sith ships, it still managed to look like a flying blade.

Dark side energy leaked from its cargo hold in palpable waves, making Relin temporarily dizzy.

"Master?"

They would be spotted in moments. He had to move.

"Have you ever gone angling, Drev?" Relin asked.

"Angling?"

"Fishing. You know."

"No, Master. I have not."

Relin tried to smile, failed. At that moment, he would have paid a thousand credits to hear Drev's laugh. "Neither have I."

"May the Force be with you, Master."

Relin picked a spot on the spine of the transport, closed his eyes, felt the Force. His mastery of the telekinetic use of the Force was not advanced enough to pull a moving ship to him, but that was not what he intended to do.

"A scanner has picked up our ship," Drev said, tension in his voice.

"Our usual encrypted channel, Drev. And minimal chatter."

"Yes, Master. And . . . don't miss," Drev said, and chuckled.

Smiling, Relin reached out with the Force, took mental hold of the Sith transport, and leapt out of the Infil-trator into open space.

"I am clear," he said, and Drev peeled off.

THE PRESENT:
41.5 YEARS AFTER THE BATTLE OF YAVIN

The screams from outside Jaden's window turned to laughter as an open-top speeder streaked past. He heard music booming from the speeder's speakers. The sounds faded as it flew away.

It took a moment for him to understand what had occurred.

Adolescents, he realized. Probably on a late-night thrill ride.

"Stang," he whispered, but he did not deactivate his lightsaber. Its hum filled the room, a comforting sound. The images from the vision remained sharp in his mind.

The whir of R6's servos announced the droid's entrance into the room. Seeing Jaden standing in his night-clothes with his lightsaber burning, R6 cut short his beeped greeting to whistle a concerned question. Jaden did not fully understand droidspeak, but he usually got the gist of R6's communications. Or perhaps he assumed R6 said or asked whatever Jaden wished him to say or ask.

"I guess that makes you my confessor," he said to the astromech. "Congratulations."

R6 beeped the question again, and Jaden smiled.

"Nothing. A bad joke. And I am fine. I had an . . . unusual dream."

But Jaden knew it had not been a dream. It had been a Force vision.

R6 hummed understanding and whistled out the first stanza of a lullaby.

Jaden smiled at the droid, though his mind was still on the vision. He had never before had one so vivid.

What had it meant?

Dead Jedi and Sith resurrected, an icy moon in the Unknown Regions, a rain of evil, and the repeated cry for help. He could not make sense of what he had seen, so he tried to recall what he had felt—the uncomfortably familiar touch of the dark side, his increasingly attenuated connection to the light side, and, bridging the two, his Master's words: the Force is a tool, neither light nor dark.

"How can that be? A tool? Nothing more than that?"

R6 beeped confusion.

Jaden waved a hand distractedly. "It cannot be," he said, answering his own question. The Force had been Jaden's moral compass for decades. Reducing it to a tool, mere potential, left him . . . rudderless. He looked at his hand, the hand from which he had discharged Force lightning.

"There be dragons," he muttered, deactivating his lightsaber.

R6 whirred a question.

"I am trying to discern the vision's meaning, but I am . . . uncertain."

He had been uncertain since the Battle of Centerpoint Station, though he had been struggling with doubt before that. His certainty had been one of the unrecorded casualties of the battle. He had . . . done things he regretted. The Corellians had simply wanted their independence. In hindsight, Jaden saw the whole affair as a political matter unworthy of Jedi involvement. He had killed over politics. The *Jedi Order* had killed over politics.

Where did that leave them as an Order? How were they different from the Sith? Hadn't they used the light side to engage in morally questionable acts? And where did that leave Jaden? He felt soiled by his participation in the battle.

"Once, we were guardians of the galaxy," he said to R6, and the droid stayed wisely silent.

Now the Jedi seemed guardians of particular politicians. What principles did they stand for anymore?

The Force is only a tool.

He shook his head as he pulled on his robes. The Force had to be more than that. Otherwise he had lived a lie for decades. His lightsaber was a tool. The Force was . . . something more. It had to be.

He feared the Jedi had come to think that because they used the light side of the Force, everything they did must therefore be good. Jaden saw that thinking as flawed, even dangerous.

Since the battle for Centerpoint, he had isolated himself from the Order, from Valin, from Kyle. He felt purposeless and unwelcome. He thought his doubt must be plain to them all. He knew he would be transparent to the Masters. He had no one with whom he could share his thoughts.

"No one but you," he said to R6.

His blaster and the small, one-handed hilt of his second lightsaber lay on his side table. He strapped on a holster, put the blaster to bed in it, and hooked his secondary saber to the clip at the small of his back. He did not know why he kept the old lightsaber, holding it close to him like a good-luck charm. He supposed its blade was the purple tether that connected him to a simpler past. He had crafted the blade when the Force had been nothing to him but a word. He had possessed no wisdom, yet he had utilized the Force to build a blade.

Didn't that mean that Kyle was right, that the Force *was* simply a tool, free-floating energy for anyone to use, no different from a loaded blaster? He shied away from the notion, because if it were true, then the light and dark side meant nothing in terms of moral and immoral, good and evil.

"I do not accept that," he said to R6. "I cannot."

Help us. Help us.

The voice from his vision echoed in his head, reminded him of who and what he was. He had stood on a frozen, dark moon in the Unknown Regions, communed with dead Jedi while evil had rained down, and someone had called to him for help. He would help. He must. Moral clarity lived in aid to others. He grabbed it like a lifeline.

What you seek can be found in the black hole on Fhost.

The words were nonsense. There was no black hole on Fhost or anywhere near it. But he had to learn what the words meant, because that would allow him to find what he sought.

"Arsix, link with the HoloNet."

The droid whistled acquiescence, extended a wireless antenna, and connected.

"Call up mapped or partially mapped sectors in the Unknown Regions," Jaden said.

R6's projector showed three-dimensional images of various sectors in the air between the droid and Jaden. There were only a few. The information was woefully thin.

"Search for any charted system with a gas giant that appears blue to the human eye, ringed, with at least one frozen moon whose atmosphere would support a human."

R6's processors whirred through the information he pulled from the HoloNet. Holographic planets appeared and disappeared so quickly in the space between them that Jaden soon felt dizzy. In a quarter hour, R6 had shuffled through a catalog of thousands of planets. None squared with Jaden's vision. Jaden was unsurprised. Most of the Unknown Regions were unmapped on Galactic Alliance star charts. The Chiss were out there. The remnants of the Yuuzhan Vong were out there. Who knew what else he would find in those uncharted systems?

"An answer, perhaps," he said. But first he had to form the question, first he had to articulate what he sought. He felt the thin edge of a blade under his feet, felt himself wobbling on it. He was off balance.

R6 beeped a query.

The Force had sent Jaden a vision, this he knew. He would follow it.

"Show me Fhost, Arsix."

The images of various systems in the Unknown Regions blinked out, gave way to a magnified image of a dusty world, one half in its sun's light, one half in darkness. He stared at the line separating the two hemispheres. It looked as thin as thread, as thin as the edge of a blade.

"Info on Fhost," he said, and R6 scrolled a readout of the planet in the air before Jaden's eyes. What little information existed was more than three decades old and came from an Imperial survey team.

Fhost was the only world in the system occupied by sentients, though none was native, and its itinerant population wouldn't have filled a sports stadium on Coruscant. Its largest population center, Farpoint, had been built on the ruins of a crashed starship of unknown origin. Jaden imagined the place to be a haven for adventurers, criminals, and other undesirables who preferred to live at the edge of known space, all of them crowded into ad hoc shelters built on the bones of a derelict ship.

But Fhost was his only lead. If he credited the Force vision at all—and how could he not?—he would have to follow it to his answer.

"Get the Z-Ninety-five ready and prepare a course to

Fhost," he said to the droid. He paused, then added, "And do not file a flight plan with the Order."

R6 beeped a mildly alarmed tone.

"Do as I ask, Arsix."

The droid whirred agreement and wheeled out of the room.

Whatever the vision wished to teach him, it would teach to *him*. He did not want other Jedi involved, did not even want the Order to know where he'd gone.

This was to be his lesson, and his alone. He would find what he sought, get his question answered for himself.

"Darth Wyyrlok," Kell said as he turned. The honorific came with difficulty to his lips. Both Wyyrlok and Krayt had adopted a title once carried by beings of greater stature.

The Chagrian Sith Lord's mouth formed a tight smile, as if he sensed the meat of Kell's thoughts. Wyyrlock stood as tall as Kell, and the left horn on his head extended half a meter more; the right horn, lost some time ago to accident or battle, was a jagged stump only a few centimenters long. To Kell, it looked like a rotted tooth. The line of a scar extended the length of the Chagrian's face, a seam connecting the ruined horn to the corner of his mouth. Wyyrlok's robe, as black as a singularity and soaked with rain, hung heavily from his broad shoulders. The hilt of a lightsaber at his belt peeked out from under the folds.

Kell imagined the insight he could gain by devouring a soup so rich as Wyyrlok's. A cyclone of *daen nosi* whirled around the Chagrian. The feeders within Kell's cheeks squirmed reflexively.

"Anzat," the Sith said, with a faint nod.

"The droid led me to believe I might see Darth Krayt

himself. The message I received purported to come from him."

Wyyrlok's eyes never left Kell's. "The Master walks in dreams. This you know, Kell Douro. What you achieve only when feeding, he achieves at will. Past, present, and future are as one to him. Therefore, I am his voice while he sleeps. This, too, you know."

Kell tilted his head as if to acknowledge the point, but he knew better. What he experienced while feeding could be experienced only by him. The Sith, like the Jedi, conceptualized the galaxy through the lens of the Force. But Kell knew the Force to be but one aspect of the greater skein of Fate. Neither the Sith nor the Jedi saw reality's truth. Kell would, when he fed on the one whose soup held revelation.

"So you say, Darth Wyyrlok."

"So I say," Wyyrlok said. Again that smile, as if he could read Kell's mind.

Thunder rumbled. Kell felt others in the darkness around them. More Sith. Servants of Wyyrlok.

"Naga Sadow walked this ground," Wyyrlok said, his clawed hand gesturing at the brick walkway. "And Exar Kun after him. Then, no crippling Rule of Two limited the power of the Sith. Wisely, Darth Krayt has undone the mistake of Bane. Therefore no Rule of Two limits the One Sith today."

Kell said nothing. He cared little for the intricacies of the Sith religion. And the Chagrian's incessant use of *therefore* drove Kell to distraction.

"Why have I been summoned?" Kell asked.

Wyyrlok took a step closer to Kell. The Sith around them in the darkness drew closer, too. Kell felt as if he were standing in the middle of a tightening knot. He muffled his presence, quelling his *daen nosi*, deflecting perception. Between his psychic camouflage and his mimetic suit, he would be nearly invisible to those around him.

Wyyrlok blinked, looked past and through him for a moment, before his eyes refocused on Kell's.

"Clever, Anzat. He gestured with his chin out into the darkness, causing his lethorns to sway. "But they will not harm you except at my command. Therefore, you have nothing to fear."

Kell nodded, but nevertheless maintained his psychic deflection.

"An opportunity has been revealed to the Master," Wyyrlok said, and took another step closer.

Kell held his ground while lightning lit up the sky. "What kind of opportunity?"

"I will show you," Wyyrlok said, and offered his fanged smile.

Concentration furrowed Wyyrlok's brow. Their *daen nosi* intertwined. An itch formed behind Kell's eyes, then a stabbing pain. He screamed as images exploded in his mind: an icebound moon in orbit around a blue, ringed gas giant, a night sky exploding in a rain of power.

He clutched his head and sagged as the images burned themselves into his memory. He lost control of his muscles and his feeders emerged from his face, squirmed like cut power conduits. Fighting through the pain, he wrapped his fingers around one of his vibroblades, drew it.

The mental intrusion ceased, as did the pain. He snarled, brandished his blade, drew its twin.

Wyyrlok made no move for his lightsaber. He stared into Kell's eyes.

"I do not require a lightsaber to kill you. Therefore, an attack would be foolish. Are you foolish, Kell Douro?"

Kell considered, calmed himself, and sheathed his blades. "What is the meaning of the vision?"

The Chagrian gave his false smile. "That is what you will determine. The vision portends something important, Anzat. And the Master has concluded that it will begin on Fhost. There, a sign will be given to you. Perhaps even the sign you have long sought."

Kell tried to hide the excitement birthed by Wyyrlok's words. He imagined lines of fate coalescing around Fhost, catching it up in a net of destiny. "I know its location."

"You will, therefore, travel there. Watch for the sign. Learn what there is to learn. And, perhaps, take what there is to take."

Kell rubbed his eyes, as if erasing them of the remembrance of pain. "Why me?" He gestured out into the darkness. "Why not one of them?"

"Because it is the Master's will that the One Sith remain quiescent. Therefore, we must use intermediaries."

Kell had had enough of Wyyrlok's *therefore*s. "To whom shall I report what I learn?"

"You will report back to me," Wyyrlok said. He frowned, as if struck with a thought, and said, "The Master believes it likely that the Jedi have received a similar vision. The Force is moving in this matter. They may, therefore, interfere. You should not allow interference."

Kell put his hands on the hilts of his blades. "I understand. What form will the sign take?"

Wyyrlok shrugged. "The Master believes you will know it when you see it. He believes in your ingenuity. And your desire to find the one that you seek."

Kell licked his lips, knowing he would get nothing more, though he had been given precious little. "Is that all, then?"

Wyyrlok held out his hands, as if to show himself harmless. "You are free to go."

Kell backed away from Wyyrlok, down the stairs, and

toward his ship. He checked his chrono as he walked. He had last fed only half a standard hour earlier, yet he felt the need to feed again, to recapture the certainty that feeding brought him. Wyyrlok's words had poked holes in that certainty. They always did. The Chagrian left him ill at ease.

From behind, Wyyrlok called out above the rain. "Why do you serve the Master, Kell Douro?"

The question confused Kell, halted his steps. He shook his head, his mind suddenly jumbled, his thoughts inchoate. "What? What did you say?"

"Consider the answer to that question, Anzat." Kell could see the Chagrian's fangs bared in a smile, even through the rain, and there was nothing false in it. "Then consider anew who sees reality's truths. You are not the only one who can shape perception."

Thunder boomed; lightning ripped the sky. Kell shook his head to clear it, started to answer Wyyrlok, but saw that he had gone. His head felt muddled. A headache nested at the root of his skull. Out of habit, he checked his chrono again.

He had lost a quarter of a standard hour since he'd last checked it moments ago. He had no idea how.

chapter three

RELIN STARTED TO LOSE FORWARD MOMENTUM THE instant he leapt clear of the air lock. He activated the magnetic grips in his gloves and boots as he fell. Time seemed to slow as he plummeted toward the transport, and an image of the transport against the background of stars burned itself into his memory. Remaining focused, holding the ship in his telekinetic grasp, he steered his descent and reeled himself in. He could not afford to slow himself with the Force and he hit the surface of the ship hard, thumping his helmet on the hull and for a moment scrambling the HUD.

The transport lurched the moment he alit, and the sudden shift in momentum nearly threw him. He cursed and grabbed the protuberances nearest to hand. The Force and his magnetic grips kept him anchored. For an instant he feared a scan by the transport crew had detected his presence, but the ship had swerved left and down, probably an evasive maneuver in response to the detection of the Infiltrator.

Drev would be under pressure soon. Relin had to move fast.

He hung on to the transport as it sped toward the

dreadnoughts. *Harbinger* and *Omen* had long sleek bodies dotted everywhere with batteries of rotating laser cannon turrets, typically used for ship-to-ship combat. As he watched, the cannons rotated in the direction of the Infiltrator, but they would have difficulty getting a fix on the small, stealth-equipped starfighter.

In moments a rapid reaction squad of Sith fighters, like flying knives, streaked from the bay.

"Incoming," he said to Drev over the encrypted channel. "Ten *Blade*-class fighters. Stay among the smaller craft and the dreadnoughts will not fire."

He glanced back but could not see Drev and the Infiltrator, could see only the dark side of Phaegon III, a handful of the transport shuttles going evasive, and the floating rock of the dead moon. He returned his gaze to the dreadnoughts and focused on his mission. The transport was making for *Harbinger*.

Interior lights from observation decks and viewports flickered here and there along *Harbinger*'s and *Omen*'s lengths. In shape, the dreadnoughts reminded Relin of gigantic lanvaroks, the bladed polearm favored by the Sith. The tumors of bubble-shaped escape pods lined the spine that connected the forward bridge section to the aft engine and landing bay sections.

Like most Jedi, he'd studied the available schematics of Sith starships. He knew their layout. And he knew where he was going once he got aboard.

The transport straightened its course, descended a bit, and headed for the bay. Relin estimated time of arrival, removed three of the mag-grenades from his flexsuit, and crawled along the transport as fast as he dared until he reached the housing for the engine nacelles. He stuck all three charges to one of the nacelles and waited.

The moment the transport cleared the landing bay's shielding and started to slow, he activated them, put them on a ten-second timer, and began counting down in his head. Two more Blades sped past him and out of the ship.

Ten, nine . . .

He worried for Drev. His Padawan was an extraordinary pilot, but the sky would be thick with Sith fighters. Relin would have to be fast.

Eight, seven . . .

The activity in the landing bay gave it the appearance of an Eesin hive. Pilots in full gear were carted in levs to their Blades. Droids wheeled and walked here and there. Organics and machines unloaded open transports and loaded what looked like raw ore onto lev pallets. The sight of the ore, the greasy feel of it, made Relin queasy.

He remembered a moment years before when he and Saes, then still a Jedi, had happened upon a crystal that enhanced a dark side user's connection to the Force. He shuffled through his memory until he recalled the name of the ore—Lignan.

The feel of it was the same. It had to be the same material.

He had never imagined there could be so much.

A female voice on the loudspeaker announced commands. "Cargo droid team four to landing bay one-sixty-three-bee."

Relin reached out with the Force and felt the minds around him as the transport settled into a landing bay and powered down its engines. Autoclamps secured its skids and gases vented with a hiss. Relin discerned ten or so beings nearby, none a Force-user, all weak-minded.

Five, four . . .

Using the Force, he entered their minds and erased himself from their perception.

Three, two . . .

He leapt from the ship, hit the floor in a roll, found his feet, and ran. Augmenting his speed with the Force, he covered a hundred meters in the tick of a chrono.

Zero.

Behind him, the mag-grenades blossomed into a cloud of flame and heat, and the secondary explosion from one or both of the transport's other engines rocked the landing bay. The concussion wave nearly knocked him from his feet. Shards of metal, chunks of flesh, screams, and sparkling motes of the transported ore peppered the area. The presence of the ore in its naked form made his stomach churn, and he took care as best he could to touch none of the particulates.

An alarm screeched and the crew near the wreckage scrambled for the firefighting gear. A medical droid wheeled past Relin.

"Firefighting team to main landing bay," announced the female voice.

Ears ringing, Relin hurried down a corridor in the direction of the hyperdrive chamber. He flipped back his helmet, letting it hang by the hinge at the rear of the suit's neck, and put the helmet's removable comlink in his ear.

A firefighting team, several curious crew members, and three towering, red-skinned Massassi in security uniforms stormed past him at intervals. He used the Force to deflect their perception as he hurried along. The interior of the ship reflected the mind-set of its Sith builders: all hard edges, sharp corners, and pure functionality, with no allowance for comfort or aesthetics.

The sound of the alarm grew fainter, and he allowed himself to feel a small sense of relief. He reached an intersection and paused for a moment to gather his bearings. He shuffled through the cards of his memory, recalling the direction of the hyperdrive chamber.

Left. And not far.

A hatch to his left slid open to reveal the muscular, vaguely reptilian form of a Massassi warrior in the deep black uniform and epaulets of security personnel. A lanvarok hung across his back, a blaster on the trunk of his thigh. Bone quills poked from his knuckles. Metal ornaments pierced his wide nose and small ears. Studs had been implanted underneath the red skin of his forearms, biceps, and hairless scalp. The Massassi's eyes fixed on Relin before he could use the Force to blind his perception. The tentacles of the Massassi's beard quivered over his broad, toothy mouth. A vein in his temple visibly throbbed.

"We need assistance in the landing bay," Relin said. "Something went wrong with the—"

The Massassi took in Relin's flexsuit, the lack of a uniform. His yellow eyes narrowed and his clawed hand clutched the hilt of his lanvarok, pulled it free. The large polearm could be spun by a wielder to release the sharpened metal disks mounted on its haft, or the jagged bladed end could serve as an ax. A crude weapon, but dangerous.

"Who is your superior?" the Massassi asked, his voice as guttural as comm static.

The Massassi put the point of the lanvarok on Relin's chest and pushed him up against the wall.

Relin understood then how things would go. He looked up and down the corridor, saw no one.

With his free hand, the Massassi pinched the comlink on his collar.

"This is Drophan, security detail five. I have a—"

"My superior is Memit Nadill," Relin said.

"Go ahead, Drophan," said the voice from the comlink.

But Relin's words had creased the Massassi's forehead and his fingers released the comlink. "Memit who? I do not know that name."

"He is a Jedi Master on Kirrek."

"A Jedi what?"

"Say again, Drophan. Your transmission fell off. Say again."

Relin's words finally penetrated the Massassi's armor of incredulity and his yellow eyes widened. He leaned into his lanvarok as his hand went for his blaster.

Relin projected a telekinetic blast from his palm, pushed the Massassi across the corridor, and slammed him against the wall. The impact summoned a gasp of pain and sent the blaster to the floor. The Massassi ignored it, growled, and lunged for Relin with the lanvarok.

Relin ignited his lightsaber and the green blade met red flesh, severing an arm on the crosscut, then the head on the backswing. The Massassi's corpse fell at Relin's feet.

"Report, Drophan," said the voice in the Massassi's comlink.

Relin saw no point in hiding the body. They would know he was aboard soon enough. Deactivating his lightsaber, he sprinted down the hall. He decided to risk a communication.

"Drev?"

"It's thick out here, Master. But I'm holding."

Relin heard the tension in his Padawan's voice. The rumble of a near miss carried through the connection, along with Drev's grunt.

"It's about to get thick in here, too," Relin said. "Not much longer. Rely on the Force, Drev. And hang on."

Saes stalked the bridge, the susurrant rush of his robes loud in the quiet. None of his crew met his eyes. On the viewscreen, the Jedi Infiltrator weaved and darted through space, upward of twelve Blades in pursuit. Laserfire crisscrossed the screen, a net of glowing lines. Frustrated comm chatter from the Blade pilots carried over the bridge speakers.

Saes used the dark side to probe the Infiltrator pilot's connection to the Force and found him more of a potential than a fully realized Force-user, though he was an extraordinarily intuitive pilot.

He could not be alone.

As Saes watched, Blades came at the Infiltrator from two sides and the bottom, a claw encirclement.

"They have him now," muttered a junior officer.

The Jedi cut hard to the left and engaged a booster, blasting one of the Blades from space as he did so, and gained some separation from the rest. Soft curses sounded from the bridge.

"He's heading for another transport," Dor observed.

The Infiltrator wheeled around and the transport pilot took evasive maneuvers but it was far too little. The Infiltrator's lasers spat energy; the transport and its ore turned to dust.

Saes's anger grew. He could not afford to lose any of his ore. Out of habit, he tapped his forefinger on the point of one of his jaw horns.

"Intensify scanning in system," Dor ordered the helm. "This Jedi cannot be alone. More will be coming."

"Yes, Colonel."

Saes ground his fangs as the Infiltrator weaved out of another trap laid for him by the Blades. He glared at the weapons officer, a human male with gray at his temples and concern in his eyes.

"Can you get a lock?"

"No, Captain. The ship has some kind of sensor scrambler. We could blanket an area and bring him down even without a lock, but he's too near our ships."

Saes nodded. "Prepare a firing solution to provide a safe corridor for the transports. Transmit it to the Blades' navicomps to keep them clear."

"Yes, Captain."

Saes turned to Dor. "End planetside operations.

Order every transport back to *Harbinger* and *Omen*. A firing corridor will be provided for them."

"Yes, Captain," said Dor with a nod, and began transmitting the orders.

"Firing solution ready, sir," said the weapons officer.

"Fire," Saes said.

Harbinger's laser cannons put a curtain of flames in space, dividing the Infiltrator and Blades from the transports. The transports took immediate advantage and sped for the landing bays.

"As soon as the transports are aboard, recall the Blades," Saes said to Dor. To his weapons officer, he said, "Then you blow him from space."

"What?" Dor said, and the exclamation turned heads on the bridge. For a moment, Saes thought Dor to be questioning his order, but he soon saw otherwise. The colonel tilted his head into his earpiece. As he listened, his skin turned a deeper red and his tentacle beard quivered with anger. "Double security around all sensitive areas. Establish search teams and comb the ship. Dor out."

"What is it?" Saes asked.

Dor's beard twitched as he leaned in close to Saes and spoke in a low tone. "The body of a security guard was found in the corridor off the landing bay. His arm and head were severed. It appears to have been the work of a lightsaber."

Adrenaline fueled Saes's pheromones, increasing their odor. "A lightsaber," he muttered to himself. "Then the explosion in the bay was not an engine malfunction."

"It appears not."

"We have a Jedi aboard."

A murmur went through the bridge crew. The smell of their sweat sweetened with excitement.

Dor tapped his palm on the hilt of the lanvarok he

wore even on bridge duty. "If these Jedi are a vanguard for a larger force . . ."

Saes nodded. He could not take the chance. Sadow would be displeased with a delay in the delivery of the Lignan. To the helmsman, he said, "Move us out of the planet's gravity well and prepare the ship for hyperspace. Plot a route to Primus Goluud and jump as soon as all our ships are back aboard." To Dor, he said, "You have the bridge."

Dor nodded. "Yes, sir. What are you going to do?"

Saes put his hand on the hilt of his lightsaber. "I am going to retrieve my mask and find our stowaway. A captured Jedi would make a nice gift to accompany the Lignan for Master Sadow."

Relin felt the mental fingers of his onetime Padawan and knew that the dead Massassi's body had been found. Saes was searching for him. Relin resisted the impulse to lower his mental screen and reveal himself. He needed to accomplish his mission, not correct a past wrong.

He hurried through the maze of corridors, using the Force on groups of two or three crew to remove himself from their perception. The crew of *Harbinger* was on alert, searching for him, and Relin found it increasingly taxing to render himself hidden from them.

Ahead, he heard the heavy tread of boots and the booming bass voices of several Massassi. From the sound of it, he put their numbers at six or seven. Given their alert status and attunement to the dark side, he would not be able to use the Force to hide from them. He checked one of the nearby hatches, found it locked, checked another, found that locked, too.

The voices drew closer. He could not make out their words. They were speaking their native language.

He pulled an overrider—an electronic lockpick—from his suit and attached it to the nearest door's control panel. Lights flashed as the equipment interfaced and the overrider tried to find the door's open code. The Massassi were around the corner. Relin would not get clear in time. He took his lightsaber in hand and ignited it.

The Massassi fell silent. They must have heard him activate his lightsaber.

The overrider flashed green and the door opened with a metallic hiss. Moving quickly, he detached the overrider and slid inside as the Massassi rounded the corner.

A meeting room. A large table surrounded by chairs and dotted with three comp stations sat centermost. A vidscreen, powered down, took up one wall. Transparisteel windows made up the bulkhead, allowing a view of the system outside.

He crouched with his ear to the door, listening to the voices of the Massassi. They sounded like they were right outside, separated from him only by a thin layer of metal, talking in hushed tones. He winced as his comlink activated and Drev spoke.

"The transports are returning to the landing bay and both dreadnoughts are moving, Master."

Relin heard laserfire in the background of Drev's transmission, but his mind was on the Massassi in the corridor outside.

"Stand by," he whispered. "Stand by."

The voices outside went silent. Had they heard Drev? A human would not have been able to hear the comlink transmission, but Massassi had keener senses than humans. Relin sat behind the door, lightsaber humming in his hand, the calm of the Force in his heart, waiting, waiting . . .

Nothing.

He glanced back out of the meeting room windows to see the background of stars shifting slightly as the ship moved away from Phaegon III and its gravity well.

"They are preparing to jump," he said to Drev. He had to get to the hyperdrive, and now.

"Get off that ship, Master, or you'll go with them."

"There is still time." He pushed the button to open the hatch. "I'm near the hyperdrive chamber and—"

He found himself staring at the uniformed chest of a Massassi security officer, who held his lanvarok in one hand. The bone spurs and studs under the Massassi's red flesh gave it a tumorous appearance.

"Here!" the Massassi shouted down the hall. Roaring, he swung his lanvarok in a downstroke for Relin's head, but Relin sidestepped the blow and it slammed into the deck while Relin drove his lightsaber through the Massassi's abdomen. The Massassi groaned, dropped his weapon. His clawed hands groped reflexively for Relin's throat as he died.

Shouts from down the hall told Relin the dead Massassi's comrades had heard his call. He took a thermal grenade from his flexsuit, stepped out of the room, and tossed it down the corridor at the onrushing Massassi, each with a blaster and lanvarok bare. Recognition of what he had thrown widened their eyes and they dived for cover, but not before one of them got off a blaster shot.

Relin deflected it with his lightsaber and ducked back into the room he had vacated as the grenade exploded.

Flames bathed the corridor in orange. The Massassi's screams were lost in the explosion and the shock wave rattled Relin's teeth. Alarms shrieked, and fire foam hissed out of valves in the ceiling.

Relin heard shouts from the other direction and the stomp of many boots. The ship's entire security force would be coming. As would Saes. He had to move.

He drew his blaster with his off hand and pelted down the hall, past the bodies of the Massassi, toward the hyperdrive chamber. The time for stealth was past.

A pair of Massassi appeared in the hallway before him, both with blasters drawn. Before they could shoot, Relin dropped one with a shot from his own blaster, opening a smoking hole in the Massassi's black uniform and sending the insignia of rank on his chest skittering across the floor. The second Massassi fired his blaster rapidly while shouting for aid and backing away.

Relin closed the distance, deflecting the blaster shots with his lightsaber as he ran, leaving a trail of scorch marks in his wake along the wall and ceiling. At five paces the Massassi tried to draw his lanvarok, but Relin lunged forward and was upon him too fast. The clean hum of his lightsaber gave way to a muffled sizzle as he cut the Massassi in two.

He did not slow, could not slow. Shouts told him that pursuit was right behind him. Alarms were sounding all over the ship. When he reached a thick blast door, an idea struck him and he drove his lightsaber's tip into the control panel. The circuitry expired with smoke and sparks and the blast door descended with a boom. He assumed his pursuers would be able to go around, but it might buy him a few extra moments.

Drawing on the Force, he enhanced his speed and ran in a blur for the hyperdrive chamber.

The young helmsman did not look up from his screen as he spoke to Dor. "Colonel, we are clear of the gravity well. System scans show no additional Jedi ships."

Dor nodded. "Begin the jump sequence."

As the helmsman obeyed, the weapons officer said, "All Blades are returned to the ship, Colonel Dor."

Dor heard the question hiding behind the comment. "The Infiltrator remains in range?"

"Yes, Colonel."

Dor stroked the tentacles of his beard. "You have until we jump to destroy it."

The helm recited the jump sequence countdown. The weapons officer gave the order to the gun crews to fire at will.

Eight Massassi warriors armed with blaster rifles and lanvaroks loitered in the large open room adjacent to the hyperdrive chamber. The quills, lumps, and scars that scored their red flesh made them look deformed.

Relin slowed only long enough to count their numbers and ensure there were no others. He did not bother to hide himself. They were too alert for that. They saw him, pointed, showed their teeth in a growl. Six pulled their blaster rifles to their shoulders to fire while another spoke into his comlink and the last headed for a wall-mounted alarm.

Without breaking stride, Relin held up a hand, took telekinetic hold of the blaster rifles aimed at him, ripped them from the Massassi's hands, and flung them across the large chamber. One fired when it hit the deck, and the shot blew the booted foot from one of the Massassi. He fell to the floor, cursing in his language, the ruins of his ankle leaking black fluid.

Relin fired his blaster and put a fist-sized hole in the back of the skull of the Massassi about to push the wall alarm. Black blood and brain matter splattered the wall as the body slid to the floor.

"Run," he said to the remaining Massassi.

The six still standing grinned mouthfuls of sharp teeth—the teeth of predators—and drew their lanvaroks, spun them with skill until they hummed. Relin knew what was coming next. He would have to take care that his suit did not get damaged.

As one, the Massassi jerked back on their lanvaroks. A shower of the sharpened disks attached to the haft, each a few centimeters across, sprayed at Relin. Ready for it, he used the Force to augment an upward leap over the projectiles and reached almost all the way to the ceiling, ten meters up. All but one of the disks flew harmlessly under him. The last scored his forearm, but it was little more than a scratch and did not seem to penetrate his suit.

He landed in a crouch, lightsaber blazing. "I said run."

The largest said, "We are six to your one, Jedi. With more coming."

Relin tilted his head, holstered his blaster, and took his lightsaber in both hands.

Through the large double doors behind the Massassi, Relin heard the hyperdrive hum with pre-jump preparation. Pressure built on his eardrums. The hairs on his arms stood on end. He had no time to waste.

"You will be fewer than six in a moment. Flee now. Final chance."

They lost their smiles but not their fire, and charged him in a loose arc, roaring. He charged them in silence, focused, the Force surging through his muscles.

When he'd closed to two paces, he bounded over them, flipping in midair and decapitating one as he landed behind their line. By the time they spun to face him, he'd put his lightsaber through a second.

Sidestepping the downward slash of a lanvarok from a third Massassi, he cut the metal weapon in half, ducked under a crosscut from another, and severed both legs of the nearest Massassi. He backflipped out of range, the screams of the dying loud in his ears.

The large Massassi put his lanvarok in the skull of the other whose legs Relin had severed, ending the screams, then all three remaining snarled and charged.

Relin threw his lightsaber at the first, impaling him through the neck. Surprise slowed the others a moment, and Relin took advantage of the reprieve to use the Force to pull his weapon back into his hands.

They licked their fangs, bounced on their feet, and charged anew.

He met their advance with his own, ducking, spinning, wheeling, slashing, killing. They could not match his speed, his skill, and within a five-count, pieces of the Massassi and their weapons dotted the bloody deck. All were dead but the one wounded on the foot by the blaster.

"You must gift me with death, too, Jedi," the wounded Massassi snarled. "This." He gestured at his wounded foot. "I will be as a child."

Relin stared at him with contempt. He knew the Massassi had been bred as warriors, but their carelessness with their own lives sickened him. "We all live with ourselves."

"Not like this! Kill me. I demand it."

The Massassi crawled a blaster rifle, leaving a line of smeared blood in his wake.

"As you'll have it, then," Relin said, and put a blaster shot in his skull.

Deactivating his lightsaber, still centered in the calm of the Force, he turned to the doors. Body and mind tingled with fatigue, but he endured. Behind the door, energy gathered around the hyperdrive. He could feel the change in the air. The dreadnoughts would jump soon. He would not be able to stop *Omen*, but at least he could stop *Harbinger*.

He slipped the overrider over the control panel and hoped it would work quickly. Lights and beeps signified the beginning of the cryptographic holo-chess match. Relin could do nothing but wait. Despite the urgency of the moment, he put his back to the door, sat cross-legged on the floor, stared out and over a chamber of dead Massassi, and held his calm.

Several corridors opened into the chamber, and Relin heard shouts down two of them. They were coming. The realization did nothing to disturb his calm. Taking comfort in his relationship to the Force, he held the hilt of his lightsaber in his hand, felt the coolness of its metal, studied its lines, recalled its making.

A long beep signaled the overrider's victory.

"Checkmate," Relin said, standing.

The hyperdrive chamber's doors parted. Dry, warm air swarmed out. The gathering energy in the chamber created extreme static electricity. Relin's hair stood on end. Insects seemed to crawl over his flesh. His robes clung to him as if trying to prevent him from entering.

The rectangular metal block of the hyperdrive hung in the center of the room from ceiling mounts and a series of power conduits as thick as Relin's arm. A large, disk-shaped concavity in the floor yawned underneath it, the open mouth into which the drive fed its power. Circuitry crisscrossed the hyperdrive's face, the circulatory system of interstellar travel.

A transparisteel window on the far side of the chamber opened onto an adjoining room. A pair of wide-eyed human engineers in the black uniforms of Sadow's forces pointed at him, shouted something, and reached frantically for communicators. Relin used a telekinetic blast to slam both men against the far wall and they slumped to the floor, out of sight.

Relin had seen a hyperdrive bisected once for engineers to study. The complexity of the circuitry, the odd geometry of its inner workings, had left him nauseous. And now that complexity, that geometry, began to do its work. Machinery clicked, connected, turned. The power conduits squirmed like snakes as more energy coursed through them. The hum increased in volume. Relin felt light-headed. Radiation filled the room, he knew. He would need treatment for radiation poisoning if he survived.

If.

He placed a hand on the hyperdrive. The metal felt warm, as slick as talc. It pulsed like a living thing, seeming to shift, to flow under his touch. A headache rooted in his left temple, intensified. His stomach flirted with nausea.

He removed three of his mag-grenades from the pocket of his flexsuit, attached two of them to the face of the hyperdrive, a third to the main power conduit connection. He checked his chrono to mark the time and rapidly set the timers.

The grenades began ticking away the remaining moments of *Harbinger*'s existence.

He turned for the door, activating his communicator. "Charges are set. Heading out now, Drev."

"Understood. The Blades have cleared out. Perhaps I have frightened them."

Relin heard the beginning of a smile in his tone.

Drev went on: "I am alone out here. Well, except for the two hulking dreadnoughts bristling with weapons."

Relin stood amid the Massassi he had slaughtered. "Jump out of the system. With their ships clear, the cannons may fire."

"They're preparing for a jump, Master. They won't risk firing."

"They may. Jump out, Drev."

"I am not leaving you."

"Jump, Drev. That is an order."

"No."

Relin cocked his head. "No?"

"I'm not leaving, Master. Both ships are in jump prep. Neither will risk firing."

Relin shook his head, incredulous at his Padawan's stand. "You are leaving. *Harbinger* will not be able to jump, but *Omen* will. There's nothing we can do about that now. But we can warn Odan-Urr and Memit Nadill about the ore and what it can do. That is your task."

"No. I won't. We go together or not at all."

Relin lost his calm for the first time since coming aboard the dreadnought.

"You will do it and do it now. That is a direct order."

"You're breaking up, Master."

"Blast it, Drev! You heard—"

"Understood, Master. I will get in close, scrape the surface of the ship. The laser cannons from *Omen* will not be able to engage me there, and for *Harbinger* it will be like using a club to swat a fly. Get to an escape pod and we'll dock. Out. And they won't fire anyway. Out, again."

The link went quiet. "Drev? Drev?"

His Padawan did not respond.

"Blast!"

"You have a way of losing your Padawans," said a coarse voice behind him, a voice that Relin still heard in the quiet, solitary moments of his life when he had only his failures for company.

"Saes." The word came out a curse, and Relin accompanied its pronounciation with the sizzling sound that came with activation of his lightsaber.

The Sith entered from the same corridor Relin had used. He wore the loose browns and blacks favored by dark side users. The red blade of his lightsaber filled the space between them. His scaly, reddish brown skin was the color of blood. He strode among the scattered Massassi parts that littered the bloody floor of the chamber, his eye ridge cocked, a sneer curling his lip over one of the small horns that jutted from the side of his jaw. His long hair, bound into a rope with bone circlets, hung to his waist.

"I should have known it was you on my ship. Who else but a Jedi? Who else but Relin Druur? I learned such things from you." He shook his head, poked a Massassi corpse with a toe. "It seems long ago now."

"You destroyed every life-form on that moon. You learned nothing from me."

Saes laughed, the sound fat with contempt. "I learned much from you, but it was not what you sought to teach. You should not have come here, Relin. But then you always were the fool."

"There are many things I should not have done."

Saes's eyes narrowed at that.

Shouts carried from three of the corridors that opened onto the chamber.

Relin said, "Your servants will arrive soon."

Saes raised a clawed hand and the blast doors closed, one after another, blocking the corridors from which Relin had heard the sounds of pursuit.

"This is between us, and is long overdue. Do you agree?"

They approached each other, circled at four paces, lightsabers blazing. Saes was the taller between them, the physically stronger, but Relin was faster.

"I do."

Relin's chrono continued its countdown. Thirty-three seconds.

"I have missed your company from time to time," Saes said, and Relin heard sincerity in the words.

"You have chosen a lonely path, Saes. It is never too late to turn away."

Saes smiled around his horns, an expression that did not reach his eyes, and the hollowness of the expression reminded Relin of the gulf between the natures of his first Padawan and his second.

"*You* have chosen the lonely path. The Jedi teach denial of self. That is their weakness. No sentient can long abide that. The Sith embrace the self, and therein lies their strength."

"You understand so little," Relin said. "The Jedi teach the interdependence of life. The understanding that all is connected."

A flash of anger animated Saes's eyes, and he spit at Relin's feet. "A lie. You tried to steal what is best in me, to make me as empty as you."

Relin sneered, but Saes bored deeper.

"When is the last time you felt anything with passion? When is the last time you laughed, Relin? Felt a woman's touch? When?"

The words cut close to bone, echoing, as they did, Relin's own thoughts about his training of Drev.

Saes must have seen it in Relin's expression. "Ah, I see you've thought of these matters yourself. And you were right to think them. It is never too late for *you* to learn wisdom. Join me, Relin. I will present you to Master Sadow myself."

"I think not," Relin said.

"Very well," Saes answered. He reached down to a pouch at his belt. "May I?"

Relin knew what he would draw forth and nodded.

Saes removed a white memory mask from the pouch, placed it before his face. It adhered, shaping itself into a likeness of the skull of an erkush, one of the largest predators on Kalee.

"You used to wear a mask of real bone," Relin said.

"I reserve that now for only special prey," Saes said, and attacked.

THE PRESENT:
41.5 YEARS AFTER THE BATTLE OF YAVIN

Jaden's ship emerged from hyperspace and the navi-comp automatically removed the tint of his cockpit window while R6 confirmed coordinates. Jaden checked the readout. They'd had a good jump and reentered real-space at the edge of the Unknown Regions.

"Well done, Arsix."

Ahead, Fhost spun through space, night side facing out. He saw only an old weathersat and commsat in orbit. Like many planets so far out on the Rim, Fhost had no orbital dock and processing station, no plane-tary defenses, no sign of Galactic Alliance bureaucracy at all. The population of Fhost was on its own.

He felt a sudden, overwhelming impulse to throw away everything and start anew on some wild, indepen-dent backworld like Fhost, free of rules and obligations, but he had enough self-awareness to recognize the feel-ing for what it was: a desire to run away from his old life, not a desire to run *to* a new one.

He engaged the ion engines on his customized Z-95 and sped around the planet, outpacing its spin, chasing the day, until he saw the system's star crest the horizon line.

"Put us in geosynchronous orbit, Arsix," he said, and the droid complied.

Jaden stared out the cockpit's window as the planet rotated into day. Light filled his cockpit and washed over the planet's surface by increments, unveiling a quilt of clouds floating over the red, orange, and tan of vast deserts, the blue smear of an ocean, the spine of a moun-tain range that ran the length of the main continent. To Jaden, it was like watching the slow reveal of a master-ful work of art, a sculpture of land and water, wondrous in its lonely, whirling trek through the emptiness of space. He always tried to see a starcrest from orbit be-fore setting foot on a planet. He wasn't sure why— maybe he wanted to see every world in its best light before putting down on its surface.

Unbidden, he recalled a starcrest over Corellia that he'd seen from a viewport aboard Centerpoint Station as he and his strike force had moved through the metal maze of its corridors.

He dismissed the memory quickly, pained by the realization that his actions on Centerpoint had polluted even this, one of the small pleasures he had long enjoyed.

Frowning, he looked out of the cockpit, past Fhost, and into the field of stars that dotted the Unknown Regions.

"There be dragons," he said, smiling.

R6 beeped a question.

"Something Kyle once said to me," Jaden explained.

What you seek can be found in the black hole on Fhost.

Fhost's largest population center was Farpoint. He would start there, keep an ear to ground, and try to figure out how something could start in the lightlessness of a black hole. He'd pose as a salvager with old Imperial–era hulks to sell for scrap. The fact that he piloted a Z-95 would add credibility to the claim.

"Why do I fly an old Z-Ninety-five, Arsix?"

The droid beeped and whistled in answer, though Jaden needed none. He flew the Z-95 for the same reasons he still bore an old lightsaber in the small of his back.

"Arsix, set the comm to standard planetary control frequency."

R6 chirped when it was done.

"Farpoint control, this is *Far Wanderer,* requesting permission to land."

A long pause and the crackle of static answered his request. Before he could repeat it, the planetary control finally answered in Basic.

"*Far Wanderer,* permission granted. Coordinates for the yard are being transmitted to you now. What is that, a Z-Ninety-five? How'd you get a hyperspace sled to stay attached to that old girl? We didn't know those antiques still flew."

"Still flies, Farpoint control. But it isn't always pretty."

Laughter carried over the channel. "Bring that bird in."

Predator settled into orbit over Fhost and Kell took in the planet. It was covered in great swaths of desert; stretches of tan and brown bisected by gashes of reds and smudges of black made the surface look scarred, bruised, wounded. He hovered over it for a time, his ship invisible to the meager scanning technology available to those onworld. He studied the planet's specs on his console a final time.

Apart from a few isolated settlements on the edge of the deserts, the planet had only one main population center—Farpoint, with a transient population of perhaps thirty-five hundred sentients. He frowned, thinking that he would have to take care to keep his feeding discreet in such a small settlement. On the other hand, the small population limited the target of his inquiry. With his talents, he would be able to gather information rapidly.

In his mind's eye, he saw the image Wyyrlok had burned into his brain—the icy moon hanging against the backdrop of the blue gas giant, its sky on fire. He stared past Fhost out at the trackless systems of the Unknown Regions. The moon could be anywhere.

Wyyrlok had demanded that he look for a sign. Kell had another idea. He intended to look for a Jedi. Thinking of the rich soup of a Jedi caused his feeders to roil in their cheek sacs. Thinking of the soup of the one who would bring him revelation caused him to drool.

He stared down at the planet as the line of night crept across its surface, swallowing the deserts in darkness.

"I am a ghost," he said.

chapter four

THE PAST:
5,000 YEARS BEFORE THE BATTLE OF YAVIN

*H*ARBINGER'S BRIDGE CRACKLED WITH ACTIVITY.

"Forty-five seconds to jump," said the helmsman to Dor, then, into his communicator, "Forty-five seconds. Confirm, *Omen*."

The speakers crackled with *Omen*'s answer. "Confirmed. Forty-five seconds. Forty-four."

Dor put his clawed hand on the weapons officer's soft shoulder. "You have twenty-five seconds to destroy that Infiltrator. Or explain to the captain why you could not."

Saes's blade spat a blurry shower of sparks as he unleashed a series of powerful blows. Relin allowed the strength of the attacks to move him backward as he dodged left, right, leapt, spun, and parried, biding his time. At last he deflected an overhand strike in a shower of energy, slid his blade free, and stabbed at Saes's middle. His onetime Padawan slid left, spun, and drove Relin's blade to the deck with an overhand strike. Saes threw a reverse elbow with his off arm, augmented with strength from the Force, but Relin anticipated the blow, parried with his forearm, lurched his blade free, and drove a Force-augmented kick into Saes's midsection. The impact lifted Saes from his feet and drove him fifteen paces across the room, though he flipped in flight and landed on his feet in a crouch.

"Your skill with a lightsaber remains wanting," Relin said, advancing. "You rely on strength over technique."

Anger tensed Saes's body, darkened his visible skin from crimson to deep red. "It is well, then, that I've learned other methods."

Blue Force lightning gathered on the black claws of his fingertips, crackled a dire promise. Before Relin could respond, Saes gestured and the energy cut a jagged path across the room.

Relin dodged too late and the energy struck him, put a cold spike into his heart, and threw him against the far wall. Despite the agony, he managed to use the Force to cushion the impact and fell to the floor, his breathing ragged as the last of the lightning crawled over him and expired.

He climbed to his feet, lightsaber held low, and eyed Saes. His Padawan had grown in the Force since they had parted.

As if reading his thoughts, Saes saluted him with his lightsaber. Relin imagined him grinning behind his mask. "More than you know, even."

The pitch of the hyperdrive's hum changed, accelerated, took on the regular cadence of a rapidly beating heart. Relin felt the vaguely nauseating swirl in his stomach that he often felt when a ship was about to enter hyperspace.

Staring at Saes, he decided that he would not bother with escape. He had accomplished his mission. Now he would right a wrong before he died.

He fell into the Force, let its energy course through his body, enhance his reflexes, his strength, his endurance. Saes answered Relin's stare with his own, his eyes black holes in the white mask, and lightning sizzled on his fingertips, tracing a spiral path up the red blade of his lightsaber.

"We end it," Relin said.

Former Master and Padawan strode across the chamber toward each other, lethal purpose in both their minds.

Relin's comlink crackled. "I am hit! Master!"

Drev's alarmed voice eroded Relin's resolve, carried away the anger that had been driving his thinking. Strength went out of him.

Saes, sensing the hesitation, bounded forward, lightsaber raised in a killing stroke. Relin parried but too slowly. Saes's blade severed Relin's left arm at the elbow.

Blinding pain exploded in Relin's mind; a scream broke through the wall of his gritted teeth. He felt himself fall, but as if from a distance. The world seemed to slow. His senses felt attenuated, all except for the throbbing, acute agony of his arm. His heart kept time with the pulse of the hyperdrive, and each beat sent a knife stab of pain up his bicep.

Saes loomed over him, his lightsaber sizzling, the masked embodiment of Relin's failure.

"No right, no wrong," his former Padawan said, and raised his weapon. "Only power."

Relin's chrono beeped a warning, and Relin smiled through his pain.

The expression caused Saes a moment's hesitation and in that moment the charges in the hyperdrive chamber exploded. A column of flame and a concussive wave burst from the chamber's doors and rolled over Saes and Relin. The blast flattened Relin to the floor—he felt his ribs crack, adding that agony to that of his arm and seared face—and blew Saes across the room, slamming him against the wall with the force of a battering ram.

Shrapnel rained down. The entire ship lurched from the explosion.

Saes and *Harbinger* fled from his mind. Relin sat up, still half dazed, but able to think of only one thing.

"Drev!"

"It is . . . all right, Master. I believe I have matters righted. Though I now admit to being wrong. The Sith appear willing to fire pre-jump." Drev laughed and Relin thought he heard the hint of hysteria in it. "What just happened aboard *Harbinger*?"

Relin could hear the continuous thrum of laserfire through the comlink, could hear the stressed grunts and rapid breathing of his Padawan. He glanced at Saes, unmoving on the floor of the chamber, and fought down his need for revenge. He could not fix himself through murder, and anger had already caused him to exercise poor judgment.

He deactivated his lightsaber, and left his arm and his former Padawan behind him on the deck of the Sith dreadnought.

"I'm coming. Stay out of the way of those guns."

"The dreadnoughts are near the end of the jump sequence. I've got to stay in their jump field until the last moment or those guns will get a clear shot."

"*Harbinger* isn't jumping," Relin said as a secondary explosion ripped through the hyperdrive chamber. Smoke poured through the double doors, and he lifted his cloak to his mouth to prevent a coughing fit that would feel like a knife stab to his broken ribs. Alarms sang their song of dismay while he sped as best he could from the chamber. Even if his charges had not completely destroyed the hyperdrive, *Harbinger* would not risk a jump with a damaged drive. He and Drev had done something to help Kirrek. Not everything. But something.

* * *

Klaxons blared on the bridge. Tension animated the faces of the bridge crew, hung in a pall over the quiet. Dor stalked over to the helmsman's station.

"Abort the jump sequence!" he ordered, his claws sinking into the helmsman's shoulder deep enough to draw blood.

"Trying, sir. Something is . . . wrong."

Crew stood from their stations, watching the helm and the viewscreen.

"Stay at your posts," Dor ordered, and stared them back into their seats. "Sit!"

They did as he bade, while Dor hovered over the helmsman's shoulder like a guardian spirit. *Harbinger* could not jump with a damaged drive. The ship would be torn apart.

"Not responsive, sir," the helmsman said, and Dor heard panic creeping into his voice.

"Emergency shutdown, then," Dor ordered, and disliked the tension in his own voice.

The helmsman worked his console, then slammed a fist on the readout. "Not responsive. Jumping in twenty-three seconds."

"Get the engineers down there," Dor said.

"I've tried," the communications officer said. "No one is responding. A security team is in Corridor Three-G, outside the hyperdrive antechamber, but they report that the blast doors are closed and sealed."

"Have them go around, and quickly!" Dor said, and the comm officer repeated his order.

The ship lurched as another explosion rocked the rear section. The distinct bass hum of the activating drive, more felt than heard, vibrated Dor's bones. He turned to the bridge security officer, a Massassi a head taller than Dor and with as much metal under his flesh as he had bone.

"Get a team to the hyperdrive with explosives and blow the power linkages! Now!"

The security officer nodded and sped off the bridge, barking orders into his comlink, but Dor knew nothing could be done in time. They were going into hyperspace, on fire and with a damaged drive. He sagged into the command seat as the helmsman counted down the seconds remaining to them all.

"Nineteen. Eighteen."

Captain Korsin's voice from *Omen* cut through the silence. "We are getting odd readings from your jump field."

Dor stared at the viewscreen and saw the bulk of *Omen* beside them. The Jedi Infiltrator did a fly-by of *Harbinger*'s bridge, twisting and turning through a shower of laserfire, smoke streaming from one of its damaged engines. Dor cursed the Jedi in the Infiltrator, cursed the blasted Jedi on board who had done a half job on the hyperdrive so that they would all die in hyperspace.

"You shoot that ship out of the sky," Dor snapped at the weapons officer. "And you do not stop shooting until I countermand the order. If we're to die, so is that Jedi."

"Sir? The jump—"

"Do it!"

The weapons officer nodded and the sky around *Harbinger* lit up with intensified laserfire.

"Sections ten, eleven, and twelve on D deck have fires," said someone. "Dispatching fire teams."

Dor waved a hand in acknowledgment. It mattered little.

"Captain Saes, did you receive my last transmission?" Korsin asked.

"Twelve. Eleven . . ."

*   *   *

Despite the ache in his severed arm and the spike of pain in his ribs, Relin used what mental strength remained to him to augment his speed with the Force. His emotions swirled: fear for Drev, anger at Saes, disappointment with himself. The Force swelled in him and he drew on it fully to pelt through the corridors, a blur of motion. Alarms sounded everywhere in the ship. Droids, crew members, and teams of Massassi security forces hurried through the corridors.

Concealed by the chaos, Relin sped toward the ship's spine and its escape pods.

"*Harbinger* is still readying to jump," Drev said. An explosion sounded in the background. Drev cursed as an alarm sang. "Engine one is down."

"They cannot jump. I destroyed the drive."

"Still showing an active drive, Master."

Relin cursed, hesitated, almost turned. But he did not. Wounded, fatigued, he would not be able to fight his way back to the hyperdrive. Perhaps he had damaged it enough to at least foul *Harbinger*'s jump coordinates.

"Get clear, Drev," Relin said. He reached one of the long corridors that connected the forward and rear sections of the dreadnought. Doors dotted its length. Each would open onto one of the ship's 288 escape pods.

"Engine two is down. I'm on thrusters only."

Laserfire still sounded in the background. Relin cursed. The Infiltrator would be an easy target maneuvering on only thrusters.

"Get out of that ship. I'll pick you up in a pod."

"I am not in a suit, Master," Drev said, coughing. "And you know how long it takes me to put one on."

Relin did know. Drev's Askajian frame made donning a flexsuit a lengthy process. He imagined the cockpit filling with smoke, imagined losing another Padawan.

Relin moved to the nearest escape pod docking door and cut his way through it with his lightsaber, nearly short-circuiting the weapon's power pack in the process, and piled into the cramped interior of the pod. He did not bother with the instrumentation or pause to strap himself into one of the four seats. Instead he simply found the emergency release button and struck it.

The pod exploded away from the dreadnought, throwing Relin against the wall. Wounded arm and shattered ribs protested the impact, but Relin endured. He reached out with the Force for his Padawan. The contact reassured him. He felt the lightness of his Padawan's spirit, his joy in life.

"I'm clear. Put the ship on auto-evasive, get into a flexsuit, and get out. I'll find you in the pod."

"No," Drev said, and Relin heard the smile in his Padawan's voice. "*Harbinger* is going to jump. Your plan did not work, Master. We cannot let both of those ships get back to Sadow. You said so yourself."

It took Relin a moment to understand what his Padawan intended. He rushed to the small viewport in the pod and scanned space for the Infiltrator. He spotted it under the dreadnought, swooping up and circling back toward the bridge. Even on thrusters Drev spun the Infiltrator in evasive arcs that danced through the laser-fire.

Relin spoke in a low tone, the same tone he might use to calm an excited bantha.

"Drev, listen to me. Listen. There is another way."

Drev's laugh, full and loud, was his only answer. Relin imagined his head thrown back, his chin bouncing with mirth.

Funereal silence hung over the bridge. All eyes were on the viewscreen, waiting for the black of realspace to give way to the star streaks of hyperspace, then to the nothingness of oblivion.

"Seven seconds to jump."

The Jedi Infiltrator came into view, operating on only thrusters, and swung around to face them. Laserfire crisscrossed the viewscreen and the Infiltrator danced among the blasts. Thrusters flared and the sleek Jedi ship accelerated directly at them, growing larger, dodging through the anti-ship fire.

"What is he doing?" someone said.

Dor knew exactly what he was doing, and despite the fatalism that had taken hold of him, he would rather die in a jump malfunction than at the hands of a Jedi.

"Blow him from space!" he shouted at the weapons officer.

"I cannot get a lock," the officer said. "I cannot get a lock!"

The ship streaked toward the bridge, twisting, turning, wheeling. Laserfire converged on it at last, struck it once, twice. Flames exploded from one wing, from the nose, but the ship grew larger, larger, until it nearly filled the viewscreen. One of the crew screamed, a defiant snarl. Dor caught a split-second glimpse inside the Infiltrator's bubble cockpit of the Jedi pilot, a young human, or perhaps an Askajian, and he was smiling, his mouth and flabby cheeks wrinkled with mirth, his eyes hard with resolve.

"Brace for impact!"

The smell of smoke and his own seared flesh brought Saes to his senses. He opened his eyes to a wailing alarm and the irregular vibrations of the damaged hyperdrive. It sounded not so much like a healthy heartbeat as one in fibrillation.

For a moment he stared up at a blinking light on the ceiling, still dazed, his thinking slowed by the viscosity of his thoughts. Events replayed in his mind—Relin, the flash of an explosion in the hyperdrive chamber. The pain of his seared flesh sharpened as the muzzy-headedness began to clear. He sat up on his elbow.

Relin was gone. He reached out with the Force but did not feel his former Master on the ship.

Smoke poured from the hyperdrive chamber. A broken power conduit spat sizzling sparks just within the chamber's double doors. Saes climbed to his feet, grunting with pain, and activated his communicator.

"Dor, shut down the jump immediately. The drive is damaged."

The dull boom of an enormous impact shook the ship, nearly knocking Saes to the ground.

"Dor! Status! What just happened?"

The whine of the hyperdrive increased in pitch; the vibrations grew more rapid, more intense, the dissonance nauseating. Saes felt the vibrations under his skin, deep in his bones. *Harbinger* was going to jump with a damaged drive. If they even made it into hyperspace, the ship would be torn apart. He limped to the hyperdrive chamber, dodging the power conduit, trying to raise Dor as he did.

"Abort the jump! Dor!"

Relin saw the tongue of fire reach out from *Harbinger*'s bridge and lick the black of space. It held there for a moment, frozen, then shrank to nothingness, as did his hope. He stared dumbfounded, the pain in his body forgotten in the wash of pain in his spirit. His Padawan's laughter, even as Drev had died, lingered in his memory, replayed again and again.

He stared out the viewport of the escape pod at the thick black smoke pouring from the scar of the ruined bridge, as if he could will time to reverse itself. But the smoke continued to pour forth and his Padawan was still dead. Bodies floated free in space, the corpses fixed forever by the vacuum into contortions of pain and expressions of surprise.

Relin felt as if he'd been hollowed out, as if he'd become a hole, as scarred as *Harbinger* by Drev's death.

And moment by moment, anger seeped into the hole and began to fill it. Anger at himself, at Drev, at Saes and all of the Sith. He felt like *Harbinger*'s floating dead, frozen forever in pain. He knew it was dangerous to give play to such feelings, but they felt too close, too real, to deny.

"You laugh too little," he said, and tears fell. He suspected he would never laugh again.

Despite the danger, he had to see the damage up close, to bear witness to his Padawan's grave, to remember. He seized the pod's controls and piloted in close to examine the destruction.

Drev had opened a hole in the dreadnought, a screaming mouth with jagged pieces of charred metal for teeth. Cables squirmed from opened bulkheads, spitting energy. Metal glowed red-hot here and there, but dimly, losing its battle against space to retain heat. He saw nothing recognizable as the Infiltrator. The ship had been vaporized by the impact.

So, too, had Drev.

Secondary explosions tore through the front section of the ship and it began to glide to starboard, toward *Omen*.

Relin imagined the dreadnoughts smashing into each other, burning like twin comets, and almost smiled. That, too, was an event to which he would bear witness. The Lignan from neither ship would get to Kirrek, and Drev's death would not be in vain.

"Good-bye, Saes."

But Relin realized quickly that neither was was aborting its jump sequence.

He saw his danger, then cursed and turned the escape pod about.

More explosions boomed in the distance, their force communicated to Saes through ominous vibrations in the hull. The ship lurched hard, turned abruptly. The gravitic stabilizers did not compensate fully for the sudden movement, and the ship's momentum sent Saes scrambling. Another alarm sounded and a mechanical female voice proclaimed, "Proximity alert. Danger. Proximity alert."

Saes ran to a viewport and the scene outside the ship pulled his mouth open.

Harbinger had listed to starboard and was accelerating toward *Omen*. Saes cursed as the *Harbinger*'s sister ship grew larger.

"Move your ship, Korsin!"

He imagined the two crews scrambling to avoid impact. Both were near the end of a jump sequence, and the ion engines were offline.

Omen did start to move at last, but Saes could see that it was too late. He gripped the viewport's frame so tightly that his claws scored the metal.

The dreadnoughts were on slightly different planes, but the bottom of *Harbinger*'s fore section scraped the top of *Omen*'s aft engine section. The scale of the collision gave it an unexpected slowness that looked almost graceful. *Harbinger* bucked as the two enormous masses fought for positional dominance. Metal strained, screamed, buckled, the sound like the rumbles of angry gods. More explosions boomed. Pillars of flame erupted here and there from the mixed metal of the collision, garlands of orange heat decorating the void of space. Explosive decompressions echoed along *Harbinger*'s length, along *Omen*'s. Here and there, bodies were blown from vented compartments and floated free in space. And through it all, *Harbinger*'s hyperdrive continued to gather energy.

"Jump sequence initiated," said the same mechanical voice that had announced the collision.

Saes turned from the viewport and saw that the air in the hyperspace chamber was distorted by the storm of loose energy. Waves of power pulsed from the chamber.

"No!" he shouted, but the mechanical voice was implacable.

"Hyperdrive activated."

Relin turned the engines to full, tried to accelerate away from *Harbinger* in time. A quiet, steady beep was the only alarm on the minimally equipped pod, and Relin's heartbeat outpaced it two to one.

He had not cleared enough distance before *Harbinger* jumped. The pod jerked to a halt, throwing Relin forward. It was stuck in the dreadnought's wake, pulled along in its energy draft. Though he suspected it was futile, he redirected more power to the engines. They whined, fought against the pull, but failed. He slammed himself into a seat and snapped on a restraining harness, fumbling with the latch.

Black turned blue and the churn of his stomach told him that *Harbinger* had entered hyperspace and dragged the pod along behind it. He could tell immediately that something was wrong, that the hyperspace tunnel was unstable. The pod began to spin, then flip over, again and again, careering wildly, a cork caught in a river's rapids.

Gritting his teeth, Relin tried to keep his bearings, but he could get no frame of reference. He caught sporadic glimpses out of the viewport and saw the black of real-space flickering intermittently with the streaks of hyperspace.

They were stuck in a bad jump. If he could not get out of it . . .

The escape pod was not built to withstand hyperspace unattached to a mother craft, and its gravitic compensators could not adequately handle the velocity. They did their best, but Relin was flattened against his seat, his blood flow affected. He was moving in and out of consciousness and tried to use the Force to keep himself sensate.

The pod shook as it spun, creaked. He would not have long before the integrity of the pod failed and it decompressed. Through squinted, watering eyes, he saw instruments that provided nonsensical readings, saw starlines swirling in and out of existence, trading time with realspace. The effect was disorienting. Each time the black of space oozed through the streaks of hyperspace, the pod lurched as if it had struck something.

Harbinger tore through space before him, swirling in his spiraling vision as if it, rather than he, were spinning wildly. Strands of energy streamed from the dreadnought's edges like glowing garlands. Pieces of *Harbinger* flew from it, and Relin winced as they sped past the pod like bullets down a barrel. Some of the debris was caught in the flashing transitions between hyperspace and realspace and blinked out of sight, presumably left behind in the black, a scattered trail of metal bread crumbs someone could follow all the way to *Harbinger*'s ruin and Relin's death.

Another jarring collision at the boundary between hyperspace and realspace rattled the pod, caused Relin to bite a wedge in his tongue. Blood warmed his mouth; pain spiked his mind.

He had to pull the pod out of hyperspace.

Mentally and physically exhausted from his efforts aboard *Harbinger,* Relin nevertheless found a final reserve of strength. Getting the pod to exit hyperspace could be done, but only with the aid of the Force.

He inhaled, dwelled in the Force, and with it fought against the pressure of the velocity as he attempted to take control of the pod's flight through the maddening swirl.

He perceived time slowing. His breathing steadied. His thoughts and reflexes came faster. He heard the beeps of the alarm but it seemed as though a standard hour passed between each. The instruments still provided no worthwhile readings, so he would have to rely entirely on feel.

He felt as if he were being stretched thin, as if he existed everywhere at once, and nowhere at all. He took hold of the pod's controls, managed to right its flight and end its spin. He waited for the right moment, waited, waited, and when he felt it arrive, he jerked the controls hard to starboard, toward the black of real-space.

Instead the black disappeared in a wash of blue and his abrupt change of direction sent the pod to spinning, worse than before. Anger and frustration built in him until it burst out in a shout that seemed to echo into forever.

"Saes!"

chapter five

THE PRESENT:
41.5 YEARS AFTER THE BATTLE OF YAVIN

KHEDRYN USED A DIGITAL CALIBRATOR TO FINE-TUNE
another power exchange relay in *Junker*'s propulsion systems. He'd been optimizing his freighter's ion
engines for hours. Like all good salvage jockeys, he was
as much tinkerer as pilot, and he refused to let a maintenance droid touch his ship.

"Has to be it," he muttered, tweaking a manifold on
the exchange.

He pulled a portascan from his belt, attached it, and
checked the relay's theoretical efficiency. The readout
showed 109 percent of manufacturer's spec, drawing a
smile.

He intoned his personal motto as if it were a magic
spell. "Push until it gives."

He pulled his communicator from his belt, smug even
in his solitude, and flicked it open.

"Marr, efficiency on number three power exchange is
one hundred nine percent. Let that settle in, my Cerean
friend. Just bask in it."

His navigator and first mate's calm voice answered.
"Basking, as ordered."

Khedryn grinned. "Didn't I say I would get it there?"

"You did. I believe that means I owe you a distilled spirit of your choice."

Khedryn nodded. "I believe it does, at that. Unfortunate that this rock doesn't have much of that in the way of quality. Pulkay it is, then."

"Are you still at the hangar?"

"Of course. Where are you?"

"I'm in The Hole. There is an empty chair at the private sabacc table."

Khedryn checked his wrist chrono. He was already late. "Stang!"

"Indeed," said Marr, calm to the point of annoyance. "I will simply continue to bask."

Khedryn slammed the relay cover closed and sprinted from the open-top hangar, shedding his tool belt as he ran.

"Pick that up," he called to a nearby maintenance droid.

"Yes, sir," said the droid.

"And don't touch my ship!"

"Yes, sir."

"I'm coming now," he said into his communicator. "Tell Himher to hold the first hand."

Marr's voice remained unperturbed.

"I will see what I can do to delay the start of the game. Reegas is here. And there appears to be some interest in our recent . . . discovery."

That halted Khedryn before his Searing swoop bike. He squinted in Fhost's sun. "The signal, you mean? How did that leak to anyone?"

"If memory serves, and I am certain it does, the leak originated in your consumption of several jiggers of spiced pulkay combined with a desire to impress a trio of Zeltron dancing girls. I believe it worked."

Khedryn ran a hand over his cheeks, rough with three

days' growth of whiskers. "Three? Zeltrons? Really?" He thought of their smooth red skin and curves, his own average appearance. "Were they drunk, too?"

"That seems probable."

Khedryn saddled up on his swoop and started it. The engine growled like a feral rancor. He had forgotten his helmet. No matter. "You still basking?"

"Yes, sir."

"Well, I should've had my mouth occupied with things other than our discovery, but I guess that's burned fuel I'll never get back. On the upside, it should make the sabacc game more interesting. Someone will offer on it, if it comes to that."

"Given your luck, I suspect it will come to that."

"Right." He revved the Searing. "You're really quite excellent for my ego. Are you aware of that?"

"I am."

"I'm en route."

"Please try not to collide with anything."

Khedryn pocketed the communicator and covered his mouth and nose in a scarf against the dust. He angled upward to fifty meters of altitude and loosened the reins on the engine. Below him, ships of questionable space-worthiness and even more questionable registration dotted the thirty square kilos of flat, dusty ground and the handful of decrepit hangars that served as Farpoint's official landing field.

A control tower built of cast-off parts and scrap metal stood sentry in the middle of the field. Landing beacons blinked here and there in the swirl. A sonic boom rolled over Khedryn's ears, indicating a ship entering atmosphere.

A few speeder bikes and another swoop darted through the sky over the field at lower altitudes than Khedryn. Treaded cargo droids unloaded goods from an old freighter, and crews in dungarees worked at their ships' engines and landing gear. Other than *Junker*, not a single vessel on the field was less than two decades old. Expensive technology trickled out to the fringe of the galaxy only after it had been replaced by something newer and became affordable on the secondary market.

Once clear of the field, Khedryn ducked low behind the swoop's windscreen and gave the Searing its head. He squinted into the spray of dust and wind and sped for Farpoint, glinting ten kilos in the distance, and looking not so much like a town as a junkyard.

The rusting, broken remains of a decades-old star cruiser formed the core of the town. The cruiser had crashed on Fhost sometime before the Yuuzhan Vong War, and no one knew what had happened to the crew. No one even knew the make of the ship, not anymore, though it must have been big. The wreckage had created a debris field eight kilometers long.

Khedryn thought it likely that it had been a wayward Chiss ship, but if so, the Chiss had never come back to recover it. Over time the rusting hulk had accreted a community of scoundrels around it, almost as though it had its own gravity that pulled only at criminals and rogues, or just those for whom the Galactic Core meant not luxury but overcrowded cities and too many laws.

Over the decades, Farpointers had torn apart, added to, and remade the ruins of the cruiser so many times over that only the more or less intact bridge section remained recognizable as something that had once flown—though now it was a warren of cantinas, brothels, and drug dens, not a command center for a starship. Of course, the vice dens of the onetime bridge *were* the command center of Farpoint, and that was about all that needed to be said.

Viewing the rickety, slipshod sprawl of Farpoint from

altitude always reminded Khedryn of the first time he had seen it. He'd been a deckhand on a cargo freighter running medicines into the Unknown Regions, and Farpoint had reminded him so much of the ruins of Outbound Flight in the Redoubt that he had been unable to breathe. In that moment, he knew he'd found a home.

Only a few clear memories of his time in the Redoubt remained to him. He had drunk most of them away in the years after his rescue. But he did remember the way the planetoid had looked as he'd been shuttled away on the transport, the rusted, ruined remains of Outbound Flight as stark against the stone as exposed bone. He remembered the anger the survivors had harbored against the New Republic and the Jedi. He had not shared it, despite the stories of C'baoth's betrayal.

He'd soon grown up, put life on the Redoubt behind him, and ridden ships from the Empire of the Hand to the Galactic Core. He had resided for a time on Coruscant and Corellia, but he had called only the Redoubt and Farpoint home, the first out of necessity, the second out of grudging affection. Everywhere else he'd been, hundreds of planets in scores of systems, had been nothing but way stops.

Rats always find a hole, he figured. And Farpoint, it turned out, was his hole.

Above him, the setting sun turned the ambient mineral dust in Fhost's atmosphere into bands of orange, yellow, and red that bisected the sky, a rainbow that wrapped around the world. Khedryn wondered how long it would be before the planet's natural beauty—not only the sunsets, but also the gashed canyons and sheer cliffs that bordered the Great Desert—turned it from a backrocket launching point to the Unknown Regions and into a tourist destination. He tried to imagine tourists and respectable citizens of the Galactic Alliance mingling with the rogues and scoundrels who skulked in Farpoint's ruins. The thought made him laugh out loud.

He decreased altitude and speed—the roar of the swoop growing throatier—as he hit the outskirts of the town. Ramshackle buildings made from cast-off materials leaned like drunks against the more sturdy structures built from the crashed starship's bones. The large reptiles native to the planet's deserts—ankaraxes—pulled carts and wagons through the packed dirt streets, snarling in their harnesses, side by side with ancient landspeeders and even a few wheeled vehicles.

Khedryn weaved his way through the street traffic— leaving a trail of curses in various languages in his wake—until he reached The Black Hole, his cantina of choice.

Corrugated shipping containers, welded together like a child's building toy, made up the bulk of The Hole. Smoke, discordant Yerk music, laughter, and conversation leaked out of the rough-cut holes that served as windows. He spotted Marr's parked speeder bike, put the Searing beside it, powered it down, activated its anti-theft security, and hopped off onto the packed-dirt road, avoiding the inevitable mines of ankarax dung.

A trio of Zabrak lingered on the street outside The Hole, the horns jutting from their heads as irregular in size and formation as Farpoint's buildings. They chatted in their rapid, coarse language, each with a tin cup of pulkay from The Hole's stills in their hand. Khedryn knew them by appearance but not name. He nodded and they returned the gesture.

A hulking Houk sat on a crate outside The Hole's door. A light blaster cannon that looked old enough to have served in the Yuuzhan Vong War—normally a crew-served weapon—hung across his scarred chest, suspended by a strap of ankarax leather.

"Khedryn Faal," the Houk said in Basic, his voice as deep as a canyon, and pulled open the metal slab that served as a door.

"Borgaz," Khedryn returned. He stopped before the door, noticing the new words painted over old ones in an uncertain hand: NOT EVEN LIGHT ESCAPES THE HOLE.

He puzzled over it for a moment, frowning. "What is that supposed to mean?"

"Milsin calls it marketing. A catchphrase."

"A catchphrase?"

Borgaz wobbled his head from side to side, the Houk equivalent of a human shrug.

Milsin owned and operated The Hole and was always trying this or that gimmick he picked up from watching vids from the Core.

Shaking his head, Khedryn entered The Hole.

The dim interior of the place smelled of unwashed bodies, stewed ankarax, the pungent cheese produced locally by a small community of Bothans, and some off-world spice that Milsin must have purchased from a passing freighter. The eclectic collection of tables and chairs, some plastic, some wood, some resin, some metal—gathered from hither and yon over the years—mirrored the eclectic clientele. Rodian, Chiss, human, even a Trandoshan, drank, ate, gamed, and argued at The Hole. A duo of well-attired Bothans sat on crates and played the twelve-stringed soundboards of their people in a tuneless attempt at Yerk music that Khedryn barely heard anymore. Old vidscreens hung on the walls, the largest over the bar. HoloNet reception was hit or miss so far out, so most of them played recordings of shows and sporting events that had aired in the Core four standard months earlier. Nothing was produced locally, not even news. It was as if The Hole, as if all of Far-point, existed in the past, four months behind the Core.

Khedryn nodded at familiar faces as he maneuvered

his way through the tables. Milsin, an elderly human as thin as a whipweed, as bald as an egg, but as tough as an ankarax, waved at him from behind the bar.

"Spiced pulkay," Khedryn called, and Milsin nodded.

"See him?" called Stellet, captain of *Starfire* and a friendly rival of Khedryn's. Stellet was speaking to his Wookiee tablemate, presumably a new add to *Starfire*'s crew. "That man's a junk jockey. Swims in engine lubricant. Handles a wrench better than he handles a woman."

Khedryn made an obscene gesture but offset it with a smile as he approached Stellet's table. "I've been on the rickety boat you call a ship, Stellet. I expect to be salvaging it when it burns out on your next run to Chiss space."

Stellet laughed, raised his glass in a mock toast. "Sit?"

"Can't. Got a game to play."

A gravelly voice from a nearby table pulled Khedryn around. "You smell of fine perfume, Khedryn Faal," said Kolas, a tawny-furred Cathar still working on the kind of banter that predominated at The Hole.

Khedryn leaned over him—he smelled of spoiled pulkay—and said, "You mean ankarax dung, or an open sewer, or something *unpleasant*. Keep trying, Kolas."

Those at the tables near Kolas jeered the Cathar. Kolas's whiskered face screwed up in confusion. He growled with embarrassment and hid behind his drink.

Khedryn thumped Kolas on his massive shoulder, picked up his pulkay from the bar, and spotted Marr down the hall, near the archway to the back room of The Hole. His first mate's elongated head seemed to float over the more vertically challenged crowd. Marr was tall even for a Cerean.

Before Khedryn could raise a hand in greeting, a human thrust himself into Khedryn's space. The man was taller than Khedryn by a head. His neatly trimmed beard and short brown hair bookended intense, haunted gray eyes, the kind Khedryn had seen in religious fanatics. Khedryn put him at forty years, maybe, about the time human men looked back on their lives, found them wanting, and turned stupid.

"You're in my gravity well, friend," Khedryn said, and tried to push past.

The man would have none of it and blocked his way. He felt as solid as Kolas. Over the man's shoulder, Khedryn saw Marr take note of the confrontation and move his way. Several other patrons took notice, too, and half stood. The man seemed to sense the precariousness of his situation.

"Captain Faal," the man said. He backed off a step and put his hands in his pockets. "If I could have a moment."

"Not now."

The man stared into Khedryn's face. "Please, Captain. I will be brief."

Khedryn took him in. From his dungarees and boots, Khedryn made him as a salvage man. He wore a blaster, but that was part of the Farpoint uniform.

"Is this business?" Khedryn asked.

The man nodded. "Potentially lucrative."

"That's the only kind I'm interested in. We should talk, but in a bit. I've got a sabacc table waiting for me."

The man held his gaze and did not give way. "It would be better if we spoke now. Please, sit."

The words sounded strange to Khedryn's ears. They bounced around in his mind, repeating, repeating. He felt a tickle behind his eyes. His vision blurred for a moment and when it cleared he figured he should at least hear what the man had to say.

"Of course, friend. Let's get a table—"

Marr's long fingers fixed on Khedryn's shoulder. "The game is waiting, Captain. Reegas is displeased already."

Khedryn felt a moment's light-headedness. "Reegas?"

"Yes." Marr put his body between Khedryn and the human. The Cerean had a hand on his blaster and a question in his eyes.

Khedryn looked into the dark eyes of his friend, shook his head to clear it. What had he been thinking?

"Reegas, right."

He looked around Marr at the man who had accosted him.

"What is your name, friend? And how do you know me?"

Disappointment colored the human's face. "I know of you. And you'll be interested in what I have to say, Captain."

"No doubt. After the game, though."

"Captain—"

"He said after," Marr interrupted.

"What'd you say your name was?" Khedryn asked.

"Jaden Korr."

"Korr here says he has a business proposition, Marr." Korr did not even look at the Cerean.

"We are always looking for business," Marr said.

"I'll find you after the game. You're welcome to watch, if you like," Khedryn said, and indicated the vidscreens. "Better'n watching a grav-ball game that was played four standard months ago."

"I suppose it is," Jaden said, studying Khedryn and Marr. "I may take you up on that, Captain."

Sitting in the corner of The Hole near the Bothan musicians, Kell watched the bearded human confront Khedryn Faal and he knew almost immediately that he had found his Jedi. He imagined the sharp tang of the Jedi's soup, licked his lips, and stood.

For two standard weeks he had prowled unnoticed among Farpoint's streets, cantinas, and gambling dens. He had fed off the stored sentients in *Predator*'s hold while gathering information about Farpoint, its people, the comings and goings of ships, always with an eye toward spotting a Jedi.

He had found nothing. Until now.

The Jedi had been posing as a scrap dealer from the Core. He must have been shielding his Force signature. But Kell had felt the flash of power when the Jedi had used the so-called mind trick on Khedryn Faal. Therefore—Kell smiled at the echo of Wyyrlok's syntax—the Jedi clearly had urgent business with Faal.

And that information allowed Kell to put together the puzzle of Krayt's vision, to see Wyyrlok's sign. And perhaps his own.

He had heard the gossip that *Junker* had happened upon a promising salvage opportunity, of course, but such stories were not uncommon in Farpoint. He had thought there was little to distinguish it from any others.

But now he suspected otherwise, because the Jedi must have thought it different from the others. And that meant that Kell had found his sign. He would get his answer when he determined where the salvage opportunity was located. He would have wagered much that it was on the icebound moon in orbit around a blue, ringed gas giant, the image of which Wyyrlok had impressed on Kell's mind.

Kell imagined lines crossing, knotting together, the warp and weft of Fate's skein meeting in the corrugated confines of The Black Hole and leading outward into the Unknown Regions and Kell's destiny.

Over the Bothans' music, over the hum of conversation, laughter, and vidscreens, Kell had heard the Jedi say his name to Khedryn Faal.

Jaden Korr.

The name sent a thrill through him. He savored the syllables, the sounds an incantation that would summon him to revelation.

"Jaden Korr," he whispered.

The Bothan musicians built their song to a climax, staring at and past Kell without seeing him. Kell allowed his perception to see fate lines as the Bothan music died. The room became a net of glowing tethers, but Kell had eyes only for the tendrils of red and green that spiraled around the gray-eyed Jedi.

He wound through the crowd, almost invisible to those in The Hole. Perhaps someone saw him for a moment, but he flickered in and out of perception with such smoothness that they probably registered him only out of the corner of an eye, as a fleeting shadow.

Or a ghost.

A table erupted in shouts as someone scored in the grav-ball game blaring on one of the vidscreens. Korr stood in place, arms crossed, staring after Khedryn Faal, motionless and placid amid the frenetic activity of dancing girls, servers, and patrons in The Hole.

Kell fell in with the activity. His feeders roiled in his cheeks as he closed on Korr. He could not take his eyes from the back of Korr's head, could not pry his thoughts from the imagined taste of the Jedi's soup, the sharp, creamy flavor implied by the power that flashed when the Jedi had used his mind trick.

Kell's appetites were driving him, he realized, making him incautious. He recognized this, but he recognized, too, that if revelation were ever to be his, it would come through the soup of a Force-user.

Perhaps this Force-user, he thought.

He glided behind Korr, near enough to touch him, and stopped there. His feeders twitched. The effort to keep himself shielded—even from a passive Force-user—strained him. His *daen nosi* tangled themselves with Korr's, squirming, silver, green, and red serpents wrestling for dominance.

The sounds and smells of the cantina fell away, leaving him and Korr alone in the swirling potentiality of Fate, the roiling mix of their *daen nosi*. Kell leaned forward, inhaled the air around Korr.

Korr cocked his head, turned. Unready for the sudden spotlight of the Jedi's Force-enhanced awareness, Kell's perception screens failed him.

Thinking quickly, he clutched at the Jedi's coat and stumbled into him as if drunk, the collision of their flesh echoing the collision of their fates.

"Pardon," Kell said in Basic, and tried to stagger past. He bumped a waitress carrying a wooden tray laden with glasses of pulkay, but she did not even break stride.

The Jedi took Kell by the bicep, held him in place. Kell's left hand fell to the hilt of one of his vibroblades.

"Are you all right?" Korr asked.

Kell looked up and met the Jedi's deep-set gray eyes, underlined by dark circles, and saw the stress and longing written in the broken capillaries of his conjunctiva. For a moment he could not speak. He knew he had met a kindred spirit, that he and Jaden Korr sought the same thing—revelation. And Kell knew that he would find it when he fed on the Jedi's soup.

"I am fine," Kell said with an affected slur. "Thank you."

The Jedi let him go. Kell weaved to an unoccupied table with a view of the sabacc table and slid into a seat.

He felt the weight of the Jedi's regard on the back of his head. It diminished only when Korr walked past him and into the back room to watch Faal play sabacc.

Kell waited a few moments, then followed him in.

*　*　*

Clutching him by the arm, Marr steered Khedryn toward the sabacc table the same way he might a balky speeder.

"You are nineteen minutes and nine standard seconds tardy," Marr said.

"You cannot just say *late*? You have to say *tardy*?"

"Nineteen minutes and *fourteen* standard seconds . . . tardy."

"Why are you worried? You do not approve of my gambling anyway."

The Cerean shrugged. "I would disapprove less if you did not lose so often."

Khedryn smiled halfheartedly. He still felt discomfited from his encounter with Jaden Korr. He looked over his shoulder and saw that Jaden was staring at him, his deep-set eyes in shadow.

"You remember that time we carried those Sacred Way pilgrims to Hoogon Two so they could see the monument built there by their founder?" Khedryn said to Marr. "You remember how they looked when they got there and there was no monument?"

Marr nodded. "Haunted."

"Right. Haunted." He indicated Jaden with his chin. "He reminds me of them. He's got that look. Like he learned something he wished he hadn't and it called into question what he believes."

"I can steer him off, if you'd like. He doesn't look like much."

Khedryn shook his head. "That's bad business. He said *lucrative,* so let's hear what he has to say."

Reegas's nasal voice pulled Khedryn's head around to the sabacc table.

"Put your arse in a seat, Faal! And get your bug eyes on some cards!"

"Did he say *bug eyes*?"

Khedryn preferred to think that his lazy eye allowed him to see the world askew, from a different angle than most.

"I believe he did."

"Huh," Khedryn said. He fixed false mirth to his face and turned to the table.

Reegas's bald head, already dampened with sweat, glistened in the overhead lights. He smiled through his paunchy jowls, and his overweight body slouched in his seat. A glass of straight keela sat before him on the table, as clear as water. His two Weequay bodyguards, their faces as dry and cracked as the leather of their blaster holsters, leaned against the back wall of the room. Both eyed Khedryn with the dead eyes of those who harmed others for a living.

"Sit! Sit!" Reegas called.

Khedryn thumped Marr on the shoulder. "Duty calls."

"But that Cerean comes nowhere near this table," said Reegas. "His brain is built for counting cards."

Khedryn lost even the false mirth. "You spent too much time in Hutt space. Gotten yourself paranoid. I don't cheat, Reegas."

"No wonder you never win," said Earsh, also seated at the sabacc table. The human's long nose and his bushy sideburns, groomed to a point, made him look like he was sniffing the wind for easy marks. He had the twitchy nature of a rodent, and Khedryn knew he was into Reegas for at least three thousand credits.

"Oh, I am not here to win. I am here to make the game respectable. Otherwise it's just a table full of thugs and scoundrels. Save you, Flaygin."

The old man smiled a mouthful of rotted teeth. An old-timer in Farpoint, Flaygin had been a salvager himself before he'd retired. Khedryn saw his own future in Flaygin's thin gray hair, sun-wrinkled skin, and serial gambling. Flaygin missed the life because he'd never had anything else. Khedryn could see that.

Earsh grunted, tapped a credit on the table, spun it under his finger. "A junk jockey don't make a game respectable. You pull any rubbish out of the sky recently, junk jockey?"

"Why?" Khedryn said to Earsh. "You lose your ship somewhere?"

Earsh's expression hardened. His sideburns pointed accusations at Khedryn, though he could rarely hold Khedryn's eyes. Khedryn figured his eyes made Earsh uncomfortable. "You calling my ship trash, Faal?"

Khedryn stood behind his chair, the comforting weight of his blaster on his thigh, his eyes all innocence. "Calling your ship trash would be an insult to trash."

Earsh stood, a callused hand on his DL-21 blaster pistol.

Khedryn lost his smile. "A man skins his weapon at this table, he best be ready to use it. You think hard, Earsh." He let his hand hover over his own IR-5.

"Sit down, Earsh," ordered Reegas, tapping the table with a finger as if summoning his pet. "We need four to play."

Earsh looked as if he had eaten something foul as he sat back down. "One day, Faal. One day."

"Any day that takes your fancy, Earsh. Any day."

"Please sit, Khedryn Faal," said the dealer droid, Himher, and one of its dexterous, metallic hands gestured at his chair. Himher's voice changed from male to female in midsentence, a manufacturing defect that had either slipped past quality control or reflected the odd sense of humor of a worker at the plant. How it had ended up in Farpoint, owned by Milsin, Khedryn had no idea. Himher was a fixture at The Hole and always had been.

Khedryn accepted the droid's invitation while Flaygin threw back a long drink of pulkay, slammed his empty glass down on the table, and said, "Now that the preliminary posturing is out of the way, maybe we can see some cards, eh?"

Everyone chuckled, but none sincerely.

"Corellian Gambit rules, players?" asked Himher.

All four nodded and Himher's mechanical appendages turned to blurs. Khedryn sank into the game as cards floated across the table: flasks, sabers, staves, and coins. Credits slid across the tabletop, one hand after another. A steady stream of dancing girls took shifts either standing at Reegas's side or sitting on his lap and sinking into the folds of his obese body. He gave a few credits to those he favored. Other spectators and hangers-on trickled in as the stakes grew larger, the game more intense. Khedryn did not need to turn around to know that Marr's eyes were boring holes into his back. He could feel their weight.

Lengthy discussion and dueling insults went by the wayside as the game turned earnest. The room became quiet but for the hum of Himher's servos and the occasional gasp or exclamation from one of those in the audience. Reegas sipped his keela with affected casualness, studying the other players over the rim of his glass. Earsh's face reddened as the game went on. He slammed back pulkay about as fast as the servers could fill his cup. Khedryn barely touched his own drink.

His sobriety was not rewarded. Over the next four standard hours, Khedryn's cards fell about as well as they usually did. He watched as bad luck and bad play eroded his pile of credits while growing Reegas's into a mountain. He kept his rising irritation from his face, but the clench of his jaw made it hard to separate his upper teeth from his lower. A headache nested in his left temple and he could not shake it. He played to push things, not to win, but it annoyed him to lose to Reegas.

"Refill me, will you, dear?" Reegas said to the haggard-looking blond dancing girl perched on his lap. He jingled his ice and wore a smug smile that Khedryn would have preferred to wipe off with a power sander.

"Me, too," said Earsh, and the dancer snorted with contempt. "Hey!"

While the dancing girl bounced off Reegas's lap and ignored Earsh, Reegas grinned at Khedryn.

"Credits are looking a little thin, Faal."

"You, however, look not at all thin," Faal returned. "Nor hirsute."

Snickers and a couple of guffaws made the rounds among the spectators who formed a ring around the table. Reegas's false smile hung on his face as if painted there, but his eyes turned hard.

As if summoned forward by his anger, Reegas's pair of Weequay bodyguards left their perch along the back of the wall and slunk through the crowd until they stood at its edge.

"You play about as usual," Reegas said.

Khredryn shrugged. "Some beings are born lucky. Some are born pretty. Never both. I suppose that makes you lucky."

Even Earsh snorted, though he tried to hide it in a cough.

"The bet is to Reegas," Himher said, its voice changing to female when it said *Reegas*.

"All in, Himher," Reegas said, pushing his sea of credits into the center of the table and staring at Faal the while.

"Reegas Vance is all in," the droid said, and an excited susurration went through the spectators.

Earsh grunted, folded his cards in disgust. "Out."

Flaygin looked first at his cards, then at Reegas, then at Khedryn. "It seems this is between you two. Good enough. Out."

"You are short, Khedryn Faal," said Himher, studying Khedryn's remaining credits. "Please produce six hundred forty-two credits, obtain credit in that amount, or cede the hand."

The crowd murmured. Khedryn stared at his credits as if he could cause them to breed and multiply through force of will, all the while seething over ceding *anything* to Reegas.

"Marr," he called over his shoulder. He stared at Reegas, daring the fat clown to object to Marr's presence at the table.

Reegas made a dismissive gesture—a king granting an indulgence—and eased back in his chair.

The Cerean appeared beside Khedryn, his face composed.

"Don't say a kriffing word about losing," he said, and Marr's mouth stayed closed. "What do we have?"

"What we have is sitting in front of you," Marr answered.

Khedryn nodded. He had figured as much. He looked up, thinking to save face by making light of the situation, and spotted Jaden Korr in the crowd. The man's gaze pininoned him, and concern carved grooves into his brow. Khedryn looked past him, smiled at some random spectator, and tried to laugh, though anger and embarrassment made his voice too tight.

"Anyone out there have six hundred and forty-two credits to loan?"

Laughter moved through the crowd. Khedryn downed his pulkay and when he looked up, he'd lost Jaden. He scanned the crowd, picked him up again, sliding around the perimeter of the room. The man was smooth. He was not sure Marr had correctly evaluated him as *not looking like much*.

"No one?" Khedryn asked.

The laughter died.

Khedryn faced Reegas and held up empty hands. "It appears I'm short."

Reegas grinned through his jowls. "So it appears. Perhaps you'd consider putting something other than credits at risk?"

Khedryn knew what was coming but played along. "Such as?"

Reegas took a sip of his drink, smacked his lips, both of them glistening wet in the overhead lights. "The coordinates of the signal you picked up. Word is there might be some value in the site. If that word is legit, we can throw those in and call it even."

"You in the junk business now? Selling narco not earning you enough?"

The crowd let out a collective *ooh* at that. Reegas lost his grin; his upper lip twitched.

"I am trying to do you a favor, Khedryn Faal."

"You don't even know what's there. I don't know what's there. It could be valueless. A crashed survey droid."

Khedryn did not think so. He thought he had stumbled upon an unoccupied base of some kind. There was bound to be lots of value there, in electronics if nothing else. And he had probably told the three Zeltron dancing girls exactly that. And they had told everyone, including Reegas. He cursed himself for a mouth that ran like a bad power manifold, always opening at the wrong time.

Reegas leaned forward, his fat folding over itself a few times. "There's always something of value floating in the black, correct? Isn't that what you salvagers say?"

Khedryn said nothing, thinking that Reegas's mouthing the salvager's motto somehow soiled it.

Reegas made a show of sighing before he stood and started reeling in the credit pool. "If you'd rather just cede the hand, then . . ."

"Fine," Khedryn said, and had to unclench jaw and fist. He would *not* cede the hand to Reegas Vance. "Done."

Reegas held his pose over the table for a moment, a bloated, half-drunk, smug dragon hovering over his hoard. He sat down and fixed Khedryn with a hard stare.

"Let's get them on the table then."

"My word is not good enough?"

"The table," Reegas said.

"The coordinates," Khedryn said to Marr, who still stood at his shoulder.

Marr hesitated a beat before he pulled a small data-pad from the dozen or so pockets in his trousers and started punching keys.

"You all right with this?" Khedryn asked him.

"You need his permission?" Reegas asked.

"Shut your mouth, fat man," Khedryn spat.

Earsh lurched from his chair, but Reegas stayed him with an upraised hand.

"You need *his* permission?" Khedryn said to Earsh. "Do it. *Do* it."

The slits of Earsh's eyes moved from Khedryn, to Reegas, then back to Khedryn, and he retook his chair. His chest rose and fell like that of a man who'd run five klicks.

"You are pushing it," Marr said to Khedryn.

"I always push it," Khedryn said.

"The coordinates if you please, Master Marr," Reegas said to Marr.

"Marr," Khedryn said, his tone soft. "Sorry."

Marr made eye contact with no one as he punched the coordinates into the 'pad. "You are the captain," he said, his tone equally soft.

Khedryn almost reconsidered—Marr's disapproval was as tangible as the heat in the room, and Khedryn valued Marr's opinion above all others'—but the smugness in Reegas's expression beat wisdom off with a stick.

"You keep all those numbers in your brains, Cerean?" Reegas asked.

Marr stared at him from under the cliff of his brow, but said nothing. The Cerean removed the storage crystal from the datapad and placed it in the center of the table. It caught the light, flickered like a diamond.

"Good luck," Marr said to Khedryn, and withdrew into the crowd. Khedryn felt his absence. Marr's presence offered Khedryn something he could not quite articulate, something solid, something . . . certain.

Word of the wager and brewing confrontation must have spread through The Hole. A few dozen spectators crowded the room, elbowing out space and craning necks.

"Give me fake coordinates," Reegas said, "and, well . . . you know."

Khedryn looked past Reegas to his Weequay bodyguards. Jaden Korr, now standing behind Reegas's bodyguards, stared back at him and slowly shook his head. Khedryn ignored him.

"Like I said, I don't cheat, Reegas. Not ever. I take my losses when that's how the cards fall."

"So you do." Reegas sipped his keela. "Deal, Himher."

"An accord over the wager has been reached," said the droid, and dealt.

Khedryn studied his hand, his heart racing. He was

not so much concerned about losing the coordinates to Reegas as about simply *losing* to Reegas in front of a roomful of people.

His first four cards included the Master and brought him to nineteen. A mediocre hand. He stared across the table at Reegas, trying to read his cards in the set of his lips. Nothing. He dared not call at nineteen.

"Khedryn Faal?" asked Himher.

He discarded his two high cards and decided to shoot low. Himher skimmed two cards across the table. Khedryn eyed them—Balance and the Evil One—and it took a few moments for their value to register. He did the math in his head again and again.

Negative twenty-three.

"Reegas," Himher said.

"Call it," Reegas said, and sat back in his seat.

Khedryn tried to answer Reegas's smugness with his own. He savored the moment, flipped his cards. "Negative twenty-three."

Gasps and applause broke out in the crowd. Only a positive twenty-three could beat him.

Reegas's face fell. He stared at Khedryn's cards a moment, his neck blotchy, before flipping his own.

"Twenty-three. To the right side of zero."

More applause.

"What?" Khedryn asked, staring at the cards, too stunned to say anything worthwhile. "What?"

Earsh's laughter was like a wood rasp on Khedryn's nerves. Flaygin just shook his head and started counting his remaining credits.

"The hand goes to Reegas," Himher said, and the room erupted into cheers, boos, and applause, all of which swallowed Khedryn's curses.

Reegas waited for the hubbub to quiet before collecting his winnings. Khedryn's mind raced. By the time the sausages of Reegas's fingers had pulled over his hoard, Khedryn had his angle.

To Reegas, he said, "I guess it'll take you a few days to hire a salvage crew and get them off to the site."

"I guess it will," Reegas said. "You need work?"

"From you? No. I was just thinking that that timetable means Marr and I will have to get out there quick. Don't worry, though. I'll leave you enough to at least pay for the fuel you burn getting there."

The room went completely silent. Reegas stared at him, face red, body tense. The Weequay put hands to blasters, waiting on the order from their boss. Jaden Korr loomed behind them, his face the only one in the room showing neither shock nor concern.

"Huh?" Earsh said, looking from Khedryn to Reegas and back again.

"Surely you did not think I was offering exclusive rights, did you?" Khedryn said to Reegas, waving a hand as if the very notion were absurd. "Himher, did I say *exclusive*?"

"Exclusivity was not mentioned in the accord," the droid said.

Reegas's mouth opened and closed a few times. Hate swam in the rage-filled pools of his eyes.

A few chuckles made their way through the audience, and Khedryn thought he might have pushed just enough for something to give. He had embarrassed Reegas badly.

The hate lingered for only a moment more in Reegas's face before he turned expressionless, as if a light had been turned off.

"Quite right. Exclusivity was not mentioned. Double or naught for exclusive rights, then?"

Khedryn did not hesitate. He leaned forward in his seat. "Deal, Himher."

The crowd shouted and cheered as the cards danced over the table, hand after hand, with neither one willing to call. Discard, deal anew. The press of bodies in the room made it hotter than usual. Khedryn took enormous satisfaction in watching Reegas daub his sweat-slicked face with a kerchief.

As Himher gathered the discards and distributed another hand, Khedryn caught sight of Jaden Korr, his eyes closed, as if he had fallen asleep on his feet.

The cards hit the table. Khedryn examined them, saw twenty-three, and tried to keep it out of his eyes. It was Reegas's turn to call or pass.

Reegas eyed his own cards, sweated, eyed his cards again.

"Call or pass, Reegas," said Himher.

"Call," Reegas said, and flipped his cards. "Negative twenty-two."

Khedryn let him sit a moment with uncertainty, then flipped his own. "Twenty-three. To the good side of zero."

The crowd erupted and Earsh jumped from his chair, bumping the table, sending credits flying. "He cheated! You are a cheating nerf! That Cerean said something to him when he came over here. I saw it."

Khedryn stood, twitchy, his legs stiff from being so long in the chair. "A lie. I don't cheat, boy. And neither does Marr."

Marr appeared at his side, solid, reassuring.

Reegas stared ice at Khedryn. "Let's talk about this somewhere more private."

"I don't think so," Khedryn said, taking a step back.

"I am not asking," Reegas said, and signaled his bodyguards with a wave of his hand. They pulled their blasters and advanced.

Khedryn and Marr pulled theirs, and Khedryn kicked

over the table as Earsh drew his weapon. Credits and the data crystal flew across the room. People started to scream, to surge toward the exit, and above the hullabaloo Khedryn heard a sound he had not heard in decades—the hum and sizzle of a lightsaber.

chapter six

THE PRESENT:
41.5 YEARS AFTER THE BATTLE OF YAVIN

THE WEEQUAY SPUN AROUND WHEN THEY HEARD
Jaden ignite his lightsaber, their eyes wide in the
nest of their wrinkled, leathery skin. Jaden was on them
before they could aim their blasters, and a downward
slash, spin, and backslash left both of them holding only
a smoking half of a weapon. The crowd milled in panic.
Blasterfire from near the sabacc table sounded above the
screams and shouts.

Jaden cursed, kicked one of the Weequay in the
chest—he felt the armor underneath his clothing—and
bounded through the churn for Khedryn and Marr.

Reegas shouted above the tumult, his voice as high-
pitched as a siren. "I want Khedryn Faal! Bring him to
me!"

Jaden spotted Khedryn and Marr retreating toward
the exit in a crouch. The sabacc player called Earsh fired
his blaster at Khedryn. It missed wildly, but put a smoking black hole in the back of one of the dancing girls.

More screams, more panicked flight.

Neither Khedryn nor Marr returned Earsh's fire,
though both held blasters. Perhaps they feared hitting an
innocent.

Earsh fired again, nicked Marr's shoulder. The impact spun the Cerean around and knocked him to the floor. Khedryn grabbed him by his good arm and tried to heave him up. Earsh aimed another shot.

Jaden fell into the Force, used it to augment an upward leap, flipped, landed in front of Earsh, and drove his lightsaber right between Earsh's surprised eyes, putting a smoking tunnel through his skull.

Jaden was already crossing lines he had hoped not to approach.

One of the cowering females nearby screamed as Earsh's body hit the floor, the hole in his forehead a third eye staring accusations at Jaden. Even Reegas stopped and stared in wide-eyed wonder at Jaden and his lightsaber.

Jaden leapt into a Force-augmented backflip, nearly hit the ceiling, cleared half the room, and landed in front of Khedryn and Marr. Up close, he sensed a faint Force sensitivity in Marr. He wondered how he had missed it earlier.

"Stay behind me," he said.

"I think we will," Khedryn said, and finally got Marr to his feet.

The Weequay bodyguards must have carried extra weapons, for they appeared out of the churn near Reegas, each wielding a blaster in each hand. Their presence seemed to renew Reegas's confidence.

"Kill them all!" Reegas shouted, his fat jiggling with rage.

The Weequay fired again and again. Jaden's lightsaber was a humming blur of green, deflecting shot after shot. He angled the deflected shots to hit the ceiling and it soon looked like the cratered surface of a moon. He feared it might collapse before everyone cleared the room.

"This way," Jaden said, and maneuvered Khedryn and Marr toward the wall.

With most of the spectators out and presented at last with a clear field of fire, Khedryn and Marr both finally answered with their own blasters. Khedryn hit one of the Weequay in the chest but the bodyguard—as Jaden had suspected—wore blaster-resistant armor under his clothing. The impact staggered him but barely put a pause in his fire.

"Heads only," Khedryn said to Marr.

"Get down!" Jaden said, and booted over another table for them to use as cover.

Khedryn and Marr hit the floor behind the table while Jaden used his lightsaber to cut an exit in The Hole's corrugated plasteel wall. The moment cost him, and a blaster shot clipped his shoulder. Pain ran the length of his arm, birthed anger. He spun, blade once more positioned to deflect the Weequay's rapid fire, and tried to regain his calm.

"Out," he said through gritted teeth.

"Cheat!" Reegas shouted after them. "You are a blasted cheat, Khedryn Faal!"

"I don't cheat, you heap of bantha dung!" Khedryn spat back.

"Yes you do," Jaden said, deflecting another pair of shots. A piece of metal came loose from the ceiling and fell to the floor with a crash. "Well, I did. I'll explain. Just go."

"What?" Khedryn said, his good eye fixed on Jaden, his lazy eye staring through the hole Jaden had cut in the wall. "Blast it all. I have a reputation here—"

Blasterfire sizzled into the wall and cut short his words. Jaden, holding his lightsaber in one hand, deflected a trio of bolts harmlessly to the ceiling.

"Go, Captain," he said.

Marr fired two shots to get the Weequay down behind

the sabacc table and then all three piled through the hole.

They hit the night-shrouded street. Glow lamps and makeshift lighting cast the street in a patchwork of shadows. Patrons of The Hole were streaming out, shouting, cursing, pointing. Passersby stopped in the middle of the street to witness the commotion. An ankarax reared up on its hind legs, growling.

"You have transportation?" Jaden asked, feeling his arm to check the damage. Minimal.

"Who are you?" Marr asked.

"Yes, who are you?" Khedryn seconded.

"Your friend," Jaden said, and deactivated his light-saber.

"Well, I can't argue with that," Khedryn said. "Though I can't say I expected to ever have a Jedi for a friend. Follow me."

They darted through the street, through the crowd, pursued by shouts, until they reached a parked swoop and a speeder bike.

"A Searing," Jaden said, admiring the raw lines of the swoop.

Khedryn nodded as he slid atop it. "Double up with me." To Marr, he said, "Back to *Junker* and then off this rock until we can get things ironed out with Reegas."

Marr fired up his speeder bike, wincing at the pain in his wounded arm.

"You all right?" Khedryn asked him.

"Yes," Marr answered. "I am all right."

Khedryn started to throttle the swoop, stopped. "Why do you stay with me anyway?" he asked Marr.

The Cerean looked puzzled by the question. "You are my friend."

Khedryn stared at him a moment, seemingly at a loss. Jaden felt as if he had witnessed something private. He wondered if Marr knew he was Force-sensitive.

"I am that," Khedryn said at last. He gathered himself and said over his shoulder to Jaden, "Meantime, whatever business you're offering, it looks like we'll take it."

Shouts from the crowd sounded above the hum of the swoop's engine.

"There! There they are!"

The Weequay burst out of the crowd, brandishing their blasters, searching the darkness for Khedryn, Jaden, and Marr.

"Time to go," Khedryn said, and Jaden grabbed the handrails as the Searing blazed into the sky. A couple of halfhearted blaster shots followed them into the air, but soon they had left Farpoint and The Black Hole far behind.

"Did you see Flaygin get out?" Khedryn shouted to Marr.

"Who?" the Cerean asked.

"Flaygin."

Marr frowned. "I do not know. I think so."

Khedryn nodded and drove. Only Jaden heard him say, "I hope so."

Kell had slid against the wall as the violence emptied the room. Screaming and shouting beings of all sorts had fled to the common area, then into the street. In the midst of the chaos, he watched Korr, Khedryn Faal, and the Cerean flee through a hole in the wall, watched Reegas, the fat human, order his Weequay bodyguards after them.

When it was over Reegas stood alone in the center of the suddenly quiet room, the king of so much flotsam, surrounded by toppled chairs and tables, scattered credits, spilled drinks, and four corpses, three of them still smoking from blasterfire.

Kell watched Reegas waddle to the body of the player at the sabacc table whom Jaden Korr had killed—Earsh.

Reegas stood over the corpse, toed it with his slippered foot, and shook his head. His breathing sounded like wind through a leaky window.

"Get me a drink!" he shouted over his shoulder to no one in particular.

No response. The common room was empty. Reegas cursed.

From outside, Kell could hear the report of more blasterfire, a few scattered shouts. He presumed Jaden Korr and the crew of *Junker* had escaped. No matter. Kell would be able to follow them. Their destination remained in the sabacc room. He would catch up to them later. He had seen the mesh of their lines, seen it intertwine with his own. He knew their fates were as one.

At the moment, he was hungry. Proximity to the Jedi had sharpened his appetite. And since he would soon be leaving Fhost, he could feed more freely. The ghost need not be so circumspect.

Reegas grunted, huffed, and slowly managed to lower himself to all fours. Still wheezing, he began scrabbling among the debris on the floor, no doubt looking for the data crystal that the tumult had sent flying.

Blocking Reegas's perception, Kell slid in behind him, following him as he sifted through credits and the grime of The Hole's floor.

"Where is it?" Reegas whispered between gasps. "Where is it?"

He threw aside credits, ice, glasses, until at last he hit upon what he sought and held it aloft as it were a trophy. The clear data crystal shimmered in the light of the overheads.

"Got you!"

With another series of grunts and wheezes, Reegas put his feet under his girth and rose.

"Now for some keela," he said.

Kell stepped around to stand before him and let his perceptual screens drop.

Reegas's eyes fixed on Kell, widened. His mouth opened.

Kell held a finger to his lips for silence while their *daen nosi* danced in the space between them.

Be still and silent, Kell projected.

Reegas sagged, his brow wrinkled in a question, but he did as he was instructed. Kell took the data crystal from Reegas's slack fingers, placed it in the pocket of his jacket. He felt Reegas resisting the shackles of Kell's command, but only weakly.

Kell smiled, took Reegas by the shoulders, stared into his eyes, and freed his feeders. Reegas's mental resistance intensified. He struggled against Kell's grasp, opened his mouth as if to scream, but managed nothing more than a stifled gasp.

The feeders squirmed up Reegas's nostrils, burst through tissue and into the brain beyond. Reegas stiffened as blood leaked from his nose.

Kell fed. His consciousness broadened, but the weak soup of Reegas's mind gave only the barest hints of Fate's purpose. Kell's consciousness drifted back to give him perspective, and he saw the network of *daen nosi* that composed the universe, the sum of the choices of all sentient beings, but he perceived no order, merely an inchoate design with no meaning.

Irritated and disappointed, he devoured all of Reegas's sentience, all he was and would be, with minimal satisfaction. Reegas was sustenance, nothing more. He withdrew his feeders, slick with the bloody stew of the human's mind, but let them dangle from his face. Reegas's body fell to the floor with a thud.

The emptiness in Kell yawned, and he gave it a name: Jaden Korr. Now more than ever he knew he would learn the truth of Fate only when he dined on the soup of the Jedi. Fate had brought them both to The Hole. Fate would bring them both to the moon of Krayt's vision. There, Kell would have revelation. The coordinates in the data crystal were the point in space–time where he would rendezvous with Jaden Korr, where he would finally learn the truth behind the veil.

A human woman, one of the dancers dressed in a gauzy green outfit that showed as much as it covered, walked into the room. Seeing Kell standing over Reegas, she froze just inside the doorway. The cup she held fell to the floor, spilling keela. Her mouth hung open, her eyes bulged. A small, abortive scream emerged from her throat. Perhaps her mouth was too dry to muster much more.

Kell's feeders snaked into his cheek sacs, leaving a spatter of blood on the floor. He eyed the woman and held a finger to his lips.

"Shh."

He blocked himself from her perception and walked out of the hole in the wall, following Jaden Korr and Khedryn Fel.

Her screams started when he hit the street.

The swoop and speeder bike blazed into the lightless airspace over Farpoint's landing field. Jaden shielded his mouth from the dust with his sleeve and looked back toward Farpoint from time to time, but saw no signs of pursuit.

A few dozen ships, freighters mostly, dotted the dusty plains of the field below, framed in ad hoc halo lighting mounted on tripods. Upturned faces greeted the arrival of the swoop and speeder.

"Start the remote launch sequence," Khedryn shouted over the wind to Marr.

The Cerean was already tapping keys on his speeder's datapad, controlling the craft with only one hand and his legs. The wound in his arm caused him to wince as he worked.

"You are used to rapid exits, I see," Jaden said over the swoop's engine.

Khedryn nodded. "Comes with the work. Where's your ship?"

"The Z-Ninety-five." He pointed to the far edge of the field at his yellow-and-white starfighter. "Over there."

Khedryn squinted against the dust and erupted into a laugh as short and abrupt as a blaster shot. "Does the Order put all their Jedi into flying cans these days? That thing's an antique even out here."

Jaden smiled. "It's a bit more than it looks."

"I hope so," Khedryn said. "Because it looks like something I'd have trouble selling for scrap." He angled the swoop for it. "I'll drop you there. Let's get offplanet, then we can talk about this business proposition you have. And you can explain to me how I—how *we*— cheated in the sabacc game."

"I'd prefer that we stay together," Jaden said.

"You would? Other than the fact that you fly a ship as old as the galaxy and I don't, why is that?"

Jaden heard the suspicion in Khedryn's tone. He assumed it came with life on Fhost. "You'll have to trust me. We can talk on your ship."

"Trust?" Khedryn smirked over his shoulder. "We don't do a lot of that out here."

"If I had meant you harm, I could have done it already."

Khedryn nodded, looked over to Marr. "This fellow better be a Jedi or we're going to be in real trouble."

"He could be a Sith," Marr said absently.

"You a Sith?" Khedryn asked, half smiling.

"Of course not."

"He says he's not," Khedryn said to Marr.

"Sith are liars," Marr said.

"That's true," Khedryn said.

"You both know better than that," Jaden said, not quite sure if they were jesting or not. "You can trust me. I am telling you both that you can trust me."

Khedryn and Marr stared at each other across the void between their speeders. Finally the Cerean shrugged.

"I trust Marr's instincts," said Khedryn. "So you're in luck. But I'm captain on *Junker*, even when a Jedi is along for the ride. Understood?"

"Understood. I have an astromech on my ship that you could—"

"I do not allow droids on my ship."

The statement took Jaden aback. "Never?"

"Never. I don't even like them dealing my cards, but there's nothing for that. Still want to hitch that ride?"

"Yes," Jaden said. He activated his wrist comm. "Arsix, activate the remote launch sequence and the autopilot. Get her into orbit around Fhost's largest moon and wait there. If you don't hear from me in two standard weeks, jump back to Coruscant and alert Grand Master Skywalker."

Jaden felt Khedryn tense at the name.

"The job will take two standard weeks?" Khedryn asked.

"That's going to depend on where it is."

"You don't know where it is?"

"No," Jaden answered. "But you do."

To Marr, Khedryn said, "This is a mysterious man."

"So it seems, Captain."

"I know what I said outside The Hole but I don't consider this a firm deal until I hear more," Khedryn said to Jaden.

"Understood."

They watched Jaden's Z-95 levitate upward on its thrusters, sending swirls of dust into the air before it turned and accelerated into the night sky. Jaden felt odd watching R6 go off without him.

"To whom will I confess?" he said, his voice overwhelmed by the swoop's engines.

"Droid works fast," Khedryn said. "Seems we're not the only ones used to rapid exits."

"Comes with the work," Jaden said. "How do you know Master Skywalker?"

Khedryn looked back at him, his lazy eye off to the side. "Let's talk about that aboard *Junker,* too. There she is now." Khedryn nodded down at a Corellian freighter visible in wall lights through the open top of one of the field's many makeshift hangars. He circled, then started to descend.

"A YT-Twenty-four-hundred," Jaden said. "Sticks out a bit here, doesn't it?"

"I salvage junk. I don't fly it."

Jaden saw. The disk-shaped freighter normally sported a cylindrical escape pod connected to the starboard side of the circular fuselage, but *Junker* featured an attached Starhawk shuttle.

"Must have taken some work to replace that escape pod with a Starhawk. How'd you manage the fittings?"

"By not using droids."

Junker's engines were already venting gas and warming. Jaden noted further modifications to the ship. A pair of universal docking rings—rarely seen outside of military rescue ships—and a complicated assembly on the rear that looked vaguely similar to a laser cannon.

"Is that a tractor array on the rear?"

Khedryn nodded. "Short-range, yeah. Sometimes we dock with a derelict and take what's worthwhile. Sometimes we have to tow the whole thing back for disassembly."

"And you make a living at that? Doesn't seem like there'd be enough floating free out there."

"You'd be surprised. You just have to know where to look."

"Indeed."

They descended through the open top of the hangar and set down beside *Junker*. Khedryn and Marr bounded off their speeders.

"How are we doing, Marr?" Khedryn asked the Cerean.

"Thrusters are already hot. We lift off in twenty-five minutes, Captain."

"Get to the cockpit and finalize the launch sequence. Then we see to that arm. Jaden, help me get these speeders aboard." He stopped. "Wait: Did you catch a shot back in The Hole, too?"

"Trivial," Jaden said, showing the wound.

Khedryn examined it with a practiced eye while Marr hurried into *Junker*.

"Looks a little more than trivial. But if you say so."

Khedryn and Jaden muscled the speeders up the landing ramp and into *Junker*'s hold. Jaden's arm screamed every time he flexed his biceps, but he bore it.

"Hurts, yeah?" Khedryn asked.

Jaden tilted his head to acknowledge as much.

"We'll see to it when we get aboard. A blaster wound, even a graze, is nothing to take lightly."

"I've had blaster wounds before."

"Yeah, me, too. That's how I know they're not to be taken lightly." Khedryn chewed his lip, as if gathering his thoughts. "You asked how I knew Luke Skywalker."

Hearing the Grand Master's first name rather than his title sounded incongruous to Jaden. He had not heard anyone other than the Grand Master's close friends and family refer to him as Luke in many years.

"My parents were children on Outbound Flight. They survived the crash in the Redoubt. I was born there, thirty-five standard years after the crash, give or take."

The admission surprised Jaden—he imagined there were few survivors still alive. He was not sure what to say. He did the math in his head. "You were an adolescent when Grand Master Skywalker and Mara Jade Skywalker rescued you."

"I was." Khedryn's expression softened, and he leaned against his swoop. "Mara was kind to me, to all of us. I was saddened when the vids reported her death."

Jaden flashed on his vision, the sound of Mara's voice in his ear on the windswept surface of the frozen moon.

"As was I. Your parents?"

Khedryn's expression turned blank, but Jaden saw the pain beneath it.

"They died there, before we were rescued."

"I'm sorry."

Khedryn waved a hand to shoo away the memory. "Long time ago. Since then, I've been doing a little of this, a little of that, but I'm mostly settled on salvage these days."

The roar of swoops flying over the hangar drew their eye, and both pulled blasters; Jaden's free hand went to the hilt of his lightsaber. The running lights from half a dozen swoops and speeders buzzed past, blotting out the stars.

"Reegas's thugs?" Jaden asked.

"Could be. Let's get these aboard and get out of here," Khedryn said.

Junker's hold was packed to the crossbeams with storage containers, raw materials, unusable pieces of electronics and vehicles, and two landspeeders.

"Over there," Khedryn said, nodding at an open space in the hold.

Once they had the speeders in the hold and secured, Khedryn lifted the landing ramp.

"You used the Force to affect that final sabacc hand?"

"I did. I would've changed the outcome of the hand when you lost the crystal, but Reegas or one of his lackeys nearby had some kind of handheld electronic cheater. By the time I realized that, you'd already lost."

Khedryn slammed a fist on the seat of the swoop. "That spawn of a diseased bantha was cheating? And he called *me* a cheater?" He regarded Jaden from under his heavy brow. "I guess I owe you then, eh?"

Jaden did not bother to answer.

"This still isn't a firm deal, though. Business is business."

Marr's voice broke over the ship's speaker. "Ready for launch."

Khedryn spoke into his collar comlink. "We are on our way up."

When they reached the tight confines of the cockpit, Marr was already seated and working the instrumentation.

Jaden took in the consoles, the scanners. *Junker* had an amplified sensor array, probably to allow more thorough reception and scanning at longer distances. Jaden eyed Marr, trying to get a better sense of his Force sensitivity. He determined it was faint. Marr probably had no idea.

Khedryn sat, activated the communicator. "Farpoint Tower, this is *Junker*. We are hot and gone."

He did not wait for an acknowledgment before flying the freighter out of the lit hangar and into the dark. Thrusters angled the ship skyward, and the night sky and its field of stars filled the transparisteel cockpit window.

"Chewstim?" Khedryn asked Marr.

The Cerean removed a square of chewstim from one of the dozen or so pockets in his jacket, offered it.

"Thanks." Khedryn unwrapped it, chewed, blew a bubble, popped it. "And we're off."

Junker's engines fired and the ship pelted toward outer space and, Jaden hoped, toward answers.

chapter seven

KHEDRYN AND MARR FLEW *JUNKER* OUTSIDE THE OR-
bit of Fhost's moons, clear of gravity wells. The
ship and cockpit took on the quiet serenity of a craft
moving through the vacuum.

"What is our course?" Marr asked. The Cerean
looked first to Khedryn, then to Jaden.

"About time for that talk, eh?" Khedryn said to
Jaden, and swallowed his chewstim.

Jaden nodded. "About time."

"Come into our office," Khedryn said, and he and
Marr led Jaden to the galley in the center of the ship.
Neither Khedryn nor Marr had removed his blaster.
Jaden understood their caution. He would have to earn
their trust.

A large, custom viewport in the galley's ceiling offered
a view of space. The stars blinked down at them. A
metal dining table and benches affixed to the floor af-
forded seating. A bar and built-in cabinets dominated
one of the walls.

Khedryn went to the bar, took a caf pot large enough
for a restaurant from an overhead storage bin, filled it
with water, dropped in three pouches of grounds, and
activated it. In moments the red brew light turned green.
Khedryn removed the lid, and the smell of caf filled the

galley. He poured two large mugs full and waved a third at Jaden.

"Caf? The ship and her crew run on it."

"Yes, thank you," Jaden said, and composed his thoughts.

Khedryn returned to the table with three steaming mugs of caf. Jaden took a sip and tried not to recoil at its bitterness.

"We prefer it strong," Marr said.

"Any stronger and you'd have to eat it with a fork," Jaden said.

Khedryn put his hands on the table and interlaced his fingers. Jaden noted the scars, the calluses. Marr put his hands under the table, near his blaster.

"Before we start," Khedryn said. "Let me ask you something. Back in The Hole, when you stopped me in the common room, did you use the mind trick on me?"

Jaden saw no point in lying. "I did."

Khedryn stared into his face, his eyes askew. "Don't do it again."

"All right."

"Now, what's your proposal?"

Jaden dived in. "The coordinates Reegas wanted. I want those, too."

Both Khedryn and Marr tensed.

"I figured," Khedryn said. He leaned back in his chair and threw an arm over its back, striking a casual pose. "You a salvager, Jedi? Or is there something else there?"

Jaden did not answer the question. "The rumors in Farpoint said the signal was an automated distress signal."

"We think," Khedryn said. "But there's no life down there. Nobody for a Jedi to save."

Except myself, Jaden thought.

"We don't know that," Marr said. "There could be life. I did not perform a thorough scan."

Khedryn stared at Marr as if the Cerean had just admitted to being a Sith. "Right. Thanks, Marr."

Jaden said, "I understand it originated on a moon at the far end of the system."

"And?" Khedryn asked.

Jaden tried to hold his calm even while he flashed back on his Force vision. He realized with alarm that he could be wrong, that Khedryn and Marr might have found a moon, but not the moon from the vision. He tried to read their faces as he said, "It's a frozen moon orbiting a blue, ringed gas giant."

Khedryn and Marr shared a glance.

"You have been there?" Marr said.

Jaden exhaled, relieved. "No. But I've seen it."

"What?" Khedryn asked.

"Tell me about it," Jaden said. "What drew your attention to it? How'd you pick up the signal?"

Marr took a long draw on his caf cup. His short, graying hair formed a ruff around the mountain of his skull. He furrowed his brow as he thought back, the lines forming cryptic characters on his forehead. "We were returning from another . . . situation and had to take a roundabout course back."

Jaden understood the Cerean to mean that they had been involved in something illicit, that it had gone wrong, and that they'd had to run. He gestured for Marr to continue.

"We stopped in a remote system so I could recalculate our course and we caught a signal of the kind you described."

Jaden's skin turned to gooseflesh. "Did you record it?"

"Of course," Marr said. "But I haven't yet been able to break its encryption."

Khedryn drained his cup, set it down on the table. "Let's slow down here." He ran a hand through his dark hair, sniffed the air. "Stang but I need a shower. I smell like The Hole."

Jaden ignored the conversational detour. "You want to get back to the *why*."

"No," Khedryn said. "I want to get to the *how much*. That'll tell me what I need to know about the why."

Jaden cleared his throat, studied his hands, finally said, "I can offer you two thousand credits now and another seven thousand after I confirm the moon is what I'm after and we return."

"Two thousand credits up front?" Khedryn leaned back in his chair, the hint of derision in the curl of his lip. "Marr?"

"Two thousand credits would barely cover operating costs."

"Barely covers operating costs," Khedryn echoed.

Jaden, in no mood for haggling, leaned forward in his chair. "I do not have time for this, Captain. Much may depend on this."

"For whom?"

Jaden stared into Khedryn's tanned, lined face. "For me."

Khedryn held his gaze for a time. "Didn't I say he had those eyes, Marr?"

"You did."

"And doesn't he?"

"He does."

"What eyes?" Jaden asked, but Khedryn ignored him.

"How do you suppose he'll look when he and his haunted eyes get out in the deep black and what he's looking for out there ain't there, after all."

"Not good, Captain."

"Not good. That's right."

"Why don't you leave that to me," Jaden said, fighting back irritation.

Khedryn stood. "Because you are sitting in my galley in my ship." He walked over to bar, refilled his caf. "Marr?"

"Yes, please," the Cerean said.

Khedryn returned to the table with the pot, refilled Marr's cup, even topped off Jaden's.

"I think this is where we part ways, Jaden Korr. This smells like some Jedi grand scheme, and I've seen what comes of those."

Jaden understood the oblique reference to Outbound Flight. Jaden had seen what came of Jedi grand schemes, too. Centerpoint and everyone on it exploded in a Jedi grand scheme.

"That's not really how we work," Marr added, and Jaden detected the hint of an apology in the Cerean's tone.

"Even after what Master Skywalker did for you?"

Khedryn stiffened, his fingers white around the handle of his caf pot. Still standing, he said, "I owe Luke and Mara Skywalker. Not the Jedi Order."

Jaden felt his plans crumbling. His own fists clenched. He saw Marr tense and took a moment to calm himself. "I don't want the salvage. I just . . . need to see it."

Marr's eyes formed a question. "Why?"

Khedryn said, "That sounds a bit more personal than you've let on."

Jaden offered the truth. "No one in the Order knows I am here. This may have consequences for the Order, but this . . . isn't about that."

Khedryn slid into his seat, and his tone softened. "Explain, please."

Jaden took a drink of caf, savoring the bitterness. "I had a vision. Given me by the Force."

He noticed Marr staring intently at him with his blue eyes and wondered if Marr had experienced his own visions.

Jaden went on: "I saw in that vision what I believe— now more than ever—to be your moon."

Khedryn smiled, shook his head. "I knew it was something like that. Those eyes."

"And?" Marr asked. "You saw it in what context? What drew you all the way out here?"

Jaden licked his lips. "The vision involved . . . symbolism that wouldn't make much sense to you." He sighed. "Listen, I am asking you to trust me. I am not interested in salvage or taking anything that's there. I just need . . . I just need to stand on it, see it, understand what it means."

The silence sat heavy between them. The stars streamed past in the viewport above. Thoughts turned behind Khedryn's and Marr's eyes. Jaden could do nothing but wait for them to render their verdict. He would not take the coordinates by force or contrivance. He had already taken a life—warranted, he thought—but he had no intention of pushing matters further.

Khedryn finished another cup of caf. "See, Marr, this I can understand. The man has something personal at stake here. And he's willing to pay five thousand credits up front to set foot on a frozen moon spinning out in the middle of nowhere. I can get behind that."

"As can I," Marr said thoughtfully.

"It's done then," Khedryn said.

"I said two thousand credits up front," Jaden said.

"Did you?" Khedryn asked.

Jaden smiled and shook his head. "All right. Five it is."

Khedryn smiled. "More caf?"

Jaden decided the man guzzled caf the way a star cruiser guzzled fuel. "No thank you," he said, and looked Khedryn and Marr in the face. "And . . . thank you."

"Marr will plot the course," Khedryn said, extending his hand. "We'll leave immediately. Done deal?"

Jaden shook his hand. "Done. And Captain . . ."

Khedryn raised his eyebrows, waiting.

"I look at you and I see the same eyes you see in me. So what is it you're looking for?"

Khedryn smiled, but Jaden saw that it was forced. "Nah, that's just my floater, Jedi." He pointed at his lazy eye. "Helps me see the angles. Me, I'm just a junk jockey flying the black. I'm happy with that."

"Of course you are," Jaden said, but he knew better. Khedryn was searching for something out in the black of space, the same as Jaden.

Jaden looked to Marr, who was staring at Khedryn. "Marr, the recorded signal?"

Marr nodded. "Certainly."

Marr disappeared for a time, returned with a data crystal and his portcomp. He inserted the crystal and pressed a few keys. The hollowness of an open channel started the recording, followed by a faint, repeated recitation, the encrypted sound unintelligible as language, but reminiscent in its repetition of an ancient rite, a magic spell of summoning.

Jaden leaned in close, his skin stippled with goose bumps, listening to an echo from the past, decades-old ghosts calling to them through time.

Marr said, "As I said, I haven't been able to decrypt it—"

"No need," Jaden said, and turned it off. "It's Imperial. I can tell from the cadence. Probably an automated distress call, as you suspected."

In the privacy of his mind, the voice from his vision sang out: *Help us. Help us.*

"Take me to this moon," Jaden said.

chapter eight

*J*UNKER WAS PREPARED TO JUMP. KHEDRYN BLEW AND popped bubbles with such rapidity, they sounded like a repeating blaster.

"You always jaw a chewstim before a jump?" Jaden asked him.

"Before liftoff, before a landing, before a jump. Sometimes just because I think things will get hairy."

Jaden smiled at Khedryn's superstition while he raised R6 on subspace. The astromech's questioning beep answered his hail. Jaden stared out into the black of the deep system as he spoke and made his last confession to his droid.

"Two standard weeks, Arsix, then return to Coruscant. Tell Grand Master Skywalker that I was doing what I thought I must. Do you understand?"

Khedryn and Marr pretended not to hear as R6 beeped acquiescence.

"Clear to jump," Marr said.

Khedryn swallowed his chewstim. "Do the math and let's turn her loose."

The Cerean tapped keys on the navicomp so quickly that Jaden could barely follow. Complex calculations appeared on the screen, numerological puzzles so baffling to Jaden that they might as well have been another language. Marr solved them as if by magic, relying on the navicomp processor only to confirm his calculations. His Force presence flared as he worked.

"Confirm," Marr said, after tapping a key, and the navicomp did so. Another string of numbers, another solution.

"Confirm."

Jaden had heard of Cerean math savants but hardly expected to encounter one on the fringes of the Unknown Regions, copiloting a salvage ship, much less one with Force sensitivity. He felt Khedryn's eyes on him.

"Like magic, ain't it?" said Khedryn, smiling.

"You have no idea," Jaden answered.

Marr seemed not to hear them, lost as he was in a world of numbers and operators. It took the Cerean longer than it would have taken the navicomp to plot their course, but not much.

"Course plotted," Marr said.

"Off we go," Khedryn said, and engaged the hyperdrive.

Stars stretched, giving way to the blue spirals of hyperspace.

"It will take three separate jumps," Khedryn said. "Why not grab some sleep? You look like you could use it. There are racks in the rooms off the galley. I will wake you when we arrive."

Jaden *was* tired, bone-tired, and still feeling the ache of the blaster wound. "I think I will. Thank you, Captain. Thanks for everything, both of you."

"No need for thanks," Khedryn said, and winked his lazy eye. "Just be sure to pay me on time."

Jaden picked his way through the ship—memorizing the layout, a habit of his—found a rack in a room off the galley, and lay down. He stared up at the metal of the low ceiling, shadowed in the dim light, wondering what he would find when he reached the moon.

Help us. Help us.
In time the exhaustion won out and he fell asleep.

Kell piloted *Predator* into the night sky and out of the atmosphere over Fhost. He placed the data crystal he'd taken from Reegas into the ship's navicomp. Using the data from *Junker* stored on the crystal, it began plotting a course. He studied the coordinates but did not recognize the system. It appeared at least three jumps away, deep into the Unknown Regions.

The ship's comp had little data on the region. Unsurprising. He would simply have to improvise as the situation demanded.

He prepared an encrypted burst transmission on the obscure HoloNet frequency he used to communicate with Darth Wyyrlok. As a matter of course, he used only audio transmissions. He sent the ping and had to wait only a few seconds before the channel opened. It was as though it were waiting for him.

"I have encountered a single Jedi and have obtained a copy of the coordinates for the moon we discussed. Something on the moon is transmitting an automated signal, but I do not yet know its content. The moon's coordinates are embedded in this message."

"You have done well, Kell Douro," Wyyrlok returned. "Therefore the Master smiles upon your efforts from his journey in dreams."

Kell ignored the praise. "Once I enter the Unknown Regions, I will be out of contact except via subspace burst. If I need to report to you, I will do so on the following subspace frequency." He tapped in the frequency and sent it.

"Received. Name the Jedi you have encountered."

"Jaden Korr."

Saying the name recalled to Kell's mind the power of

Korr's soup. His feeders leaked partway from his cheeks, but he retracted them.

"We know of him. He was apprenticed to Katarn and is, therefore, dangerous."

"I want him," Kell said.

The channel hung open for a time, the silence a chasm. Kell imagined Wyyrlok somehow communing with Krayt.

"You believe his mind holds the truth that you seek."

The words were not a question.

"Our lines are intertwined. I have seen it."

"As have we," said Wyyrlok, and Kell heard a smile in the Chagrian's tone. "In him you will find your truth. He is, therefore, yours to do with as you will. Good-bye, Kell Douro."

Kell closed the channel, activated his sensor cloak, and started his jump sequence.

Only afterward did he think it odd that Darth Wyyrlok had not ordered him to report back on what he found on the moon. No doubt Wyyrlok assumed Kell would do so of his own accord.

The hyperdrive activated and he watched stars turn to lines, implying the grid of *daen nosi* that undergirded the universe. He would understand the truth of the grid when he fed on Jaden Korr.

THE PAST:
5,000 YEARS BEFORE THE BATTLE OF YAVIN

The misjump tore at *Harbinger*'s superstructure, clawed at the durasteel. The scream of stressed metal turned the maddening, flickering tunnel of hyperspace and real-space into a shouting throat without end. The ship was flying down the gullet of the universe.

Harbinger bucked from side to side, shook as pieces

of it flew free of the front section and slammed into the trailing end. Escape pods tore free from their berths and hurtled into oblivion.

Saes barely heard the alarms. He held on to the bulkhead, watching the dismemberment of his ship. Panicked, distorted chatter carried through his comlink, voices of the dead from beyond the grave. He seized at the Force to find calm and took comfort in its power. As it filled him, his perception sharpened. He felt the terror in some members of his crew, the fearful resolve in others. He wondered, in passing, what might have happened to *Omen*. Had Relin sabotaged its hyperdrive as well? In any event, the collision of the two Dreadnaughts would surely have disrupted *Omen*'s jump.

Sensation tickled the back of his skull. Realization lingered at the edge of his consciousness. He became aware that the air felt charged, pregnant with potential. At first he attributed it to the twisting of space–time occurring as a result of the misjump, but then he recognized its true source.

The Lignan.

Despite Sadow's prohibition against using the ore, Saes did not hesitate, not for a moment. The Lignan offered salvation.

He attuned himself to the potential offered by the ore, immediately felt it augment his relationship to the Force, sharpen it. The emotional rush felt similar to the flood of feeling he'd experienced after his first kill.

But the increased power was not enough. He could sense that. He was only drawing from its emanations, its penumbrae. He needed to be closer to it to utilize it fully.

He took a final look out the viewport at the chaos outside, then turned and sped through *Harbinger*'s corridors, down its lifts, through its hatches. Time was his enemy. *Harbinger* was dying.

Along his route he passed crew members working frantically at their stations.

"The bridge is gone, Captain!" someone shouted, but Saes paid the words no heed.

"A third of the landing bay was damaged in the collision, sir!"

A protocol droid appeared before him, tottering on the shifting floor.

"Captain, it appears something has gone wrong with the hyperspace jump. I believe that—"

Saes blew past the droid, sending it clattering against the wall and to the floor.

Before he reached the cargo hold, the ship began to shake violently, its solidity responding to some destructive vibratory frequency created by the velocity and the jump error. He had only moments. With his Lignan-enhanced perception, he felt the rising tide of terror sweep through the crew. He ran into a Massassi security team emerging from a side corridor. Even their sharp ferocity had been dulled by concern over events. Still, they recognized him and bowed their heads as the ship shook under their feet.

"Accompany me to the cargo bay! Quickly!"

Bred and trained to obey, the hulking Massassi asked no questions. They ran before him, their boots thunderous on the deck, lanvaroks bare, gravelly voices shouting.

"Out of the way! Captain coming through! Out of the way!"

Crew hugged the walls as the Massassi and Saes stormed past. Many fell in behind them. By the time Saes descended the lift and reached the double doors that opened onto the cargo hold, he had more than a score of his crew trailing in his wake—engineers, security personnel, even a few Blade pilots still in flight gear.

The cargo bay doors did not respond to his open code, so the Massassi pried them open with their clawed hands and lanvaroks. Power blew out of the hold, enough to cause Saes to rock on his feet.

"Sir?" asked one of the Massassi, wide-eyed, too, from the ambient dark side energies.

The ship lurched, throwing many of the crew against the wall. As one they uttered an alarmed moan.

Saes squeezed through the open doors into the vastness of the cargo hold. Loading droids dotted the deck, several stuck on their sides, wheels and treads spinning helplessly. The stacks of storage containers lay in disordered piles like the ruins of some lost city.

He did not need a droid or crew member to point him to the containers containing the Lignan. It drew him like a lodestone drew iron shavings. With each step he took closer to the ore, his mind and spirit opened further until he could not contain a laugh. It was as though he had been drawing power from a nearly exhausted well, and now drew it from an ocean.

He was vaguely aware of his crew trailing after him as he followed the power back to its source, to the stack of rectangular storage containers that held mounds of the ore. He felt giddy, rapturous from its effects.

He drew on the power the ore offered, filled himself with it, sank ever more deeply into the Force. Power coursed through him. His crew backed away, eyes wide—all except the Massassi, who fell to one knee and bowed their heads.

The ship screamed outrage at the stresses of the misjump. With a minor exercise of will, Saes used his enhanced telekinetic power to throw open several of the storage containers holding the Lignan. Ore spilled out onto the deck, bounced around. Power spilled out into the air, collected around Saes. He reached deeper until he was nested fully in the Force, alight with the Lignan's power.

An impact jarred the ship. The hollow boom of an explosion told of some distant destruction to fore. The buck of the ship sent three of the shipping containers skidding along the deck toward him, toward the crew. The Lignan allowed him to use his telekinetic powers to stop them cold with minor effort.

He reached out with the Force, with his augmented power, until his consciousness encapsulated the entire ship. The task challenged him. Dark energy swirled around him. Force lightning shot in jagged lines from his curled fingers, from his eyes. His crew turned and ran, all except the Massassi. They remained, though uncertainty filled their bestial faces.

Grunting, Saes took mental hold of the dreadnought, the pieces of it floating in its wake. His mental fingers closed over the hull and reinforced it, then righted the ship's course.

As he exerted himself, the loose Lignan ore on the deck flared red, sizzled, and crumbled to dust. Apparently it could offer only so much before burning out. He burned through it like a wildfire through brush, like the mining cruisers through the crust of Phaegon III's moon.

He gritted his teeth, his entire body shaking with the challenge of keeping the ship intact. The effort squeezed more Force lightning from his hands, his eyes, his entire body, and soon he was sheathed in a swirling cyclone of the energy. He roared as his power alone kept the ship from shattering.

More and more Lignan burned out around him until he stood in a field of dull gray rock, miniatures of Phaegon III's moon. His heart pounded against his ribs, gonged in his ears. Corded veins and sinew made a topographic map of the exposed flesh of his forearms. The strain bore down on him, drove him to his knees. He was failing. He had to pull the ship out of its jump or they would all die.

He drew from the last well of his strength. The cargo

hold lit up like a pyrotechnic display as more of the Lignan flashed and died. He held *Harbinger* in his mind's eye and felt the intermittent, flawed tunnel of hyperspace around it, felt the ship as a needle through the fabric of space and time, darning in and out of hyperspace and realspace.

Using the Force to time a moment when the ship moved into realspace, he tried to deactivate the damaged hyperdrive, but failed. The pitch of the damaged drive turned to a scream as it poured radiation into the ship and burned out as completely as the used Lignan.

Saes answered its scream with one of his own, straining to hold the ship together and jerk it back into realspace. With a roar of Force power, he changed its course and tore it from the grips of the misjump.

The ship was steady beneath him. The scream of strained metal was silent.

Exhausted, he sagged fully to the ground, his breath ragged but his mind exultant.

"Sir?" said one of the Massassi.

Saes inhaled and stood on wobbly legs. The Massassi moved to assist him but he waved them off. He gathered himself and walked across the cargo hold to a viewport.

Outside, he saw the calm of realspace, a distant blue planet, an orange sun. The stars in the background of space did not look familiar to him, though. He did not know where in the universe they were, but he knew he had saved the ship. The power of the dark side had saved the ship.

THE PRESENT:
41.5 YEARS AFTER THE BATTLE OF YAVIN

Jaden awoke to the metallic shriek of a thrown hatch lever. The door opened to reveal Marr's lined face and smooth gray hair. The Cerean's goatee was so precisely groomed that Jaden imagined Marr gave its angles and length as much attention as he did jump solutions.

"We will be there soon," Marr said.

"How long was I out?"

"Six standard hours and eleven minutes. There is caf in the galley."

Jaden stood, chuckling at the Cerean's precision. Marr turned to go, but Jaden halted him with a question.

"How did you and Khedryn meet, Marr? With your gifts, it seems as if . . . you might have done something else."

"My gifts," Marr said softly, and trailed off. He looked up. "Perhaps I did do something else."

"Of course. I meant no offense."

"I took none." He turned once more as if to go, but stopped himself and faced Jaden. "When I was young, I once spent a week calculating the probabilities that my life would take this or that turn." He smiled, and Jaden noticed for the first time that one of his front teeth was badly chipped. "I even deduced a small possibility that I would become a Jedi. Amusing, isn't it?"

Jaden chose his words carefully. "Perhaps you could have been."

Marr seemed not to hear him. His deep-set eyes floated in some sea of memory where he had experienced a loss. "I was wrong about all of it, of course. It was a silly exercise. Life does not follow a predictable path. There is no way to capture the infinite variables involved. I think it reflected more my view of myself, or maybe my hopes back then, than anything else."

"Life is not predictable," Jaden agreed, thinking of the course of his own life, thinking of an air lock activation switch he wished he'd never seen.

"Later I decided that I needed to *live* life, not think

about living it, not mathematically model living it. Not long after that I met Captain Faal. He's a good man, you know."

"I see that. And so are you. Where did you receive your training in mathematics?"

Marr frowned. "Not at a university. I had a series of private tutors, but I am mostly self-taught. Born to it, I guess."

"It's intuitive," Jaden said, unsurprised.

"Yes."

Jaden nodded, considered the idea of telling Marr that he was Force-sensitive, but decided against it. Why burden him? Jaden had been happier using the Force in ignorance. "Come on, let's get to the cockpit. I need to see this moon."

They found Khedryn already in the cockpit, his feet up, relaxed in his chair. He nodded at the cerulean swirl visible through the window.

"Beautiful, isn't it? I've heard it can drive you mad to stare at it. I've been doing it for years, though."

"That may not support the claim you suppose it does," Marr said, smiling, and took his seat.

Khedryn grinned. "Six years I've put up with this, Jaden. Six years."

"Six standard years, four months, and nineteen days," Marr corrected.

"You see?" Khedryn said to Jaden, and Jaden could not help but smile. The camaraderie between the two was infectious. Long ago Jaden had felt similarly in the company of his fellow Jedi, but those feelings had vanished. In the company of two rogues on the fringe of space, he found himself feeling as light as he had in months.

"Coming out of hyperspace," Marr said. "In three, two, one."

"Disengaging," Khedryn said, and disengaged the hyperdrive.

Blue gave way to black. Stars appeared in the dark blanket of space. The day side of a blue gas giant filled half the viewport. Clouds of gas swirled in its atmosphere, echoing the swirl of hyperspace. A midnight-blue oval, a storm hundreds of kilometers wide, stared out of the planet's equatorial region, an eye that would bear witness to Jaden's fate. Thick, churning rings of ice and rock, the largest ring system Jaden had ever seen, whirled around the planet at an angle fifteen degrees off the equator.

"Nothing on the scanners," Marr said. "We're alone."

"No way Reegas gets someone out here this fast," Khedryn said. "We're on the chrono, though."

Jaden tried to speak, found his throat dry, tried again. "The moon?"

"Coming around now," Marr said, and they watched an icy moon, as pale and translucent as an opal, come into view, under the scrutiny of the planet's dark eye.

Seeing it stole Jaden's breath. He stared in silence for a time before he finally managed, "That is it. Marr, put it on the speakers."

"Put what on the speakers?" Khedryn asked, but Marr understood. The Cerean flicked a few switches, tapped a few keys, and the repeating signal of the Imperial distress call fell over the cockpit, not a recording but the real thing, as faint and regular as an infant's heartbeat.

Help us. Help us.

"You all right?" Khedryn asked Jaden, taking him by the arm. "It's just a distress beacon, right?"

It was more than that to Jaden. "I need to get down to the surface of the moon."

"What is down there?" Marr asked.

"I do not know," Jaden said. "I only know that I am supposed to find it."

Khedryn and Marr shared a look before Khedryn shrugged.

"We'll take *Flotsam*," Khedryn said, Jaden assuming he meant the attached Starhawk. "I'm not landing *Junker* down there."

"We'll need to break out the enviro-suits—" Marr said.

The rhythmic beep of the proximity alarm cut short their conversation, joining its clarion to the distress signal coming from the moon. Marr spun in his seat to the scanner console. Khedryn leaned over his shoulder.

"What do we have?"

Marr bent over the sensor screen, his brow lined with concern. "Unknown, but coming in fast. Very fast."

"From where?"

"From out of the system," Marr said.

Harbinger was still moving under its own power, blazing through the star system at full speed but no longer lost in the nether region between hyperspace and realspace. It was damaged, but repairable.

Pleased, Saes turned and found himself facing not only the Massassi but also many of those of the crew who had fled when he had drawn on the Lignan.

As one, they stood to attention and saluted. Saes returned the gesture and activated his communicator to the channel that would carry his voice across the entire ship.

"This is the captain. All members of the night-watch bridge crew assemble on the secondary bridge."

He assumed Los Dor and his bridge crew had died when *Harbinger* had lost its primary bridge. He needed to figure out where the ship was, then figure out how to get his wounded dreadnought and its remaining ore to Primus Goluud.

Without warning, the pod ceased shaking and Relin, his equilibrium still off, struggled to right the spinning craft. A planet flashed in and out of the viewport, a blue gas giant with thick, busy rings of rock and ice, and a large, ice-covered moon that hung against the black of space like a shimmering gemstone. Relin did not recognize the planet or the system.

Gripping the controls with his remaining hand, wincing at the pain in his ribs, he activated the reverse thrusters to slow the pod and gradually righted it. Using the pod's rudimentary sensor array, he scanned the area around him. He picked up *Harbinger,* apparently intact and slowing, and another ship near the moon. He did not recognize its signature and turned the pod so that he could see it out of the viewport.

"Who are you?" he murmured.

He'd never seen a ship like it—disk-shaped, with an attached boat off the starboard side and what looked like some kind of docking rings aft. He wondered where in the universe the jump had stranded him.

Wheeling the pod around, he brought *Harbinger* into view and almost collided with the dreadnought. The Sith ship filled the viewport as it passed under the pod, the charred scar of its destroyed bridge the hole into which Drev had fallen, into which Relin had poured his rage.

He stared at the ship a long while, the need for revenge a fire in his gut. He knew *Harbinger* would be blind until Saes got a secondary bridge up and running, so he had a short window of time to operate out of view. He would get back aboard, finish what he had started. He owed Drev that much.

But he could not do it with a damaged escape pod. It would never survive the jolt through the deflectors.

His mind made up, he turned and accelerated toward the unknown ship, hoping the pod's small size would allow it to get lost in *Harbinger*'s sensor shadow as he approached.

He came at the ship from aft, somewhat below its ecliptic plane, and piloted for the docking ring. At best he would get an awkward mating with the pod's universal docking port, but he hoped he could make it last long enough to board the ship. He secured the helmet on his flexsuit, oriented the pod, and piloted it toward the ring.

"I have never seen a signature like this," Marr said, studying the enhanced readout from *Junker*'s sophisticated sensor array. "I am getting odd readings." He tapped a few keys, then shook his head in frustration.

Khedryn examined the readings. "Big ship. Not Reegas. Cruiser size, but that signature is no cruiser I've ever seen. Look at that. One of yours?" he asked Jaden.

Jaden moved to the scope, looked over Marr's shoulder, and studied the ship's erratic signature. "No. And it's not Chiss or Yuuzhan Vong. What is—"

Sudden nausea cut off Jaden's words, made his stomach squirm. Marr put two fingers to his left temple and winced with pain.

"You all right?" Khedryn asked Jaden. "You look a little green. Here, sit."

Jaden nodded, took the seat Khedryn offered. He realized he was sweating. He felt a tingle in his fingertips, the beginning of a discharge of Force lightning. He fought it down, putting the hand in his pocket as if it were a proclamation of his guilt.

"Marr, you all right?" Khedryn asked.

"I am fine," Marr said, but squinted as if at a bright light.

Khedryn tapped the scanner screen. "What are you doing in my sky, big girl? Especially right here, right now?"

Marr shook his head as if to clear it, inhaled. "No hails. Getting closer, Captain."

"Keep us clear of it, Marr. Get us on the other side of the moon if you have to."

"Copy."

"Have they pinged us?"

"No."

"Odd," Khedryn said.

"Perhaps not," Marr said. "The ship is showing a lot of damage. I see fires and decompressed compartments all over it."

"A derelict?" Khedryn asked, brightening, presumably at the possibility of profit.

"No, sir. Lots of living crew aboard."

Jaden fought the nausea, the muscles gone weak, and tried to understand his feelings. He finally recognized the source—the power of the dark side. Having put a name to the problem, he put up a defensive screen and the ill feeling passed immediately. He felt it as a pressure in his mind, but it no longer affected his body.

"Get the ship clear of that cruiser," he said. "Now!"

"What is it?" Khedryn asked.

"Sith," Jaden answered.

"Sith? Get us clear, Marr!" Khedryn glared at Jaden. "I thought you said this was not a Jedi grand scheme?"

Relin slowed the pod only at the last instant, slamming on the reverse thrusters and hitting the ship in a crush of booming metal. He activated the magnetic seal on the pod's docking port, hoping that it would hold as he scrambled out of his seat and opened the air lock.

He had a tiny leak in the seal between ships—he could hear its hiss, but not see it—but he had some time before the pod would be depressurized and out of oxygen. He left the pod's inner air lock doors open to increase the amount of oxygen in the linkage. His damaged flex-suit would not protect him from a vacuum—Saes's lightsaber had taken off both arm and suit below his left elbow—but it still functioned enough that it would maintain his body temperature for a time.

He double-checked his gear: his lightsaber, a few more mag-grenades, his overrider, and his blaster. Good enough.

He knelt before the other ship's emergency external air lock control panel—the writing used an odd, stylized version of the Galactic Standard alphabet, but he could make it out—and attached his overrider to it. He had to strip the overrider's tines and improvise a connection because the panel's architecture was nonstandard. He activated it and waited, willing the red light to turn green. He figured he'd blow the inner doors with his remaining grenades.

"I had no idea," Jaden protested.

Marr started to bring *Junker* around when it shook with an impact, knocking Khedryn to his rump and slamming Marr's head against the console. Alarms sounded.

"What was that?" Jaden asked.

"Unknown," Marr said, dabbing at a bleeding gash in his forehead and tapping keys.

"Something hit us," Khedryn said.

"Debris, maybe," Marr said.

"Not debris," Jaden said, and activated his lightsaber.

"What are you doing?" Khedryn said, backing away from the green line of Jaden's saber.

A second alarm rang out. Marr spun in his seat. "Something has attached to the port docking ring. Someone is trying to board us."

"Stang!" Khedryn cursed, and drew his blaster.

chapter nine

KHEDRYN AND JADEN SPRINTED THROUGH THE SHIP'S corridors, Khedryn leading, alarms blaring along the way.

Marr's voice sounded over Khedryn's comlink. "They are docked and have overridden the external doors. They are in the air lock."

"The cruiser?"

"Now at a full stop. It still has not scanned us as far as I can tell."

Jaden imagined the tiny freighter facing the huge cruiser across the void of space, a lava flea staring down a rancor.

"Keep me updated," Khedryn said.

They sped through the cargo hold, down a hall, and into a side compartment. Jaden could see the black of space through the occasional viewport. Ahead, he saw the twin hexagonal pressure doors that opened onto the air lock and the docking rings. Both remained closed. The green light above the far door indicated a successful dock.

Jaden put a hand up to slow Khedryn. He pressed his cheek against the nearest viewport and tried to get a look at the ship docked on the ring, but the angle provided poor visibility. The docked ship looked tiny, a small sphere like an escape pod, but no make that Jaden recognized.

To Khedryn, he said, "Probably best you keep your distance—"

An explosion blew the inner air lock door from its fittings and knocked Khedryn and Jaden to the ground. The impact of the falling door sent vibrations through the deck. Smoke filled the corridor, the sizzle of exposed, severed wiring.

Jaden's ears rang, but he still heard the dull clarion of the alarm and, through it, the hum of an activated lightsaber. Adrenaline allowed him to climb to his feet, groggy, his lightsaber in hand. Beside him, Khedryn did the same, blaster in his fist, his other hand on the bulkhead for balance.

Marr's voice crackled over Khedryn's comlink. "What was that? Khedryn?"

A human male in silver armor bounded through the breached doors, a green—not Sith red—lightsaber glowing in his fist. Oddly, a cable attached the hilt of the lightsaber to a power pack on his belt. His left arm was a stump below the elbow, the suit—not armor—black and frayed at the joint, as if it had been recently cut.

Khedryn did not hesitate and fired a series of blaster shots. The intruder's lightsaber turned from line to blurred circle as he weaved a defense that deflected each shot into the bulkheads.

"Stay back," Jaden said to Khedryn. He augmented his speed with the Force and rushed forward, feinting high and stabbing low.

Parrying the low stab as he sidestepped, the intruder spun into a reverse strike at Jaden's head. Jaden interposed his blade, met the man's hard eyes through the transparisteel of his helmet, and put a Force-augmented kick into his abdomen.

The impact slammed the intruder into the wall, elicited a wince and a grunt of pain. He doubled over for a moment, favoring his side. Taking advantage of the opening, Jaden unleashed an overhand slash, but the man spun aside and Jaden's blade cut a black groove in the bulkhead.

Jaden backflipped high into the air to avoid the intruder's reverse backslash and landed on the other side of the corridor, three meters away, trapping the intruder between Jaden on the one side and Khedryn on the other.

Jaden could not quite place the man's fighting style. He had seen nothing like it before.

Khedryn, now with another clear shot, leveled his blaster to fire but the intruder, his eyes on Jaden all the while, gestured with the stump of his left arm and the weapon flew from Khedryn's hand and skittered along the floor until it reached the man's feet.

Jaden and the man stared at each other, eyes narrow, blades held before them. The intruder's breath came hard, and his hunched posture indicated that Jaden's kick had done lasting damage to his ribs. His eyes moved alternately between Jaden's face and his blade.

Surprisingly, Jaden felt no additional pressure against his mind from the dark side. He would have expected a more acute thrust in the presence of a Sith.

Khedryn smashed the glass on an emergency tool bin and removed a hand sledge and ax. Jaden gave him credit for courage if not sense.

The intruder held his ground, breathing heavily, favoring his side. Seconds passed and no one moved to attack.

"How's this going to go, then?" Khedryn said, hefting hammer and ax.

The rhythm of the alarm kept time with Jaden's heart-beat, his breath. He felt the man testing his Force presence, as Jaden did the same to him.

Instead of the bitter tang of a Sith, he felt the kindred nature of an advanced light-side user, perhaps polluted a bit by anger, but definitely a light-side user. No doubt the intruder felt something similar from Jaden, though Jaden knew it was doubt and not anger that infected him.

"Who are you?" Jaden and the man asked simultaneously.

Both lowered their blades, puzzled looks in their eyes. The man touched a button on the control pad on his chest and threw back his helmet. Long black hair streaked with gray contrasted markedly with pallid skin. Dark circles under his eyes tried to bridge the hues of hair and skin.

"You are a Jedi," Jaden said, the words only half question.

"As are you," the man said, his voice a thickly accented dialect.

"Now it's a party," Khedryn said, lowering the hammer and ax.

Jaden deactivated his saber. "Did Grand Master Skywalker send you?"

Perhaps R6 had contacted the Order without Jaden's orders—

"I know no Grand Master Skywalker." The man glanced around the ship. "Where am I? What system? I do not know this make of ship and you both speak oddly."

"*We* speak oddly?" Khedryn said.

"You do not know the name of Grand Master Skywalker?" Jaden asked, incredulous.

"I have been away from Coruscant and the Order for some time, on a mission for Master Nadill."

"Master who?" The name bounced around in Jaden's mind, seeking purchase in his memory. He felt as if he should have known it.

"There is no time for this," the man said. "My name is Relin Druur. I need to get back aboard *Harbinger*."

Khedryn stepped forward. "Back aboard? That damaged cruiser, you mean?"

"Sith dreadnought," Relin said, nodding. "I tried to bring it down with my Padawan and managed only to damage its hyperdrive. I was caught in its draft when it misjumped. We ended up here."

"Your Padawan?" Jaden asked, and wished he had not.

Relin's jaw tightened. Pain stained his eyes. "He's dead."

"Sorry," Khedryn said awkwardly. "And sorry about shooting at you, but you did ram my ship and—"

"What are your names?" Relin asked.

"Jaden Korr. This is Khedryn Faal and this is his vessel."

Relin took a deep breath, wincing with pain as he did so. "Listen to me, Jaden and Khedryn. *Harbinger* cannot be allowed to jump away. The cargo it bears, a special ore, enhances the power of those who use the dark side and could turn the battle for Kirrek into a rout. Unless you wish the galaxy to fall under Sith dominion, you will assist me."

"Ore? What are you talking about?" Khedryn said. "You need medical attention, man. Look at you."

Relin's eyes flared and he advanced a step on Khedryn. "There is no time! If Naga Sadow is victorious on Kirrek, we may not be able to stop the Sith at all."

Jaden's mind tried to make sense of Relin's words. Some kind of ore on the cruiser enhanced the power of a dark side user. The presence of the ore explained the free-floating dark side energy that had caused Jaden such unease as the cruiser had approached.

"I need to commandeer this ship," Relin said. "I am sorry but—"

"You aren't commandeering so much as a caf pot, Jedi," Khedryn said, his fists bloodless around hammer and ax. "This is *my* ship."

More of Relin's words registered with Jaden, but he could not shape them into anything coherent.

"Did you say Naga Sadow?" he asked distantly.

Sadow's name triggered memories of ancient history lessons from Jaden's time in the Jedi academy.

"Yes, Sadow," Relin said. "His forces marshal at Primus Goluud even now while we debate trivialities. Hear me, Jaden. I need your help and I need it now."

The pieces of Relin's story started to fall into place—Kirrek, Nadill, Sadow, his ignorance of Grand Master Skywalker, his obsolete lightsaber, the oddly made blaster he bore.

Jaden's suspicion hit him like an unexpected punch in the stomach. How could this be? How?

"This is not possible," he whispered.

Relin mistook his meaning. "It is not only possible, it is essential. I need to get back onto *Harbinger*." He looked at Khedryn. "Unless this ship can bring it down?"

Khedryn scoffed, put the hammer and ax back into their wall mounts. "This is a freighter, not a warship. I don't have ship-to-ship weapons. Jaden, are you all right?"

"Nothing at all?" Relin asked.

"Nothing," Khedryn said to Relin. "Jaden? Are you all right?"

Jaden swallowed through a throat gone dry. When he spoke, his voice sounded as mechanical as that of a protocol droid. "The Battle of Kirrek was fought more than five thousand years ago. Naga Sadow has been dead for centuries. If what you've told us is correct, your misjump didn't just move you through space." He let the moment hang there for a moment, allowing Relin to brace himself, before he said, "It moved you through time."

"You are mad," Relin said, but he took half a step back. His eyes flicked to Jaden's lightsaber, his blaster, the ship, to Khedryn, his blaster.

"Seconded," Khedryn said to Jaden, his lazy eye and good eye seemingly split between Relin and Jaden. "That cannot be right. Can it?"

"Look at my lightsaber," Jaden said, and held up the hilt of his blade. "Lightsaber technology left the power pack behind long ago."

Relin took another step back, resisting the evidence before his eyes. "You have a more advanced lightsaber, but it means noth—"

"Look at this ship, Relin," Jaden said. "His blaster. Mine." He held up his own DL-44.

Relin's eyes widened, his pale skin growing a shade more pallid. "This is . . . a mistake. I . . ."

He visibly concentrated, once more testing Jaden's Force presence.

"I *am* a Jedi," Jaden said, understanding his purpose. "You are not being misled."

Relin sagged and Khedryn stepped forward as if to help Relin keep his feet, but the Jedi waved him off.

Jaden continued: "The galaxy just endured a civil war caused by a Sith Lord named Caedus, but he was defeated by the Order and its allies. My Jedi Order. Before that, the Jedi were instrumental in overthrowing a galaxywide Empire ruled by a Sith Lord named Palpatine."

"Jaden . . . ," Khedryn said, holding out a hand to Relin as if to steady him. "Come on, let's tend to those ribs. We can work this out later. I am sure there's an explanation."

"I just gave it," Jaden said, more convinced than ever.

Relin stared at Jaden, started to speak, and then stopped. He shook his head.

"How can this be?"

Jaden had no idea. It seemed impossible, yet he sensed no lie in Relin, and the facts he had were the facts he had. "Get Marr," he said to Khedryn, thinking the Cerean, with his mathematical gifts, might be able to explain what had happened.

Khedryn licked his lips. "Just so I know what to tell him: you're saying I have an old Imperial distress call coming from a moon no one's charted before, a five-thousand-year-old Jedi aboard my ship, and a five-thousand-year-old Sith dreadnought with some evil ore aboard flying through my sky?"

Neither Jaden nor Relin said anything. Jaden understood Khedryn's need to make light. That was how he coped.

"If this is work to you, Jaden," Khedryn said, "I'd love to see what you do for excitement." He activated his communicator. "Marr, you will not believe this."

Saes hurried through *Harbinger*'s corridors, bays, and lifts. Damage-control teams saluted him as they hurried by.

The bone rings holding his hair in a long tail bounced against his back with each stride. He still felt a joyous light-headedness, an aftereffect from his use of the Lignan.

When he reached the secondary bridge, he found the night watch already taking their stations. The viewscreen remained dark. *Harbinger* was blind. All of them, males and females, human and nonhuman, stood and raised a fist in a salute. They smelled of stale fear.

"Captain on the bridge," said Lieutenant Llerd, standing at attention and sticking out his barrel chest.

"As you were," Saes said to the crew, and they returned to work. "You are acting executive officer, *Colonel* Llerd."

"Thank you, sir," said the human.

"Status?"

"Most of our instrumentation is down, so I've ordered a full stop," Llerd said. "Repair teams are trying to repair blown bulkheads. The primary bridge has been sealed off."

"Get our instrumentation operational and get a scan under way. I want to know where we are. And get the viewscreen up."

"Copy, sir," the human answered.

Someone activated the bridge's communications system. Static crackled for a moment; then the damage reports started pouring in. Saes noted them absently, but his mind was on Relin. He recalled the mirth in Relin's eyes in the moment before the charges on the hyperdrive had blown. The recollection summoned anger. He put a finger to the tip of the horn jutting from his jaw, pressed until the finger bled and he had his anger controlled.

His onetime Master had probably escaped before the jump, though Saes figured it was possible that he could still be aboard.

Saes reached out with the Force and tried to feel Relin's presence, but picked up nothing. Of course, he knew Relin could mask his presence when he wished. Saes tapped his bleeding finger against his jaw horn.

Llerd watched him, frozen, as if hypnotized by the motion.

"Colonel Llerd?"

Llerd came back to himself. "Sir?"

"Have security perform a room-by-room sweep of the ship. We may still have a Jedi aboard."

"Yes, sir."

Saes sat in the command chair, issuing orders and letting his surviving crew do the work of resurrecting *Harbinger*. One by one its systems came back online.

"Scanners operational," said Llerd at last. His tone sharpened. "Picking up a ship, sir. Odd signature. Viewscreen coming online."

A white line formed in the center of the screen, expanded to show the black of space and stars, a nearby ringed gas giant, and a small ship shimmering in the glow of the system's orange sun.

"Magnify the ship," Saes said.

The image centered on the ship and expanded. A flattened disk, with an ancillary vessel attached to it side. He saw no obvious weapons. Not a warship, then. Saes had never seen a ship of its make before.

"That is one of our escape pods," Llerd said, pointing. "There, aft."

Saes rose from his seat, understanding instantly what it meant. Relin had escaped *Harbinger* in a pod right after the jump and was now rendezvousing with his Jedi allies.

"Close on that ship and fire main batteries, Colonel. Bring it down."

"Weapons are still offline, sir."

Saes clutched the edge of his seat, unable to take his eyes from the ship and the pod. He would not let Relin escape again, not again.

"Scramble two squadrons of Blades. I want that ship on fire."

* * *

As Khedryn, Relin, and Jaden hurried toward the bridge, Marr's voice rang out from Khedryn's comlink.

"Incoming, Captain. Sixteen fighters have launched from the cruiser."

"You must be kidding me!" Khedryn said. He looked at Jaden and Relin as if it were their fault, and Jaden supposed it was. "This started as a kriffing sabacc game!"

"Saes must suspect I am here," Relin said matter-of-factly.

"Then leave," Khedryn said, but recovered himself almost instantly. "I do not mean that. Sorry. I've no love for Sith. Especially really old ones." He spoke into his communicator. "Plot a jump, Marr. This is unsafe sky for rascals."

"No!" Jaden and Relin said as one.

That stopped Khedryn in his steps, and he turned to face them. "No?"

"I have to get down to that moon, Khedryn," Jaden said.

"And I need to stop *Harbinger*," Relin said.

Kheydrn looked at them as if they were crazed. "You heard sixteen, yes?" To Relin he said, "The Battle of Kirrek already happened." To Jaden he added, "And that moon isn't going anywhere."

"Cruiser's on the move, too," Marr said.

"You hear?" Khedryn asked, eyebrows raised.

Jaden heard desperation in his own voice and made no effort to hide it. "The Force directed me here. I cannot leave until I see what's on that moon."

"Maybe you were sent here just to find Relin," Khedryn said, obviously hoping that would convince him. "Maybe you've both already done what you're supposed to do."

Jaden shook his head. Relin joined him.

"This is incidental," Jaden said.

"Incidental?" Khedryn responded. "That's what you call this? You are both madmen. Worse than fanatics. Those haunted eyes." He shook his head, paced a few steps, snapped into his comlink. "Marr, can we outrun them without jumping?"

"Outrun them to *where*, Captain?"

"Good question," Khedryn mumbled to himself. He looked to Jaden and Relin. "Ideas?"

Jaden did not hesitate. "We use the rings for cover. Scanners will never find us and the fighters will not follow."

"That's because we'll be space dust," Khedryn said. "Last time I tried, I wasn't able to walk between raindrops. So unless you can—"

"I can," Jaden said. "And I'll pilot *Junker*." Seeing Khedryn's hesitation, he said, "I can do it, Captain."

"Force-piloting?" Relin asked, one eyebrow raised.

Jaden nodded.

"Stang, man," Khedryn said, shifting on his feet. "Stang."

"Still closing," Marr said, his voice somehow staying placid. "Orders, Captain? Sitting still seems unwise."

"You think?" Khedryn snapped. He stared at Jaden. Finally he said, "Head into the rings, Marr. Ahead full until we hit them, then Jaden gets the stick."

A long hesitation. "Flying into the rings is madness, Captain."

"Yes. It seems to be going around. Just do it."

Jaden thumped Khedryn on the shoulder. "I appreciate the trust."

Relin said, "You said you have no weapons, but what *do* you have?"

"Nothing. A tractor beam mount on the rear. We use it for towing derelicts."

"Take me to it."

"What do you have in mind?" Jaden asked him.

"Perhaps nothing. But perhaps something. Jaden . . . *Harbinger*'s captain and I have a personal connection. The fighters will follow you into the rings."

"Understood."

"Nearing the rings," Marr said. "The fighters are fast, Captain."

"They're kriffin' antiques! How can they be fast?"

"Antiques? I don't under—"

"Never mind, Marr. Jaden is on his way up."

Jaden thumped Khedryn on the shoulder again. "I'll be sure to get a piece of Marr's chewstim."

"Get two."

The Blades poured out of *Harbinger*'s belly and swooped into view on the viewscreen, streaking toward the Jedi ship. The ship turned, its engines flared blue, and it accelerated toward the gas giant's rings.

"Where is he running to? The rings?" Llerd asked. "There's not much room to fly in there."

Saes watched the Blades bear down on the ship. "If he goes into the rings, order the Blades to pursue. I want that ship destroyed. He will try to jump if we allow him to clear the planet's gravity well. The Blades are not to allow that."

Llerd did not hesitate. "Yes, sir."

Saes turned to 8L6, the replacement science droid. "I want a course back to Primus Goluud as soon as possible. And I want a subspace transmission on the ship-to-ship frequency. See if you can raise *Omen*."

He doubted he was anywhere near *Omen*, but he needed to confirm.

"Captain, I am getting very odd readings," said 8L6.

Saes leaned forward in his chair. "Specify."

"Astronavigation is unconnected to *Harbinger*'s base chrono."

The words pulled Saes away from his chair to 8L6's side. He made sure Llerd was occupied before continuing the conversation. "How can that be?"

"Unknown, but standard astronavigational markers are not where they should be given the time."

Saes studied the readings for himself. Everything was out of place. "Something fouled the ship's chrono. Double-check it."

"I ran several diagnostics before bringing this to your attention. The chrono is functioning correctly."

A nervous tingle moved up Saes's spine. "Then you have mislocated us in space. Astronavigation was damaged."

"I have located our new position with ninety-nine point nine nine percent confidence. I know *where* we are."

The implication of the words hung in the space between them, unmarked on 8L6's expressionless face. Saes's yellow eyes reflected off the droid's surface, stared back at him.

Saes spoke in a low tone and asked the question, though he already knew the answer. "What are you saying, Elsix?"

The droid, too, spoke in a quiet tone. "I am saying that given our position, my long-range astronavigation scans strongly suggest that significant time has passed since we entered hyperspace."

Saes glanced around to ensure that no one was listening. "How significant?"

"More than five thousand years."

The words settled like weights on Saes's mind, heavy with meaning. He put a hand on a nearby chair and locked his knees. The tingle creeping up his spine spread to his entire body. His legs felt weak under him but the chair kept him up. He turned and stared at the viewscreen, at the stars that looked the same to him as those he had left behind but were five millennia out of position.

"How?" he said.

"The most likely explanation is that the misjump resulted in *Harbinger*'s never quite entering hyperspace. We had a hyperspace tunnel in front of us but never entered it. Instead, the ship accelerated to near lightspeed only. For us, only a short time passed. For the rest of the galaxy, five thousand years passed."

Five thousand years.

Thoughts bounced around in his mind, unconnected, inchoate. His mind felt unmoored.

Five thousand years.

He struggled to focus, to analyze the situation, but he knew nothing. He had no information with which to perform an analysis. He had no knowledge of the state of the galaxy. What of the Sith Empire? The war with the Jedi? His homeworld?

It occurred to him that he and his crew were artifacts, living fossils heaved from the strata of a misjump.

"Anything could have happened in five thousand years."

The droid said nothing, merely cocked its head as if intrigued by Saes's reaction.

Saes's connection to the Force began to ground him. Five thousand years had passed, but the Force remained constant. He fought down the panic.

"Say nothing of this to anyone," he said to 8L6. "I must think."

The droid nodded, its servos whirring, and turned back to its station.

"Blades are entering the rings in pursuit," Llerd said,

the eagerness in his voice betraying a desire to see something die.

Saes realized that Relin would be as lost as he, two men of purpose suddenly left purposeless. Neither had an Order to which to report. The Battle of Kirrek was long over. Yet it suddenly seemed more important than ever that he kill Relin.

In the need for that act he found his purpose.

Meanwhile, he had a damaged but functioning dreadnought, a hold filled with Lignan, and a full crew of soldiers. He had little doubt he could make his presence felt. Once he understood the state of the galaxy, he could make contact with the current Sith Order, if it existed. He could use the Lignan as a way either to secure a place in the hierarchy or seize control of the Sith himself.

And if an Order no longer existed, he would remake it.

Finding his mental footing, he said to Llerd, "Do not monitor or scan local subspace channels. Understood?"

Llerd looked puzzled but acknowledged the order.

Saes did not want local comm chatter, should there be any, to prematurely indicate to the crew what had happened to *Harbinger*.

He turned his eyes back to the viewscreen, watching his Blades hunt his former Master through a storm of stone and ice.

He wondered, in passing, who else was aboard the ship with which Relin had docked. Not other Jedi, surely.

Kell had watched, his spirit aflame, as the damaged cruiser streaked out of the darkness toward *Junker,* as fighters of a kind Kell had never before seen launched from the belly of the cruiser and pursued *Junker* into the thick bands of rock and ice that caged the blue gas giant.

"Lines intersect and grow tangled here," he said. His heart was racing.

He needed only to unknot them and revelation awaited. This he knew. And he knew Jaden Korr to be the key.

He used a nose cam to take pictures of *Junker,* of the cruiser, of the fighters, and stored them in a holocrystal. He watched *Junker* dart toward the rings, watched the sleek fighters follow. He did not fear that Jaden would die in the rings. Jaden's destiny was to die while Kell fed on his soup.

He scanned all frequencies until he picked up the signal from the moon that had started it all, the signal that would, in the end, summon Kell to the altar of understanding.

He amplified it, let the heartbeat of its repeating cadence fill the cockpit. Having performed services for the Empire decades earlier, he recognized the signal as Imperial in origin. *Predator* possessed an advanced decryption package, and Kell loosed it upon the message. In moments he had it decrypted.

"Extreme danger," said a female voice. "Do not approach. Extreme danger. Do not approach."

Pelting through *Junker*'s corridors, Khedryn led Relin to the tractor beam control compartment at the rear of the ship. A small, rectangular viewport provided a view outside the ship. They could see the fighters from *Harbinger* gaining on them, narrow slivers of black and silver metal hurtling through space toward *Junker* with ill intent. Khedryn noted the laser cannons mounted on each wing. The cruiser loomed behind the fighters, huge and dark.

"Lose the escape pod, Marr," Khedryn ordered over his comlink. "I don't want Jaden flying my girl with a sack on her back."

"Copy that," said Marr.

Seconds later they saw Relin's escape pod spinning through space in *Junker*'s wake. One of the Blades fired its wing-mounted laser cannons, and green lines turned the pod into flame and scrap.

"Stang, those things are fast," said Khedryn.

"Blades are flying cannons," Relin said. "They have low-powered deflectors. One hit is all it takes."

"TIE fighters," Khedryn said. "Sith designs are the same no matter the time."

"Do you have deflectors?" Relin asked, strapping himself in at the console.

"Didn't I already say that this is a salvage ship?" Khedryn said, watching the Blades grow larger. "I have nothing that can even slow that kind of firepower."

Relin examined the controls. "Can the tractor beam be aimed with any precision?"

"Aimed, yes." Khedryn showed the Jedi the scan and lock display, the fire controls. "But precision? I use it for towing. It's not a weapon."

"It will be today. How do I communicate with the cockpit?"

Khedryn thought he knew what Relin intended. "Tell me you're not planning to do what I think you're planning to do? We'll be in the midst of the rings. The mass shifts alone—"

"If they follow us into the thick of the rings, we'll need to try something. The communicator, Captain."

Khedryn swallowed his protest. He activated the on-board intercom.

"Cockpit, do you read?"

"Clear, Captain," Marr answered. "Fighters are closing. We are in the outskirts of the rings."

In his mind's eye, Khedryn imagined the rings around the gas giant. Taken together, they were a storm of enormous size—five kilometers thick, more than a thousand kilometers wide, and riddled with chunks of rock and ice that varied in size from pieces less than a meter to mammoth hulks 150 meters in diameter. *Junker*'s deflectors could handle the tiny particles, but if Jaden hit anything of size . . .

"Don't let that Jedi ruin my ship, Marr," Khedryn said. "Increase power to the forward deflector—for whatever good it will do."

"Yes, Captain."

"You don't ruin my ship, either," Khedryn said to Relin.

Relin ignored him, inhaled, closed his eyes, and seemed to lose himself in meditation for a moment.

Through the viewport, Khedryn watched the Blades swoop in behind *Junker*. The slits of their cockpit covers looked like a cyclopean eye squinting to aim.

Laser cannons fired and green lines cut the space between the two ships. Jaden dived *Junker* so hard and fast that Khedryn's stomach waved a greeting to his throat.

"I told you not to ruin my ship!" he said into the intercom. He scrambled into a seat and strapped himself in as Jaden pulled hard on the stick and put *Junker*'s nose up.

Relin snapped open his eyes.

"Jaden, when we get into the rings, I plan to use the tractor beam against the Blades. Can you compensate?"

A long pause. "You tell me when and which way to expect the drag. I can compensate."

"Copy that." To Khedryn, Relin said over his shoulder, "Maybe they won't follow us in."

Khedryn nodded but knew better. He had not been born lucky.

A patter of ice and small rocks, the steady beat of a snare drum, announced their entry into the fringe of the rings. Khedryn felt *Junker* decelerate and allowed himself a relieved breath. At least Jaden wasn't crazy enough to try to run the rings at full speed.

The Blades devoured the distance between them. They moved in and out of view as *Junker* flew deeper into the rings and the debris field thickened. One of the Blades hit a chunk of ice, spun wildly, and exploded in flame against a spinning rock that reminded Khedryn in shape of a clenched fist.

Ever-larger chunks of ice and rock whirled by, a blizzard that would allow Jaden no room for even a single mistake.

"Stang," Khedryn said, clutching the base of his seat in a white-knuckled grip. He reminded himself to breathe and tried to slow his heart.

"Getting thick now," Marr said.

"Stop stating the obvious!" Khedryn shouted, but forgot to activate the intercom. It was just as well.

As if to make Marr's point, another of the Blades struck a chunk of rock and exploded into a shower of flaming metal.

"Ready yourselves," Jaden said, and *Junker* began to spin.

Jaden dwelled in the comforting warmth of the Force. He barely saw the swirl of ice and rock whirling through the space before *Junker*. He felt each rock, each bit of ice, large or small, as if it were an extension of his body. All were connected to one another and he was connected to them. He abided in the cohesiveness of the universe, the ship an extension of his will.

Action preceded conscious thought. His hands were a blur on the console. *Junker* dived, climbed, spun, wheeled, and careered through the empty spaces between ice and rock. The patter of particles against the cockpit viewport sounded like applause.

Laserfire cut glowing lines along their port side and Jaden turned starboard, dived, then burst out from the bottom of rings and into open space. For a moment he caught the glimpse of the frozen moon of his vision, a pearl against the black of space, before he veered hard right and lost sight of it.

Laserfire once more turned the sky green, crisscrossed the space before them, cut the darkness aft and starboard. Jaden put *Junker* into a spiraling roll as he nosed the ship back up through the rings.

Marr, his voice tight, spoke into the intercom. "What do you see back there?"

"Two are down," Khedryn said, his voice as sharp as a vibroblade's edge. "The rest are in pursuit. These jocks are good."

Jaden knew. Several of them were Force-sensitive.

But they were not as good as he was.

The ship's internal compensators could not keep up with *Junker*'s rapid shifts and the g's pasted Khedryn to his seat. His vision clouded now and again when blood rushed too quickly to his head or too quickly out of it. Jaden had *Junker* wheeling so wildly through space that Khedryn feared for the ship's integrity, never mind the rocks.

"Hold together, girl. Hold together."

The Blades appeared and disappeared in the viewport, flickering in and out of sight like a faulty image on one of The Hole's vidscreens. Rocks and bits of ice large and small moved in and out of his field of vision with dizzying speed. The rapidly changing visual field made Khedryn nauseous. Before him, Relin seemed as impassive as stone.

"Ever gone angling?" Relin said softly to no one. His hand gripped the tractor beam controls.

Junker spun and veered hard to starboard. Khedryn tried not to think about the stress the vessel would endure between Jaden's piloting and Relin's use of the tractor beam.

"Engaging the tractor beam, Jaden," Relin said. "Drag on starboard."

He aimed the tractor beam at a large planetoid in the rings. *Junker* lurched hard and slowed as the beam tethered it to the chunk of rock. *Junker*'s momentum pulled the rock out of its orbit, and Relin held it for only a fraction of a second before cutting it loose.

Junker lurched hard the other way but Jaden somehow compensated, and the rock, now spinning, crashed into another large rock, then another, and the leading Blades, unready for the sudden movement of the planetoids, wheeled out of the way too late. Two more vanished in a spray of metal and flames.

"Another two down," Khedryn said into the intercom, his voice cracking.

Laserfire split the sky, exploding a large rock to *Junker*'s aft, spraying the ship with particulates. More laserfire lit up the sky. Jaden wheeled down, spun, pulled up hard. Relin aimed the tractor beam again, latched on to one of the Blades themselves. *Junker* lost velocity from the drag and the other Blades gained.

"Port," Relin said to Jaden, and used the beam to foul the Blade's trajectory. With no room for error, the fighter hit a rock and broke into two flaming bits, one of which spun into another Blade, sending it into a rock.

The rest of the Blades, swooping and diving in and

out of the field of rock and ice, fired. Jaden nosed up but one of the beams hit *Junker* along the port side, shaking the entire ship. The lights flickered and an alarm rang.

"I cannot keep this up for much longer," Jaden said over the intercom. Khedryn could hear the stress in his voice.

Khedryn agreed. It was only a matter of time before they caught a laser. He spoke loud enough to be heard on the intercom.

"Jaden, can you get us out of the fighters' sight line for a moment?"

Jaden did not hesitate. "Yes."

"What are you going to do?" Relin asked.

"I am going to space what's in my hold. It'll hit a rock, explode, maybe fool the fighters if we can stay out of their sight. They can't scan us in here. We make them think we're dead, then lay low."

"I'll have to accelerate to full to open some space," Jaden said. "It will get iffy."

"Do it," Khedryn said, his mouth dry. "And the price of my cargo is added to the price you owe me."

Relin said into the intercom, "A hard dive out the bottom, we space the cargo, then a hard climb back in. We'll have moments."

"Good thought," Jaden said.

Laserfire exploded a nearby rock, spraying *Junker* with debris. Jaden climbed hard.

"Will what's in the hold explode with enough pop?" Relin asked Khedryn.

"I don't know," Khedryn said. He had speeders in there. They'd blow, though the thought of spacing his *Searing* made him almost as ill as Jaden's flying.

Relin pulled two oval-shaped metal devices from his pocket as laserfire shook the ship. "These are mag-grenades. Attach them to a speeder and press that

button. They'll blow when the speeder does. Understood?"

Khedryn nodded, and another wild turn nearly caused
him to pass out.

"Go," Relin said, then to Jaden, "Khedryn is on his
way to the hold. Open up some space, Jaden."

Khedryn unstrapped himself and wobbled like a
drunk through the corridors, using safety rails to keep
his feet as the ship answered with exclamation points to
Jaden's commands. He felt *Junker* accelerate, twist,
turn, wheel, and he imagined his ship dancing through
hundred-ton raindrops. The superstructure creaked and
moaned under the strain.

"Don't get wet," he said, tapping a bulkhead as he
opened the cargo bay hatches.

Everything was secured and in order, held down with
magnetic clamps or stored in containers integrated into
the walls or floor. He had two nearly complete landspeeders, his Searing swoop, Marr's speeder, several
containers of electronics, and other pieces of assorted
scrap. He ran to the landspeeders—he could not space
his Searing—and affixed the mag-grenades. A press of a
button turned both of them hot.

"Quickly, Khedryn," Jaden said through the comlink.

Khedryn did not bother to respond. He hurried across
the bay to the air lock doors and activated the venting
sequence. A beeper started ticking off the thirty seconds.

"Thirty seconds to vent," he said into his comlink.

"We have the readout up here," Marr said, in his
calm, certain voice. "Tell us when you are clear."

Khedryn ran back to the speeders, lost his footing,
scrambled to his feet, heart racing, and decoupled them
from their magnetic mounts. For good measure, he
opened one of the storage containers that held scrap
electronics. Too late he realized that if the speeder

bumped hard against something else in the bay, it might trigger the grenades while they were still in the ship.

He started to go back, but Marr's voice halted him. "Ten seconds to venting."

"Stang," he cursed. He exited the cargo bay, secured the hatch, and then grabbed a safety rail with both hands. "Clear."

Jaden turned *Junker*'s engines loose and slammed the nose down. The g's flattened Khedryn against the wall, and the overhead siren screamed the imminent venting of the cargo hold. He imagined the speeders skidding across the bay floor, live grenades attached to them.

"You've lost them for the moment," Relin said over the intercom.

"Venting," said Marr's voice.

Khedryn stood and stared through the transparisteel viewport in the hatch doors as the air lock opened and months of work, including the speeders, flew out into the void of space. Through the open air lock doors he caught a glimpse of the edge of the rings as *Junker* burst out of them. He also caught a flash, presumably from the explosion.

Jaden nosed back up hard, throwing Khedryn to the floor as he angled back into the rings, still spinning and wheeling.

"A good explosion," Relin said, as if he were evaluating a grav-ball shot. His vantage at the rear of the ship would have allowed him to see it directly.

Jaden said, "We'll stay flying hard until we see whether they buy the ruse."

Khedryn sat in the core of his ship, listening to her strain, waiting for the telltale shake from a laser cannon's near miss.

Nothing.

"There is nothing behind us," Relin said.

Khedryn looked to the ceiling, and exhaled. He patted his ship. She had saved him again.

"Find something big enough to accommodate us," he said. "And set her down. Then everyone get to the galley. We need to talk."

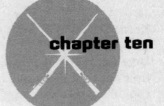

chapter ten

SAES WATCHED ON THE VIEWSCREEN AS THE REMAIN-ing Blades peeled out of the gas giant's rings. Llerd monitored the chatter among the pilots through an earpiece, then relayed it to Saes.

"The target has been destroyed, Captain," Llerd said, his round face flush with the news. "Collided with rocks in the rings. We lost six Blades in the pursuit."

Saes nodded, surprised to find himself so unmoved by Relin's death. He supposed whatever attachment he might have had with Relin had been eroded by time and lost long ago. He reached out his consciousness for his Master, trying to recall the feelings he'd had when he'd realized that Relin had been aboard *Harbinger*. He felt nothing, only emptiness, a hole.

He was alone now, five thousand years in the future. His onetime Master had died a fool. Saes regretted the loss of the Blades, particularly since he would not be able to replace them, but he'd needed to end matters with Relin.

"Put us in orbit around the planet's moon. I will be in my quarters."

"When repairs are completed, should the helm plot a course to Primus Goluud?" Llerd asked.

Saes heard 8L6's servos whir as he stood and looked at the captain.

"No," Saes said. "Plans have changed."

* * *

Khedryn tried to slow his still-racing heart as Jaden set *Junker* down in a deep, sheltered declivity on one of the large asteroids in the rings. His equilibrium was still off from the wild flight, and he swayed as he stood. After confirming that the cargo hold's air lock had resealed and repressurized, he opened the hatch to check on his *Searing*.

Still there, along with Marr's speeder bike. Good. Khedryn loved that swoop.

By the time he reached the galley, Relin was already there, sitting at the central table. Sweat glistened on his face, and his eyes looked like glassy, distant pools sunk in the deep pits of his sockets. His breathing came fast, like that of a rabid animal.

"You are sick," Khedryn said.

Relin looked up, squinting at Khedryn. "Yes. Radiation."

Khedryn tried to look sympathetic. "I have nothing aboard, but we can do something for it back on Fhost." He left a *maybe* behind his teeth, seeing no reason to further burden the Jedi over Farpoint's limited medical facilities.

Relin stared at him for a long moment. "Thank you."

"And the ribs? The arm?"

Relin looked at his stump. "I am all right."

Khedryn could see otherwise but did not push. He held up a caf cup and changed the subject. "Caf? It's a bitter, uh, caffeinated beverage served hot."

"Tea?"

"Sure," Khedryn said, and prepped some tea for the Jedi. It was old, something he'd picked up on a whim months ago, but it was tea.

Jaden and Marr entered, neither talking. Jaden looked drawn behind his beard. Sweat dampened the fringe of his brown hair. Marr, of course, looked like Marr—

solid, calm, as certain as an equation. Khedryn wondered how the Cerean managed such balance.

"I will take some of that caf," Marr said, staring at Relin with unabashed curiosity. "Jaden explained . . . matters to me."

"I'll take some, too," said Jaden. His voice had the sound of a man who had not slept in a few days.

"Take a seat, please," Khedryn said to them both, his tone more formal than he intended.

Marr looked a question at him as he crossed the room but Khedryn, still composing his thoughts, ignored it. He spiked his caf with a jigger of pulkay, then poured caf for Jaden and Marr, joined it on a tray with Relin's tea, and took it to the table.

"Nice flying," he said to Jaden.

"It was," Relin said, wincing in answer to one pain or another. "Well done, Jaden."

"Thank you," Jaden said. He seemed to notice Relin's physical condition for the first time. "Are you . . . all right?" he asked, the question as loaded as a charged blaster.

Relin sat up straight, cleared his throat, and it turned into a soft cough. "I am fine."

Khedryn distributed the drinks. "He's not all right. He's sick. Radiation. And the arm and ribs."

"I know all that," Jaden said, his eyes still on Relin. "That's not what I mean."

Khedryn realized that the Jedi were having a conversation at some level invisible to him.

"I am fine," Relin repeated, but he glanced away.

Jaden sipped his caf and looked unconvinced.

To Relin, Marr said, "Assuming both ships got to near lightspeed, you would have traveled . . . a long way for five thousand years to pass relatively."

Khedryn knew Marr must have been discomfited to use words like *near* and *a long way*.

"Yes," Relin agreed. He looked at Marr. "My name is Relin."

"Marr. I have so many questions."

"They'll have to wait," Relin said.

"I suppose so," Marr said.

"Good caf," Jaden said to Khedryn, holding up the mug.

"Thanks," Khedryn said as he took station at the head of the table. He swallowed, then dived in headfirst. "I have been thinking hard about this, and . . . we are done. This is over." He cut off whatever Jaden and Relin would have said with a raised hand and a raised voice. "*Junker* is my ship. Mine. And I am not risking her, or my crew, over a salvage job."

"This is more than that," Relin said, his glassy eyes fixed like glow lamps on Khedryn.

"You know that already, Captain," Jaden said.

Khedryn gave no ground. "I know it is to you two. To me, this is just another job, and it's gotten too hairy. Do you know why I don't have weapons on *Junker*, Relin? Because I run." He wagged a finger between himself and Marr. "*We* run. I am a salvager. This is a salvage ship."

He realized that he was breathing heavily, that his tone was overly sharp. He took a moment to control himself. Between the calmness of the Jedi and the placidity of Marr, he felt like he was the only one who grasped the danger they had been in.

Jaden started to speak, but Khedryn pointed a finger at him as if it were loaded.

"And don't you even consider trying that mind trick nonsense on me again."

Jaden half smiled, put his hands on the table, and interlaced his fingers. He studied them as if they were of interest, then looked up at Khedryn. "You were going to take me down to the moon. We had a deal, Khedryn."

That hit Khedryn where he lived. He did not renege on deals. "I know. But . . ."

Jaden continued in his infuriatingly calm voice. "But our agreement aside, I want you to step back and consider what has happened here. You and Marr discovered a distress beacon on a backrocket moon in the Unknown Regions."

"Chance," Khedryn said, but Jaden continued.

"I received a Force vision of that same moon. In it, voices pleaded with me for help." His voice intensified a degree. "For help, Captain."

"You received a Force vision?" Relin asked. "Did you see anything that suggested my presence or *Harbinger*'s?"

Jaden had eyes only for Khedryn as he drove home his point.

"We meet under extraordinary circumstances in Farpoint, then journey here, and at almost the exact moment of our arrival an ancient Sith ship appears."

Relin piled on. "And that ship bears an extremely dangerous cargo."

Khedryn's response was knee-jerk defensiveness. "So you say."

"So I *say*?" Relin said, heat leaking into his tone.

Jaden held a hand up. "Please, Relin."

Khedryn shook his head. "Look, this was supposed to be a simple job. Instead it's . . ."

"Something bigger," Jaden said.

"I was going to say *complicated*," Khedryn said. "But if it is about something bigger, then that makes it a Jedi concern. Not mine. Not ours. Right, Marr?"

Marr drummed his long fingers on the table, taking it all in. He gave a noncommittal grunt that Khedryn liked not at all.

"No, this isn't just a Jedi concern," Jaden said. "It concerns you, too. Consider all the things I mentioned, the synchronicity of them. It is not chance that we are here together at this moment."

"It could be chance," Khedryn said halfheartedly, but he did not believe his own words. "Marr could put a probability to it, had he a mind. No, I am not doing this."

Relin slammed his fist on the table with the suddenness of a lightning strike, startling them all. Caf and tea jumped over cup brims. "You are a stubborn fool, Khedryn Faal."

Khedryn could handle anger more easily than Jaden's inexorable reasonableness. "Better a live fool than a dead fanatic, which is the course you've charted for yourself. You've got radiation poisoning, broken ribs, a severed arm. You haven't even paused long enough for treatment. You haven't even asked for some pharma for the pain or bacta to help the healing."

Relin rose to his feet, anger in his eyes. Khedryn's mouth went dry but he held his ground and made certain nothing on him shook.

"I do not stop for treatment because I will not shirk doing what needs to be done. Even if it causes me pain. You cannot always run, Khedryn."

Khedryn stared into Relin's haggard face, saw there a deeper pain than that of his wounds. He wilted under its weight, sighed, sat.

"You spilled your tea," he said quietly.

Silence took the head chair for a time, everyone letting time deflate the tension. Relin sat, too, his anger at Khedryn seemingly dispelled as fast as it had appeared.

"Marr is Force-sensitive," Jaden said. "Did you know that? Did either of you?"

Khedryn spilled some of his own caf. "What?"

"How do you know that?" Marr said, and Khedryn thought he did not sound overly surprised.

"I can sense it. Relin can as well, I am sure."

Relin nodded absently, mostly lost in the depths of his teacup.

Jaden looked to Marr. "I apologize for springing this on you. I thought I would tell you after we returned to Fhost. If I mentioned it at all."

"What does that even mean, *Force-sensitive*?" Khedryn asked.

"It means he has an intuitive connection to the Force," Jaden said. "Were he younger, it would mean he was trainable. But given your age, Marr, even with your mathematical gifts, training is probably out of the question."

The possibility, even if remote, of losing Marr to the Jedi Order opened a hole under Khedryn's feet, and he started to slip. He held up his hands. "Whoa. Aren't we getting ahead of ourselves a bit?"

"Yes, we are," Marr said, and looked at Jaden. "Why did you tell me this now?"

"Because I want all of us to realize that the Force brought you to that signal. You may not have known it, but that is what happened. You selected the route back to Fhost, didn't you? Didn't you?"

"He's the navigator," Khedryn said.

"I chose the course," Marr acknowledged.

Jaden nodded, obviously unsurprised. "It was not chance that you chose this system. The Force is moving through you, through all of us."

"Not through me," Khedryn said before he could wall the words off behind his teeth. He knew they sounded petulant. He felt the odd man out on his own ship.

Jaden put a hand on Khedryn's shoulder, and that only made it worse. "The Force touches all of us. Look at us. Look."

Khedryn did, and had to admit that it would have taken an odd coincidence to bring all of them together, at that place, at that time.

Marr, staring at his hands, said, "I do not wish any training."

Jaden did not seem surprised. "Understood. I simply wanted you to see what is happening here. I want all of us to see it."

"Jaden is right," Relin said.

Khedryn tried to get his head around events, but could not. He faced the fact that perhaps Jaden was, in fact, right. Could he simply run as he usually did?

"Time is our enemy," Relin said. "Khedryn, please."

Khedryn downed the last of his caf, pleased to find the final sip heavy with bitterness from the pulkay. He was almost to the point of surrender. "What are you asking us to do?"

"Help us accomplish what needs to be accomplished," Jaden said. "I need to get down to the surface of the moon. There is someone down there who needs help."

Khedryn fired the last of his ammo. "And if you go down there and there's nothing? Have you considered that? I've seen that happen before."

Jaden shook his head, a bit too fast, a bit too forcefully. "That won't happen. Something is transmitting that signal."

"Jaden—" Khedryn began.

Relin cut him off. "I cannot go down to the moon."

Khedryn set down his caf cup and stared across the table. "No, you want to get aboard the cruiser. You said that. It remains crazy even when repeated often. Antique or not, that ship packs more firepower in its shuttles than we do on all of *Junker.*"

"Relin," Jaden said. "I don't think—"

Relin held up his stump, perhaps forgetting that it had no upraised hand attached. "You seemed surprised when I mentioned Lignan earlier." He swirled his cup. "Were you?"

"Yes," Jaden said.

"And that tells me that you have never before heard of it or its power. Yet Khedryn mentioned Sith, so I know they still exist in this time. Putting the Lignan in their hands would be dangerous, yes?"

Jaden nodded. "It would, if it does what you say."

Relin's voice frosted. "You felt it. Do you doubt what I say, too?"

"No," Jaden admitted. "But . . ."

Relin ignored him, continued. "And Saes, the captain of *Harbinger,* should he figure out what has happened, may try to do exactly that: take it to the Sith. Or he may hoard it for himself. But he is very dangerous in either case. I need to destroy either the Lignan or the ship. And if he leaves this system, we may never get another chance. I do not have much time. *Harbinger*'s hyperdrive is damaged. The whole ship is reeling from the misjump. This is the moment."

Khedryn thought he could see Jaden bend under some weight known only to him. The Jedi very much wanted to go down to the moon's surface. When his expression fell, Khedryn knew that Jaden, too, had just surrendered.

"You are right," Jaden said. "The ore is the greater concern. I am being influenced by . . . personal concerns. The moon can wait. I will accompany you aboard *Harbinger.*"

Relin stared into his teacup. "No. Unless you can suppress your Force presence altogether, you are unwelcome. Saes will detect you easily."

"You could screen me."

"Your presence is too strong, Jaden," Relin said. "Masking it from Saes would be difficult and an inefficient use of my power."

Listening to their exchange, Khedryn perceived two

men trying to give the other an excuse to do what he wished, all while purporting to want its opposite.

"Heed your own words," Relin said to Jaden. "The Force called you to the moon, and that is where you should go. Look to your feelings."

"I don't trust my feelings."

The admission seemed to take Relin aback. "You cannot accompany me, Jaden. This is for me to do."

"My Force presence is not strong," Marr said, his words surprising everyone. "I could accompany you."

For a long moment, no one said anything.

Khedryn was too stunned to speak. Finally, he said, "Why would you do that?"

Marr sighed over his caf, shrugged, tilted his head, finally found words. "I told Jaden how I once calculated the probability that my life would go this way or that. Do you remember me telling you the same thing?"

Khedryn nodded.

"Do you know why I did that? It was not just the math. I wanted to confirm that my life would mean something, that I would do something important. But then . . . other things got in the way."

"Marr . . . ," Khedryn said.

"I do not regret a moment. You are my great friend. But is salvage all I want to have left behind me? This is a chance to do something meaningful. I concur with Jaden that something other than chance brought us to this moment. It is more likely that you'd win at sabacc than all of this to happen by chance."

Khedryn smiled despite himself. "That's sayin' something."

Marr continued, "Our lives have led us up to this place at this moment. How can I run away from that?"

Marr did not say it, but Khedryn understood Marr to be asking him the same question, and he had no good answer. For him, running away was simple habit. He'd been running away from roots and responsibility since he'd become an adult. It had worked pretty well for him.

Marr looked to Relin. "I will go, if you will have me."

Jaden started to speak, stopped.

Relin stared across the table at Marr. "You've only just met me, and you do not know what I have in mind."

"Whatever it is, it will require a ship. You'll need a pilot who knows the ship, not to mention one with two hands."

Relin tilted his head to acknowledge the point. "The Lignan will affect you more strongly up close. You've felt some . . . unease since *Harbinger* appeared?"

Marr nodded. "A headache, mostly."

"The feelings will be more acute when you are near its source."

"For you, too," Jaden said to Relin.

Marr's brow was smooth, his eyes untroubled. "Even so."

"You're certain?" Relin asked.

"Too certain, I'd say," Khedryn said.

"Yes," said Marr, eyeing first Relin, then Khedryn. "I am certain."

"Very well," Relin said.

Khedryn shook his head, finished off his caf. "We are all crazy on this boat. I need another caf. Anyone else?"

Everyone nodded.

"Drinks all around, then," Khedryn said, and started to rise.

"I will get it, Captain," said Marr. The Cerean rose, placing his hand on Khedryn's shoulder as he passed, the small gesture a reminder of the years they had been friends.

"Let's talk specifics," Khedryn said to the Jedi. "What are your plans?"

Relin gestured for Jaden to go first.

"I fly down to the moon. Find what I am supposed to find."

"Alone?"

Jaden nodded.

"No," Khedryn said. "I am not leaving my ship down on that moon if you . . . find something unexpected. I can shuttle you down in *Flotsam*. We'll be able to dodge the cruiser's sensors and get you into the atmosphere. From there you can locate the source of the beacon. But I expect more when we're done. The Order owes me. Another five thousand on top of what we already agreed. Yes?"

"Agreed."

"You hear that, Marr?"

"Heard it, Captain."

Haggling over fees made Khedryn feel more like himself, more in control of events. He looked to Relin.

"And what about you? How do you plan to get aboard that cruiser?"

"I need Marr to fly me in."

"In where?"

"Into the ship."

Khedryn scoffed, then frowned when he saw that Relin was serious. "That isn't happening."

Relin's jaw tightened, and loosened, masticating his thoughts. "My Padawan died trying to bring that ship down. I am going back aboard and destroying what needs destroying. There's only one way for me to do that. We fly this ship right down its throat."

"Fly *my* ship, you mean."

"Yes, your ship." Relin's tone turned earnest. "Listen to me. *Harbinger*'s weapons systems are down. They have to be. Otherwise they would have blown your ship from space already. Saes had to deploy fighters to attack you rather than his batteries. So Marr flies your ship out of the rings and into the landing bay before they can stop us."

"You look a lot less sick when you're talking about risking lives," Khedryn said. "The ship has active deflectors. How do you propose getting through those?" He felt a pang of guilt even asking the question.

Relin's expression fell. "The shields? I . . . don't know."

Khedryn did know but could not bring himself to mouth the words.

"There has to be a way," Relin said.

Khedryn stared at Marr, who was pouring caf, willing him to hold his silence, but the Cerean ignored him. "We could use the power crystal to open a temporary hole in the shields."

Khedryn blew out an irritated sigh.

Jaden looked startled. "You have a power crystal?"

Khedryn glared at Marr, at Jaden, at Relin. "We've used it twice, to board uncrewed derelicts when the autopilot kept the shields operational."

"Where did you get it?" Jaden asked.

"There's a whole lot of things floating in the black, Jedi. I told you that. Just need to know where to look."

Jaden looked around, as if he expected a power crystal to burst out of a closet. "Where is it?"

"In my pocket," Khedryn snapped, then recovered himself. "Mounted on the beam projector behind *Junker*'s dish."

"It is a power sink," Marr said. "We'll have to divert most of our power to operate it. But it should work."

"The problem appears solved," Relin said. "Thank you, Marr."

"Yes, thank you, Marr," Khedryn said.

Relin went on as if he had not heard Khedryn's sarcasm. "Saes will not expect it. He thinks we're destroyed. The Blades flying patrol will be too far out and none of the fighters on the ship will scramble in time to intercept us."

"That is madness," Khedryn said. "Marr, did you hear this?"

"I heard it, Captain." Marr returned to the table, distributed the caf.

Khedryn raised his eyebrows. "And?"

"What other choice is there?"

"We go back to Fhost, forget this whole thing," Khedryn said, but everyone responded as if he had not spoken at all. Events had passed him by.

"That gets you aboard," Jaden said. "How do you get back?"

Relin hesitated a beat too long, Khedryn thought. "Marr need only drop me off and get back out. He could jump anywhere he wanted to after that. Or he could flee back into the rings until you and Jaden return from the moon."

Marr pulled back a chair, sat. "The fighters will pursue and I cannot pilot *Junker* through the rings. I'd have to jump out and return later."

Khedryn tried to sip his caf but his hand was shaking. Embarrassed, he put the cup down. "You are seriously entertaining this? This is not a plan. It's madness."

"That tells us how Marr gets out," Jaden said, and leaned forward. "How do *you* plan to get out?"

This time Relin answered a beat too quickly. "Escape pod, same as before."

Jaden and Relin shared a long look before Relin buried his eyes in the depths of his tea.

"When does all this happen?" Khedryn said, dreading the answer.

Relin looked up. "Now."

*   *   *

Kell held *Predator* at a distance from the cruiser and followed on his scanner as the fighters nosed up and out of the rings and returned from their pursuit of *Junker*. There were several fewer than had entered.

Kell decided that they had either lost the freighter or simply called off the pursuit. He knew they had not destroyed it. The skein of Fate was too strong. Jaden Korr's destiny was not to die in laserfire. It was to die in Kell's hands, as Kell devoured his soup and transcended.

Content that his destiny was unfolding as it should, he engaged *Predator*'s low-output ion engines and piloted the ship near the edge of the rings. His baffles and screens would keep him invisible to the scanners of the cruiser. There he waited, a lurking spider.

The opalescent moon glittered against the black of space. He watched it turn, the featureless ball where his life would find fulfillment. He could have surveyed the moon, reported his findings back to Darth Wyyrlok. But he would not. He would wait, watchful, and descend to its surface only when Jaden Korr did so. Their lines were knotted together in a common fate, tethered to each other, and he would put down on the moon only when pulled down by Jaden. He could no more go to the moon's surface without Jaden than a Twi'lek could separate its lekku.

His hands were shaking, partly from hunger, partly from exaltation. He had not fed since leaving Fhost, nor would he. His next meal would be, *had to be,* Jaden Korr.

He powered down *Predator* but for the scanners, life support, and the speaker, which played the Imperial beacon, the sound that had summoned all of them to this one place, at this one time, and waited.

"I will prep *Junker,*" Marr said, and rose to leave.

Khedryn put his hands on the table, pushed himself

up as if he weighed a thousand kilos. "And I will . . . do something else. Stang, I cannot believe I agreed to this."

The two Jedi said nothing, and he turned to go. When he stood in the hatch leading out, Khedryn glanced back and said to Relin and Jaden, "Listen, when we get back to Fhost, we gamble, all of us together. Yes? As reckless as you two are, I might actually win some credits. As long as Jaden doesn't cheat. You have credits in your time, Relin?"

"Yes, of course."

"Then you've got something I can win. You play sabacc?"

"I don't know it."

"I will teach you." Apparently thinking better before his exit, he returned to the food locker, poured and drank a final jigger of pulkay. "I'll get *Flotsam* prepped. Then I will pray."

Jaden smiled him on his way. After Khedryn had gone, Relin, too, rose but Jaden halted him with a word.

"Stay."

Relin eased back into his chair, grimacing at the pain in his ribs.

But Jaden knew that physical pain was not driving him. He waited until he was sure Khedryn would not return.

Before Jaden spoke, Relin said, "You do not need to say it."

But Jaden did. "Anger is pouring off you. I feel it more strongly than I do the effect of the Lignan."

"Saes must pay. My Padawan—"

"You will lose yourself, Relin. And you cannot do that. You have made yourself steward of Marr on this mission."

Relin's lip curled in a snarl. "He understands the risk. And it was your words that encouraged him to do something *meaningful*."

Jaden heard the contempt in Relin's tone and knew the man was nearly gone. Yet he could not deny Relin's accusation. "You bring him back with you. Understood? I want your word."

Relin brushed his dark hair off his forehead, and Jaden was struck with how pale and drawn the man appeared. "I will see that he returns."

Jaden knew he would get no more. The silence sat heavy between them. More than just five thousand years separated them.

"What did you do, Jaden?" Relin asked at last.

At first Jaden did not understand, but when he saw the knowing look on Relin's face, his heart jumped at the implicit accusation. "What do you mean?"

Relin leaned forward, his watery, bloodshot eyes nailing Jaden to his chair. "Anger pours off me? Well, doubt pours off you; uncertainty. I know what gives birth to that. *What did you do?*"

Jaden drew on his caf, hiding his face behind the mug's rim. In his mind's eye, he saw the faces through the viewport, pleading with him not to do it.

Relin smiled, though he managed to make it look unpleasant. "Something that shattered your image of yourself, yes?"

Jaden set down his cup and confessed. "Yes."

Relin chuckled, the first genuine mirth Jaden had heard from him. "The Jedi have not changed in five thousand years. Our expectation of ourselves always exceeds the reality. I have no wisdom for you, Jaden." He stood, extended a hand. "Good luck. I need to figure out a way to get my lightsaber charged."

Jaden stood, took his hand, a bit puzzled by Relin's parting words. He considered offering Relin the lightsaber he had crafted as a boy on Coruscant, since it required no power pack. But he knew Relin would not accept it.

"Marr will be able to help, I'm sure," Jaden said.

"I am sure," Relin said.

Before he exited the galley, Jaden said to his back, "May the Force be with you, Relin."

Relin did not slow.

Khedryn found Marr in *Junker*'s cockpit, checking its instrumentation, testing systems. Khedryn hesitated in the doorway, thinking of all the flights he and Marr had sat beside each other in the cramped space while *Junker* hurtled through the black. The ship had carried them through some dangerous times. He cleared his throat.

Marr glanced over his shoulder but did not turn to face him.

"She ready?" Khedryn asked.

"Indeed," Marr said. "The damage was minimal, and she weathered the strain on the engines remarkably well. Probably due to your fine-tuning."

Khedryn recognized the praise as a gesture of reconciliation. He put a hand on the wall, felt the cool durasteel of his ship under his hand, and offered his own gesture. "Been a while since she's flown without both of us sitting up here."

"Indeed," Marr said, more softly.

Khedryn shook off the sentimentality, stepped forward, and performed a cursory glance over the instrumentation, not really seeing it.

"These Jedi go all-in, don't they?"

Marr smiled, stood, turned to face him. "They do. Push until it gives, right?"

"Right." Khedryn smiled, too, but it faded quickly. "I am still not entirely sure why we are doing this."

"It is the right thing," Marr said.

"How are you always so certain, Marr? This isn't math."

"I am not *always* certain, but I am about this."

"Because you learned you're Force-sensitive?"

Marr colored. "Maybe. Partially."

Khedryn did not press. He thought of all the scrapes he and Marr had been through the past six years and realized that all of them had been of his own making. Marr had simply followed his lead and respected Khedryn's call. Khedryn figured he owed Marr the same, at least this once.

"Try not to get *Junker* shot up, eh? And you are on shuttle service and that's an order. If it gets too hairy, you abort and jump out of the system, no matter what Relin says. If you get aboard that cruiser, you drop off that Jedi and get out. *Flotsam* can get Jaden and me out of the system if need be."

Marr did not respond, and Khedryn liked the silence not at all. "That's an order, Marr. Understood?"

"I will do my best," Marr said.

Khedryn gave him a gentle shove. "You come back with the same look in your eyes as these Jedi and I'm throwing you off the ship for good."

Marr smiled, the tooth he'd chipped in a brawl Khedryn had started on Dantooine a jagged reminder of his loyalty. Khedryn looked out the cockpit window at the grainy, rough surface of the asteroid on which Jaden had set *Junker* down.

"This didn't exactly go as planned, did it?" he said.

"It rarely does," Marr said. "Variables. Always variables."

A fist formed in Khedryn's throat. He stared at his reflection on the transparisteel and swallowed it down. He wanted to say more to the best and only real friend he'd had since leaving the Empire of the Hand as a young man, but managed only to turn, reach out, and say, "Good luck."

Marr took Khedryn's hand, shook it. "And you."

Khedryn took one last look around *Junker*'s cockpit,

moved past Marr, and started to go, but Marr's voice pulled him around.

"Captain. For you."

Khedryn turned to find Marr holding out a stick of chewstim.

He took it, supposing it said all that needed to be said.

When Khedryn had *Flotsam* prepped and loaded with envirogear, he got on *Junker*'s shipwide communicator.

"All hands to the galley one more time. Attendance is mandatory."

He took a roundabout way to the galley, walking *Junker*'s corridors, cognizant of the fact that it, and Marr, might not return from *Harbinger*'s landing bay.

If they made it to the landing bay.

He knew he was getting sentimental; knew, too, that he could not afford to do so. He was the captain and as such had certain obligations.

Beginning with this one, he thought.

When he reached the galley, he found Jaden, Relin, and Marr standing at the table, looking questions at one another.

"Time is short," Relin said.

"Gotta make time for this," Khedryn said.

He went to the food locker, pulled four drink glasses, and poured all of them a double from the only bottle of decent keela he kept on the ship. He carried the glasses to the other three men, handed one to each in turn. Relin sniffed at the glass.

"I do not consume alcohol," he said.

"You do now," Khedryn said. "Captain's orders."

Relin half smiled and relented with a shrug.

Khedryn held aloft his glass, and the others mirrored his gesture. With nothing better to say, he recited an old spacers' toast he remembered from his adolescence.

"Drink it down, boys, for the black of space is cold.

Drink it down, boys, for it's always better to live hard and die young than live not and die old."

Everyone smiled. No one laughed. All drank.

Khedryn slammed his glass down on the table. "We go."

chapter eleven

KHEDRYN TOOK THE COPILOT'S SWIVEL SEAT IN *FLOT-sam*'s tiny cockpit. It had been a while since he'd sat in the Starhawk's cockpit, and the tight confines made him feel like he was sitting in a metal coffin.

Instrumentation was live. He shook off the sense of foreboding and performed a final preflight check. Everything showed green. He stared out the tapering transparisteel window, eyeing the swirl of rock and ice, faintly backlit by the cerulean balloon of the gas giant. They were coming around to the planet's dark side. The deep blue oval of the superstorm was nowhere in sight. They would pass unmarked by the planet's giant eye.

"We are go for release," he said.

"Go for release," Jaden said from the pilot's seat. "Warming engines. Disconnecting."

The modified couplings released with a series of deep clicks and *Flotsam* floated free of *Junker,* just another piece of debris floating in the gas giant's belt of ice and rock. Repulsors carried them safely away from *Junker* and the asteroid.

Khedryn felt a moment of intense vertigo as they moved off, and he knew it had nothing to do with motion sickness. Jaden must have noticed his feelings.

"When is the last time you sat in the cockpit of something other than *Junker*?"

"Been a while," Khedryn acknowledged. Usually Marr flew *Flotsam,* if it proved necessary on a job. "Marr will take good care of her."

"Of course he will," Jaden said. He activated the comm and raised *Junker.* "We are clear."

"Copy that," said Relin. "You are clear."

Hearing Relin's disembodied voice struck Khedryn oddly, made him experience the same sense of disconnectedness he sometime did while watching time-lagged events on the vidscreens in The Hole.

Except in Relin's case the lag was five thousand years rather than only a few months. It was as if Relin had already happened, as if he were a foregone conclusion that Khedryn could only watch but not affect.

He cleared his mind, his throat, tasted the afterburn of keela in his phlegm.

"Do you find it odd that Relin asked nothing of the current state of the galaxy? I'd be as curious as a spider monkey."

Jaden fiddled with the instruments, and Khedryn imagined him putting a filter around his thoughts. "I am not surprised, no."

"No?"

"He knows he is going to die," Jaden said, his tone matter-of-fact. "Whether he succeeds or not, he is dead. The radiation will kill him."

Khedryn's voice was not matter-of-fact. "What about Marr?" He reached for the comm, not sure what he would say, but Jaden's hand closed over his.

"Relin will ensure Marr's safety as best he can. He is a Jedi."

"Jedi." Khedryn spat the word as if he were trying to rid himself of a foul taste. He recalled stories of C'baoth's betrayal of Outbound Flight, and feelings he had not known he possessed bubbled up from his gut and slipped between his lips. "You Jedi think you know right from wrong, always making life-and-death decisions for others. How can you be so certain about it? These are lives, people."

"I am certain of nothing," Jaden said, and Khedryn heard a surprising resignation in the Jedi's tone. Khedryn's anger floated away with the rocks and ice.

"Why are you really here, Jaden? I mean, why really? The vision, yes, but it's more than that."

Jaden licked his lips, stared out the cockpit glass, then finally turned in his seat to face Khedryn.

"You really want to know?"

Khedryn sensed that Jaden wanted him to really want to know. He nodded.

Jaden stared straight at him, no evasion, and spoke in a tone as flat as a droid's.

"During the civil war, when the Jedi assaulted Centerpoint Station, I led one of the teams."

"I heard of that. The whole station was destroyed."

"My orders were to move fast and leave no one behind us as we advanced. At one point, we met stiff resistance from the Confederation and some Corellian sympathizers. Eventually we forced them back and they fled into a cargo hold and sealed the doors."

Khedryn could see that Jaden was not seeing the present. He was looking at Khedryn, but his eyes had followed his memory back into the past. He was seeing whatever ghosts haunted him.

"You blew the doors? Cut through them?"

Jaden's voice gained volume, as if he feared he would not be heard. "I activated the air lock and spaced all of them."

For a moment, Khedryn thought he might have misheard.

"You spaced them?"

Jaden nodded, his eyes narrowed, fixed on some distant point in his past where his guilt lived.

"Most were Confederation soldiers," Jaden said. "But there were noncombatants there, too. Engineers. Women. But I could not take the time to dig them out or negotiate a surrender. Leave none behind me. Those were my orders. From a fellow Jedi. I followed them."

Khedryn watched Jaden's jaw and fists clench and unclench, his tracheal lump rise and fall in his throat like a heartbeat.

"Stang," Khedryn said, the word pathetically unsuited to the job of articulating the mix of emotions he felt.

Jaden's eyes refocused on the present.

"So, Khedryn, when it comes to knowing right from wrong, I do not profess to knowing anything. Not anymore."

Khedryn searched his mind for some words that might offer solace. "It was war, Jaden. People die in war. What difference does it make if it's by blaster, lightsaber, or the vacuum?"

Jaden inhaled deeply and looked past Khedryn. "It makes a difference."

Khedryn thought about that. Finally he nodded. "I suppose it does."

Jaden wore a pained, self-conscious smile behind his beard. "You have sins you want to confess, Captain? Now seems to be the time. Something about this cockpit, maybe."

Khedryn laughed, and it dispelled some of the mood. "If I started confessing my sins, Jedi, we'd never get this party started. You ready?"

Jaden looked out the glass at the churn of the rings, the gas giant. "Engaging ion engines," he reported to *Junker*.

"Confirmed," responded Relin.

"At this speed it will take us an hour to get around the planet and be ready to go," Khedryn said over the comm.

"One standard hour, seventeen minutes, and thirty-six seconds," Marr answered, eliciting a smile from Khedryn.

"Mark," he said, and marked the in-ship chrono to count down the timeline.

They would navigate slowly through the rings—an easy task at low velocity—come around the gas giant's dark side, and try to come at the moon from the opposite side, undetected by *Harbinger*'s sensors, while *Junker* burst out of the rings and flew right down the cruiser's throat.

Relin felt his body failing, his cells popping under the weight of the radiation poisoning. Fatigue and emotional exhaustion made his vision blur from time to time. Sweat dampened the tunic and trousers under his robes, pasted them to his flesh. He sought comfort in his connection to the Force, but it, too, was under assault, popping under the weight of his anger.

He found it difficult to maintain a passive screen against the Lignan's ambient energy. It leaked through his defenses in dribs and drabs, though it no longer caused him the same degree of discomfort it had previously. He had become inured to its worst effects. The radiation had polluted his body. The Lignan had polluted his spirit. He was failing all over.

Marr had *Junker*'s controls. Even if Relin had not lost a hand, the unfamiliar instrumentation would have made it difficult for him to fly. The chrono in the HUD counted down the timeline as they moved into position.

He flashed back to the past, *his* past, recalled sitting beside Drev in the Infiltrator, countless times, recalled his Padawan's laughter, his joy. It seemed long ago, yet to Relin it had been only a day. The wound of his grief still bled freely, unscabbed, unscarred.

"You are thoughtful," Marr said, adjusting course.

"I was thinking of my Padawan."

"I see," Marr said.

Hunks of rock and ice floated past the cockpit window. Marr did a fine job of steering them through the debris. No doubt he was an excellent pilot.

Just like Drev.

"Before our assault on *Harbinger*, Drev piloted our ship through an asteroid belt not unlike this."

"At speed?"

"Yes, using the Force." Relin remembered Drev's smile and tried to answer it with one of his own, but he simply could not summon it. His lips twisted into something he imagined looked more like a bared snarl than a smile.

"He must have been an extraordinary pilot," Marr said. "I have never seen anything like what Jaden Korr did with *Junker*. You must have been an exemplary teacher."

Relin appreciated what Marr was trying to do but it brought him no comfort. He shook his head. He had lost one Padawan to the dark side and another to battle. "I was a poor teacher, I fear."

To that, Marr said nothing.

"You have not consulted the navigation computer," Relin said. "You do all of the computations in your head?"

Marr nodded.

"I have never seen so narrowly focused a gift from the Force. I suspect it has a purpose you do not yet see."

Marr smiled, Relin noticing his chipped tooth. "Perhaps this moment is its purpose."

"Perhaps," Relin said, liking Marr despite himself.

Moving at one-eighth power while watching the HUD chrono, Marr maneuvered them through the rings until they neared the edge.

"Far enough," Relin said. He did not want them hanging out there too far, visible to *Harbinger*'s passive scans. The debris in the rings would give them cover until *Flotsam* got into position. Meanwhile, they could gather some situational intelligence.

Through the debris field they could see the milky glow of the gas giant's moon.

"I will magnify on the HUD," Marr said.

The moon, filling a section of the cockpit window, grew larger with each press of a button—larger, larger, until it filled about half the window. Rock and ice floated before them and blocked a clear view, but Marr could see it well enough to note the long, dark form silhouetted against the moon's glow.

"The cruiser has moved into orbit around the moon," he said.

"That is more distance that we'll need to close," Relin said. "*Harbinger* will have more time to respond to our approach."

Marr tapped a few keys on his console. "Two hundred eighty-one thousand three hundred two kilometers from here to there."

Relin estimated the math in his head. "How fast does *Junker* fly at sublight?"

"We can cover that distance in about a minute."

"A minute," Relin said, thinking. "Too long. The high-alert Blades will scramble."

Marr licked his lips. "Alternatively, we can attempt to jump right under *Harbinger*."

Relin's thoughts collided with Marr's suggestion. "Jump? We are still in the planet's gravity well, as is *Harbinger*. And there's the moon's well, too."

"We are at the outside of the gas giant's well, and the moon's is weak. I can account for all of that in such a short jump." He paused, cocked his head. "Maybe."

"Maybe?" Relin looked at the HUD. Debris from the rings blocked the moon and *Harbinger* from view. "You are talking about using the hyperdrive to jump between a planet and its moon. A second in hyperspace, maybe less."

"I do not see an alternative. Do you?"

Relin did not. "I have never heard of this being done."

"Nor I," said Marr. "But maybe now we see the actual purpose to which my talent is to be put."

Relin decided that he would have to trust in Marr's gift, have to trust in the Force. Hypocrisy stabbed at him.

"Do it," he said. He looked at the chrono, counting down the time. "You have less than an hour to get the calculations done."

Marr leaned forward in his seat and started to turn off the magnified HUD display. *Junker* had shifted some, and he could once more see the moon and *Harbinger*.

"Leave it up," Relin said.

As Marr began his work, Relin sat in his seat and gazed at Saes's ship, letting memories put a spark to the kindling of his anger. Staring at the dreadnought, he recalled the black scar of twisted metal, all that remained of its primary bridge, all that remained of Drev.

The pain in his ribs and arm faded in the flames from the pain in his heart. The ambient energy from the Lignan stoked his quiet rage and he let the flames grow, heedless of what they were consuming.

He magnified the HUD further, growing *Harbinger* in

his sight as anger grew in his core. And the alchemy of that anger transformed the pain of loss into the power of hate. He held it in and gave no outward sign of his feelings, though he thought he must soon burst.

"Hurry, Marr," he said, his voice choked by the emotional turmoil within him.

Marr said nothing, simply continued his calculations. Even with his mathematical gifts, he relied heavily on assistance from the navigation computer. Relin could not follow all of the formulae, but he could see that Marr was making remarkable progress.

Jaden glided through the rings at one-half power, *Flotsam* twisting and turning to avoid rocks and ice as necessary.

Khedryn eased back in his chair, hands crossed behind his head. "A bit more controlled than your previous piloting, Jaden."

Jaden smiled distantly as he stared out of the slit of the cockpit window, his mind on something else altogether. Khedryn wondered if the Jedi regretted confessing to him.

Khedryn said nothing more as they circumnavigated the gas giant, using its rings for cover. Eventually they caught up with the blue superstorm that looked like the planet's eye, half of it lost in the night side, the other half still in light and staring. Jaden watched it as if hypnotized.

"You all right?" Khedryn asked, concerned that Jaden might drift *Flotsam* into a rock.

"Fine," Jaden said, his voice soft.

They planned to come around the gas giant and put the moon more or less between them and *Harbinger*, hoping that their small size would allow them to hide in the moon's scanner signature.

A HUD in the cockpit window showed the countdown. If all went as planned, *Flotsam* and *Junker* would break from the rings at the same time.

Khedryn took out the chewstim Marr had given him, ripped it in half. He held a piece out.

"Jaden?"

"Yes, thanks."

"Hold it until we actually go," Khedryn said.

Jaden nodded. Together they watched the chrono and waited.

Marr completed the calculations with ample time to spare, then double-checked them.

"I am confident in these calculations," the Cerean said.

Relin only nodded, his mind already moving to what he would do when his feet hit *Harbinger*'s deck. He felt an unexpected exhiliaration at the thought of destroying the ship and killing so many aboard, including Saes. He would turn Drev's grave into a burning pyre that would consume them all. He would—

Marr's hand closed on his shoulder, and he flinched at the touch. His skin felt hypersensitive.

"Relin, you are unwell."

Relin knew he was sweating, breathing too rapidly. "I am all right."

He looked at the chrono: ten seconds.

He had traveled five thousand years into the future to have his life hang on the thread of the single moment they would spend in hyperspace. He flashed on the wild trajectory of the escape pod when it'd been caught in *Harbinger*'s wake, the sickening twists and turns of the misjump.

Marr put his hand on the lever that would engage the hyperdrive.

"I will power us down the moment we emerge from hyperspace. Are you ready?"

Relin took a deep breath, feeling it against his broken ribs. "Yes."

They stared at the chrono as it counted down the final seconds.

"Prepare yourself for the Lignan," Relin said.

Marr engaged the hyperdrive.

Khedryn and Jaden popped the chewstim in their mouths as Jaden took *Flotsam* out to the edge of the rings. Open space beckoned before them, the moon bifurcated by the sun's light. Khedryn dared not scan for *Harbinger* lest the cruiser's passive scans pick up the probe.

Both of them watched the HUD chrono roll to zero.

"Mark," Khedryn said.

Jaden accelerated to full and blazed through space for the moon.

Kell lurked in the black between the moon and the gas giant's rings. He had positioned *Predator* as best he could to ensure that his scanners would pick up any ship exiting the rings in the direction of the moon.

Predator's cockpit had grown cold, but Kell modified his metabolism to maintain a comfortable body temperature. He sat in the darkness of his cockpit, staring into the void of space, wondering at its hidden meanings, seeking the truth of its many lines.

His mind drifted on clouds of memory. He thought of the other Anzati he had met through the centuries. They did not see the *daen nosi*. One had thought Kell mad. In return, Kell had slowly consumed his soup for a standard month, keeping him alive until the very end.

Kell was not mad. He was blessed, unique, chosen to see the truth of existence as written in the lines of the universe's fate. And soon he would have its cipher.

When he heard his sensor console beep to indicate a contact, he knew it was Jaden Korr. He knew, too, where Jaden was going and that he would kill him there.

He examined the scan signature of the small craft darting out of the rings. A Starhawk, moving fast, heading for the dark side of the moon. Not *Junker*, but its attached shuttle.

Where was *Junker*?

Kell pushed the thought from his mind, waited a ten-count to give the Starhawk a nice lead, then brought *Predator* back online and fell in behind it.

The Imperial beacon indicated danger on the planet's surface, but given the age of the beacon and the extreme environmental conditions of the moon, Kell expected to find nothing but ice-choked ruins.

Still, he would prepare for any eventuality, as always.

Relin did not blink but felt as though he had. His visual senses registered only a blue afterimage rather than a hyperspace tunnel. One instant *Junker* floated at the edge of the rings, the next it floated under *Harbinger* and the cold metal and hard angles of the dreadnought filled his sight lines.

Power from the Lignan filled the space around the dreadnought like a fog. Relin felt it seep into him, feeding his seemingly boundless anger, his limitless need for revenge. He resisted at first, but it was halfhearted.

It was *right* that he feed his anger, feed it until it grew into a monster. Drev's fate merited anger. To feel something else would be to disgrace the memory of his Padawan.

"Do you feel it, Marr?"

Marr bared his teeth between clenched jaws, the chip in the incisor like a tunnel through which the Lignan's effects could leak.

"I feel it," Marr said, taking a moment to angle the ship properly and verify velocity. "Powering down. Diverting everything to the power crystal array."

He hit the emergency shutdown for almost every system on the ship, including life support, and repurposed the power to the crystal array. *Junker*'s cockpit turned as dark as space and only their breathing broke the sudden silence, Relin's ragged with pain, guilt, and power, Marr's smooth but elevated. The ambient temperature dropped several degrees in a moment. The viewscreen remained active, though its clarity faltered and static clouded the image. A thick red beam from *Junker*'s top split the screen, slammed into *Harbinger*'s shields, and exploded into a spiral of red lines, an antique corkscrew boring into the Sith ship's deflectors.

"Is it supposed to look like that?" Relin asked.

Marr inhaled deeply and put a hand over his stomach. "I am nauseated. The ore does not affect you?"

"Not like it does you," Relin said, and left it at that. "I could screen you."

Marr shook his head, his face wrinkled with discomfort. "Do not waste your energy. I can bear it."

Relin recalled one of the first lessons taught to Force-sensitives by the Jedi. He remembered being taught it himself by Imar Deez, remembered teaching it to Drev. The words came out of his mouth without thought, a reflex, as *Junker* coasted through the cold of space toward *Harbinger*.

"Imagine in your mind a fortress of stone and steel, with crenellated walls. Within it stands a keep, itself walled."

Marr looked a question at him.

"Do as I say," Relin snapped. "It is a simple lesson and it will help."

"All right."

Relin mouthed the words spoken by generations of Jedi while his heart beat false in his chest, while the Lignan ate at his spirit. He was a liar and he did not care.

"Again, imagine a strong fortress, walled, unbreachable. Within it stands a keep, similarly fortified. Do you see it?"

"I have no training. I—"

"Do you see it?"

"I . . . can imagine it, yes."

"You are the keep, Marr. The Force is the fortress. Feel it."

"This—"

"Feel it. Open yourself to it." He had said the same words to Drev, once. Remembering his Padawan threw coal into the oven of his rage, but he kept it from his voice.

"Do not analyze it. Feel it."

Marr held Relin's eyes for a moment, then closed his eyes and steadied his breathing.

Relin walked him farther down the path, feeling each moment more of a hypocrite. "Imagine how you feel calculating a course through hyperspace. Focus on that feeling. Hold on to it."

It took almost no time, as Relin had known it would not. A Force-sensitive was usually habituated to drawing on the Force unconsciously. Marr did it every time he did mathematics. It usually took only a nudge to open up someone sensitive to simple uses of the Force. Through five thousand years it had remained just so.

Marr opened his eyes, the thickets of his eyebrows

raised in wonder. "That is . . . surprising. This is what you do to keep it out?"

Relin hesitated, because he could not tell Marr that he no longer kept it out. Instead, he uttered another lie. "Yes."

Junker glided under the smooth metal of *Harbinger*'s underside, past viewports, idle laser cannon turrets. Relin imagined that their sudden appearance under the ship had caused no small consternation among *Harbinger*'s crew. They would be scrambling to respond.

The landing bay, illuminated with lights around its perimeter, yawned ahead of them, the mouth of a beast. In moments they would be swallowed.

"We are near enough to hit the deflectors," Marr said, his voice still filled with the wonder caused by his first conscious use of the Force.

As Marr steered *Junker* through the hole carved by the power crystal, Relin felt as if he were going down a drain.

Flotsam's belly hit the moon's upper atmosphere and the entire ship vibrated in the turbulence like shaken dice. Flames formed around the heat shield, licked up the sides, sheathing the ship in fire. Jaden could see nothing but orange out the cockpit window as the ship skidded through the atmosphere. In his mind, he heard the repetitious call of the beacon. He found himself staring at his fingertips, the fingertips on which his anger or fear sometimes formed Force lightning.

He did not trust himself anymore, he realized. Doubt was the fundamental core of his being. Relin had sensed it in him.

"Twenty seconds," Khedryn said. "Switching to repulsors."

Jaden leaned forward in his seat, wanting to see the

surface the moment the fires dissipated, hoping that something on the moon would dispel his doubt, return him to certainty.

The orange gave way to a thick swirl of clouds. As they descended and the air thickened, the stresses on the ship changed from the steady, intense vibration of atmospheric entry into the the irregular buffeting of powerful winds. Snow and ice streaked past the cockpit transparisteel, frosting its exterior.

Jaden recalled his Force vision, remembered the feel of the wind against his skin, the frost collecting in his beard, the surface under his feet.

"Winds upward of ninety kilometers per hour," Khedryn observed as gusts rocked *Flotsam*.

Jaden stared through the swirl, heart thumping madly. They broke through the clouds, but the blowing snow and the ice-covered surface allowed him to distinguish nothing. All he saw was a blur of white. There was no revelation in sight.

"Get a fix on the beacon," he said to Khedryn.

"Triangulating," Khedryn said. He tapped a button and the beacon sounded on the interior speakers, louder than ever.

Jaden leveled *Flotsam* off at 150 meters and slowed its speed. Topographic scans showed vast, frozen plateaus, oceans of ice, bordered by enormous mountains.

"Got it," Khedryn said, and the words put a flutter in Jaden's stomach. "South-southwest, a quarter hour out. Near the moon's equator."

When Khedryn had linked the location of the signal to the navicomp, Jaden adjusted course accordingly. He realized that he was sweating. He accelerated to full in-atmosphere speed, and *Flotsam* cut like a knife through the wind, ice, and snow.

"Like following bread crumbs," Khedryn said, nodding at the speaker through which the beacon's call carried.

Jaden nodded. The hairs on the nape of his neck stood on end. He felt as if he were being watched. Before he could trace the source of the feeling, Khedryn asked, "What do you hope to find here, Jaden?"

Jaden did not hesitate. "An answer."

He needed one. He could not continue as he had. He ran a sensor scan to ensure they were not being followed. Nothing.

Khedryn stared blankly out of the cockpit. "What is the question?"

Jaden smiled, thinking how close the words cut to his own thoughts.

When Jaden did not answer, Khedryn said, "I hope Marr and Relin are all right."

"The Force is with them both," Jaden said.

Khedryn nodded, absently reading the topographic scans, meteorological reports, atmospheric readouts.

"Trace elements in the atmosphere suggest volcanic activity here," he said.

Jaden imagined hot spots on the surface of the planet where heat and magma leaked up to turn ice into bathing water. He imagined, too, that the oceans under the ice could be thronged with life.

"Air is frigid but breathable," Khedryn said. "We'll still need enviro-suits, though."

Jaden only partially heard Khedryn. The navicomp showed them closing on the coordinates from which the distress signal originated. He leaned forward in his seat, straining to see through the weather.

He could not breathe when it emerged from the static of the weather like a lost city.

Khedryn squinted, staring through the cockpit transparisteel. "What is that?"

* * *

Junker coasted, dark and cold, through the hole made by the power crystal.

Relin stared into the tunnel of the landing bay, remembering the last time he had entered it, five thousand years ago, riding the back of a shuttlecraft. Then, he'd had a comlink connection to Drev. Now he would enter it alone, unconnected to anyone, centered not in a sense of duty but in a sense of rage.

Content with that, he drank the power of the Lignan the way *Junker*'s crew drank caf.

"We are through," Marr said, blowing out the words as if he had been holding his breath. "Powering up."

Light returned to the cockpit, and the instrumentation went live with an audible hum.

"*Junker* is live," Marr said.

"If they haven't already, *Harbinger* will certainly pick us up now," Relin said, not caring.

Marr nodded. "Engaging repulsors. In we go."

Saes sat in meditation on the floor of his chambers, lost in the Force, trying to plan a role for himself in the new time. His comlink beeped to life, disturbing his calm. Ordinarily he removed it when meditating, but under the circumstances he had not wanted to be out of contact for even a moment.

Llerd's voice carried over the frequency, barely controlled tension in the tone. Saes heard the bleat of an alarm in the background, the proximity alert.

"Captain, a ship jumped directly under us, and coasted through our deflectors into the landing bay."

Saes opened his eyes, inhaled deeply. "A ship? What ship?"

"I have dispatched all available security teams and

isolated the area should the craft prove to be loaded with explosives."

"What *ship*, Lieutenant?"

A pause, then, "I believe it is the ship we pursued into the planet's rings, sir."

"Our pilots reported that ship destroyed," Saes said.

He stood and threw on his robes, his anger building, narrowing down to a point.

"Yes, sir," Llerd said. "It appears they were . . . incorrect."

"They were duped," Saes said.

"Yes, sir."

In ordinary times, Saes might have executed the Blade pilots, but the times were not ordinary. He needed his crew, at least for the time being. He would devise a suitable, nonlethal punishment later.

"I will speak with the pilots later," he said.

"Yes, sir."

Saes cut off the connection to Llerd and opened another, through the Force. He reached out, but tentatively, the way he might have gingerly touched a fingertip on an object that he feared might be too hot.

Immediately he felt a familiar presence.

"Welcome back, Relin," he whispered, surprised to find himself pleased.

He went to one of the display cases built into the wall of his quarters. Five ancient Kaleesh hunting masks leered out from behind the glass, each of them hand-carved from the bones of an erkush, a fierce reptilian predator native to Kalee. Shamanic runes covered the brow and cheeks of each mask, invoking the spirits to lend the wearer strength, speed, skill.

Saes opened the case, took a familiar, age-yellowed face from the ancient gallery, fitted it over his own face, and tied it on. He felt himself transformed in that single act, reconnected to the wondrous, faceless savagery of his ancestors.

He would confront Relin while wearing the mask he had worn when he had been Relin's Padawan. It seemed fitting that things end just so. He strode from his chamber, hunting a Jedi.

chapter twelve

SNOW DRIFTED HALFWAY UP THE METAL AND DURA-crete walls of the facility. Spears of ice hung in thickets from every overhang. Three-quarters of a communications tower jutted upward from the tundra like an accusatory finger blaming the sky for its fate. A faint, snow-blotted light at the tower's top flashed intermittently, keeping time with the beacon playing over *Flotsam*'s cockpit speaker, keeping time with Jaden's heart.

"Looks abandoned," Khedryn said.

Jaden came back to himself, swallowed in a mouth gone dry. "Yes."

"Definitely looks old enough to be Imperial," Khedryn said.

Jaden forced a nod, though a sense of déjà vu gripped his gut. For an instant he lived in the dreamspace between his Force vision and his real senses and he was suddenly unsure that he wanted to set foot on the moon.

Fighting down the doubt, he reached out through the Force, expecting to feel the bitter recoil of contact with the Sith from his vision.

Nothing.

He took his hand from the stick, made a claw of his fingers, looked at their tips, the fingertips that leaked Force lightning when he was overcome by anger or fear.

Nothing.

"Are you all right?" Khedryn asked, taking the co-pilot's stick. "What are you doing?"

Embarrassed, Jaden made as though he were flexing his fingers against stiffness. "Nothing. I am fine."

"Maybe a flyover before we set down?" Khedryn said. He did not release the stick and seemed pleased to be in control of the ship.

"Agreed," Jaden said.

Khedryn decreased altitude and speed, flying low over the complex.

With many of the buildings having lost their battle to the snow, Jaden found it difficult to make out the contours of the complex. Small mounds suggested tertiary structures, though it was hard to tell.

"Could be a shield generator," he said, pointing at a dome-shaped mound of snow.

"You would know better than me," Khedryn said.

The central building, a rectangular, single-story mass of ice-rimmed metal, looked like any number of facilities Jaden had seen before. The structure could have been anything from a hazardous materials storage depot to a training complex.

"That looks like an entrance," Khedryn said, pointing at a shadowed portico on one side of the central facility. "Can't see if there's a hatch."

Khedryn fiddled with the instrumentation, tweaking his scanner. "There is still power in the main complex, though not much of it. Life support is online but barely. Some kind of backup or emergency power probably. Good construction to last this long."

"Yes," Jaden said absently, looking at the blowing snow, remembering the ghostly touches of Lassin, Mara, Kam Solusar. The beacon still played over the cockpit speakers, their pleading voices—*Help us. Help us.*

"If life support is functioning, someone could still be alive in there."

"Unlikely," Khedryn said. "It's been decades. Can we turn that off, Jaden? *Jaden?*"

Jaden killed the sound of the beacon.

They completed their flyover, having learned little.

"Well?" Khedryn said, and looked across the cockpit at Jaden, one eye on him, one eye off on some distant point. "Having second thoughts?"

"No. Let's put her down," Jaden said. He knew he would not find his answer sitting in *Flotsam*'s cockpit.

The repulsors engaged, pressing Relin and Marr into their seats as *Junker* streaked toward the landing bay. Leaving the piloting entirely to Marr, Relin sorted through *Harbinger*'s schematics in his mind, and decided on the best approach for his attack. Agitated, he unstrapped himself, stood, and checked his lightsaber and gear, speaking to Marr as he did so.

"About one hundred and fifty meters in, you will see a wide corridor open off the landing bay on our starboard side. It is a freight corridor. Put *Junker* down against it with the port cargo bay door facing it."

Sweat dampened the wall of Marr's brow. "If you want to block the corridor, it will have to be a belly landing. No skids."

"Right," Relin agreed. He had not thought of that. "No skids."

Were *Junker* to land on its skids, *Harbinger*'s crew could simply walk or crawl underneath to get into the corridor and at Relin.

"You should strap yourself back in," Marr said. "That will be a bumpy landing."

Relin sat, and buckled himself in. "I will not need long. A few minutes at most and you get *Junker* out of there. Lots of side corridors open off the freight corridor. They will not know where I have gone, and I am . . . skillful at avoiding detection."

"Understood," Marr said as they sped down the throat of the landing bay, the guide lights casting the cockpit in red. Marr did not slow once they were within the launch tunnel, and *Junker* scraped one of *Harbinger*'s bulkheads. Metal shrieked and Relin imagined a shower of sparks trailing in their wake. Marr cursed and got the ship off the wall.

"Calm, Marr," Relin said, though he did not feel it himself. The touch of the Lignan had his spirit churning.

They cleared the launch tunnel and moved into the broader landing bay, pelting past a few shuttles on landing pods and a couple of treaded cargo droids. A few of *Harbinger*'s black-uniformed crew scrambled out of ships or trotted along the landing bay deck, watching them pass, questions on their faces. Relin imagined the reports that must have been heading to Saes and the command crew.

"It's enormous in here," Marr said, eyeing the whole scene with a look of faint wonder, perhaps realizing that he was flying in the landing bay of a ship that had fought in a war five thousand years previous. Or perhaps just surprised that they had made it that far.

Relin pointed with his stump when he saw the freight corridor.

"There."

Marr nodded and did not slow.

"Brace yourself," the Cerean said.

Three droids were unloading cargo from a lev pallet. Marr slammed into them, crushing all three, while spinning *Junker* on its repulsors and slamming its port side against the freight corridor opening. The impact rattled Relin's teeth. *Junker* protested with a groan of stressed metal. Relin protested with a grunt of pain. It felt as if someone had stuck a knife in his ribs.

"Are you all right?" Marr asked, unstrapping himself.

Relin caught his breath, unbuckled his safety straps, rose, and thumped Marr on the shoulder. "Yes. Well done."

Marr activated the security system right away. Metal shields slid over every viewport: *Junker* closing its eyes.

"That will protect the ship from small-arms fire. But she is still vulnerable to more powerful weapons. I should not leave her here long."

"I do not think they will try to blow her up on their own landing deck, at least not before they surround her with a makeshift blast wall. We could have loaded her with explosives for all they know. No, I think droids build a blast wall while a security team tries to gain entry."

As if to make Relin's point, blasterfire barked from outside the ship, dull, harmless thumps against the bulkheads.

"None of which will stop some fool pilots from taking shots at the ship," Relin said. "We must hurry."

He turned to go but Marr's hand pulled him back around. The Cerean did not make eye contact.

"How often do Cereans fall to the dark side? In your time, I mean."

Relin understood the origin of the question. The touch of the Lignan, and Marr's conscious use of the Force, had brought him face-to-face with the two poles of potential. Relin remembered that feeling himself from his early days in the Order, the feeling that he stood on a very thin line, and that he might step over it at any moment.

"The dark side can reach anyone," Relin said, pained by the truth of the words.

Marr considered, nodded, released Relin's arm.

"Thank you," he said. "For showing me what you showed me."

Relin was touched, but kept his feelings to himself. "I need to go, Marr. Now."

* * *

Relin and Marr sprinted through *Junker*'s corridors, Marr leading, until they reached the port cargo bay. The bay felt cavernous, as empty as Marr had seen it in years. His speeder bike, Khedryn's Searing swoop, and a few sealed shipping containers were all that remained. They had spaced everything else.

They hurried across the bay, their boots beating staccato on the metal floor, until they stood before the cargo door. Marr put his finger on the red button that would lower the door and looked to Relin. He could see that the Jedi was not well. Sweat glistened on his pale skin, pasting his black hair to his scalp. His breathing was labored, pained, like that of a wounded animal. His deep-sunken eyes looked clear, though, lit by some inner resolve, and that heartened Marr.

"Ready?" Marr asked.

Relin inhaled and bounced on the balls of his feet, staring at the cargo bay door as if he could burn holes into it with his eyes. He ignited his lightsaber, the green blade humming in the quiet of the bay.

"Open it."

Marr hit the button and the bay door started to descend. The wail of *Harbinger*'s alarm carried through the opening.

"Five minutes and go," Relin said without looking at Marr.

Before the door got halfway down, blasterfire from the freight corridor sizzled into the bulkheads, scorching the metal. Marr threw himself against the wall, out of the line of fire. Relin did not so much as move while the door continued its trek. More blasterfire poured through the opening. Relin deflected two shots with his lightsaber, almost casually sending the bolts into *Junker*'s bulkheads.

Looking straight ahead, Relin started to speak, stopped, then started again, his lips barely moving.

"May the Force be with you, Marr."

Marr heard sadness in Relin's words, saw tears pooling in the Jedi's eyes.

"Relin . . . ," Marr began, but before he could say more the bay door opened fully and Relin bounded out into a hail of blasterfire, the glowing line of his lightsaber transformed into a figure-eight by the speed of his defense. He roared like a rancor as he sped down the corridor.

Blasterfire forced Marr back against the wall and he lost line of sight to the corridor. He heard Relin's shouts answered by throaty growls, heard enough blasterfire to know that Relin was facing a large number of enemies. Blasts carried through the cargo bay and blackened the storage containers.

A lull in the fire allowed Marr a moment to peek out and down the corridor.

A pair of bodies—large, red-skinned humanoids in black uniforms—lay in a pool of blood eight meters down the corridor, both decapitated. One of the heads faced Marr, yellow eyes still open, a fleshy beard of finger-length appendages partially concealing a fanged mouth. Marr had never seen such creatures before.

Relin sheltered in a crouch in one of the many doorways that lined the hall, maybe fifteen meters from *Junker*'s gangway. More of the red-skinned humanoids, all of them armed with large blaster pistols, crouched at intervals in the other doorways and alcoves that dotted the length of the corridor. Two more sheltered in the middle of the hall behind a treaded droid, which beeped plaintively at its predicament. Marr assumed the creatures to be some kind of security detail. He counted fourteen of them.

The smoky air carried the acrid tang of blaster discharge and scorched metal. *Harbinger*'s alarm contined to scream.

The creatures shouted at one another in deep, gravelly voices, though Marr did not understand the language. Now and again, one of them fired a blaster shot in Relin's vicinity, but none made as though to advance. They appeared content to keep Relin pinned down. Probably they had already called for reinforcements.

Relin crouched with his back to the wall, facing Marr, favoring his cracked ribs. Anger twisted his expression so much he could have been another man altogether. His eyes looked like holes. The light from his lightsaber cast his pale skin in green.

He must have felt Marr's eyes on him. He looked up and made an angry gesture with his stump, ordering Marr to seal *Junker*.

When Marr made no move to comply, Relin snarled and leapt out of the doorway, moving so fast he looked blurred. His lightsaber weaved an oblong shield of light around him. The security detail opened up in full and blaster shots filled the corridor. Relin spun like a top, deflecting the shots with rapidity but no control. Blasts slammed into the ceiling, into overhead lights, sending a rain of glass to the floor, into the cargo bay, close enough to Marr's face that he felt the heat of its passage.

Relin closed on the nearest pair of the red-skinned humanoids, gesturing with his stump as he neared them. The creatures' blasters flew from their hands and they backed off a step, eyes wide, fumbling with the huge metal polearms on their backs.

Before they could bring them to bear, Relin redirected the blasterfire from their fellows at them and blew holes in both their chests, spattering the bulkheads with their black blood.

Relin ducked into the alcove where the two dead creatures had sheltered, using their corpses as partial cover. Marr saw him in profile, the pained grimace on his face, the angry set of his jaw. A blaster had winged his arm with the severed hand, though it appeared a minor wound. Scorch marks ringed the frayed holes in Relin's robes and shirt.

Blasterfire pinned him to the wall.

He was moving too slowly, Marr knew. He should already have been gone. They had not expected so much resistance right away. *Harbinger*'s crew knew where he was, where *Junker* was, and more and more of them would marshal here to stop him. Relin looked back at Marr and again gestured angrily for him to seal the ship.

"Close it!" Relin shouted.

Blasterfire forced him to press himself against the wall.

From outside in the landing bay, something heavy thumped against *Junker* and the high-pitched whine of some kind of motor carried through the bulkheads. Marr knew the crew in the landing bay would soon either try to cut their way in or simply blow the ship from the deck. He had little time. If they got into *Junker*, he'd never leave *Harbinger*.

He reached for the button that would close the cargo bay door, let his hand hover over it, and . . . stopped.

He remembered the greasy touch of the Lignan on his spirit, its coldness, its sharpness. He did not fully understand its danger, but he knew Relin's warnings about what the Sith could do with it were true. Relin could not be allowed to fail. He lowered his hand and met Relin's gaze.

Perhaps Relin saw Marr's resolve.

"No!" Relin shouted. "Go, Marr! Go!"

Marr nodded, but not at Relin.

"I am the keep," he said to himself.

* * *

Pulses of blasterfire slammed into the bulkheads near Relin, turning the metal black and warm. Anger, frustration, and pain warred for predominance in Relin. Every breath made his side feel as if he were being stabbed. He was moving far too slowly, he knew. More Massassi would be coming. Saes would be coming. He had underestimated their ability to respond.

A shout of rage crept up his throat, but he held it in, pulled it close, used it to focus his mind. The Force flowed strongly through him, but he was unable to use it to reduce his fatigue or replenish his spirit or body. His power, heightened by the Lignan, answered only to his anger, only to his hate. With it, he could only destroy and kill, not heal.

He knew what that meant but no longer cared.

He had left what he once was five thousand years in the past. Now he was something different, someone else. He *wanted* only to destroy and kill, to avenge Drev's death, to redeem the two great failures of his life in a conflagration of fire and blood. His grief had metamorphosed into hate, and the change pleased him.

But first he needed to get out of the corridor and deeper into the ship. He'd inhaled as best he could and readied himself to move when a roar from *Junker*'s cargo bay drowned out the sound of blasterfire. For a moment he could not place the origin of the sound, but then it occurred to him—it was an engine.

Flotsam set down twenty meters from the large central structure. The craft's landing threw up a cloud of snow. Jaden unstrapped himself from his seat. Khedryn did the same.

"You needn't come, Khedryn."

Khedryn smiled, his floating eye staring out the cockpit viewport, his other on Jaden's face.

"That's as true a statement as you've uttered, Jedi. But I think I'll come along anyway." He winked his lazy eye. "There might be something here worth salvaging."

Jaden smiled, grateful for the companionship. "Let's gear up, then."

Both donned environment suits, sealed the helmets, tested the comlinks, and opened the starboard side exit.

The frozen air and snow of an icy world blew in and dusted the floor at their feet. The enviro-suits blunted the force of the cold, but Jaden's skin still goose-pimpled. He stood at the top of the ramp, staring out at the drifts and the swirling snow.

Khedryn's voice sounded in his helmet. "Jaden? Let's move. Even with the suits we don't want to be out in this any longer than necessary."

But Jaden needed to feel the air, taste it. He deactivated the seal on his helmet, and it disconnected with a slight hiss.

Khedryn took him by the arm. "What are you doing?"

"I need to do this, Khedryn."

"Why?"

Jaden did not answer, but Khedryn let him go, muttering about eyes and cursing randomly.

Jaden lifted off the helmet and gasped at the smell of the air, the cut of the wind against his skin. He was living his Force vision, the imagined and the real melding into one in the frozen air of the moon.

He inhaled. The air felt like fire in his throat and he imagined himself purged by the pain. Moisture from his breath formed clouds in the air before him, collected in his beard, froze there. The wind hissed past his ears. In the distance, he heard the crack of ice.

All of it as it had been in his vision.

He knelt, removed a glove, and took a handful of

snow from the deck, letting it melt in his hand. He looked out through the swirl and saw the red light of the communications tower looming over the rest of the complex, blinking at him through the snow.

Help us. Help us.

He would.

Standing, he slid his glove back over his freezing hand, resealed his helmet, then activated his lightsaber. The heat it threw off warmed him.

"Follow me," he said to Khedryn.

Khedryn drew his blaster and followed him toward the facility. "I am increasingly concerned that all Jedi are crazed."

Jaden smiled but otherwise left the comment alone. Khedryn tapped a control pad on his suit's forearm and remotely closed and secured the Starhawk.

The deep snow clutched at their feet, as if trying to slow their advance and give them time to reconsider. Jaden looked up, eyed the slate of the sky, imagined not snow falling but reified evil.

"Do you think they're all right?" Khedryn said over the comlink, apparently misunderstanding his look. "Would you know if . . . something happened?"

"The Force is with them," Jaden said.

"You said that before, but it's not an answer."

"I do not have many of those."

The facility looked to Jaden not like an ordinary building, but like a tomb that held an enormous evil better left alone. He was unsure that he should dig it up, yet he felt he had no choice. He faltered in his steps.

Khedryn stepped to his side. "Come on, Jaden. Keep moving. There is a hatch ahead."

Jaden continued on, walking beside a skew-eyed salvager on a moon not found on any star charts.

"Hey, was I in your vision?" Khedryn asked him.

"No."

"That's not reassuring," Khedryn said, and chuckled.

Jaden laughed, too, glad once more for Khedryn's presence.

They neared the hatch, and Jaden was certain that whatever fate the Force had for him lurked behind it.

Marr held a blaster in one hand and with his other the steering bars of Khedryn's Searing swoop. The swoop's motor was so loud it sounded like an ongoing explosion.

Marr's heart beat so fast he could hardly breathe. Recalling Relin's words, he turned inward, focused his mind on the keep within him, thought of how he felt when immersed in a difficult calculation, a distant, warm isolation that brought him calm.

His heart and breathing slowed, replaced by a pleasing serenity.

Centered, resolved, he revved the swoop's engine and bolted out of the cargo bay into the corridor, firing his blaster as fast as he could pull the trigger, hoping the Force would guide some of his shots.

Blasterfire from *Harbinger*'s security forces answered his own, sizzled past his ears, and thumped into the swoop. It bucked under him like an angry bantha, but he held his seat. He picked a spot in the hall—where the two humanoids sheltered behind the loading droid—ducked low behind the windscreen and, still firing his blaster wildly, flew right at them.

Jaden expected to find the hatch rusted shut, or protected by a security system. Instead they found it propped open a few centimeters. Khedryn and he stared at the hatch for a long moment, the wind howling past their helmets.

"What do you make of that?" Khedryn asked, nodding at the item holding the door open.

Jaden knelt and picked it up—the back hand plate from a suit of Imperial stormtrooper armor.

"Is that from a stormie suit?"

Jaden nodded, turning the plastoid plate over in his hand. "It is. Odd."

"Probably been there for decades," Khedryn said, but he did not sound as if he believed it. He looked over his shoulder as if he expected a squad of the 501st to come charging out of the snow.

"Probably," Jaden agreed. On edge, he pulled the heavy metal door open the rest of the way. It opened onto a small foyer. A transparisteel observation window on an inner wall opened onto a guard station. Another hatch, thrown open, revealed a hallway that led deeper into the facility. Over the hatch, written in Basic in stenciled letters, were the words:

WEST ENTRY. AUTHORIZED PERSONNEL ONLY.

Jaden reached out with the Force, seeking any Force-sensitives within range, but felt none.

"Follow me," he said, leading Khedryn past the post and through the hatch, his lightsaber a torch in the otherwise dark corridor. Khedryn activated a glow rod and added its light to the weapon's glow.

Walking those metal-floored, abandoned halls, Jaden felt as if he had stepped into the past as surely as Relin had stepped into the future.

"Ten degrees Celsius," Khedryn said, taking the information from his suit readout. He unsealed his helmet, letting it hang from its connectors down his back. "Someone is keeping the place warm."

Jaden unsealed his own helmet, his breath steaming in the air. They walked on, their feet moving through the detritus of a rapid retreat: scrap electronics; flimsiplast, the ink long faded; stray data crystals; oddly, a hairbrush.

Khedryn cleared his throat, a nervous sound. "What do you suppose happened here?"

Jaden shook his head.

They moved through hall after hall, room after room, and everywhere it was the same—debris littered the floor in the silent, cool air. They found nothing to indicate the facility's purpose.

In time they came to a series of small, sparely furnished personal quarters where clothing still hung in closets, where beds remained unmade. The whole facility felt to Jaden like a doll's house in which a child had lost interest and just left off in midplay.

He examined the clothing and shoes in the closets. In addition to ordinary clothing, he found a neatly pressed Imperial uniform and several lab coats. The label sewn onto the coat's breast read DR. BLACK.

"Thrawn-era uniform," Jaden said, noting the cut of the cuffs, the rank insignia. "Imperial Medical Corps."

"Medical corps?" Khedryn said, his breathing a bit too rapid. "A bioweapons research lab, you think? I did not think to scan for an aerosolized bioweapon."

"You had no reason to," Jaden said. "And what's done is done. If there were something in the air, we'd be suffering effects already. I feel fine. You?"

"Fine."

"Then I think we're all right."

"Maybe we should put our helmets back on."

"We're all right."

Khedryn seemed to accept that, and the two of them searched the chest of drawers, the side table. Jaden felt awkward pawing through another's personal effects, but saw no other choice. He rifled through toiletries, a reading light, a gift set of novels on data crystals inset into an elaborate box. Eventually Khedryn pulled a personal vidlog from the back of one of the drawers.

"Here," he said in an excited tone. He tapped at the buttons, soft at first, then harder. "Not functional. With some time Marr could probably recover the data."

"Leave it," Jaden said. He started to move on when something struck him and halted him in his steps. He looked around the room to confirm his thought, then spoke it aloud.

"There are no pictures."

"No what?"

"No pictures, no holograms, no vids. Of friends, family. Look around."

Khedryn turned a circle, his eyes askew. "You're right. Maybe they took them with them?"

"Maybe," Jaden said, but thought not. They seemed to have left in a hurry, abandoning all manner of personal effects. They would have left at least some pictures or holograms.

"Let's keep moving," Jaden said.

They soon came upon a recreation room where two card games and a match of sonic billiards appeared to have ended abruptly. Khedryn examined the cards at one of the tables.

"Sabacc," he said, and flipped over the cards for all but one of the hands. "Cheap deck and not a good hand among them. Unlucky bunch." He seemed to hear his words only after he said them and colored at their implication. "At cards, I mean."

A galley off the recreation room still had sludgy caf in two of the pots, stores of dry goods, fresh food long rotted. Jaden eyed the walls and saw a large square speaker beside one of the air filtration vents. He imagined an alert blaring out of it, everyone leaving what they were doing to respond, but ultimately fleeing the facility in a hurry.

Assuming they had gotten out. He was no longer so sure.

"What is this place?" Khedryn said, his outstretched arms taking in the whole of the complex. "Have you noticed that there's nothing to indicate what it is? Nothing. But Imperials used to put labels on *everything*. Normally the hallway walls would be crowded with written directions and arrows pointing to weapons lab this, research area that. This place is secret even from itself."

Jaden agreed. Something about the facility felt off. Too secret.

"There has to be a central computing core," Jaden said. "Let's find it."

Continuing through the corridors, they found still more sleeping quarters for laboratory personnel. The lab coats again had names sewn onto the breasts. After seeing a few more the pattern became clear—DR. BROWN, DR. RED, DR. GREEN, DR. GRAY.

"What the kark?" Khedryn asked, holding up another lab coat to read the name—DR. BLUE.

A picture started to develop in Jaden's mind. "None of them knew the real names of the others. That's why there are no pictures or holograms in their quarters. Nothing personal, nothing with which one could later identify another."

Jaden knew that at some top-secret Thrawn-era facilities the participating scientists would be forced to endure surgical alterations of their facial structure while on assignment, changing back to themselves only after their work was completed. None would be able to recognize another afterward. He wondered if that had happened in the facility, and if so, why.

"And no instructions on the walls," Khedryn said.

"Visitors knew nothing. Probably the doctors had the facilities map imprinted into their memory." He licked his lips nervously and stared at Jaden for a long moment, even his lazy eye fixed straight ahead. "I think we should leave, Jaden. There is something wrong here."

Jaden agreed, but he could not leave, not yet. "I cannot, Khedryn. But you are not obliged to remain."

Jaden saw shame and resolve battle in Khedryn's expression. His fingers opened and closed reflexively over the handle of his blaster. His lazy eye floated off for a time before returning to fix on Jaden's face.

"I said I was with you and I'm with you. Blast it, if Marr can fly into *Harbinger* with Relin, I can walk some abandoned halls with you."

"Thank you," Jaden said, moved by Khedryn's loyalty.

"What do you think they were working on here?"

"Something high priority. Top secret."

"Something dangerous."

"Yes."

They continued on, caution slowing their progress. Eventually they passed through a large botanical garden where cold-stiffened, time-browned vegetables and flowers sagged in their pots like desiccated corpses. Sunlamps hung from the ceiling, eyeballing the death of their charges. The faint smell of soil and organic decay filled the cavernous garden.

They walked through, trying not to smell the death, seeking the central computing core. They passed what Jaden figured to be a barracks: wall-mounted double racks, military-issue blankets, a central table for recreation. Bits of stormtrooper armor lay strewn about here and there. None of the armor exhibited unit identifications. Jaden imagined the troopers had been elite soldiers plucked from various units to serve as security in the facility. They would have been mindwiped after leaving the facility, he imagined.

A weapons locker adjacent to the barracks had only empty racks save for a lonely BlasTech E-11 on one of the rungs, a heavy blaster commonly used by storm-troopers. Jaden and Khedryn left it alone.

They passed through more corridors, more rooms, but Jaden barely saw them. He wanted to reach the central computing core. He would find an answer there, if anywhere, to the question of the facility's purpose.

"Look at this," Khedryn said, nodding at the walls.

Jaden came back to himself and saw what had caught Khedryn's eye. Scorch marks on the walls, lots of them, even a few on the ceiling. Khedryn ran his gloved fingers over them.

"Blasterfire," Jaden said.

"Looks like quite a battle," Khedryn said. He turned about, examining the walls, floor, ceiling. There were marks everwhere. "Some wild shots taken here. Desperation fire."

"Yes," Jaden said. "Let's keep moving."

The signs of a pitched battle grew more pronounced as they continued deeper into the complex. More scorch marks from blasters, entire suits of stormtrooper armor cast in pieces across the floor with holes in the chest or helmets.

"No bodies," Khedryn said, toeing an empty breast-plate. "Pieces look scattered, as if by an animal." He crouched on his haunches and studied a breastplate. He picked it up, put his finger through a narrow hole that showed only the smallest scorch ring around the entry. "Look at this. What kind of blaster makes that neat of an entry wound?"

"That is not a blaster hole," Jaden said. "It's from a lightsaber."

*   *   *

Marr's appearance on the swoop drew some of the Massassi's fire. Blaster shots tore smoking holes in the speeder but Marr drove straight at them, blazing past Relin, the swoop's engine changing pitch and sputtering from the blaster damage.

Amazement did not paralyze Relin. He augmented his speed with the Force and charged out from cover. The nearest pair of Massassi, aiming at Marr's back as he passed them by, never saw the Jedi coming. Relin decapitated both of them with a spinning crosscut before they turned around.

The swoop's engine screamed and Relin turned in time to see Marr roll off its side a moment before it slammed into the loader droid and exploded. Fire, smoke, and a hail of metal parts showered the corridor. The blast wave blew Relin against the wall. Flames engulfed the speeder, droid, and the two Massassi who had sheltered behind it. They staggered down the hall, screaming and burning, making it only three strides before their legs gave out and they fell facedown to the deck.

One of the loader droid's arms protruded from the flaming amalgam of plastic and metal, waving in slow motion as if in farewell. The stink of burned flesh, blaster discharge, and melted plastic filled the hall.

The unexpectedness of the explosion froze the action for a moment. Even the Massassi's blasters went temporarily silent. Marr lay in the center of the hall, a dazed look on his face.

The moment passed; violence re-erupted.

The Massassi near Marr recovered first and trained their blasters on him. But before they could fire, Relin drew on the power he had gained from the Lignan to target a Force blast—a telekinetic burst of concussive force—on the two of them.

His raised hand and a violent impulse drove a focused

blast into their throats and visibly crushed both of their tracheas. They fell to the floor, clutching at their ruined windpipes. One discharged his blaster into the ceiling as he went down.

"Cover, Marr!" Relin shouted, in a hard, sharp voice that did not sound like his own.

He realized only then that he was smiling. He was outside himself, someone else.

Marr, his face blackened, bleeding from the nose, heeded Relin's words and scooted against the wall, firing at anything that moved. He hit one Massassi down the hall in the face, another in the leg, then went fully prone in a nearby doorway while blasterfire soaked the air around him.

Relin stepped into the center of the hallway, near the ruins of the swoop and loader droid, his lightsaber blazing, his spirit on fire from the Lignan, his rage the fuel of the conflagration. He laughed aloud, embracing the full power running through his body, drawing on the sea of energy available to him.

The Massassi focused their fire on him, but he deflected it almost casually. Walking down the hall, repelling blaster shots as he went, he moved methodically through the ranks of the security team, crushing throats and shattering chests as he went. The last surviving Massassi threw down his blaster, pulled his lanvarok from the scabbard on his back, snarled, and charged. Relin took mental hold of the Massassi's throat and drove him to his knees, gasping, two paces away.

Relin stared into his yellow eyes, took in the bared fangs dripping saliva, the piercings of steel and bone that disfigured the Massassi's face, the map of veins in his straining arms and neck. He drove his lightsaber into the Massassi's chest and the body fell facedown at his feet.

Around Relin, *Harbinger*'s alarm wailed, the loader

droid offered distorted, slurred beeps, and the few stubborn Massassi gasped away the moments that remained to them. In the privacy of his mind, Relin heard Drev's laughter and the irresistible call of his own rage.

The weight of what he had done and how he had done it, what he had become, settled on him. He stood up straight and bore it. He deactivated his lightsaber and Marr's hand closed over his shoulder.

"We should go," the Cerean said. "Now. More will be coming. You lead."

Marr's touch grounded him. His legs went weak and he sagged, but thought of Drev and did not fall. Turning to face Marr, he saw the blood leaking from the Cerean's nose. Marr seemed not to notice it. A contusion was purpling on his right cheek.

"Thank you," Relin said to Marr. "My injuries have . . . slowed me."

Marr gestured at the corpses. "What kind of creatures are these?"

"Massassi," Relin answered absently. "Warriors bred by Sith alchemy from original Sith stock."

Marr nodded. "Something similar occurred with clones in a recent war in this time." He knelt over one of the dead Massassi and took its blaster, testing its heft in his hand. Seemingly satisfied, he slid it into his thigh holster, keeping his own blaster drawn.

"I do not have much of a charge left in mine," he explained.

Overhead, the alarm continued its wail.

Marr tried to push Relin along. "You lead."

Relin stood his ground, shook his head. "No, Marr. Go back."

"I know what you will say, but I can help you." He tried again to nudge Relin forward. "There is little time. You are sick, Relin. You cannot make it alone."

Relin *was* sick, but not only in the way Marr meant. And he had to do it alone.

"I have lost two Padawans already, Marr. One to darkness and another to fire. I will not be responsible for anyone else."

Marr stood up straight. "It is my choice to make."

Relin's temper flared and he poked a finger into the Cerean's chest. "It is not. You are to return to *Junker* and get off this ship. Now."

Marr looked as if Relin had struck him. His expression fell. "But . . . what you taught me in the ship, about the Force. I did not . . . I felt the power of the Lignan. I know this ship needs to be destroyed."

Relin's anger leaked over the brim of his control. "You felt *nothing*, Cerean! Nothing!" He felt a burning in his fingertips, looked down to see blue Force lightning leaking from them, snaking around the hilt of his deactivated lightsaber. He felt himself color with shame. He did not look up when he spoke, though he managed a gentler tone.

"Go, Marr. Please."

"But I felt the Force . . ."

"Then let your awakening be my legacy. But I can teach you nothing more. You must go."

He felt Marr's eyes on him, studying him, as if Relin were a computation Marr needed to solve. "You do not intend to escape."

Relin did not deny it. "I am no longer a Jedi, Marr. I am just . . . a murderer. And there's yet more murder that I must do."

Marr kept his face expressionless. "You do not have to do this in this way."

"Good-bye, Marr. Seal up *Junker* and go. Things will end as they must."

Marr hesitated, but finally extended his hand. Relin

tucked his lightsaber hilt under his left arm and clasped Marr's hand.

"May the—" Marr stopped himself, started again. "Good luck, Relin."

Relin winced over the verbal detour and what it meant. "And you, Marr. Do me a service. Tell Jaden that he was right. And tell him that he was also wrong. There is nothing certain. There's only the search for it. Things only turn dangerous when you think the search is over. He will know what I mean."

"I will tell him," Marr said.

Relin allowed himself that maybe those words, too, could be his legacy.

Without another word, he turned from Marr and headed down a side corridor. The moment he had his back to Marr, the moment that shame no longer reined in rage, he embraced fully what he had become.

Kell trailed the Starhawk by fifty kilometers, well out of visual range given the snowstorm. And the Starhawk's scanners would never pierce *Predator*'s sensor baffles. Jaden's ship showed up clearly on *Predator*'s scanners, though, and Kell traced its flight as it closed on the source of the Imperial beacon. He knew when they reached it, for the Starhawk slowed, circled. Kell kept *Predator* as a distance, waiting for Jaden to set down.

He did not have to wait long.

He delayed a quarter hour before piloting *Predator* in the direction of Jaden's ship, but stayed high enough to make visual detection difficult.

Below, he saw a building complex, its walls gripped in ice, the spike of the communications tower blinking red through the storm. He snapped photos with his ship's nose cam, intending to send them to Wyyrlok via subspace when he got back into outer space.

Despite the beacon's warning, he expected little danger

from anything or anyone other than Jaden. He supposed there could be some leftover and still-functioning automated security apparatus, but he could not imagine anything organic surviving for long on the moon.

He set *Predator* down a kilometer away from the Starhawk and hurried to the hold. The stasis chambers stood empty—he had fed on all his stored meat—but they piqued his hunger for Jaden. His feeders twisted in his cheek sacs.

He donned his mimetic suit and activated it, holstered his blaster, sheathed his vibroblades. He threw a thick enviro-suit over the whole and climbed into his covered speeder.

Wind buffeted the cargo bay the moment he opened the door. The speeder rocked on its repulsorlifts. Snow and ice blew in, dusting the windscreen. Kell activated *Predator*'s security system as he drove the speeder out of the bay.

Gliding over the frozen landscape, he downloaded the Starhawk's location from *Predator*'s computer and accelerated to full speed, chasing Fate. He stopped the speeder fifty meters from Jaden's landing site, threw up the hood of his weathercloak, and climbed out.

The wind and cold rifled his cloak, wormed under his insulation, and stabbed at his skin. The faint aroma of sulfur hung in the freezing air, probably due to volcanism.

With an effort of will, he elevated his core body temperature until he felt comfortable. He trudged to the top of a snow dune—the wind tried to pull him from his perch—and glassed the Starhawk's landing site with a pair of macrobinoculars.

The ship sat on its skids atop a clear field of packed ice, apparently sealed tight. He increased the magnification of the binoculars and confirmed that security screens covered the viewports.

Most likely Jaden had already exited the ship.

Examining the area around the ship, he thought he might have seen indentations in the snow that could have been footprints leading toward the facility, but he'd have to get closer. He glassed the facility itself.

Snow covered all but the communications tower and the rectangular central facility. He noted the single-story steel-and-duracrete construction, the lack of windows, the sealed hatches for doors. The whole place sweated Imperial functionalism, with nothing wasted on aesthetics.

Probably a research facility of some kind, Kell supposed. He imagined a lower level or two belowground. An experiment gone awry would explain the beacon's message.

Walking sideways down the dune, he returned to the speeder and used its onboard scanners to check the complex for radiation. His body could endure radiation exposure that would kill most other sentients, but he saw no reason in taking chances.

Detecting nothing dangerous, he drove the speeder up to the Starhawk. He stripped off his enviro-suit, exposing the mimetic suit, and pulled up its hood and mask. As he disembarked the speeder, he upped his core temperature still more. The mimetic suit turned him white, even mimed a tumble of blowing snow.

Drawing his blaster, he walked the area around the ship until he found the footprints. They were so deep that the wind and snow had not yet effaced them. Two pairs of boots dug a chain of little pits in the snow in the direction of a large entry hatch in the main complex.

Jaden was not alone. He was accompanied by either Khedryn Faal or Marr Idi-Shael. Their soup Kell did not crave, not anymore. His appetite was limited to Jaden Korr.

He hurried back to the speeder, parked it out of sight of the Starhawk, and headed for the hatch.

His mimetic suit turned him into just more blowing snow.

He was a ghost.

chapter thirteen

WHEN JADEN AND KHEDRYN FOUND THE CENTRAL computer room, it had been ransacked. All of the comp stations appeared to be destroyed, some obviously slashed by lightsabers, others simply smashed with something heavy. Ruined display screens, servers, and CPUs dotted the floor. Pieces of shattered data crystals crunched underfoot like caltrops.

"Someone did not like computers," Khedryn said.

Jaden had hoped to find an answer in the core computing room. Instead he'd found the same ruin that characterized the rest of the complex. He felt pressure building in his chest, at the base of his skull.

For the first time, he began to worry that the complex had nothing to show him.

But how could that be?

He went from table to table, sorting through the debris.

"Anything usable, Khedryn. There has to be something here. Look! Look!"

Khedryn joined him, the two of them sifting the strata of destruction like archaeologists.

Khedryn pulled a water-stained hard-copy schematic from the debris, holding it gently by one corner. "Looks like the layout of this facility." He studied it for a moment, turned it over, slowly unfolding it.

"Careful," Jaden said.

Khedryn got it unfolded in one piece and studied it. "It mentions a lower level in the key but does not show it."

"Good find. Keep looking."

Jaden needed something more solid, something that would show him where the Force wanted him to go. He could not consult his feelings. They were too clouded with doubt. He wanted facts. He wanted—needed—to understand the facility's purpose, the reason for all the mystery.

Reaching under a desk against the wall, he found some stray data crystals, frayed power cords, and a single computer that was not obviously damaged. The batteries would be long dead.

"I need a power cord," he said over his shoulder.

"Here," Khedryn said, grabbing one from the floor near his feet and tossing it to Jaden.

Jaden held his breath as he plugged one end into the computer, the other into an outlet, and turned on the power.

He blew out a relieved breath when it hummed to life. He thought Khedryn must surely have heard his heartbeat.

"There are data crystals under that desk. Grab them. Any that are intact."

Khedryn did. There were dozens.

They tried one after another, quickly finding all of them encrypted or unusable. Jaden's elation faded. The facility seemed intent on keeping its secrets.

"Second to last," Khedryn said. "Holocrystal."

He tossed it to Jaden. Jaden snatched it out of the air and shot him a glare for being so careless. Khedryn responded by making bug eyes.

Jaden inserted the crystal into the functioning computer and tried to extract usable data. As he had with all the others, he moved through a series of files and found most of them corrupted. He executed two or three and the computer's holoplayer projected only a scrambled image and indecipherable audio.

Khedryn shook his head and walked away in frustration.

Toward the end of the file string, Jaden hit on a log of files that appeared less damaged than the others.

"Here," he said to Khedryn, and ran the files.

"What do you have?"

"Let's see."

The computer holoprojector lit up, and a shaky hologram materialized before them. Dr. Black—they could read the name on his lab coat—a paunchy, graying human with a receding hairline and eyes set too close together, spoke without much inflection.

". . . of us will keep a log. This is mine. Experiment log. Day one. Dr. Gray was finally able to recombine the sample DNA into a usable form. I told him that he'd earned a drink from the whiskey stores. Dr. Green and Red agree on the growth medium. Subjects A through I are born."

He gave a tiny smile, nodded slightly as if satisfied, and the log entry faded out.

"DNA?" Khedryn said. "Clones or a bioweapon, then."

"Seems likely," Jaden said, though he dared not follow the thread of his thoughts to its conclusion. Instead he continued the holo-log. Long portions of it were ruined. They saw still moments captured in time as if frozen by the ice of the moon: Dr. Black's face motionless in an expression of triumph or defeat, his pronouncement of a single word or phrase that meant little absent context.

"Jedi and Sith," Dr. Black said, the words floating

alone in the cold space of the ruined data crystal, nothing before or after them to give them meaning.

Jaden stopped the holo, reset the recording to an earlier point, at the same time rewinding in his head the voices and imagery from his vision.

"Jedi and Sith," said Dr. Black.

Jaden, said Mara Jade Skywalker.

Jaden played it again.

"Jedi and Sith," said Dr. Black. "Jedi and Sith."

Jaden, said Master Solusar.

"There is no more in that bit, Jaden," Khedryn said. "Keep going."

Jaden, said Lassin.

"Jaden," Khedryn said, louder, and put a hand over Jaden's. "Speed it forward."

Jaden came back to himself and nodded, his mind spinning, then continued the holo. He felt knots drawing close, puzzle pieces falling into place. Another single word chilled his blood.

". . . Palpatine," Dr. Black said.

"I thought this was a Thrawn-era facility," Khedryn said.

"It was," Jaden answered, but said no more.

"Keep going," Khedryn said, warming to the mystery.

Jaden did, and they hit on a longer entry.

"There," Khedryn said.

Jaden replayed it.

". . . thirty-three. The experiment has been an unqualified success. We retarded the maturation process as much as possible to ensure an appropriate rate of growth, but the subjects still grew to maturity much more rapidly than our models predicted. Memory imprinting will begin soon, though the subjects appear to have been born with extant knowledge of their Force sensitivity. All have exhibited mastery of basic and moderately advanced Force techniques. Testing reveals an extraordinarily high midi-chlorian count in all subjects. Grand Admiral Thrawn has been apprised of the results."

The entry ended, and neither Khedryn nor Jaden said anything.

Ignoring the feel of Khedryn's eyes on him, Jaden sped forward through the log, looking for something else coherent, rushing toward whatever catastrophe befell the facility.

A broken entry sometime later showed a haggard-looking Dr. Black. His entire body drooped, as if borne down by a great weight. A few unidentifiable stains marred his lab coat.

"He looks like he has lost ten kilos," Khedryn said.

Jaden played the hologram. Dr. Black spoke to them from out of the past.

"Subject H was killed by the other Subjects in an incident of collective . . . rage. We are unsure what sparked the incident."

The holo faded. Jaden sped it forward but encountered nothing for some time. Then Black appeared again, the circles under his eyes dark enough to have been drawn in ink. He licked his lips nervously as he spoke.

". . . appear to have an unusual connection to one another, empathetic certainly. Possibly telepathic. This was unexpected. Dr. Gray believes that . . ."

The image faded again and in the next available entry, Dr. Black's voice audibly quavered. "We discovered today that Subject A had smuggled enough spare parts into his living quarters to build a rudimentary lightsaber. A subsequent search of the other Subjects' living quarters revealed that all of them had partially constructed lightsabers at one or another stage of development. Security has been . . ."

The entry turned black. So did Jaden's thoughts.

"Lightsabers?" Khedryn asked, his voice low. "Were they cloning . . . Jedi?"

For a moment, Jaden's mouth refused to form words. In his head he saw Lassin, Kam, Mara, all of them with Force signatures more akin to Sith than Jedi. How could Thrawn have gotten their DNA? Mara would have been easy, but Kam? Lassin? The others?

"I do not know for certain," he said, while the words from Dr. Black's original entry stuck in his brain as if tacked there by a nail: *recombine the sample DNA.*

The DNA of whom? Or what?

Jedi and Sith.

Palpatine.

Jaden's mouth was as dry as a Tatooine desert. He continued through the holo-log, a pit the size of a fist opening in his stomach. He stopped when a human woman in a lab coat appeared before them. She wore her dark hair short and looked younger than Dr. Black. Her left hand twitched as she spoke. Jaden read the name on her coat—DR. GRAY. He wondered what had happened to Dr. Black, then supposed he did not want to know.

". . . their hostility toward their confinement is growing, as is their power. Even the stormtroopers seem frightened by them . . ."

A final entry followed. Again, Dr. Gray spoke.

". . . lost control. The lower level is sealed and I have requested of the Grand Admiral that the experiment be terminated along with the Subjects by way of a trihexalon gas protocol. All of the surviving staff members agree with this recommendation."

The holo-log stopped, though the frozen image of Dr. Gray hung in the air before them like a ghost. Jaden and Khedryn sat in silence, each alone with the jumble of his thoughts. Jaden spoke first.

"There is a lower level. There must be a lift."

"They had hex here," Khedryn said, his brow wrinkled with concern. "If they used it, even the residuum could be harmful. I saw a holovid that showed what that stuff can do. We are in deep here, Jaden."

Jaden barely heard him. "We need to find the lift, go down, see if anyone is there." He pictured the shape of the facility. They had covered most of it already. The lift had to be nearby.

Khedryn stepped through the image of Dr. Gray to stand before Jaden. "Did you hear me?"

"Did you hear the holo-log? They had prisoners here."

"Subjects," Khedryn said. "Clones. Lab rats."

"They were confined against their will."

"From the sound of it, that was the right thing to do. They thought them dangerous enough to gas them with hex, Jaden."

Jaden fixed Khedryn with a thousand-kilometer stare. "I need to go down."

Khedryn's good eye followed his lazy one away from Jaden's face. "They combined Jedi DNA with something else and grew it into clones. Dangerous clones."

Jaden inhaled, then dived in, speaking to Khedryn the way he might have to R6, the way he did when confessing a transgression. "I suspect they recombined the DNA of Jedi with the DNA of Sith."

Khedryn's lazy eye floated in its socket, fixing on nothing, as if it did not want to see. "Why would they do that? Being a Jedi or a Sith is a choice, isn't it? It's not biology."

Jaden shook his head. "We didn't know all there is to know about how biology meshes with Force use. Perhaps they sought to create some kind of breakthrough Force-user, one unbound by the limitations of light and dark."

"How is that possible? Light and dark sides are exclusive, aren't they?"

Jaden turned off the computer and Dr. Gray disappeared. "The line between light and dark is not as clear as many think."

"More reason we should go, Jaden. They created some kind of monsters here and—"

"Not monsters!" Jaden said, and the harshness of his tone took them both unawares. He hung his head. "I need to go down, Khedryn. If any of them are still alive, I need to . . . help them."

"Help them!" Khedryn exclaimed, then, more softly, "We are not talking about them. And you and I both know it. Jaden, you made a mistake on Centerpoint. An understandable one. Fine. Don't make another one here. It's time to go."

"I cannot."

Khedryn continued, his words like hammerblows. "Subjects A through I. One is dead for certain, but that leaves up to eight clones that could still be alive. I have seen what you can do, but you are one man. Eight, Jaden. And we have reason to suspect they will be hostile."

"I know all that."

"You are asking me to risk my life so you can save your conscience."

"I did not know things would turn out this way, Khedryn," Jaden said, and meant it. "Go back to *Flotsam* and wait for me there."

"I don't quit, Jaden. That's not—"

Jaden's thoughts crystallized around the fact that he had asked far too much of Khedryn already. Relin had done the same with Marr. They—the Jedi—were exacting too high a price from those around them. Jaden wanted no more blood on his hands.

"Listen to me, Khedryn. You are right. This has been and is about me learning something about myself. I . . . can use light and dark side powers and I do not know what that means for me."

The words caused Khedryn to take a half step back, as if Jaden had struck him. His eyes widened. "You can what? Like the clones?"

Jaden bulled forward without acknowledging the question. "But I think there's an answer here, in this place. And I do not want you risking anything more than you already have—"

"I said I do not quit, Jedi."

Jaden nodded. "And I'm not asking you to. I'm asking you to recognize the fact that you will be able to do nothing for me should I meet the clones. They will be dangerous, too dangerous for you. Go back to the ship. We can stay in contact via comlink. If something happens to me, you can leave, rendezvous with Marr and Relin."

Khedryn shook his head, pure stubbornness taking over. "Relin is not coming back. You and I both know that, too. But Marr better."

"Go back," Jaden said. "Go back, Khedryn."

Khedryn continued to shake his head, but Jaden saw his resistance crumbling.

He put his hand on Khedryn's arm. "Go. Back."

"You using that mind trick on me again?"

Jaden smiled. "Yes, I am. You know why you have no weapons on *Junker*?"

"Because I run," Khedryn said softly, and his lazy eye looked past Jaden and off to the side, no doubt seeing the world askew. He refocused on Jaden. "You are certain?"

"I am."

"I don't intend to leave without you, though."

Jaden knew he had done the right thing. He saw the relief in Khedryn's body language, his expression. Khedryn seemed to draw a deep breath for the first time since leaving *Junker*.

"Understood, Khedryn. Go on."

They settled on a comlink frequency and Khedryn headed out, while Jaden studied the schematic that showed the facility's layout. He put his finger on the drawing of the lift that led to a lower level.

"There be dragons," he said.

Kell slid through the open hatch of the facility, past the guard post, and down the dark hallway. He activated the light-amplifying implants in his eyes and glided through the dim corridors. His mimetic suit rendered him all but invisible against the featureless gray walls. His skill rendered him all but silent.

For a time, he was easily able to track Jaden and his companion by way of the wet tracks they left behind. When those disappeared, he relied more heavily on his skills. He examined patterns in the dust, depressions in the carpet, noted items—a computer station, a closet door—that appeared recently disturbed. He also kept his keen hearing focused on the way ahead.

From time to time he heard the hiss of distant voices, the squeak of an opening door, the tread of boots on metal.

The facility was some kind of secret research lab, though its particular purpose was lost on Kell. He spent little time thinking about it. His appetite pulled him forward. He imagined himself casting a line of fate into an ocean of possibilities and hooking Jaden Korr. All he needed to do now was reel him in and feed.

His hunger grew with each step.

Marr slammed his palm into the button that closed *Junker*'s cargo bay door on the dead Massassi, on the ruins of Khedryn's Searing, on the ruins of Relin.

There is nothing certain.

Once the door began its descent, he took one last look down the freight corridor at the corpses and the destruction, then turned and sprinted for the cockpit. He stopped dead when he hit the galley, his chest rising and falling like a forge bellows.

The caf pot on the table had been toppled, the caf still dripping off the edge, pattering on the floor. He stared at it as if the spill pattern were a deep mystery whose solution promised wisdom.

The hard landing had spilled it.

He started to walk, stopped again.

If that were true, the caf would not still be dripping to the floor.

Something else had spilled it. Very recently.

The clang of an opening hatch sounded from somewhere behind him, one of the corridors on the stern side of the galley.

His heart revved faster than the Searing. For a moment, fear froze him. His thoughts turned chaotic, coming so fast and inchoate that they made no sense.

They had gotten in the ship from the landing bay side. They must have pried open an exterior hatch, or cut their way in, or something.

Another hatch sounded, closer. He heard the soft tread of boots on *Junker*'s metal floors, a ginger footfall trying and failing to move with stealth.

The proximity of the danger freed him from his paralysis and he bolted from the galley, clutching his blaster in a sweaty hand as he ran. After he'd cleared the galley, reason overcame fear and he realized that pelting through the corridors would both telegraph his position and potentially send him right into the arms of whoever was aboard. He had no idea where they were, *what* they were.

He slowed, his heart still thumping madly, and ducked into a seldom-used crew quarters. The small room featured nothing but twin, wall-mounted bed racks and a round viewport blocked by the gray steel of a security shield.

He had to to get himself under control, think rationally.

Recalling what Relin had taught him, he tried to retreat into the keep but found it barred. Fear worked against him. He could not seem to catch his breath.

Gathering himself, steadying his breathing, he thought of the calculations that proved Vellan's theorem and tried again.

He relaxed as he fell into the Force. Its touch comforted him, warmed him, steadied him. The Force crowded out his fear, leaving him clear-headed and calm.

Marr realized that Relin had been wrong. There *was* something certain. The Force was certain, as constant as the speed of light.

He considered his options and realized that all of them led to a single place—the cockpit. But first he needed to get to the storage locker near the forward air lock.

He put his hand to the cool metal of the hatch, turned it, and pushed it open. Cringing at the squeak, he exited the quarters and moved in fits and starts along *Junker*'s corridors. Every windowless hatch was an exercise in controlled terror since he had no idea what he would find on the other side. As best he could, he peeked around corners, listened before he moved. From time to time he heard sounds of movement behind him, the soft chatter of a quieted comlink. Whoever was aboard sounded louder now, more careless than before, as if *Harbinger*'s crew thought the ship empty.

He reached the air lock, opened the storage locker, and grabbed an oxygen kit and his vac suit. Not quite a hardsuit designed for long-term exposure to the vacuum, this was a flexible mesh-and-plate garment used for short-term space walks. He'd used it to travel between ships on salvage jobs, make quick repairs to *Junker*'s exterior, and the like.

He considered donning it then and there but felt too exposed in the corridor. Instead, he slung it over his shoulder, grunting under its weight, and humped it through the corridors.

Before he had gone ten meters, a guttural voice shouted behind him. He did not understand the language, but he understood the tone.

He whirled, saw two of the Massassi in black uniforms, and fired a shot with his blaster. It clicked and fizzed, the charge exhausted. He cursed, dropped it, drew the blaster he'd taken from the dead Massassi back in the freight corridor, and fired.

He missed badly and threw himself against the wall as the two Massassi tore down the hall toward him, their blasters sending pulses of green energy into the bulkhead near him.

The spinwheel of a hatch pressed into his back. He fired a couple of shots, forcing the Massassi to slam themselves against the wall for cover, and threw open the hatch. He ducked inside the corridor and closed the hatch behind him. It had no lock. Cursing, he looked around for anything he could stick into the spinwheel's spokes, but saw nothing.

He heard the Massassi on the other side of the door, and then the wheel started to spin. Marr grabbed it, but the creatures were far too strong. Desperate, he stuck the Massassi blaster into the spinwheel, wedging it between the wheel and the pull handle. It stuck, halting the wheel's spin, but Marr knew it would not hold for long.

Heedless of the danger of bumping into more Massassi, he ran as fast as he could for the cockpit. Adrenaline lent him strength, but the vac suit and oxygen kit weighed him down. By the time he saw the cockpit door ahead, his lungs burned and his legs felt like lead.

Blasterfire from behind sizzled past his ears and slammed into the bulkhead. The shouts of the Massassi, more than two, rang out behind him. He dug deep, surprising himself when the Force gave him strength and speed, and staggered into the cockpit.

Pain lit his back on fire as a rain of small metal disks, dozens of them like flying razors, richocheted around the space. Warm blood streamed down his back and he hoped he had not taken a hit to a kidney.

He threw the vac suit and oxygen kit to the ground, the momentum pulling him to his knees, and turned to close the cockpit security door. Three Massassi sped down the hall, the trunks of their legs chewing up the distance, the thump of their boots like blaster shots on the metal floor. Two others behind the charging three whirled their polearms above their head, jerking them back as Marr hit the security door release. A rain of the tiny metal disks flew from the end of the polearms over the other Massassi, but the door closed and they chimed against it like tinny rain.

Marr's breath sounded loud in the close confines of the dark cockpit. A bout of dizziness caused him to sway. He was losing blood rapidly.

Impacts challenged the security door—shoulders or booted feet—but it held for the moment. Marr did not have much time. He could hear the Massassi growling in their language on the other side of the door.

He needed to get off *Harbinger* but he dared not lift the security shields for fear the deck crew would shoot out *Junker*'s viewports. He would have to fly her on instruments only.

He climbed to his feet, put the autopilot into launch prep, and methodically donned the vac suit and oxygen kit, all while blasterfire from the Massassi pounded against the security door. Judging from the noise, Marr thought more of the creatures must have joined the first five. Blaster shots challenged the door but did not penetrate it.

The autopilot completed pre-launch and Marr squeezed into the pilot's seat. He engaged the repulsorlifts and *Junker* rose off the deck.

For a moment, the Massassi left off their attack on the cockpit security door. Perhaps they had felt the liftoff.

Marr's mouth turned dry as he rotated *Junker* on its vertical axis, using only his instrumentation to orient him.

An explosion from outside the ship rocked it sidelong into *Harbinger*'s bulkhead. Marr fell from his seat as metal scraped against metal. For a terrifying moment the power on the ship went brown and *Junker* started to sink, but emergency reserves kicked in and brought it back online.

He cursed as he climbed back into his seat, fearful that he had perforated his suit, but he had no time to examine it. He checked his board, cursed again when he saw that the explosion had scrambled the readout from his instrumentation. Nonsensical information streamed from the scanners. He activated a diagnostic but could not wait for it to resolve itself.

In his mind, he pictured the layout of *Harbinger*'s landing bay. To him, it was all angles, proportions, distances in meters. As he fell into the geometry of his mind, he felt his connection to the Force strengthen. The connection had always been there, but now that he recognized it, he could more readily use it. Mathematics was his interface with the Force.

Another explosion slammed *Junker* against *Harbinger*'s bulkhead. In the corridor outside the cockpit, the Massassi renewed their assault on the door, a more frantic, desperate assault.

Marr remained calm, though blood loss turned him mildly dizzy. Thinking of Jaden piloting *Junker* through the rings, he strapped himself into his seat as best he could—his vac suit did not allow for full use of the harness—closed his eyes, trusted his instincts, and piloted *Junker* in the direction he thought was out. If he was wrong, he was flying not out but deeper into the landing bay. In that case, he would soon be dead.

He fought down the doubt and continued his course.

Blasterfire from the landing bay thumped against the ship, like someone knocking urgently for entry. The Massassi outside the security door beat against it like rancors in a bloodlust.

Blind but not-blind, Marr felt *Harbinger*'s bulkheads, felt other ships nearby, the faint pulse of *Harbinger*'s crew around *Junker*. He was going the right way.

He understood the interconnection of all things by the Force, understood how Jaden had piloted *Junker* through the gas giant's rings. The realization made him smile as *Junker* flew on its repulsors toward the mouth of the landing bay. He held the smile as blood poured from his back and he began to see spots.

When he had put some distance behind him and the deck crew, he raised the security shields. The mouth of *Harbinger*'s landing bay was just ahead and, beyond it, the black of space and the partial arc of the gas giant's moon.

The squeal of straining metal turned him around in his seat and sent his heart racing. The Massassi had forced the security door open a centimeter and wedged one of the metal studs they wore in their skin between the door and the bulkhead. One of them must have pulled it from his flesh. Their voices sounded loud and close—too close—through the slit. He could see motion through the gap and ducked as they tried to get the barrel of a blaster through. The opening was not quite wide enough, but it would be soon.

He heard an exclamation and saw the work end of a pry bar slip into the gap. They had taken it from one of the wall-mounted emergency equipment cases.

He cursed and engaged the ion engines. *Junker* raced out of *Harbinger*'s landing bay and into open space. He presumed *Harbinger*'s deflectors would work on the same outward-facing principle as their modern counterparts so he did not power down and coast. Instead he kept the engines at full and blew through them.

The door creaked open more, its springs and levers groaning against the Massassi's strength. Marr looked over his shoulder and saw the hole of a blaster barrel pointed through the slit, one yellow eye of a Massassi fixed on him.

Marr hunched in his seat out of reflex, though the seat would not so much as slow a blaster shot. He pulled back on the *Junker*'s control and accelerated to full as the ship went vertical. The sudden shift in direction and velocity poured him flat into his seat and sent the Massassi backward from the door. The crowbar slipped free and the sound of a blaster's discharge accompanied their frustrated roars.

Weakened from his injuries, Marr almost passed out from the maneuver. The view through the cockpit window shrank to a tunnel with a few stars as he tried to hold on to consciousness. His blood pumped like a drum in his ears. The drumming gave way to a soft, steady rush, white noise that reminded him of the surf on Cerea. The tunnel of his awareness reduced to a pinpoint. He was falling . . .

He fought his way back, seized awareness with both hands, and reached for the lever and buttons that would activate the emergency vent sequence. He seemed to be moving in slow motion, watching himself on a vidscreen.

He hit the control sequence and an alarm beeped. Designed to put out an electrical fire shipside, the emergency vent would cause rapid depressurization and vent all oxygen in the ship into space. The Massassi would be dead in less than a minute while the vac suit would protect Marr.

In theory.

The beeping alarm turned into a prolonged keen, indicating imminent venting. Marr realized that he had never had the opportunity to check his suit. His fall could have pierced it, or one of the Massassi's sharpened disk projectiles could have damaged it.

There was nothing for it.

The alarm fell silent as the interior of *Junker* turned into a vacuum. Marr listened to the sound of his breathing inside his helmet, the hiss of the oxygen kit feeding him air. He watched the life-support readout on the console show the absence of oxygen.

He turned in his seat and found himself staring at the muscular, red-skinned form of a Massassi. The cockpit door was open behind the creature, an open mouth that had vomited the Massassi into the cockpit. Broken capillaries turned the Massassi's yellow eyes into a mesh of black. The creature swayed on its feet, already dying from lack of oxygen. For what seemed an eternity, the Massassi stared at Marr and Marr stared at the Massassi through his suit's visor.

Baring its fangs, the creature lunged for Marr, clawed hands outstretched. Marr tried to grab the Massassi's wrists as the creature fell on him, but blood loss had left him with little strength, and the creature got its hands free of Marr's grasp. The Massassi tried to pull Marr from his seat but the straps secured him.

Marr reached for his blaster with a free hand, then

realized he had no blaster. The Massassi, mouth wide and gasping for nonexistent air, hit the emergency release on Marr's strap and both of them fell to the cockpit floor in a heap.

The Massassi scrambled atop, his weight a vise on Marr's chest. Its clawed hands pawed at Marr's suit. Marr's breathing rasped in the echo chamber of the helmet. He tried again to grab the Massassi's arms but his strength was no match for the alien's. He punched the creature in the face, shoulders, but the blows were so weak the Massassi barely seemed to notice them.

The creature's face loomed into Marr's faceplate. Droplets of black blood fell from the Massassi's ears, eyes, and nose, smearing the screen. Marr once more felt the odd sensation that he was watching events happening to someone else on a vidscreen. The Massassi's claws closed on the suit's neck ring, then tighter, around Marr's throat, and started to squeeze.

Marr's body failed him. Strength rushed out of him as if through a hole. He could not lift even an arm to defend himself. He stared up through the smeared faceplate, barely able to see, barely able to breathe.

The Massassi squeezed Marr's throat, squeezed, then . . . released its grip and collapsed atop him, dead. The vacuum had done what Marr could not.

For a time, Marr heard only the sound of his own rapid breathing. After a few moments, he rolled the Massassi's bulk off him and sat up, feeling instantly dizzy. Every muscle in his body screamed. He tried to stand, but his legs would not support him and he sagged back to the floor. His body seemed disinclined to answer his demands.

Crawling on all fours, he climbed over the Massassi and went to the instrument panel, intending to deactivate the emvent and repressurize *Junker*. He tried to wipe away the blood on his faceplate but that only made it worse. His eyes seemed unable to focus. So, too, his mind. He could not remember which buttons did what.

Only then did he notice the hiss.

His vac suit was bleeding air.

He looked down and saw a gash in the suit's belly, a laughing mouth put there by a Massassi claw. He stared at it dumbly, watching the edges flap as the oxygen kit fed air into the vacuum.

He put both hands on the instrument console, leaned over it as if he could intimidate it into cooperating. Forcing himself to focus on the instruments, he tried to clear his mind enough to remember which sequence of buttons would repressurize the ship.

When he thought he had it, he pushed them, then pulled the lever.

Nothing happened.

He sagged into the pilot's seat, his vision fading. He was going to die unless he did something. He flicked on the autopilot and it blinked at him, awaiting a course.

Focusing on the navicomp, blinking through his pain and dizziness, he hit a random button and stared at the coordinates displayed on the screen. He did not recognize them at first, then realized them for what they were: the provenance of the distress beacon coming up from the gas giant's moon.

It occurred to him that he would get shot down by *Harbinger*'s fighters before he ever hit the moon's atmosphere but he realized it did not matter. Oxygen deprivation and blood loss were already killing him.

He transmitted the coordinates from the navicomp to the autopilot.

He looked out the cockpit window as *Junker* came around. The moon came back into view, the gas giant and its rings, *Harbinger*. He wondered briefly how Relin was, then sank into his chair, into the Force, and did not move.

His mind wandered. He smiled, thinking that Khedryn could have at least allowed a medical droid aboard. But the captain was as stubbon as a bantha when it came to droids.

He found breathing difficult, tiring. He just wanted to close his eyes and sleep.

Relin stalked *Harbinger*'s corridors, more predator than prey. It was as if Marr had been the compass for his conscience, the Cerean's presence the needle that pointed to right and wrong. Now, alone with his anger, with the Lignan, Relin gave full play to the darkness of his emotions. The shipwide alarm continued to howl but he tuned it out, hearing only the call of revenge. He did not bother to hide his presence in the Force; he transmitted it. He wished for Saes to find him. The power of the Lignan saturated him, eager to be used in service to his rage.

While thinking through his attack in his time aboard *Junker*, he had planned to return once more to *Harbinger*'s hyperdrive chamber and rig the hyperdrive to irradiate or explode the entire ship. But now, flush with power, he had another idea.

Moving through *Harbinger*'s corridors reminded him of the last time he had been aboard. He imagined he would hear Drev's voice over his comlink—Drev's laughter—but he knew he would never hear his Padawan's voice again. His anger grew with every step. His power grew with every step. He used his growing connection to the Lignan to steer him through the ship, a left turn here, there a lift down or up.

Laugh even when you die.

Laughter bubbled up between Relin's gritted teeth, steam through an escape valve, venting the overflow of his anger lest he explode from it.

He turned a corner and found himself staring at three humans, all men, and a treaded mech droid. The humans wore helmets and surprised expressions. They stopped in their steps when they saw Relin and his lightsaber. One of them lifted the portable tool chest he bore to his chest, as if it could protect him.

Nothing could protect them.

The droid beeped a question.

Relin smiled.

All three of the humans dropped their tool chests, turned, and ran, shouting for help.

Relin augmented his speed with the Force, leapt over the droid, caught up to the humans, and put his lightsaber through each of them, one after the other. He barely noticed their screams.

A single Massassi security guard, perhaps hearing the tumult, trotted around the corridor to investigate.

"You!" the Massassi said, reaching for his blaster. "Halt right there!"

Relin gestured with his stump, closed a mental hand around the Massassi's windpipe, and crushed it with a thought. The creature fell to the ground, legs drumming the floor, clawing at his throat.

Stepping over and past the writhing Massassi, Relin continued on. He looked down at his hand and saw long fingers of Force lightning dancing out of his fingertips.

He laughed louder, shouting his hate through *Harbinger*'s walls.

"Saes!"

Ahead, perhaps twenty meters, the doors of a turbolift opened to reveal six of *Harbinger*'s crew, all humans. He did not see a blaster among them.

One started to step off, saw Relin, and stopped cold. His mouth opened, but he said nothing. Instead he retreated into the lift, said something to his fellow passengers, and frantically tapped at the control panel, trying to close the lift doors.

"Quickly!" another said, while one in the back spoke into her comlink.

Relin roared, increased his speed with the Force, and sprinted toward them. The six members of the crew flattened themselves against the far side of the lift, made themselves a living mural, but there was nowhere for them to run. Terror filled their eyes and blood fled their faces. The doors began to close but Relin held them open with telekinetic force.

Seeing that, the crew shouted for help, pressed themselves against the walls as if trying to meld flesh with metal. Relin stepped through the lift doors, laughing. The hum of his lightsaber competed with the screams, but not for long. He spun a circle, stabbing and slashing, pleased when his lightsaber met the soft resistance of human flesh. In a few moments the screams fell silent and only the hum remained.

Relin stared at the carnage he had caused. Tears warmed his face, mingling with the blood of those he had killed. Without warning he vomited, *Junker*'s caf and his last meal joining the gore on the lift's floor. That, too, he stared at for a time, until his eyes dried.

Whatever had remained of him as a Jedi had just left him in a spray of puke.

On the control panel he saw a button for the lower-level cargo bay. He knew he would find the Lignan there. The touch of the ore was the fishhook he'd swallowed and it was pulling him along by his guts.

Ever gone angling, Drev?

He had said those words a lifetime ago.

He pushed the button.

"When is the last time I felt anything?" he said, echoing Saes's challenge to him in their last duel.

"When indeed," he said, chuckling darkly.

* * *

Alarms blared from speakers overhead, the sound muted by the erkush bone mask Saes wore. With each step, he felt more attuned to his tribe and ancestors than he had in a long while. He had lost himself entirely when he had joined the Jedi Order, forced by Jedi teachings to renounce the fierceness of character and passionate spirit that made him who he was. He had partially recovered himself when he had spurned the Jedi and embraced the teachings of the Sith. But he had never felt closer to whole than he did now, moments before he would murder his former Master. He was a hunter, a warrior, a Kaleesh.

He threw back his head and screamed an *ingmal* hunting cry through the fangs of the mask. Startled faces emerged from hatches and side corridors, but he strode past them without offering an explanation.

Through his connection to Relin, he felt his onetime Master's growing anger over the loss of his Padawan. For a moment, but only a moment, Saes felt a flash of sympathy for Relin, a flash of kinship. He was pleased that Relin had felt the sting of loss, rather than only the distant, attenuated, abortive emotions the Jedi allowed themselves.

Saes knew that all men should feel the pain of loss before they died. In that way, they would know they had lived. Relin was no exception, and Saes was pleased for him. Now he could kill him with true affection in his heart.

Relin's anger would lead him to only one place. There, Saes would confront him, and their story together would end. He activated his comlink.

"Sir," Llerd said. "Other than a trail of bodies, we do not yet have any idea of the Jedi's location."

"He is on his way to the cargo bay," Saes said. "The Lignan is drawing him."

"I will alert security and—"

"No," Saes said. "Order the bay evacuated. I will face him there. Alone."

"Yes, sir."

The lift hummed as it descended several levels to *Harbinger*'s cargo bay. Relin's lightsaber sizzled, warmed the close confines of the lift. He stared at its light, hypnotized by the swirl of green. He knew it should have been red. He *wished* it were red.

The doors opened and the naked power of the Lignan filled the lift compartment, filled Relin. Light-headed, giddy with power, he stepped into the cavernous cargo bay. Stacks of storage containers lined the walls. If the stresses of the misjump had knocked some to the floor or otherwise put the ship's cargo into disarray, the crew had cleaned it up.

Pieces of human-operated lift gear—lev pallets, treaded lifters—sat abandoned on the metal floor. He saw no one in the bay, not even a cargo droid, and he knew exactly what the emptiness meant. He walked across the floor, the lift closing behind him, the tread of his boots loud in the soaring chamber.

Following the string of his rage, he walked through a maze of storage containers until he found the several dozen that held the Lignan ore. They were stacked several high, arranged in a box shape, so that they described the perimeter of an open square of deck ten meters on a side. Several of the containers had been partially crushed and remained open. A pile of ore bled onto the deck through the open seals. He walked gingerly among the ore, touching none. He did not need to touch it with his flesh. He was connected to it in his spirit. It *knew* him, and knew what he needed.

The power in the air nearly lifted him from his feet.

He was swimming in it. Elated rage buoyed his body, lit his spirit on fire. Force lightning formed flowing serpents around his fingers and forearms.

He sat down cross-legged among the ore, amid the embodiment of his need to murder one Padawan to avenge another, and awaited Saes and battle.

chapter fourteen

JADEN FELT THE WEIGHT OF HIS SOLITUDE THE MO-
ment he and Khedryn parted. He was surprised at
how much he had come to rely on the presence of
Junker's crew. He had isolated himself for so long that
he had forgotten the value of simple companionship.
They were good men, Khedryn and Marr. Rascals, yes,
but quality rascals.

He moved as rapidly as he could through the facility.
The beam of a glow rod and the glow of his lightsaber
augmented the dim illumination from the emergency
lights. He did not need to consult the folded schematic
in his pocket to know the direction of the lift. The way
there was engraved in his brain.

Without Khedryn at his side, the metal walls of the
narrow corridors felt increasingly oppressive, their un-
broken gray smoothness a winter sky that sunlight never
pierced. He wondered how the Imperial scientists had
remained here for any length of time without going
mad.

Perhaps they hadn't, he thought, recalling the pro-
gressively deteriorating physical condition of Dr. Black
in the holo-log, Dr. Gray's nervous hand spasm.

His exhalations steamed in the cool air. The echo of
his boots on the floor seemed to carry everywhere. And
somewhere in the complex, at the base of the communi-

cations tower, the facility sent its heartbeat pulsing into space.

Help us. Help us.

He swallowed and ran a hand through his hair, taking a moment to gather himself. He was not fearful of encountering the clones, if any yet survived. Like all Jedi, he did not fear battle or death. But he was growing ever more fearful of encountering an answer to his question, and he felt certain the lift would take him to it.

Static crackled over the open comlink connection he maintained with Khedryn. Something in the facility's makeup must have interfered with short-range communication. Between outbursts of static, he heard Khedryn's breathing, an occasional whispered curse, the thump of Khedryn's boots on the floor as he made his way back to the ship. The sounds reminded Jaden that he was not alone, that he was still connected.

"Everything all right?" he said in response to another of Khedryn's curses. Static roared in to fill the silence after he'd spoken.

"Fine," Khedryn said, his voice a whisper, as if he feared to awaken whatever slept in the facility. "I'm tripping over debris, is all. This glow rod isn't exactly a—"

Static ate the rest of his reply.

"Let me know when you get to the ship," Jaden said.

"Will do," Khedryn said through the interference.

Serenaded by ever more static, Jaden continued through the facility. Doors and side passages opened here and there. He caught a glimpse of a kitchen that smelled faintly of food rotted long ago, another recreation room with rusted exercise equipment, conference rooms—all of the mundane trappings of a research facility anywhere in the galaxy.

Except for the blaster marks that scored the walls and

ceilings, the black lines a cryptic script that chronicled the death of the facility.

Ahead, at the end of a long corridor, he saw the closed double doors of the lift, blackened and scarred by a barrage of blasterfire. A headless body lay on the ground near the lift doors, half propped against the wall, the arms thrown out wide as if to embrace. He noted the lab coat.

Segments of stormtrooper armor containing bits of desiccated body parts littered the corridor between Jaden and the lift. Large pieces of security droids lay strewn about the hall, likewise dismembered—here a leg, there a torso, there a head, the eyes gone dark. Jaden recognized the work of a lightsaber, and a skilled combatant at that.

Guilt dogged Khedryn's steps. He knew Jaden was right—Khedryn would be no help facing any of the clones, should any have survived—but he still felt as if he was abandoning the Jedi.

For all Jaden's power, all his talent, he still struck Khedryn as remarkably fragile and entirely alone. And for all Khedryn's cynicism, he liked Jaden.

"Because I run," Khedryn murmured, embarrassed to have ever uttered the words, notwithstanding their truth. He wished that he understood himself less well, that he could live in ignorance of his character flaws.

He felt himself a coward.

Yet his fear was warranted. He had gotten in much deeper than he had intended, and whatever had happened in the facility was better left undisturbed. He no longer felt like he was walking through a research facility. Instead, he felt like he was walking through the scene of a mass murder.

Sweat soaked his clothes under his enviro-suit. His fingers girdled the handle of his blaster too tightly, and he consciously relaxed them. He soft-stepped his way back through the complex, trying even to quiet his breathing, hyper-aware of his surroundings.

The holo-log had unnerved him. He had seen the concern root in the eyes of the doctors, seen the root blossom into fear.

If the Force had led Marr to choose a course that brought them to the moon, then the Force could karking well curl up in a corner and die. Khedryn wanted nothing more than to be off the moon, back aboard *Junker* drinking pulkay.

Marr had turned some corner around which Khedryn could not see. He'd given up Khedryn's skewed view of the galaxy for the straightforward view of the Jedi. He had seemed eager to fly with Relin. Eager.

Khedryn worried for Marr.

And despite himself, he worried for Jaden.

I do not quit, Jedi. He had said those words. They sounded like self-mockery, like a bad joke. He did quit. He was quitting.

Unbidden, Relin's words bubbled up from the soup of his memory, the Jedi wan, haggard, the walking dead— *You cannot always run, Khedryn.*

But he always had. Not so much from fear of danger as from fear of standing still.

He cursed under his breath as he walked, each stride punctuated with a soft expletive. The guilt did not relent and he could not believe what he had come to. He was seriously considering turning around to stand next to a Jedi he'd only just met and possibly face foes against which he could do nothing.

Maybe he had turned a corner, too.

And maybe he'd stared out too many viewports while moving through hyperspace and gotten the madness.

The comlink blurted static, putting his already racing heart in the back of his throat.

"Stang," he hissed, his steps already starting to slow. He was still moving in the same direction but only by way of inertia, not propulsion.

Time to change course.

Jaden studied the scene, imagining the battle in his head. Security droids, backed by a squad of stormtroopers, had been waiting when the clones came up the lift. Blasterfire and smoke had filled the hall. The clones, deflecting the shots with their lightsabers, had cut their way through both men and machines. When all had gone quiet, one of the medical corps's doctors had approached the clones, perhaps pleading for mercy or arguing for reason and calm.

They had decapitated her.

He suspected no staff had escaped the facility and, for the first time, he seriously considered the possibility that no clones remained on the moon—that they had taken whatever ships had been available to the staff and fled into the Unknown Regions.

As the dire implications of that settled on him— Jedi–Sith clones roaming space—a burst of static exploded from the comlink. He winced as if it were blasterfire.

"Say again, Khedryn?"

More static. Perhaps they were losing contact altogether.

He picked his way through the aftermath of the battle, feeling as if he were walking through a graveyard, the large pieces of the droids the metallic tombstones. When he reached the doors, he looked down at the corpse. Time had drawn the skin tight over the bones and discolored it to ash. The trousers and lab coat, stuffed with a headless body, struck him as obscene. He read the name on the coat—DR. GRAY.

He flashed back to the holo-log, the fear he had seen in her eyes when she had recorded the final entry.

She had been right to fear. A clone had decapitated her, probably while she stood there unarmed.

Jaden stared at the lift doors and flashed back to the air lock door on Centerpoint Station, the frightened eyes staring at him through the tiny viewport. They had been those of someone who, though armed, was not dangerous.

He reached for the button to summon the lift, cognizant that the same hand and the same gesture had spaced more than two dozen people on Centerpoint.

Somewhere behind the walls a mechanism hummed. The lift still functioned. He stood there awaiting it, living for a moment in his past, in his guilt.

The lift arrived, opened. Dr. Gray's head lay in the center, the open eyes on the mummified visage staring holes into his soul.

For a moment his feet remained stuck to the floor, pinioned there by Dr. Gray's eyes. Random static from the comlink freed him from his paralysis.

"I am heading down," he said to Khedryn.

He entered the lift, turned his back to Dr. Gray, and watched the doors close. He tapped the button on the control panel for the lower level. The lift began to sink, and Jaden with it.

By the time Khedryn reached the recreation room and its sabacc table, he had resolved to stop.

"I'm coming back," he said to Jaden, but feared the static in the connection had disrupted the transmission. On impulse and without looking at them, he took the cards from the single sabacc hand he had left unturned on the table and stuffed them in his pocket. He decided they totaled twenty-three, no matter what they showed. Someone in the facility must have been lucky.

His comlink coughed more static but he caught the tail end of whatever Jaden said.

". . . down."

"Say again, Jaden?"

A voice spoke in his ear, and breath that smelled of rotting meat warmed his neck.

"He said he was heading down."

Khedryn whirled, bringing up his blaster. Kell seized the human's right wrist and held the arm out wide while the blaster discharged, putting a smoking hole in the sabacc table. Cards fluttered into the air like freed birds.

Kell's and Khedryn's *daen nosi* whirled around them, the arms of their personal spiral galaxy. Staring into Khedryn's misaligned eyes, Kell projected, *Be still.*

The human showed surprising resistance, swinging an overhand left that caught Kell on the temple. The punch might have knocked a human unconscious, but it only surprised Kell.

Frowning, he squeezed Khedryn's wrist hard, felt the bones start to crack.

Khedryn winced with pain, grunting through the wall of his clenched teeth. He tried to twist his cracking wrist free from the vise of Kell's grip but did not have the strength. The human punched Kell in the face once, twice, again, again. Kell absorbed the blows, his nose trickling blood, and squeezed as hard as he could.

The bones of Khedryn's wrist snapped at last and the human shrieked with agony, spraying saliva. Kell did not release his grip, but instead ground the bone shards against one another, the coarse friction a music of pain under the human's flesh.

Khedryn's scream went on and on, ending only when Kell took him by the throat with his free hand and lifted him from his feet. The human hung in his arms, clawing with his one good hand at Kell's grip, trying to draw breath, his legs spasming with the effort.

Kell watched his *daen nosi* twist around the human's and overwhelm them, strangling Khedryn's possible futures just as Kell strangled his body. He looked into Khedryn's pain-dazed eyes.

Be still, Kell projected, more forcefully, and Khedryn at last went limp. One of the human's eyes focused on Kell, the other off to the left, perhaps seeing the end approach.

Out of habit, Kell opened the slits in his cheeks and his feeders slipped free. The human, lost in his pain and the maze of Kell's mental command, did not appear to notice them until they began to slide up his nostrils.

He kicked feebly and shook his head, fighting against Kell's mental hold. But his struggles proved futile. Kell's feeders knifed their way through the nasal tissue. Khedryn's eyes watered. Blood leaked around the feeders, out the human's nostrils, and into his beard and mouth.

Only then did Kell realize what he was doing, that he felt nothing, that he was risking revelation by surrendering to his appetite prematurely.

The possibility of feeding on the human's soup elicited no longing, no yearning expectation of revelation. He looked at Khedryn's *daen nosi,* found them uncomplicated entirely, lines of fate that did nothing more than curl back on themselves forever, leading nowhere, offering nothing.

Khedryn Faal did not offer revelation. No one did.

Except Jaden Korr.

Their lines were connected, Kell's and Jaden's. Only Jaden's lines, once enwrapped by Kell's, would map out the road to understanding, would scribe characters of revelation for Kell to read. Only then would Kell have what he had sought for centuries.

Disgusted with himself—and with Khedryn—he pulled back his feeders. They came clear of Khedryn's face with a wet, slurping sound. A flood of blood and snot poured from Khedryn's nose. Kell lowered Khedryn to the floor, loosening his grip on the human's throat.

Attempting to draw in some air, Khedryn instead aspirated some of the blood and snot and began to cough. When he finished, he looked up into Kell's face. The human's eyes watered; a network of popped blood vessels made a circuit board of his eyes; blood and mucus slathered his mustache and beard.

"What are you?" he asked, his voice as coarse as a rasp.

Kell almost answered by reflex, *I am a ghost,* but stopped himself.

"I am a pilgrim," he said instead.

Khedryn's face screwed into a question and Kell, distracted, drove his fist into the center of it. Khedryn did not make a sound. His nose shattered, blood sprayed, and Kell let him fall on his back to the floor unconscious. He gathered up Khedryn's blaster, searched him for other weapons, found none, stripped him of his comlink, and left him on the floor.

He considered slitting Khedryn's throat with his vibroblade, but realized that he was indifferent to Khedryn Faal. And he would no longer murder with indifference. Perhaps his apathetic butchery had been the reason revelation so long eluded him. He must kill only with his spirit on fire.

And he was burning for Jaden Korr.

And Jaden had headed down.

Kell left Khedryn behind and followed after Jaden. His pilgrimage was nearing its end.

Khedryn swam in pain, drowning, flailing, seeking release . . .

He awoke on the cold floor of the recreation room, coughing blood. Each cough drove a spike of pain through his nose and nasal cavity. The metallic taste of blood clung to the roof of his mouth, near the back of his throat. He winced with remembered pain and terror, recalling the pointed appendages that had squirmed from his attacker's cheeks and wormed up his nose. He'd been unable to breathe, unable to think, violated.

Nausea seized him. He sat up, vomited blood, snot, and his last meal onto the deck, where it steamed in the cold. Forgetting the details of his injuries, he steadied himself with a hand on the floor and his broken wrist screamed in protest. The pain from bone grinding against bone almost caused him to pass out. He held on to consciousness through sheer force of will.

After the room stopped spinning, after the pain in his wrist grew bearable, he used a chair from the sabacc table to help him to his feet. His shattered nose did not allow air to pass, so his breath wheezed through his mouth, left hanging open like a cargo bay door.

As he rose, he fixed his eyes on a sabacc card that had fallen from the table, staring at the image on it—a grinning clown face in an absurd hat. The Idiot. He almost laughed.

His body ached from the beating. The adrenaline dump and the aftereffects of the terror he'd felt left him weak, shaking, barely able to stand. He tried to collect his wits, gather his thoughts, endure the pain in his wrist.

Had the creature been one of the clones? It had seemed a Force-user. He'd felt it slip into his thoughts and command him to be still. The greasy feeling of being mentally violated had been reminiscent of Jaden's use of the mind trick.

Why had it left him alive?

He did not know and did not care. It was enough that he was alive.

He reached for his comlink, thinking to warn Jaden, and found it gone. The creature had taken it. He looked around the room for his blaster, saw that it, too, was missing.

The creature seemed concerned only that Khedryn be unarmed and unable to warn Jaden. He had no particular interest in Khedryn, apparently. Khedryn understood the message—*Leave and it's all over.* He had just been in the wrong place at the wrong time.

It had seemed exactly so since he had first met Jaden Korr.

"One problem after another," he murmured.

Dizziness overcame him. His legs gave way and he sagged gingerly into a chair at the sabacc table, struck with the fact that the last people to sit there were all dead.

He daubed his nose, wincing at the pain, and slowly drummed his fingers on the table. He thought of Marr, of Relin, of Jaden. All were putting their lives in danger for . . . what?

For something bigger than themselves, he decided. For something they believed in.

What did Khedryn believe in?

His drumming fingers waited for an answer. He decided they could wait a long time.

He flashed on his last conversation with Marr. His friend had said that helping the Jedi was the right thing. He'd been certain of it.

Khedryn stopped drumming his fingers.

He could not always run.

"Kriffin' son of a murglak broke my kriffin' nose."

He stood, fought down the dizziness, and headed back the way he had come. His wrist throbbed with agony. His nose leaked blood and felt as if it had been smashed with a hammer. But he was through running.

He remembered the way to the lift, but he had a stop to make on the way.

Jaden felt light-headed as the lift sank into the moon. He grounded himself in the Force while the hum of the lift's motors proclaimed its rapid descent. By the time it slowed, he figured he had descended a hundred meters or more.

The doors parted, the aged mechanism squeaking loud enough to make him wince. Air ten degrees warmer than that in the surface installation flowed into the lift compartment. It bore the whiff of things dead a long while.

He stepped out and into a circular room with an overturned desk and chair near the single door that provided egress. Dried blood, brown and crusted, stained the walls.

It was not a spray pattern, Jaden realized. Someone had slathered it on the walls as if it were paint. The shapes and patterns made no sense to him, their meaning plain only to the mad.

The lift doors closed behind him. He activated the comlink.

"Khedryn, do you read?"

In the silence, his voice sounded as if he were speaking through a voice amplifier. Water dripped somewhere behind the walls, the rhythm that of the distress beacon.

The comlink exploded in static.

"Khedryn, do you read?"

More static. He was too far underground. He muted the comlink and walked into the room. He realized with horror that he was walking on clumps of hair, lots of it. Human hair. Brown, black, blond, gray. It was scattered all over the room, like fallen snow.

He knelt down and took some in his palm. Ragged pieces of the root clung to the clumps, little brown bits of dried scalp that made Jaden's mouth go dry. The hair had been ripped out in handfuls.

Dread settled on Jaden like a funeral shroud. The ceiling suddenly seemed too low, the light too dim, the whole of the complex as oppressive as a tomb. Whatever had happened in the facility had been not merely violent, but macabre.

A large brown stain covered the floor near the desk, as if someone had bled out there. Other than the unsettling scattering of hair, he saw no sign of any bodies.

Licking his lips, he put his hand on the door control— not a hatch but an ordinary door—and it slid open. The stink of old death—a stale, sickly sweet stench—wafted through, stronger than before. He wondered when he would encounter the bodies. He knew it was only a matter of time.

A wide, curving corridor stretched in either direction. From the angle of the arc, he surmised that the corridor formed a circle and came back on itself.

Putting his free hand on his blaster, as tense as a coiled spring, he went left. Blaster marks scored the white duracrete walls here and there. Blood spattered the walls. Together, the scorches and blood looked like some ancient, indecipherable script, pictographs of violence. Again, he found stray pieces of stormtrooper armor, souvenirs of the slaughter that had occurred. Again he found no bodies.

At intervals he encountered double doors along the inner wall. All were closed and would have required a card reader to pass, but the readers had been destroyed by either blasterfire or lightsaber.

Wanting to understand the layout of the complex, he delayed opening any of the doors until he walked the entire corridor. As he had suspected, it formed a circle.

Each pair of double doors stood opposite another pair. Drawing a line between each would neatly bisect the circle ringed by the corridor, another example of the Imperial fetish for symmetry.

He walked to the nearest set of the metal double doors. In addition to the destroyed card reader, the doors also had a manual lock and bar. The bar, a rod of titanium alloy, lay on the ground near the doors, bent.

Whatever was behind those doors, the doctors had not wanted it to get out.

But it had gotten out, and it had slaughtered everyone in the facility.

Jaden took a handle in hand, conscious of how cool the metal felt in his palm, and pulled it open.

A narrow corridor led straight about ten meters before ending at another metal door. Above it was written:

OBSERVATION DECK

Hallways and rooms opened along the corridor's sides, and Jaden noted them in passing—a few offices with chairs and desks overturned, loose flimsies cast over the floor, destroyed computers and data crystals scattered everywhere; a conference room, its chairs toppled, the conference table cut into pieces by a lightsaber. A wall-mounted vid display had a burn hole like a singularity in its exact center. He assumed that there was a laboratory somewhere, but he did not stop to look for it. His feet carried him of their own accord to the door that led to the observation deck.

A half-full caf pot sat on the floor in the corner of one office, somehow completely unaffected by the chaos. Caf mugs, too, littered the floor here and there, all of it the ruins of ordinary activity and interaction.

His eyes caught an unexpected shape and he stopped, staring at it.

Set atop an overturned desk was a single shoe, a woman's shoe browned with dried blood and still wrapped in an age-yellowed steri-slipper, the kind worn by laboratory techs.

The scene struck a visceral chord in Jaden, repulsed him. Someone or something had to have consciously *placed* the bloody shoe there, as if its presence exactly there were important, as if it were some kind of trophy, as if it made some kind of sense.

A realization struck him. He was seeing reified madness.

Dr. Gray's head, the hair on the floor, the shoe, all of it the acts of deranged minds.

The clones had gone mad. Perhaps they had been unable to reconcile the two poles of their origin, Jedi and Sith. Perhaps a misstep along the sword-edge a Force-user walked would lead not to a fall into the dark side so much as a descent into madness.

Jaden's mind turned to Khedryn, to the stories he'd heard of Outbound Flight's failure. Master C'baoth had gone mad, and his actions had led to many deaths.

Jaden feared he was slipping himself; he felt an abyss to either side. Yet he could not stand still. He craved certitude, yearned for it the way a drowning man did air. He unmuted his comlink, and static shouted at him.

"Khedryn," he said, knowing it was hopeless but wanting to say something aloud, a human sound to break the funereal silence of a facility that felt like a crypt.

A metallic clang from somewhere ahead caused him to tense. Moving slowly, he muted his comlink again and approached the door that led to the observation deck. He stood before it for a moment, his lightsaber sizzling in his hand, his other hand on his blaster, but the sound did not repeat. He slid the door open, crouching to reduce his silhouette.

A large, round chamber opened before him. The lights suspended from the high ceiling had all been shattered, their glass littering the floor like broken ice, so he flashed his glow rod around the room. It had to have been one hundred meters in diameter. Waist-high computer console towers rose here and there from the floor like stalagmites, each one an eerie simulacrum of the communications tower that screamed into space for help.

He stepped inside, and the feel of the floor immediately struck him oddly. He crouched and shined his glow rod directly at it.

It was transparisteel, dimmed the way *Junker*'s cockpit viewport could dim when the ship entered hyperspace. He also noticed a latticework of hair-fine filaments that ran through it, capillaries of unknown purpose. He knelt and looked through the transparisteel; he could just make out the ghosts of shapes in the room below, but nothing distinct.

On the far side of the room, he saw the dark hole of an open lift shaft, the door only half shut, an eye frozen in the act of closing.

He rose and walked to one of the computer consoles. The interface was intuitive and controlled the lighting in the room he was in, as well as the lighting, temperature, and noise in the rooms visible through the floor. He turned on the power to the rooms below, expecting the lights to be nonoperational. They functioned, illuminating the equivalent of a fishbowl. He pressed another key to eliminate the dimming effect on the floor.

The observation deck overlooked a subcomplex of rooms that Jaden assumed to have been the clones' living quarters. Hallways radiated outward from a central meeting room and attached mess hall. Two dejarik sets sat atop a table in the meeting room, the static-laden holographic creatures facing each other across the battlefield, the games unfinished. The chairs in both rooms had been pushed neatly under the table. Plates and eating utensils sat in orderly stacks atop the serving counter in the mess. Unlike the rest of the facility, everything in the clones' rooms was in place, tidy, and invariably white, cream, or some shade of gray.

"Womp rats in a maze," he murmured.

Jaden walked the observation chamber, his steps slow, staring at the rooms below his feet, tracing them as if he were walking in them himself. The hallways led to sparsely furnished personal quarters, nine of them. Each contained a bed, a desk, two chairs, some old books in hard copy.

He had not seen an actual book in a long time and he puzzled over their presence—a single data crystal could hold an entire library of information and take up essentially no space at all—until he remembered Dr. Black's words from the holo-log.

The doctors had given the clones hard-copy books so they'd have no datapads from which to scrounge parts. In fact, Jaden realized for the first time that there were no computers of any kind in the clones' rooms. They'd managed to construct lightsabers anyway.

He continued his walk, noting little assertions of individuality in each of the personal quarters—a potted plant, long dead, a remarkable clay sculpture of a human hand, a shelf on which sat four green bottles, their color a contrast with the grays and whites of the complex.

He stopped cold when he stood over the last bedroom, the hairs on the back of his neck rising. Words had been written on the ceiling—Jaden's floor. They were in Basic and underlined, the jagged letters the dried brown of old blood.

Stop looking at us!

Jaden suddenly felt guilty for walking in the footsteps of the doctors. He imagined the clones living in those quarters, day in and day out, the feet of the gods who had made them walking across the ceiling. No privacy, no freedom. Small wonder they had grown so hostile. The thick durasteel walls that encased the clones' area might as well have been bars. Despite what they had done to the others in the complex, Jaden pitied them.

He walked to the nearest console and powered down the lights. The rooms below went dark. He thought they should stay that way.

Somewhere down the lift shaft, a can or metal drum fell, rolled across a hard surface, and rattled itself still.

Startled, Jaden flashed his glow rod around the room. The beam pierced the darkness but illuminated nothing. His fingers warmed as thin tendrils of blue Force lightning snaked from his fingertips and swirled around the glow rod.

He stilled his mind, fell into the Force, and calmed himself. He reminded himself that the clones had been prisoners, victims. He reached out through the Force, feeling for another Force-user nearby, but encountered nothing.

"I am here to help you," he called, his voice echoing around the large chamber, its own version of the distress beacon.

Help you, help you, help you . . .

No response.

He moved to the open doors of the lift, lightsaber at the ready. The control panel had been destroyed. A charnel reek drifted up through the doors, fumes from some forgotten hell. Shielding his nose with his forearm, he beamed his glow rod down the shaft. It descended perhaps thirty meters. The lift compartment sat at the bottom, its interior visible through a large rectangular hole in its top. He guessed that a lightsaber had cut the hole.

He hung over the void for a long while, smelling death, listening to nothing but his own heartbeat. He had to go down. Metal rungs ran the length of the near side of the shaft, but he did not bother with them.

Drawing on the Force, he picked his spot atop the lift compartment, and leapt. The Force cushioned his impact and he hit the top of the lift in a crouch. Without pausing he lowered himself through the hole in the roof and into the lift proper, lightsaber to hand.

The smell of death was stronger. He started to call out again, but thought better of it.

His glow rod lit a long, narrow corridor that sloped downward. The air felt humid, moist with putrescence. Long, thick streaks of dried blood stained the duracrete floor. Jaden followed them as he might a trail of bread crumbs.

They led to a wide stairway that dropped another ten meters. A large metal hatch waited at the bottom of it. He descended sidelong, his back against one wall. A card reader hung from the wall to one side of the door, its wires and circuitry hanging loose like innards.

Twenty or thirty stormtrooper helmets lay on the floor to either side of the door, stacked into a rough pyramid. Some of them still had heads in them, for Jaden could see dead eyes behind some of the lenses.

The scene reminded Jaden of an offering.

Stenciled on the wall over the doorway:

AUTHORIZED PERSONNEL ONLY BEYOND THIS POINT

Across the hatch, written in an enormous, diagonal scrawl of dried blood, were three words. Jaden felt chilled when he read them.

Mother is hungry.

Jaden stared at the hatch a long while, rooted to the last stair. Moving from it seemed a fateful step, a portentous act. Holding his ground, he again reached out through the Force, feeling for the presence of any nearby Force-users.

Making contact almost instantly, he winced at the bitter recoil caused by the touch of a dark sider—but not a pure dark sider. Jaden felt the dark side as though it were adulterated with . . . something else, the same way his own signature was that of a light-side user adulterated with . . . something else.

Sentience curses us with a desire to categorize.

He looked down at his hand as if it were a thing apart from him, a piece of him that had betrayed the rest and thereby corrupted the whole. Tiny streamers of Force lightning curled around the glow rod, twisting like things alive.

The regard of the Force-user on the other side of the hatch fixed on him. The mental touch felt as greasy as the air, just as infected with putrescence.

He descended the step and opened the hatch.

chapter fifteen

THE STINK HIT HIM FIRST, THE REEK OF OLD DECAY. Computer stations lined the walls of the large, rectangular chamber. Blank readout screens dotted the walls here and there. Loose wires hung from everywhere, the entrails of science.

A hole opened in the center of the room, a perfect circle several meters in diameter, like the gullet of some gargantuan beast. Machinery hung from armatures above the hole. Jaden recognized the apparatus immediately—a Spaarti cloning cylinder.

"You have come to pay homage to Mother," said a voice, a dry, rough version of Kam Solusar's voice.

A figure stepped from the darkness on the far side of the chamber. Shaggy white hair—the color of Master Solusar's—hung loose almost to the clone's waist. Most of his features, too, reminded Jaden of Kam—the high forehead, angled cheeks—but not the eyes. The clone's eyes were as dark and lifeless as pools of stagnant water.

"Kam Solusar," Jaden said, the words slipping free before he could stop them.

The clone sneered, and in that expression lost any resemblance to Master Solusar, who so often wore a smile.

"I do not know that name," the clone said. "I am Alpha."

Alpha wore mismatched attire: clothing salvaged

from the facility, bits of stormtrooper armor on both shoulders, the forearms, and the hands, and a rough, handmade cloak fashioned from the hide of some creature that must have lived under the ice in the moon's seas. In the clone's movements, Jaden caught the suggestion of an imposing physicality, controlled savagery. He looked larger than Kam, more *there*.

Jaden cleared his throat, stepped forward. He lowered his lightsaber but did not deactivate it. "I have come here to . . . help you."

The clone held his sneer. "We require no help from you. Only the ship that brought you."

"We?"

"Are you Jedi or Sith?"

Jaden took a half step sideways, as if to avoid the ugly import of the question. He reached the edge of the cloning cylinder and winced when he saw within it.

Bodies lay piled in a grotesque heap, a tangle of decayed limbs, torsos, heads, and tattered clothing—a compost heap of butchery. Empty eye sockets stared up at Jaden. Age-ruined lips showed teeth bared in snarls.

"Beautiful, is it not?" asked the Kamclone. "Mother is where life begins and ends."

The stink caused Jaden's eyes to water. He guessed that almost every person in the facility had ended up inside the cylinder, inside Mother.

Fighting down his disgust, he asked, "How many are you? How many survived?"

"How many of them?" the clone said, and a knowing malice slinked into his dead eyes. "Or us?"

The clone stepped to the edge of Mother and started walking the circumference of the cylinder toward Jaden.

Instinctually, Jaden walked the circumference in the same direction, away from the clone, the two of them pacing the face of a chrono, keeping time under the shadow of the inevitable.

The clone nodded at the cylinder, an insane reverence smoothing his expression. "We return here from time to time to thank Mother for our lives. She can create it from the root of a hair, Dr. Green once told me. You were right, Dr. Green," he said to one of the corpses.

Jaden felt entirely exposed. More of them could appear at any moment. He reached out with the Force. He perceived no one else, but it was possible they could screen their presences.

They continued their circling, the pace quickening. Jaden knew what must come but he delayed it, discontented with the realization that all he had endured, all he had asked others to endure, had resulted in no answers. The clones had showed him nothing. The Kamclone was mad. Perhaps they all were. Perhaps he himself was, too.

"Why do you walk away from me?" the Kamclone said.

"Because it does not have to be this way."

"It does," the clone said, his right hand twitching. "Mother is hungry."

Jaden stopped pacing, and his abrupt stop seemed to take the clone by surprise. "I cannot help you," he said.

"You can," the clone said, also stopping. "And you will. You will give us your ship."

"No."

From under his cloak, the clone drew his lightsaber and activated it. A long, unstable red blade cut the shadows, spitting angry sparks.

The clone's façade ran like candlewax, the heat of his rage melting the calm mask of his expression to reveal the savagery beneath. Eyes narrowed, teeth bared, he snarled . . . and in the sound Jaden heard the violent nature that had slaughtered hundreds of people and thrown their corpses into a cloning pit turned mass grave.

"Mother is hungry!"

Jaden prepared himself, sank into the calm of the Force.

The clone ran one way around the pit and Jaden ran the opposite. They met after fifteen strides, still on Mother's edge, both lightsabers humming. Jaden ducked low under the clone's decapitating cross-stroke and stabbed at his abdomen.

The clone reverse-backflipped, balancing on the pit's edge, then immediately charged Jaden again. He feinted low and unleashed a vicious overhand blow, then another, and another. Jaden parried each one, but the blows began to numb his arms. He let the Force soothe his muscles and augment his strength, and answered with a flurry of blows of his own.

The clone gave no ground, and Jaden could not penetrate his defenses. They crossed blades at the chest, weapons sizzling, the sparks from the clone's blade searing scorch marks into Jaden's suit. The clone grunted, shoved Jaden two meters backward, and lunged after him.

Jaden leapt over his head, flipping, his blade slashing down as he flew over the clone, but the clone parried. Jaden landed on his feet on the edge of the pit and the clone was upon him, forcing his lightsaber high and landing a Force-augmented kick in his chest. Ribs snapped and Jaden staggered backward.

Following up on the opening, the clone leapt forward and cross-cut Jaden at the knees. Jaden leapt over the slash, used an overcut to drive the clone's blade into the deck, where it threw up a shower of sparks. Jaden spun, and angled a reverse-cross-cut for the clone's head.

The clone lurched backward but the tip of Jaden's blade opened a gash in his throat. Staggered, gasping, the clone swung wildly with his lightsaber while unleashing a telekinetic blast against Jaden's chest.

Jaden used the Force to deaden the blow, but his broken ribs ground against one another and he hissed with pain. By now the clone had recovered enough to charge. He attacked high, low, overhand, cross-cuts. Jaden parried them all while backing off. The clone did not relent, pressing Jaden further, faster. Jaden answered where he could but the clone's blade seemed everywhere. Jaden parried left, right, again, again, until he felt a sharp, stinging sensation and both his lightsaber and three fingers went flying off into the darkness.

A side kick from the clone ruined his already broken ribs and sent him down into Mother. He fell amid the corpses, swimming in the gore, feeling as if dead hands were clutching at him. Stinking, wet fluid soaked him. Before he could sit up, the clone leapt into the pit after him and landed on his feet with his legs to either side of Jaden. Jaden could not see the Kamclone's face, could see only the sparking line of his red lightsaber held high for a killing stroke. Jaden focused his mind on the blade as it came down. He threw up an arm, grabbed the clone's wrist, and steered the blade wide.

The clone grunted in frustration, knelt, and grabbed Jaden's throat with his free hand.

"Do not resist. You should be honored to provide sustenance to Mother," he said, and began to squeeze.

Desperate, and still holding the clone's right wrist to keep the sizzling red line of his lightsaber at bay, Jaden used his wounded right hand to claw at the clone's grip, trying to dig his remaining fingers under the clone's and pry loose some space for an inhalation. Failing that, he tried to roll aside, to shift his weight and gain some leverage, or free a leg to kick out, but the clone's Force-augmented strength was greater than Jaden's.

Jaden gagged, tried to shake loose by flailing his head, but failed. His lungs forced him to try to draw air. Unable to pull in oxygen, he saw spots. The clone grunted against Jaden's fading grip, his dark eyes wild, saliva dripping from his gritted teeth.

Jaden's arms were deadwood hanging off his shoulders. As he lost strength, the clone's lightsaber moved closer to his throat. The sparks from the unstable blade struck Jaden's face and arm, pockmarking his skin with tiny scorch marks, igniting little flashes of pain. His heart banged in his ears. He was failing. He was going to die.

The realization summoned something from deep within the dark crevices of his mind where he kept secrets even from himself. Force lightning exploded from his hand, squeezed out by the exigency of his circumstances. The blue lines spiraled around the clone's hand and lightsaber.

The clone gasped with surprise, loosened his grip, disengaged. Jaden gulped a lungful of air while the darkness within him swelled and the outburst of Force lightning intensified. Jaden knew that fear had unlocked the darkest part of himself, knew, too, that he could free that part, surrender to it, and save his body while destroying himself.

But he thought of Kyle, of his training, of Relin, and denied the impulse. The Force lightning died.

The clone recovered, growled, raised his lightsaber high.

Jaden reached behind his back, pulled out the lightsaber he had built in his youth, his ignorant youth, a lightsaber not so different from that held by the clone.

The clone lunged forward.

Jaden activated his lightsaber and drove the point into and through the clone's abdomen.

The clone's roar turned to a groan, but his momentum carried him forward along Jaden's blade, and as death turned his eyes glassy, he completed his overhand stroke.

The sparking red blade cleaved the bodies beside

Jaden and fell from the clone's hand. It lay there, a red line spitting sparks. It had no auto-off, and its energy burned into the corpses and sank part way into the muck. Jaden stared at its red swirl a long time, the dead eyes of the clone fixed on his face all the while.

Finally Jaden thumbed off his lightsaber and the clone's body fell free. He pushed the corpse to the side. Grunting with pain, he bent and picked up the clone's lightsaber, held it beside his own purple blade as best he could with his damaged hand.

Purple and red lines—two lines, two choices.

He deactivated both weapons, slowly stood. Exhaustion made his body shake. Pain turned his vision blurry. He limped to the edge of the cloning cylinder, of Mother.

Desiccated skulls and empty eye sockets bore witness to his passage. Open mouths screamed at him to cast himself in, to join them. The stink made him wince. At least he thought it was the stink.

With effort, grunting with pain, he slowly climbed out of the pit.

When he reached the top, he turned and stared down at the chaotic mass of bodies, all of them twisted together, contorted, as if frozen in a struggle to move over and past one another, or perhaps just pressed into one common mass where struggle no longer mattered. He thought all of it must be a metaphor for something, but his pain- and fatigue-addled mind could not decide for what.

He started to cast the clone's lightsaber back into the mass of flesh at the bottom of the pit, put it to rest beside his own, but decided against it. Instead, he latched it to his belt, turned, and found himself staring into the eyes of an Anzat. Surprise almost caused him to step back and fall again into the pit.

*   *   *

In the silence of the cargo bay, drenched in the power of the Lignan, Relin dwelled on his failures. He had failed Saes, failed Drev, failed the Order. He'd even failed Marr, awakening him to the Force so that his first experience with it was the touch of the Lignan.

Anger turned to rage turned to hate. He welcomed it. The proximity to the Lignan intensified the feelings.

His world zeroed down to three things only—himself, his hate, and the object of his hate, Saes. His life had been nothing more than a series of failures. He intended to end it by rectifying the worst of them—Saes.

The hum of the cargo bay lift penetrated the haze of his emotional state. He stood, lightsaber in hand, Lignan in his being, and waited. He heard the lift doors open, heard the sound of boots on the cargo bay floor, and felt Saes's presence through the Force, the black hole into which Relin had poured his early life. The stacked cargo crates blocked Saes from view, but Relin knew he was there.

Saes's voice carried from somewhere behind the containers. "Your anger pleases me. Your handiwork in the lift would earn admiration even from the most savage of my Massassi. Well done, Master."

The last word struck Relin like a punch in the stomach, and he knew Saes intended it to do exactly that. "I am not your Master."

"No, but you taught me everything I know. Perhaps not the way you intended, but it is to you that I owe my freedom from the slavery of the light side."

Through the Force, Relin tried to pinpoint Saes's location. Augmenting a jump with the power of the Force, he leapt atop one of the storage containers. The vantage gave him a better view of the cargo bay. Above the maze of storage containers, he saw the closed lift doors. But no Saes.

"Show yourself," he said. "Let us finish this."

The overhead lights flickered, dimmed, casting the bay in shadow.

Saes's voice carried from behind him. "Do you know what has happened, Relin? Do you know where we are? *When* we are?"

Relin turned toward the sound of the voice, his body coiled. "I know. It does not matter. Nothing matters now."

"Because your Padawan is dead?"

Rage clenched Relin's jaw so tightly his teeth ached.

Saes chuckled. "Your anger runs deep, not just about your Padawan, but about . . . me."

Relin swallowed the fist that formed in his throat. Words rushed up from deep inside, words he'd never said even to himself—*Your betrayal broke my heart*— but he held them behind the wall of his gritted teeth. He saw now that his descent had begun with the doubt that had rooted in him after Saes had turned to the dark side. His slide had simply been slow but, ultimately, inexorable.

"Come out," he said. "It is time we finished things."

Saes's voice came from Relin's left. "It is not too late. Join me. This is a new time, a new place, ripe for a new beginning."

Relin was already shaking his head.

But Saes continued: "Have you considered that it was never the purpose of the Force that you save me, but that I save you instead? Join me, Relin."

The idea pulled at Relin. He felt rudderless, lost. He could join with Saes—

"If you do not, your Padawan will have died in vain."

And with those words, Saes overstepped. Relin's rage bubbled over into action. He took telekinetic hold of the storage containers near the sound of Saes's voice and slammed two of them together. Metal twisted, crashed;

the doors of the containers broke open from the impact and more Lignan ore spilled out onto the deck.

He slid another container into them, then another. He realized he was shouting, an incoherent roar of rage with its provenance in a life he now deemed wasted. He stopped, his breath coming hard.

"Come out!"

Saes leapt atop a storage container opposite the one on which Relin stood. A sea of Lignan covered the deck between them, dividing them. Shadows played over the ridges on Saes's bone mask. His lightsaber hung from his belt.

"You stink of rage," Saes said. "Where is the calm of the Force of which you so often spoke? The placidity of combat? Or perhaps that was all a lie, as so much you said and believed was?"

Relin let his anger consume his spirit, fill him entirely, and with it he drew on the Force, adding to his strength, his speed.

"Addictive, is it not?" Saes said. "The Lignan, I mean."

With that, Saes raised his hand and blue Force lightning exploded from his fist. Relin did not try to avoid it. Instead, drawing on the Lignan and fueled with hate, he interposed his lightsaber, drew the lightning to it like iron to a magnet, then spun the blade once over his head and flung the dark side energy back at Saes. More Lignan flared on the floor below as Saes drew on it and absorbed his own Force lightning to no visible effect.

Standing in the shadows of the cargo bay, they regarded each other across the deck of Lignan.

"How should we proceed then?" Saes said.

Relin answered by deactivating his lightsaber.

He was no Jedi, not anymore, and would not fight with a Jedi weapon. Besides, only one form of combat could sate his rage. He tossed his lightsaber down into the pile of Lignan ore below him.

Saes took his point, tilted his head in acknowledgment. He detached his curved lightsaber from his belt and tossed it after Relin's. He flexed his clawed fingers, inhaled deeply.

"So be it, then."

Relin shouted and used a Force-enhanced leap to launch himself into the air toward Saes. Answering with a growl, Saes leapt into the air to meet him. They met midway, colliding over the Lignan, both of them filled with the dark side, stronger, faster.

Relin wrapped one arm around Saes, slammed his brow into Saes's face with the other. The bottom half of the bone mask shattered, raining shards down on the Lignan. Saes's lower tooth tore a ragged hole in Relin's forearm before it dislodged and added itself to the mask fragments raining onto the deck.

Saes slashed his claws across Relin's face. Relin used the Force to resist the blow, but it still dug jagged furrows into his forehead and tore into an eye, though he barely felt the pain.

They fell together, twisting, punching, slashing at a speed and with a force that looked blurry even to Relin. They hit the ground in a tangle of punches and kicks. Hate fueled their blows. Blood sprayed, bones cracked, the Lignan flared all around them as each drew on it in turn.

"I hate you for what you did," Saes spat between his fangs.

"I hate me for what I am," Relin said. He rolled away from Saes and from his knees fired a telekinetic blast that drove Saes through the Lignan ore and into a storage container. "But I hate you more."

He took mental hold of an entire storage container—

Lignan ore fell from its open door like droplets of blood—lifted it from the deck, and dropped it on Saes.

Saes caught it in his own mental grasp before it hit. Grunting, Lignan ore flaring to life around him, he threw it back at Relin.

Relin dived aside and the container slammed into another. For the first time, Relin felt the waves of controlled rage radiating from Saes, an anger to match his own. Odd that Relin had never felt it before, in all the time they had spent together as Master and Padawan.

Saes stood and stalked through the Lignan scattered across the floor, the ore flashing as he passed it, consumed by his hate.

"You think rage days old can match mine, nurtured over decades? You think power born of infantile anger can equal mine? I have whet the blade of my hate for years, for this moment!"

He lifted a hand and a concussive wave struck Relin like a sledgehammer, drove him through the Lignan, and slammed him against the storage container. Ribs cracked and his lungs evacuated in a wheeze of pain. Saes continued to close the distance, his eyes dark holes behind the mask, his mouth twisted into a symbol of hate. He held up two fingers and Relin felt Saes's mental grasp close on his throat and begin to squeeze, pinching off his wheezes. Relin answered with a Force choke of his own, but it only slowed Saes for a moment before he resisted it with his own power.

Relin's vision grew blurry. Spots appeared before his eyes. He could not even gasp for breath.

Saes stopped before him, loomed over him, his eyes burning.

Feeding tendrils hung from the Anzat's cheeks, their ends a vicious nail of keratin. For a moment, it seemed as if the Anzat's head floated free in space, detached from any body, but Jaden realized that the creature wore a mimetic suit and had thrown back the mask and hood. The rest of his body simply blended in with the background, even up close.

Wrung out from his battle with the clone, Jaden raised his mental defenses too slowly and the Anzat projected his will into Jaden's mind.

Be still.

The words bounced around in Jaden's mind, found purchase in the ancient reptilian structures in the deepest part of his brain. His higher functions screamed for him to act, to defend himself, but the Anzat's mental projection lodged like a leech on Jaden's brain stem, froze his voluntary muscles and chained his will. He felt as if he might be dreaming, his mind in the grip of a nightmare, his body too paralyzed to react.

The Anzat's eyes flashed, the nostrils on his slightly upturned nose flared. He leaned in close, his face only a centimeter from Jaden's, but not quite touching, as if denying himself for a moment some treat he'd longed for. The Anzat's eyes impaled Jaden. He fought against the Anzat's hold on his mind, trying to dislodge the mind leech, but his mind, depleted from the battle with the clone, could not get free.

The Anzat sensed his failed struggle and smiled.

"I am Kell Douro," the Anzat said, his voice thick with an accent that Jaden could not place. "You are my salvation, Jaden Korr."

The Anzat took Jaden by the shoulders and the cables of the alien's appendages burrowed into Jaden's nostrils, the sharp point of the tip slashing sensitive tissues. Pain exploded in his mind, setting off a spark shower of agony before his eyes, but he could not move.

Kell inhaled deeply as he drove his feeders into the blood-slickened tunnels of Jaden's nostrils. He shuddered each time they pierced a membrane or slashed tissue. The lines of their *daen nosi* swirled around them, their motion rapid, chaotic, a reflection of Kell's own excitement. They became so tangled he had trouble distinguishing the silver of his own lines from the red and green that denoted Jaden's potential futures. His legs weakened at the thought of consuming the Jedi's soup, of understanding at last, after centuries of seeking, the map of the universe and his purpose in it.

He watched his lines enmesh Jaden's, strangle them, wipe out whatever future the Jedi might have had. His feeders pierced a membrane and squirmed for the Jedi's brain, his soup. Jaden's body shuddered.

Kell stared at the *daen nosi,* expecting to see Jaden's green and red end, overcome by the silver net of Kell's future.

Instead he saw Jaden's lines endure, saw his own lines knotted off and consumed by the dull gray strands of another. The three sets of lines resolved into a noticeable pattern. Behind the pattern, within the pattern, Kell saw the meaning of life, his purpose.

A blaster barrel pressed up against his temple. He felt it only distantly, thickly.

"Thank you," he said.

At first Jaden did not think he was seeing clearly, thought, perhaps, that his mind had retreated into dreams while he died. He saw Khedryn materialize beside the Anzat. Blood dripped from Khedryn's shattered nose, and his eyes were so swollen Jaden was surprised he could see at all. He held the BlasTech E-11 in his hands, the blaster they had seen in the armory off the barracks. He had its barrel pressed against the Anzat's head.

The Anzat's feeders started to retract from Jaden's nose.

"Thank you?" Khedryn said, stress raising his voice an octave higher than usual. "Frag you."

He squeezed the trigger and turned the Anzat's head into a fine red mist. The Anzat's body fell to the floor, blood pouring from the neck stump. The feeder appendages, severed from the nearly vaporized head, still dangled from Jaden's nose. Jaden sagged, wobbled. Khedryn steadied him.

"Are you all right? Jaden?"

Khedryn's voice sounded from far away. But it was drawing closer and Jaden was returning to himself.

"I am all right," he said to Khedryn. "Thank you."

Khedryn smiled. "That is a thank-you I'll accept."

Wincing, Jaden jerked the feeders out of his nose and dropped them on the Anzat's body. Nausea seized him and he vomited onto the floor. Khedryn put a hand on his shoulder and nodded at the Anzat's corpse.

"That thing got to me before it got you. What is it?"

Jaden wiped his mouth with the back of his hand and straightened on shaky legs.

"An Anzat. I think he followed us from Fhost, but I'm not sure."

"You sure you're all right?"

Jaden took in the ruin of Khedryn's face.

"I should be asking that of you."

Khedryn took Jaden's arm and helped support him. "I've been beaten worse than this, Jedi." He looked down into Mother, at the slain clone and the grizzly contents of her gullet.

"What happened here? Are those the doctors and stormies? Stang."

"Yes," Jaden said, and deliberately did not look into Mother. "I'll explain the rest on the way out. We must hurry. There are more surviving clones, Khedryn. They want a ship and we cannot allow that. We need to get back to *Flotsam*. Now."

Khedryn cleared his throat, spit blood and phlegm onto the floor. "If they take my ship anywhere, I will hunt them across the 'verse."

"Yes," Jaden said, and activated his purple-bladed saber. He could barely hold it in his wounded hand. "We will."

"Where did you get that lightsaber?" Khedryn asked.

"Long story."

Together they hurried back through the facility, both holding weapons built decades earlier—Khedryn a stormtrooper-issued blaster, Jaden a lightsaber he'd built as a boy. They retraced their steps past one scene of slaughter to another. The facility seemed less ominous to Jaden now, but it still felt haunted by ghosts.

Jaden told Khedryn what he'd learned from the clone: that other clones had survived on the moon for decades, that they wanted desperately to get off, that they were mad and dangerous.

"Did they have any children?"

Khedryn's question slowed Jaden's steps. He had not considered that. "I . . . don't know."

By the time they neared the West Entry, Jaden had recovered some of his strength. He did not have the time or capacity to interpret all he'd learned—about the facility and himself—but he would, later.

"Did you get the answer you wanted?" Khedryn asked as he pulled up his helmet and sealed the neck ring.

"I don't know," Jaden admitted. He deactivated his lightsaber and started to pull up his helmet, realized that his suit was so damaged from combat with the clone that sealing it was pointless.

Seeing that, Khedryn said, "You will be cold."

"I'll abide," Jaden said.

*   *   *

Relin was going to die, was going to add another failure to the long line of failures that composed his life as a Jedi. The rage went out of him as if drained through a hole in his heel. Despair replaced it, black and empty.

Saes held out a hand, and his lightsaber flew from the deck to his palm. He ignited it. In its hum, Relin heard his death pronounced.

"You understand now, at the end," Saes said. He removed the remains of his mask and regarded Relin with yellow eyes that looked almost sympathetic. "That pleases me."

Relin dwelled in the bottomless void of his despondence. And in the void, in its endlessness, he saw his purpose fulfilled.

He drew on the Lignan, fed its power into the hole at his core. The emptiness in him was insatiable, drinking the power as fast as he could pull it in, yet never getting filled.

His body and mind swelled with the influx. The ore dotting the deck flared in answer to his desires. Sneering, Saes drew on the Lignan himself.

Relin gripped Saes's throat in his mental grasp. Saes tried to swat away the Force choke with his own power. His eyes widened when he realized he could not. He gasped, staggered. Relin sat up, thought of Drev, and squeezed.

Saes stumbled forward, lightsaber held high. Filled with power, Relin used the Force to pull Saes's lightsaber from his fist. It leapt through the air and landed in Relin's hand. He rose to his knees and Saes fell to his before Relin, still clutching his throat.

Relin had nothing more to say to his former Padawan. He drove Saes's own lightsaber into and through his chest. Saes fell face-first to the deck without a sound.

Relin stared at the red lightsaber blade in his hand. He had resolved that he would not fight with a Jedi weapon and he had not. He had fought with a Sith weapon and it had been appropriate.

His body felt charged, so filled with the dark side of the Force that he no longer felt human. He had transcended. He sagged to the floor among the flaring ore. The metal of the deck felt cold under him. Blood poured out of his face, his nose. Chunks of Lignan dug into his flesh. With Saes dead, he suddenly felt his injuries, and agony accompanied each breath.

But the pain of his body paled in comparison with the pain of his spirit.

He shouted, trying to purge the pain and despair in a wail that shook the crossbeams of the cargo bay. But both were infinite. He could have shouted for eternity and found no relief.

Still, he refused to fail again.

Saes had called his rage *days old,* but it was more than that. It was a conflagration, the sum total of all the repressed emotion of Relin's life compressed into a tiny singularity of self-consuming anger and despair from which nothing could escape, not even him.

And that, he realized, was the unspoken, unacknowledged pith of the dark side—it consumed all who turned to it. Yet he did not turn away. He wanted nothing more than to be consumed, to be reduced to oblivion, annihilated. He welcomed it.

But he would not go alone.

He continued to draw in the power of the Lignan, to feed it into the hole he had become, to let it amplify his hate and despair even as he died. Power burned in him. He was vaguely conscious of the remaining crystals around him flaring, a brief flash of life before he consumed their power and turned them dull and dead.

Unbound by concern for his continuing survival, he took in as much energy as he could control. Spirals of energy formed around his body. He felt his torso growing lighter, the flesh becoming diaphanous, transformed by power to become one with the energy.

Barely able to feel his own flesh, he nevertheless reached out for his dead Padawan. His fingers closed over Saes's forearm and slid along until he held his former Padawan's hand.

Tears flowed as energy gathered, turned on itself, grew stronger. Coils of blue power, like long lines of Force lightning, shot out from his flesh, roiled in the air above him, striking the ceiling and the storage containers, penetrating the ship.

He drew in more power, more, until the entire cargo bay was lit with a network of twisting, jagged lines of energy, a circulatory system through which flowed his rage. The lines spread from the cargo bay and through the ship like veins, like an enormous garrote that would strangle *Harbinger* to death. Relin's mind became one with them. Power and hate pulsed along them with each beat of his heart. They were an extension of him and he felt them as they squirmed through the ship, wrapping it in their net, from the rear section, along the spin, to the forward section with the black scar of Drev's grave gouged into its face.

He was ready, then.

He knew he was lost, and yet he was found.

"Laugh even when you die," he whispered.

He squeezed Saes's cold, scaled hand, imagined Drev's face, and laughed for joy as the power crescendoed and began to consume *Harbinger* in fire.

Marr perceived a light through his eyelids. He struggled to open them but they felt as if they weighed a kilo. Finally able to pry them open, he winced against the glare blazing through *Junker*'s cockpit viewport.

Harbinger fell into the moon's thin atmosphere and skidded along, an ever-lengthening spear of flame in its wake. Bleary-eyed, he saw fire consume the entire ship until the massive vessel exploded in a cloud of smoke and flame.

Relin had done it, he realized, but he felt no elation.

There is nothing certain.

The autopilot was flying *Junker* straight into the aftermath of the explosion but Marr did not trust himself enough to change the ship's course. He needed to reach the surface and hope that Jaden and Khedryn would see him and help him.

He was dying, he knew. Already the pain in his back was diminishing—not a good sign—and he felt a creeping cold enshrouding his body.

He tried to reach for the emergency distress beacon, thinking he would activate it and that matters would end as they had begun, with the beep of someone in distress.

But he could not reach it. His body no longer answered his commands.

Pain and blood loss drew him back into darkness.

Jaden and Khedryn stepped through the hatch and into the blowing snow and ice. Jaden welcomed the elements, the freezing air, and the pain. He inhaled deeply, hoping to cleanse his lungs of any residuum of Mother or the facility. Khedryn pointed ahead.

"*Flotsam* is still there." His voice sounded metallic through his helmet's external mike.

Jaden saw. Shields still secured the ship's viewports. The clones had not gotten in, which meant they had not gotten off the moon . . . yet.

"The Anzat had a ship."

"Right," Khedryn said, and started trudging through the snow. "Let's get aboard *Flotsam* and get into the air. We can find it that way."

They had not taken five strides before a ship streaked

into view, flying low, its engines a barely audible hum over the wind. Jaden recognized the silhouette immediately from the low profile and wide wings—a Cloak-Shape fighter, modified with a hyperspace sled and coated in the black fiberplast typical of a StealthX. It would have been almost invisible against a field of stars. In atmosphere, it looked like a piece of outer space had descended planetside.

Jaden knew that it was too late to seek cover. Khedryn must have realized the same thing. He took station beside Jaden, freed the shoulder stock on the E-11, and aimed it at the ship's cockpit. Jaden activated his lightsaber and held his ground. The weapon's hilt was unsteady in his two-fingered grasp. He switched to his left hand, where it felt awkward, but at least he could hold it.

The CloakShape slowed, maneuvered over them, and hovered at maybe ten meters. The energy from the engines warmed the air. The barrels of the laser cannons looked like tunnels that went on forever. Jaden and Khedryn stood still on the frozen ground, cloaked in the fighter's faint shadow. The ship dipped its nose so that the cockpit had a clear view of them and they of it. The transparisteel was dimmed so that they could not see within. Jaden reached out with the Force—even that small effort tried him, after all he'd been through—and felt the Force presences of ten beings.

"They do have children aboard," he said. "Or there were more clones than we thought."

Khedryn lowered his blaster, a symbolic gesture only. The blaster could not have penetrated the CloakShape's hide.

"Maybe they don't know who we are or what . . . happened."

Jaden shook his head, his eyes fixed on the cockpit. "No. They know I killed one of them. The holo-log said they had an empathic connection, maybe even a tele-pathic one. They know."

"Stang," Khedryn murmured.

For a time they stood there, staring up at the unseen crew through the swirl. Finally Jaden shouted up at the cockpit.

"If you leave I will have to come after you."

He gave that a moment to register and still received no response. He deactivated his saber, turned away from the fighter, and walked through the cold and snow for *Flotsam*.

"Let's go, Khedryn."

"Go?" Khedryn said, and hurried after him, looking back over his shoulder at the fighter.

"We are either dead or we're not. Their choice."

Khedryn fell in beside him, partially hunched as though in anticipation of a blow.

Jaden did not flinch—though Khedryn did—when a shriek tore through the sky, not the cannons on the CloakShape fighter, but the wail of engines failing, of su-perstructure collapsing.

Jaden turned, already flashing back to his vision, and looked up to see the sky on fire. An enormous ship—it could only be *Harbinger*—streaked across the upper at-mosphere, leaving a fat line of fire kilometers long.

"Stang," Khedryn said in a hush.

With the suddenness of a blaster shot, the cruiser ex-ploded, the fireball starting in the rear engine section and racing forward along the length of the ship until the entire vessel vaporized into a billion-billion tiny, glow-ing particles that lit the sky like pyrotechnics.

Jaden watched, not breathing, as they started to fall to the surface, a rain of evil. He lived alternately in the pre-sent and the memory of his vision. He felt the oily touch of the Lignan, the familiar nudge in his very being impelling him to darkness. The feeling did not elicit in him the horror he remembered from his vision and he wondered what that meant. He resisted the pull—his will, his ability to choose, was something internal, unconstrained by the external.

The CloakShape fighter's engines fired and Khedryn and Jaden watched it accelerate skyward, its form a black silhouette against the still-glowing sky.

"It is heading right into the debris," Khedryn said. "What are they doing?"

Jaden understood exactly what they were doing. They were taking in the Lignan's power.

"I will have to come after you," he said again, more softly, unsure how he felt about the words.

Another boom sounded far above them, not an explosion but a sonic boom, a ship entering or leaving atmosphere. At first Jaden assumed it was the CloakShape exiting the moon's atmosphere, but instead he saw a familiar disk cutting its way through the sky, falling out of the ruin of *Harbinger*'s death. *Junker* looked wounded, incomplete without *Flotsam* attached to its fittings and Khedryn in its cockpit.

Jaden imagined it passing the CloakShape fighter and its crew of dark side clones on its way down, imagined paths crossing, lines meeting at angles, currents intersecting. He thought of Relin and felt profound sadness. He knew the ancient Jedi would not be aboard *Junker*.

"That is *Junker*!" Khedryn said. He took Jaden by the shoulder, shook him with joy. Jaden winced from the pain but could not stop smiling himself.

With the ship so close, Khedryn tried to raise Marr on his suit's comlink. No response.

"Look at the way she's flying," Khedryn said, joy giving way to concern in his tone. "She's on autopilot."

Jaden reached out with the Force, felt Marr's faint Force presence, felt, too, that the Cerean was near death.

"Let's move," he said, and they ran for *Junker* as it started to set down.

K HEDRYN'S VOICE EXPLODED OVER THE COMLINK. "He's awake!"

Jaden jumped up from the table in the galley, spilling caf, and hurried to the makeshift medical bay aboard *Junker*. Khedryn had converted one of the passenger berths off the galley into a rudimentary treatment room. Transparent storage lockers held a disorganized array of gauze, scissors, stim-shots, antibiotics, bacta, synthflesh, and any number of other miscellaneous medical supplies and devices. Jaden had to credit him for thoroughness if not orderliness. Khedryn and Marr had already seen to their wounds as best they could. They could get better treatment when they returned to Fhost.

Marr lay in the rack, a white sheet covering him to the chest. He blinked in the lights, trying to shake the film from his eyes. Khedryn held his hand the way a father might a son's.

"Jaden," Marr said, and grinned through his pain. Jaden had never been so pleased to see a chipped tooth and could not contain a grin of his own.

"It is nice to see your eyes open, Marr. Things were touch-and-go for a while. You'd lost a lot of blood."

Marr looked away and spoke softly. "My eyes *are* opened."

Jaden did not know how to respond, so he filled the

moment with a question for which he already knew the answer.

"Relin did not get off *Harbinger*?"

Marr shook his head, still looking away. "He never intended to."

"No," Jaden said. "He didn't."

Jaden saw in Relin his own fate. A slow drift toward the dark side. He had never gotten an answer to his questions. He remained as adrift as he had before receiving his Force vision. He wondered at the purpose of it all.

Wireless pads attached to Marr's body fed information to the biomonitoring station beside his bed. Jaden eyed the readout. Khedryn followed his eyes.

"Not bad, eh?" Khedryn said, smiling. Deep purple colored the skin under his eyes. His broken nose looked more askew than his multidirected eyes. A flexcast secured his shattered wrist, though he'd need surgery when they reached Fhost. "Tough as ten-year-old bantha hide, this one."

Marr smiled. Blood loss had left him as pale as morning mist. Jaden sat next to the bed, looking on two men who had shed blood for his cause.

"That nose looks bad," he said to Khedryn.

Khedryn nodded. "I thought I'd wear it this way for a while. Goes with my eyes. But maybe it's a bit much. What do you think, Marr?"

"Keep it as is," Marr said. "Then I won't have to worry about you spilling secrets to dancing girls."

"Good point. Fix it I will. As soon as we get back to Fhost. The nose and the wrist."

"How did you break it?" Marr asked Khedryn.

Khedryn swallowed, put a finger to the side of his nose. "Long story, my friend. I will tell you the whole thing over our third round of keela back in The Hole."

"We found the bodies on *Junker*," Jaden said.

"Massassi," Marr said. "That's what Relin called them."

Jaden knew the name, though he had never thought to see one in the flesh. "What happened on that ship, Marr? They looked to have died from decompression."

"Long story, my friend," Marr said. "I will tell you everything over our *fourth* round of keela. Good enough?"

"Good enough," Jaden agreed.

"You're buying, Jedi," Khedryn said.

"I am, indeed."

Silence descended, cloaked the room. Only the rhythmic beep of the monitoring station broke the silence. Jaden knew he had to report back to the Order, tell Grand Master Skywalker of the cloning facility, the escaped clones, the Lignan and what it could do, but for the moment he simply wanted to enjoy the company of the two men who had bled with him.

"What's next for you, Jedi?" Khedryn asked. "You're welcome to fly with us for a time."

Marr nodded agreement.

Jaden was touched by the offer. "Thank you, both. But I'm not sure that will work well. As soon as possible, I will report back to the Order via subspace. Then I'll have to track down the clones."

"Clones?" Marr asked. He started to sit up, hissed with pain, lay back down.

"Like Khedryn said," Jaden said. "Long story."

Khedryn ran a palm along his whiskers. "No reason we can't help with that, Jaden. Few know the Unknown Regions as well as us."

"What?" Jaden and Marr asked as one.

"You heard me," Khedryn said. "Man can't salvage his whole life, right?"

"There's no pay in it, Khedryn," Jaden said, and immediately wished he had not.

Khedryn winced as if slapped. "I am not a mercenary, Jedi. I just try to get by. But I value my friends."

Jaden noted the plural. "I do, too. Hunting those clones will be dangerous work."

"Yeah," Khedryn said, and stared off into space.

"How about some caf?" Marr said to Khedryn, lightening the mood.

"Sure," Khedryn said. "Jaden?"

"Please."

Khedryn patted Marr's arm, rose, and left the room. The moment he exited, Marr spoke.

"Relin taught me how to use the Force."

Jaden was not surprised. "I wish he had not."

Marr's brow furrowed. "Why?"

"Knowledge can be painful, Marr. It just raises questions."

Marr looked away, his eyes troubled, as if remembering a past pain. "Yes. But what is done is done. I am not sorry he taught me."

"Then I take back my words. I am not sorry, either."

Marr studied Jaden's face for a moment. "Will you teach me more?"

The question took Jaden aback. "Marr, as I explained—"

Marr nodded. "Yes, my age. The narrow focus of my sensitivity. I understand all of that. But still I ask."

Jaden heard the earnestness in Marr's question. "I will confer with the Order."

"I can ask nothing more. Thank you."

Khedryn's shout carried from the galley. "A spike of pulkay?"

Marr nodded at Jaden, and Jaden shouted back to Khedryn.

"Yes. For both of us."

"I knew I liked you, Jedi," Khedryn called, and Jaden smiled.

"Relin asked me to tell you something," Marr said.

Marr's tone made Jaden feel like an ax was about to fall. "Say it."

Marr closed his eyes, as if replaying the encounter in his mind. "He said that there is nothing certain, that there's only the search for certainty, that there's danger only when you think the search is over." Marr paused, added, "He said you would know what he meant."

Jaden digested the words, his mind spinning.

"Do you know what he meant?" Marr asked.

"He thinks—thought—that doubt keeps us sharp. That we should not consider its presence a failure."

Marr chewed his lip. "I saw what happened to him, Jaden. I think he was wrong."

Jaden had seen what happened to him, too, and thought he might be right. And as his thoughts turned, Marr's observation became the gravity well around which the planets of recent events orbited, aligned, and took on meaning. In a flash of insight Jaden surmised that events had not been designed to rid him of doubt; they had been designed for him to embrace his doubt. Perhaps it was different for other Jedi, but for Jaden doubt was the balancing pole that kept him atop the sword-edge. For him, there was no dark side or light side. There were beings of darkness and beings of light.

He smiled, thinking he had found his answer, after all. He looked at Marr, seeing in Marr so much of himself when Kyle Katarn had agreed to take Jaden as Padawan.

"I will teach you more about the Force, Marr."

Marr sat up on an elbow. "You will?"

Jaden nodded, thinking of Kyle. Had his Master known that breaking down certainty was the only thing that might save Jaden from darkness in the long run? He suspected Kyle had known exactly that.

"You may come to wish you'd never learned from me."

Khedryn walked in, cursing, hot caf splashing over the rims of the cups. He distributed the caf, took a long sip, sighed with satisfaction.

"This is the life, gentlemen," he said to Jaden and Marr. "An open sky filled with opportunities for rascals."

Jaden chuckled, looked out the viewport, and grew serious. "There be dragons."

"What does that mean?" Marr asked.

"We will see," Jaden answered, and drank his caf.

Read on for an excerpt from
Star Wars®: Fate of the Jedi: Outcast
By Aaron Allston
Published by Del Rey Books

ONE BY ONE, THE STARS OVERHEAD BEGAN TO DISAP-
pear, swallowed by some enormous darkness inter-
posing itself from above and behind the shuttle.
Sharply pointed at its most forward position, broad-
ening behind, the flood of blackness advanced, blotting out more and more of the unblinking starfield,
until darkness was all there was to see.

Then, all across the length and breadth of the ominous shape, lights came on—blue and white running
lights, tiny red hatch and security lights, sudden
glows from within transparisteel viewports, one large
rectangular whiteness limned by atmosphere shields.
The lights showed the vast triangle to be the underside of an Imperial Star Destroyer, painted black, for-
bidding a moment ago, now comparatively cheerful
in its proper running configuration. It was the *Gilad
Pellaeon*, newly arrived from the Imperial Remnant,
and its officers clearly knew how to put on a show.

Jaina Solo, sitting with the others in the dimly lit
passenger compartment of the government VIP shut-

tle, watched the entire display through the overhead transparisteel canopy and laughed out loud.

The Bothan in the sumptuously padded chair next to hers gave her a curious look. His mottled red and tan fur twitched, either from suppressed irritation or embarrassment at Jaina's outburst. "What do you find so amusing?"

"Oh, both the obviousness of it and the skill with which it was performed. It's so very, *You used to think of us as dark and scary, but now we're just your stylish allies.*" Jaina lowered her voice so that her next comment would not carry to the passengers in the seats behind. "The press will love it. That image will play on the holonews broadcasts constantly. Mark my words."

"Was that little show a Jagged Fel detail?"

Jaina tilted her head, considering. "I don't know. He could have come up with it, but he usually doesn't spend his time planning displays or events. When he does, though, they're usually pretty . . . effective."

The shuttle rose toward the *Gilad Pellaeon*'s main landing bay. In moments, it was through the square atmosphere barrier shield and drifting sideways to land on the deck nearby. The landing place was clearly marked—hundreds of beings, most wearing gray Imperial uniforms or the distinctive white armor of the Imperial stormtrooper, waited in the bay, and the one circular spot where none stood was just the right size for the Galactic Alliance shuttle.

The passengers rose as the shuttle settled into place. The Bothan smoothed his tunic, a cheerful blue decorated with a golden sliver pattern suggesting claws. "Time to go to work. You won't let me get killed, will you?"

Jaina let her eyes widen. "Is that what I was supposed to be doing here?" she asked in droll tones. "I should have brought my lightsaber."

The Bothan offered a long-suffering sigh and turned toward the exit.

They descended the shuttle's boarding ramp. With no duties required of her other than to keep alert and be the Jedi face at this preliminary meeting, Jaina was able to stand back and observe. She was struck with the unreality of it all. The niece and daughter of three of the most famous enemies of the Empire during the First Galactic Civil War of a few decades earlier, she was now witness to events that might bring the Galactic Empire—or Imperial Remnant, as it was called everywhere outside its own borders—into the Galactic Alliance on a lasting basis.

And at the center of the plan was the man, flanked by Imperial officers, who now approached the Bothan. Slightly under average size, though towering well above Jaina's diminutive height, he was dark-haired, with a trim beard and mustache that gave him a rakish look, and was handsome in a way that became more pronounced when he glowered. A scar on his forehead ran up into his hairline and seemed to continue as a lock of white hair from that point. He wore expensive but subdued black civilian garments, neck-to-toe, that would be inconspicuous anywhere on Coruscant but stood out in sharp relief to the gray and white uniforms, white armor, and colorful Alliance clothes surrounding him.

He had one moment to glance at Jaina. The look probably appeared neutral to onlookers, but for her it carried just a twinkle of humor, a touch of exasperation that the two of them had to put up with all these delays. Then an Alliance functionary, notable for his blandness, made introductions: "Imperial Head of State the most honorable Jagged Fel, may I present Senator Tiurrg Drey'lye of Bothawui, head of the Senate Unification Preparations Committee."

Jagged Fel took the Senator's hand. "I'm pleased to be working with you."

"And delighted to meet you. Chief of State Daala sends her compliments and looks forward to meeting you when you make planetfall."

Jag nodded. "And now, I believe, protocol insists that we open a bottle or a dozen of wine and make some preliminary discussion of security, introduction protocols, and so on."

"Fortunately about the wine, and regrettably about everything else, you are correct."

At the end of two full standard hours—Jaina knew from regular, surreptitious consultations of her chrono—Jag was able to convince the Senator and his retinue to accept a tour of the *Gilad Pellaeon*. He was also able to request a private consultation with the sole representative of the Jedi Order present. Moments later, the gray-walled conference room was empty of everyone but Jag and Jaina.

Jag glanced toward the door. "Security seal, access limited to Jagged Fel and Jedi Jaina Solo, voice identification, activate." The door hissed in response as it sealed. Then Jag returned his attention to Jaina.

She let an expression of anger and accusation cross her face. "You're not fooling anyone, Fel. You're planning for an Imperial invasion of Alliance space."

Jag nodded. "I've been planning it for quite a while. Come here."

She moved to him, settled into his lap, and was suddenly but not unexpectedly caught in his embrace. They kissed urgently, hungrily.

Finally Jaina drew back and smiled at him. "This isn't going to be a routine part of your consultations with every Jedi."

"Uh, no. That would cause some trouble here and at home. But I actually do have business with the Jedi that does not involve the Galactic Alliance, at least not initially."

"What sort of business?"

"Whether or not the Galactic Empire joins with the Galactic Alliance, I think there ought to be an official Jedi presence in the Empire. A second Temple, a branch, an offshoot, whatever. Providing advice and insight to the Head of State."

"And protection?"

He shrugged. "Less of an issue. I'm doing all right. Two years in this position and not dead yet."

"Emperor Palpatine went nearly twenty-five years."

"I guess that makes him my hero."

Jaina snorted. "Don't even say that in jest . . . Jag, if the Remnant doesn't join the Alliance, I'm not sure the Jedi can have a presence without Alliance approval."

"The Order still keeps its training facility for youngsters in Hapan space. And the Hapans haven't rejoined."

"You sound annoyed. The Hapans still giving you trouble?"

"Let's not talk about *that*."

"Besides, moving the school back to Alliance space is just a matter of time, logistics, and finances; there's no question that it will happen. On the other hand, it's very likely that the government would withhold approval for a Jedi branch in the Remnant, just out of spite, if the Remnant doesn't join."

"Well, there's such a thing as an unofficial presence. And there's such a thing as rival schools, schismatic branches, and places for former Jedi to go when they can't be at the Temple."

Jaina smiled again, but now there was suspicion in her expression. "You just want to have this so *I'll* be assigned to come to the Remnant and set it up."

"That's a motive, but not the only one. Remember, to the Moffs and to a lot of the Imperial population, the Jedi have been bogeymen since Palpatine died. At the very least, I don't want them to be inappropriately afraid of the woman I'm in love with."

Jaina was silent for a moment. "Have we talked enough politics?"

"I think so."

"Good."

HORN FAMILY QUARTERS, KALLAD'S DREAM VACATION HOSTEL, CORUSCANT

Yawning, hair tousled, clad in a blue dressing robe, Valin Horn knew that he did not look anything like an experienced Jedi Knight. He looked like an unshaven, unkempt bachelor, which he also was. But here, in these rented quarters, there would be only family to see him—at least until he had breakfast, shaved, and dressed.

The Horns did not live here, of course. His mother, Mirax, was the anchor for the immediate family. Manager of a variety of interlinked businesses—trading, interplanetary finances, gambling and recreation, and, if rumors were true, still a little smuggling here and there—she maintained her home and business address on Corellia. Corran, her husband and Valin's father, was a Jedi Master, much of his life spent on missions away from the family, but his true home was where his heart resided, wherever Mirax lived. Valin and his sister, Jysella, also Jedi, lived wherever their missions sent them, and also counted Mirax as the center of the family.

Now Mirax had rented temporary quarters on

Coruscant so the family could collect on one of its rare occasions, this time for the Unification Summit, where she and Corran would separately give depositions on the relationships among the Confederation states, the Imperial Remnant, and the Galactic Alliance as they related to trade and Jedi activities. Mirax had insisted that Valin and Jysella leave their Temple quarters and stay with their parents while these events were taking place, and few forces in the galaxy could stand before her decision—Luke Skywalker certainly knew better than to try.

Moving from the refresher toward the kitchen and dining nook, Valin brushed a lock of brown hair out of his eyes and grinned. Much as he might put up a public show of protest—the independent young man who did not need parents to direct his actions or tell him where to sleep—he hardly minded. It was good to see family. And both Corran and Mirax were better cooks than the ones at the Jedi Temple.

There was no sound of conversation from the kitchen, but there was some clattering of pans, so at least one of his parents must still be on hand. As he stepped from the hallway into the dining nook, Valin saw that it was his mother, her back to him as she worked at the stove. He pulled a chair from the table and sat. "Good morning."

"A joke, so early?" Mirax did not turn to face him, but her tone was cheerful. "No morning is good. I come light-years from Corellia to be with my family, and what happens? I have to keep Jedi hours to see them. Don't you know that I'm an executive? And a lazy one?"

"I forgot." Valin took a deep breath, sampling the smells of breakfast. His mother was making hotcakes Corellian-style, nerf sausage links on the side, and caf was brewing. For a moment, Valin was transported back to his childhood, to the family breakfasts that had been somewhat more common before the Yuuzhan Vong came, before Valin and Jysella had started down the Jedi path. "Where are Dad and Sella?"

"Your father is out getting some back-door information from other Jedi Masters for his deposition." Mirax pulled a plate from a cabinet and began sliding hotcakes and links onto it. "Your sister left early and wouldn't say what she was doing, which I assume either means it's Jedi business I can't know about or that she's seeing some man she doesn't *want* me to know about."

"Or both."

"Or both." Mirax turned and moved over to put the plate down before him. She set utensils beside it.

The plate was heaped high with food, and Valin recoiled from it in mock horror. "Stang, Mom, you're feeding your son, not a squadron of Gamorreans." Then he caught sight of his mother's face and he was suddenly no longer in a joking mood.

This wasn't his mother.

Oh, the woman had Mirax's features. She had the round face that admirers had called "cute" far more often than "beautiful," much to Mirax's chagrin. She had Mirax's generous, curving lips that smiled so readily and expressively, and Mirax's bright, lively brown eyes. She had Mirax's hair, a glossy black with flecks of gray, worn shoulder-length to fit readily under a pilot's helmet, even though she piloted far less often these days. She was Mirax to every freckle and dimple.

But she was not Mirax.

The woman, whoever she was, caught sight of Valin's confusion. "Something wrong?"

"Uh, no." Stunned, Valin looked down at his plate.

He had to think—logically, correctly, and fast. He might be in grave danger right now, though the Force currently gave him no indication of imminent attack. The true Mirax, wherever she was, might be in serious trouble or worse. Valin tried in vain to slow his heart rate and speed up his thinking processes.

Fact: Mirax had been here but had been replaced by an imposter. Presumably the real Mirax was gone; Valin could not sense anyone but himself and the imposter in the immediate vicinity. The imposter had remained behind for some reason that had to relate to Valin, Jysella, or Corran. It couldn't have been to capture Valin, as she could have done that with drugs or other methods while he slept, so the food was probably not drugged.

Under Not-Mirax's concerned gaze, he took a tentative bite of sausage and turned a reassuring smile he didn't feel toward her.

Fact: Creating an imposter this perfect must have

taken a fortune in money, an incredible amount of research, and a volunteer willing to let her features be permanently carved into the likeness of another's. Or perhaps this was a clone, raised and trained for the purpose of simulating Mirax. Or maybe she was a droid, one of the very expensive, very rare human replica droids. Or maybe a shape-shifter. Whichever, the simulation was nearly perfect. Valin hadn't recognized the deception until . . .

Until *what?* What had tipped him off? He took another bite, not registering the sausage's taste or temperature, and maintained the face-hurting smile as he tried to recall the detail that had alerted him that this wasn't his mother.

He couldn't figure it out. It was just an instant realization, too fleeting to remember, too overwhelming to reject.

Would Corran be able to see through the deception? Would Jysella? Surely, they had to be able to. But what if they couldn't? Valin would accuse this woman and be thought insane.

Were Corran and Jysella even still at liberty? Still alive? At this moment, the Not-Mirax's colleagues could be spiriting the two of them away with the true Mirax. Or Corran and Jysella could be lying, bleeding, at the bottom of an access shaft, their lives draining away.

Valin couldn't think straight. The situation was too overwhelming, the mystery too deep, and the only person here who knew the answers was the one who wore the face of his mother.

He stood, sending his chair clattering backward, and fixed the false Mirax with a hard look. "Just a moment." He dashed to his room.

His lightsaber was still where he'd left it, on the nightstand beside his bed. He snatched it up and gave it a near-instantaneous examination. Battery power was still optimal; there was no sign that it had been tampered with.

He returned to the dining room with the weapon in his hand. Not-Mirax, clearly confused and beginning to look a little alarmed, stood by the stove, staring at him.

Valin ignited the lightsaber, its snap-hiss of activation startlingly loud, and held the point of the gleaming energy blade against the food on his plate. Hotcakes shriveled and blackened from contact with the weapon's plasma. Valin gave Not-Mirax an approving nod. "Flesh does the same thing under the same conditions, you know."

"Valin, what's *wrong?*"

"You may address me as Jedi Horn. You don't have the right to use my personal name." Valin swung the lightsaber around in a practice form, allowing the blade to come within a few centimeters of the glow rod fixture overhead, the wall, the dining table, and the woman with his mother's face. "You probably know from your research that the Jedi don't worry much about amputations."

Not-Mirax shrank back away from him, both hands on the stove edge behind her. "What?"

"We know that a severed limb can readily be replaced by a prosthetic that looks identical to the real thing. Prosthetics offer sensation and do everything flesh can. They're ideal substitutes in every way, except for requiring maintenance. So we don't feel too badly when we have to cut the arm or leg off a very bad person. But I assure you, that very bad person remembers the pain forever."

"Valin, I'm going to call your father now." Mirax sidled toward the blue bantha-hide carrybag she had left on a side table.

Valin positioned the tip of his lightsaber directly beneath her chin. At the distance of half a centimeter, its containing force field kept her from feeling any heat from the blade, but a slight twitch on Valin's part could maim or kill her instantly. She froze.

"No, you're not. You know what you're going to do instead?"

Mirax's voice wavered. "What?"

"You're going to *tell me what you've done with my mother!*" The last several words emerged as a bellow, driven by fear and anger. Valin knew that he looked as angry as he sounded; he could feel blood reddening his face, could even see redness begin to suffuse everything in his vision.

"Boy, put the blade down." Those were not the woman's words. They came from behind. Valin spun, bringing his blade up into a defensive position.

In the doorway stood a man, middle-aged, clean-shaven, his hair graying from brown. He was of below-average height, his eyes a startling green. He wore the brown robes of a Jedi. His hands were on his belt, his own lightsaber still dangling from it.

He was Valin's father, Jedi Master Corran Horn. But he wasn't, any more than the woman behind Valin was Mirax Horn.

Valin felt a wave of despair wash over him. *Both* parents replaced. Odds were growing that the real Corran and Mirax were already dead.

Yet Valin's voice was soft when he spoke. "They may have made you a virtual double for my father. But they can't have given you his expertise with the lightsaber."

"You don't want to do what you're thinking about, son."

"When I cut you in half, that's all the proof anyone will ever need that you're not the real Corran Horn."

Valin lunged.